TAKEN
FOR
GRANTED
A NOVEL

LESLYN AMTHOR SPINELLI

Cover design by Claire Ogunsola
Cover photography © Claire Ogunsola

ISBN: 1482684357
ISBN-13: 9781482684353

For Nick,
my Renaissance man

CHAPTER ONE

—ɯ—

Monday, September 10

I was locked in the six- by eight-foot interrogation room with him. The burly inmate—stinking of unwashed hair and rotting teeth—sat on a gray plastic chair across the table from me, his thick wrists handcuffed to a chain around his waist, his feet shackled to a hasp in the cement floor. I suppressed a gag when his lips parted to form a smile.

"He told me where the body's buried," he said. "You get me a time cut. I'll tell you what I know."

As I nodded my head in reluctant assent, the overhead light went out. Guided by the meager emergency lighting, I hurried toward the door and pushed the intercom button for the control center.

"We're done here. Please let me out," I said, making every effort to sound calm.

No response. No movement on the electronic lock mechanism. Nothing.

The inmate snickered.

Through the window of the steel door I saw thick smoke in the hallway. The fire alarm sounded. With perspiring hands I yanked on the door handle. It didn't budge. I'm going to die here with this snitch!

Disoriented and terrified from my recurring nightmare, I struggled to consciousness. In the bed beside me, Lily stirred. "Mom! Your phone." *Not a fire alarm, a telephone.* A glimpse of the bedside clock jerked me up cold. Three-thirty. *Oh, dear God!* David was in New York on a security assignment. *Please, please, let him be all right.*

Grabbing the phone, I rushed to the bathroom and closed the door—trying desperately not to upset Lily, who often crept into my bed on nights when her dad was away.

"Hello?"

"You've got to come, Caroline! They've arrested me. The girl's dead and they think I'm responsible."

With a wave of relief that my husband was okay, I leaned against the sink, pulled my sodden nightgown away from my skin, and paused to get my bearings—attempting to make sense of the call.

"Caroline? Are you there?"

"Who is this?" I asked, incredulous the unknown caller had used my name not once, but twice.

"It's me. Kate."

Kate Daniels never identified herself when she called, which, over the years, I'd occasionally found irritating. But it wasn't usually a problem, since I always recognized her deep, commanding voice—a voice born of confidence and class. This voice was constricted, a half-octave higher, and very, very afraid.

Kate's talking about a dead girl?

"Take a deep breath and tell me what's going on," I said. "They told me I can only use the phone for a minute. Just come, please! I need you."

This could not be happening. In the several years I'd spent as an Assistant District Attorney, the bizarre had become commonplace to me. I was used to having inmate informants telling me where to find a body, or a kilo of cocaine, or a cache of stolen guns. I'd prosecuted a woman for trading her twelve-year-old daughter to a pornographer for an ounce of heroin. I'd put a crooked judge behind bars for five years. But I found it unthinkable that Kathryn Daniels—prominent medical researcher and university professor—would be a murder suspect.

I had left the DA's office for private practice only eighteen months earlier and still knew a lot of the cops. "Let me talk to the arresting officer," I said, eager to calm my friend's hysteria as my own unease grew.

"She wants to talk to you," Kate said, between sobs, to someone on her end.

I listened to snatches of conversations in what I imagined was the squad room. All the while, a thousand thoughts darted through my brain, the most prominent quickly emerging: I have to go if she needs me, but what will I do with Lily? My chest tightened. My stomach churned. When the officer finally picked up the phone, I willed myself to shove the panicky feelings down.

"This is Patrolman Trevor Williams," said an officious voice.

I didn't recognize the name. "Hello. This is Caroline Spencer and I'm—"

"Your client says you have questions?" he interrupted.

Questions? Hell, yes, I have questions, I wanted to reply. *And there's no need for you to be rude.* But with a calming breath, I summoned my friendly-yet-efficient lawyer's voice. "What, specifically, are you holding Ms. Daniels for?"

"She's not under arrest," he said. "She was at the scene of a suspicious death and voluntarily came in to give a statement. The detectives are on their way in as we speak, but now your client is saying she won't cooperate without an attorney."

"Which detectives drew the case?" I asked.

"Connaboy and Jacobs."

I knew them well—both good guys. "Please tell them and my client I'll be there as soon as I can. They're not to start the interview without me. Understood?"

"Yes, Ma'am," he said and hung up.

I shook my head in frustration and turned to my immediate predicament: When you're new to a neighborhood, who do you call to watch your precious, anxiety-prone child in the middle of the night? All my close friends were thirty minutes away—and were working moms with kids of their own. I scrolled through my contacts and finally summoned the courage to dial the number that Lily's friend Megan's mother had given me to set up a play date. It went straight to voice mail.

Suddenly our decision to move to this idyllic cul-de-sac, nestled amid the rolling hills of suburban yet rural Middleton, seemed so wrong. The Madison area's four lakes—while picturesque and a natural magnet for the University of Wisconsin—did little to facilitate travel between Point A and Point B. My trip to rescue Kate at the eastside police station would be akin to traveling from Point A to Point W. *What could we possibly have been thinking, moving way out here?* Just as I'd decided to wake Lily and take her with me, I looked out the bathroom window and noticed an upstairs light in the house next door. *Maybe Mrs. McKinley'd be willing to come stay with Lily.* And I breathed with deep relief when I dialed directory assistance and the robo-operator recited the number. A widow in her seventies, our neighbor had served me coffee a couple of times and had invited Lily to accompany her on several walks with her dog. I had no qualms about trusting her.

"Oh, heavens, you're not disturbing me," Ida McKinley said when I explained the reason for my call. "I often get up about this time to stretch my arthritic back. Sometimes I'm able to go back to sleep, sometimes I'm not, and tonight was one of those nights."

Within minutes, she appeared at my kitchen door, wearing a pink velour warm-up suit and smelling of Ivory soap. Together we roused Lily and told her I'd be leaving. Ida would take her to school if I were delayed. Thankfully, Lily was not at all fazed by being entrusted to a relative stranger. As I stroked her silky dark-brown hair, she clutched the tattered blanket she'd slept with every night of her seven years and went right back to sleep. But I couldn't hide my trembling hands.

"Why don't you take a quick shower before you leave?" Ida asked in a soothing tone. "It'll only take a few minutes, and it'll clear the cobwebs."

She was right. Water temperature and pressure set to the max, the pulsing spray and steam relaxed my constricted muscles and restored my equilibrium—and with it my confidence. Stepping out of the shower, I wiped the fog from the mirror and took a glance. My short sandy-colored hair would air dry in the car with the blower turned up. I couldn't spare the time for mascara or lipstick. I threw on a pair of slacks and a long-sleeved silk t-shirt and headed downstairs.

Ida sat at the kitchen table, her hands warming around a mug of tea. "Better?" she asked as I gathered my purse and briefcase to leave.

"Uh-huh. Much better. How did you know that's just what I needed?"

She smiled and got up to walk me to the door. "I think I've told you I was a psychologist before my retirement. But beyond that, my late husband struggled with panic disorder for years, often to the point where he couldn't leave the house. Sometimes I was able to see the early signs and help him ward off the attacks. How long have you suffered from this?"

"Since college," I said, taken aback and more than a little embarrassed that she'd recognized the problem I constantly struggled to hide. "I haven't had a knock-down drag-out attack for almost a year. But I haven't conquered my fear of them, and I guess I'm hyper-vigilant—especially when unexpected things like this happen."

"Let's talk more about it when we get a chance," she said with a gentle hug. "In the meantime, don't worry about Lily. We'll be just fine."

Driving had often been a trigger for my panic attacks, and I didn't feel like tempting fate tonight. So I avoided the freeway and instead opted for slower-going University Avenue. I rolled down the window in my tank-like '97 Volvo and drank in the crisp fall air, eliminating any chance of claustrophobia. I needn't have worried about panicking, though—within blocks I was consumed with trying to make sense of Kate's call.

She'd said "the girl." Did she mean a child? A young woman? And what was Kate's relationship to the deceased? She didn't have family in the area. The officer had said "suspicious death." Not a car accident, then. Murder? Suicide? Rape, robbery or domestic violence gone from terrible to worse? Was Kate, herself, in physical danger? By the time I reached the parking lot, I was more puzzled than ever. Professor Kathryn Daniels simply didn't fit into any of the possible scenarios I imagined.

—✦—

It was impossible to hide my shock when I encountered Kate sitting alone in a waiting area at the police station. Fluorescent lights are never kind, but every flaw in Kate's waxy white complexion was clearly illuminated. Her wavy black hair, normally lustrous, hung in lifeless, dry tangles around her vacant eyes. She'd lost weight, and her rumpled jeans and stained cotton sweater—now two sizes too big—stank of stale smoke. For an instant I doubted this was, in fact, my long-time friend.

Kate stood and fell into my embrace. I cringed inside. Kate had always been strong and self-assured. Tonight she felt breakable, more vulnerable than I'd ever seen her. The task of helping her might be more than I bargained for. Was I up to it?

"Are you okay?" I asked.

"I just want this to be over with. I want to go home," she said. Kate no longer sounded afraid, but her lack of affect was perhaps more alarming.

As I eased her back into her chair, Detective Doug Connaboy strode into the room, preceded by his signature Old Spice aftershave. In his late forties, Doug had developed a slight paunch, and his closely cropped hair was thinner than when I'd last seen him. But his clear blue eyes sparkled as ever when he looked at me. "Sorry it's under these circumstances, but it's good to see you, Caroline," he said. "Can we talk alone first?"

"Sure." I turned to Kate. "Sit tight for a minute, okay?"

Although she nodded, I wasn't at all certain Kate had heard me.

I followed Doug through a labyrinth of cubicles to a sparsely furnished, institutional beige office and took the straight-backed chair he offered. "Who's dead, and what's it got to do with Kate Daniels?" I asked.

"I always appreciated your disdain for small talk," he said with a half-smile. "So I'll give it to you straight. Your client—or friend or whatever she is to you—is in deep shit."

"Tell me how deep."

With nail-bitten fingers, he flipped through the pages of a battered notebook. "At 0130 hours, our officers responded to a 911 at an apartment on Willie Street and found Kate Daniels giving CPR to a non-responsive adult female. The victim's roommate—who made the call—said she'd just gotten home and had no idea what happened. Said Daniels shook her head when she asked if she'd called for help. The EMTs got there within five minutes and didn't even bother to transport. Rigor had already begun, so they called in the M.E. to pronounce. We secured the scene and brought in Daniels and the roommate to take their statements."

I shook my head in disbelief. No way could I envision Kate in this picture.

"In answer to your first question," Doug went on, "the deceased is Yvonne Pritchard, age twenty-three, and apparently a grad student working on one of Daniels' research projects. Daniels said she'd only gotten there about ten minutes before the roommate and found Pritchard unconscious on the floor, not breathing."

"Cause of death?"

"If I had to guess, I'd say drug overdose," he said, shifting uncomfortably in his chair. "But, as you know, at this point I'm here to gather information, not give it out."

"You said she's in deep shit. Why? Do you have any reason to suspect my client of wrongdoing?"

"I think it's somewhat suspicious she didn't call 911 before trying to revive the victim. And why is she going to a student's apartment at one in the morning? But the thing I find most unusual is what she's got with her: no purse, no ID, just five-hundred bucks in cash and a car key in her pocket."

"Did you search the car?"

"C'mon, Caroline!" Doug said with a deep chuckle. "Everyone in this department knows better than that. She pointed out the car to Patrolman Williams as they were leaving the scene, and he made sure it was locked. We'd like her consent to let us search it, but that's for you to decide—unless or until we have cause to get a warrant."

My alarm mounted as Kate and I began talking in a private conference room. More harsh lighting—this time accompanied by a high-pitched persistent hum—made it impossible to ignore her ill health. *Could she be in shock?*

"What the hell is going on, Kate?" I asked, unable to hold back the harsh words.

"Yvonne called me at the lab at about nine-thirty," she said in a quivering voice. "I could hardly understand her—she couldn't stop crying. She'd been depressed for weeks, and there'd been rumors going around she was pregnant. We talked for a while, and she seemed better. But after we hung up, I kept worrying. So I decided to go check on her."

"You knew where she lived?"

"Yeah. I'd been to a party there a month or so ago."

You party with your students? I thought but didn't ask. I needed immediate details. "What time did you get there? How did you get in?"

"I guess it was about one-fifteen. There were lights on in the apartment. No one answered the door, but it was unlocked so I just went in. She was on the floor..." Kate choked back a sob.

"Why didn't you dial 911?"

"I don't know," she said, shaking her head. "Maybe my medical training just kicked into gear? But later I realized I'd left my cell phone at home, and I didn't see Yvonne's. So I guess I just didn't think of it."

Something about that answer, too, was unsettling to me, but I forged ahead without calling her on it. Kate was vague about the roommate's arrival but remembered she had done CPR until the EMTs came. She said she hadn't noticed any drugs or paraphernalia on the premises.

"Why did you have five-hundred dollars in your pocket? It looks incredibly suspicious," I said.

"I know it sounds crazy, Caroline, but I was going to offer to give it to her for an abortion. Her boyfriend dumped her, and Yvonne was always strapped for money."

Abortion? Great solution for depression. Again, I bit my tongue.

There were countless questions to be asked, including what was physically wrong with Kate, but Doug Connaboy knocked on the window, signaling it was time to take her statement. I raised one finger and nodded.

"Before we go in," I said to Kate, "I need to know the truth. Did you have anything to do with Yvonne's death?"

"Absolutely not."

"And will they find anything illegal or conceivably incriminating if we give the cops permission to search your car?"

"No. Nothing," she said with quiet conviction. Despite the circumstances and the little red flags raised by a few of Kate's answers, I believed her. I'd known her almost twenty years, and I'd never known her to lie.

—⁓—

Doug's young partner, Sam Jacobs, was already seated in the interview room when we walked in. I couldn't help but smile when he stood to shake my hand. With his head of unruly black curls, bent wire-framed glasses and protruding Adam's apple, I'd always thought he looked more like a slapstick comic than a police officer. No way could Sam ever play the "bad cop" role in this duo.

As it happened, neither detective played that part in Kate's interview. The four of us sat around a Formica-topped table, and Kate answered their questions without hesitation. Doug asked most of them, and Sam took the more copious notes.

At one point, Doug asked Kate to tell them what she knew of Yvonne's family background. I noticed deep creases in her forehead as she decided where to start. "Yvonne was a first generation college student—her parents are blue collar folks. I think maybe they pushed her and her brother a little too hard to succeed. She graduated from high school at seventeen and went on to get her bachelor's degree in three years. Yvonne was brilliant but somewhat immature and managed to get herself into some iffy personal situations."

To my shame, it was only during this answer that it finally hit me: the realization a young woman—someone's daughter, sister, friend—was gone, and way before her time. I'd been so focused on Kate's predicament that I'd lost sight of the real tragedy. Doug and Sam had the specter of Yvonne's death indelibly etched in their minds, and I knew they wouldn't rest until satisfied they knew what had happened and who was responsible.

As the interview proceeded, I grew more and more confident Kate was telling the truth. The details she provided helped. So did her almost constant eye contact with the detectives. "I think that about covers it," Doug finally said, pushing back from the table. "I'll be back in a minute with the consent form for the search of Kate's car, and then you can both go get some sleep." Sam followed him out of the room.

I glanced at the clock on the wall—it was almost six o'clock. Lily would still be asleep, and I didn't want to call home and wake her. Kate and I—exhausted and emotionally spent—sat in silence while we waited for Doug to return with his paperwork. She picked at a snagged thread on the elbow of her sweater. I looked over the notes I had made during the interview, but nothing really registered. Ten minutes stretched to fifteen, then twenty. *How long can it take to type up a simple search authorization?*

When Doug returned to the room, I got an inexplicable sinking feeling in my stomach. "Caroline, a word, please?" he said, nodding toward the hallway.

"I'm sorry," he said as the door closed behind us, "but I'm afraid your client isn't going anywhere for awhile."

CHAPTER TWO

—␣␣—

"What do you mean she isn't going anywhere?" I asked Doug. "Are you telling me you're arresting her for this? She's answered all your questions and been completely cooperative. You don't even know the cause of death yet and already you're jumping to the conclusion my client was involved. This makes no sense. No sense at all!"

"Hold on a minute," Doug said, touching my shoulder to bring me out of my tirade. "I'm not arresting her for Pritchard's death. We did a routine computer check and found Kate has two outstanding warrants."

"You've gotta be kidding," I said, leaning back against the cold cinderblock wall.

"For your sake, I wish I were kidding. The local warrant is for failure to appear on a second-offense OWI. You know how I feel about drunk drivers, especially repeaters, so I'm thinking less of her for it. But the other warrant's the troublesome one for you. It's from the feds. They've got a sealed three-count indictment against her for theft, and if they didn't consider it pretty fucking serious they would've just summoned her to court."

I caught my breath, trying to comprehend this increasingly incomprehensible set of events. *A second drunk-driving arrest for someone who rarely drinks? And a federal indictment? For Kate?*

"I'm sorry I snapped at you, Doug. This just all feels so surreal. What happens next?"

"We'll run her over to the county jail. They'll put her on the intake docket at eight-thirty to set bail on the OWI. Who knows how long that'll take? Just to be sure, I sent a message to the U.S. Marshals saying they shouldn't set the appearance in federal court till sometime after noon. Do you want to break the news to her?"

I nodded. It was the right thing to do, but fierce resentment rose in my throat. What had Kate gotten herself—and me—into? "Come with me if you would, though," I said to Doug. "In case she has questions I can't answer." My own head was reeling with unanswered questions. I felt overwhelmed and wanted nothing more than to go eat Cheerios with my daughter in the peace and quiet of our sunny kitchen.

It took every ounce of energy I could muster to walk back into the interview room. No sense mincing words. "Kate," I said, "you're not going home after all." She stared past my shoulder as I explained her situation and wordlessly nodded when Doug asked if she understood. He and Sam would be the ones to take her from the station to the Dane County Jail. There would be no opportunity for me to visit between her being booked in and court, but I'd meet her in the courtroom.

My gray gabardine pants and black shirt looked professional enough for Dane County Circuit Court, especially with the blazer I'd had the foresight to throw in the back seat. There might be time to get to Middleton to change and be back before Kate's first court appearance, but I didn't want to risk being stuck in a rush-hour traffic jam. And, frankly, I didn't have the emotional energy to undertake the drive. Even a little panic attack would be unbearable.

—✺—

Williamson Street, a ten-block thoroughfare on the narrow isthmus between Lakes Mendota and Monona and leading to downtown Madison, houses an eclectic population: aging hippies, yuppies, students and blue-collar families. Until two months ago, the neighborhood had been mine. At thirty-five, I was too young to be an aging hippie, and I'd never really considered myself a yuppie. I was no longer a student, nor was I a blue-collar worker. But the area had welcomed me, and later David, and then Lily. Our cozy bungalow was just right—that is, until we decided to expand our family. And until we decided the local elementary school wasn't a good fit for Lily.

Traveling down Williamson Street that morning, heading to the Dane County Courthouse, I couldn't help but miss the neighborhood. I drove slowly, savoring "home" and half-heartedly looking for the house with the yellow crime scene tape—where Yvonne Pritchard had spent her last hours. I noticed Lazy Jane's Café was just opening. Coffee and a fresh-from-the-oven morning bun might be the ticket out of my trance. A parking spot in front of the door beckoned, and the aroma of cinnamon welcomed me at the counter.

Enjoying the first buttery bite of the bun, I remembered to turn on my cell, planning to call Ida and Lily in a few minutes. Almost immediately it began to vibrate. David.

"What in *hell* is going on?" he asked before I'd even said hello. "I call home at seven a.m. only to learn you're out and someone we hardly know is watching our child? A child we've had in therapy because she's over-anxious? Tell me what you were thinking."

Fighting the urge to hang up, I swallowed and breathed. *Use your "I" statements*, I told myself. "I think you're over-reacting, David. It was an emergency. Lily wasn't freaked by my leaving, and Ida McKinley's perfectly reliable. I didn't feel I had a choice."

"What kind of client emergency could you possibly have in the middle of the night?" he asked, unappeased.

"It's Kate. She found one of her students dead and needed me with her when she talked to the cops."

"Ah—Kate," he muttered. "And the cops couldn't have waited until Lily was at school?"

"No, they couldn't," I said, although the question had never crossed my mind. What had been the urgency? Why hadn't I thought it through?

"We don't need Kate Daniels complicating our lives," he said, "especially with the decisions we're trying to make. And the sooner you come to see that, the better. I'll be home about five."

I kept the silent phone to my ear, wishing I'd never answered his call. Or Kate's, for that matter.

I pushed away the remains of my morning bun, wiped sugar from my fingers, and put on my upbeat voice to call home. Lily answered. "G'morning, Mom! We're just leaving to go next door and get Mrs. McKinley's dog. They're gonna walk me to school. Can I talk to you later?" "Sure, kiddo," I said, smiling as I hung up. *See, David? She's fine.*

As I finished my coffee, I thought about my friendship with Kathryn Daniels, whom I met when we were freshmen at Shenstone College in Northern California. We had each been paired with what we later called terminally perky roommates and spent a lot of time together smoking menthol cigarettes in the perpetually hazy lounge at the end of our dormitory hall. Kathryn was decidedly not the perky type. She made it clear she was "Kate," not "Kathy," and—even at eighteen—she had an air of sophistication most of us only dreamed about. Almost six-feet tall, she walked purposefully—never slouching—her bearing matching that commanding voice. Kate was in the pre-med program. Her father and an older brother were surgeons, and it seemed inevitable Kate would follow in their footsteps. Her other brother attended Harvard Law, and her sister aspired to be a concert pianist. Kate related all this reluctantly and without conceit. The Daniels family was one of "old money."

By contrast, my family seemed so ordinary. Dad was a section chief with the Department of Transportation. Mom was a housewife or—to be politically correct—a home-maker. Unlike Kate's mother, who served on boards of various foundations and hosted luncheons for charitable causes, my mom served as the Girl Scout leader and organized the neighborhood car pool. My only sibling, an older brother, had played second string on the high school football and basketball teams—when he was able to keep up a C average. Later a plumber, he had a factory-worker wife and three kids. Our family was comfortable, stable, and totally unremarkable.

Though lacking Kate's pedigree and style, I did share her sense of humor, her intelligence, and her competitive nature. We loved the same books, the same movies, the same people. We quickly became best friends.

On my way to meet her at the jail, I tried but could not imagine how Kate had gotten into this situation.

—⟋⟋—

The parking ramp was already close to capacity and it was only eight. It shouldn't have surprised me. A Monday in early September, and the court dockets would be chock-full with jury trials that the plaintiff and defense lawyers had been able to wheedle continuances for all summer. I'd gotten similar postponements a few times as an ADA, and the workload always piled up in the fall. Impatiently, I drove up and further up the dark confines of the parking structure until I finally found a spot. It would have been quicker to park at my sterile office building on the opposite side of the square and walk over.

The concrete steps of the long stairwell were urine stained and littered. Covering my nose against the stench, I hurried to the street level, thankful I no longer had to deal with this on a daily basis.

The security line at the courthouse was blessedly short, and I breezed through the metal detector without a hitch.

Regretting I'd left my laptop at home, I dashed into the court clerk's office to run a CCAP check on my friend. The public database would give me basic facts about her pending case. After four slapdash attempts, I managed to fill in the blanks to the computer's satisfaction, and Kate's record flashed on the screen. I'd expected the two entries for driving while intoxicated, but my heart sank when I saw a list.

"What the f—"

"That ain't no way for a fine upstanding lawyer to be talkin'!" came a big booming voice from behind me.

Spinning around with alarm and burning cheeks, I was greeted with a welcome sight—Tom Robbins, a jailer I'd worked closely with as an assistant DA, grinning from ear to ear and ready to lift me off my feet with his hug. Tom stood about six-four and his biceps threatened to burst through his short polyester shirtsleeves. It had taken me awhile to get used to his pseudo-macho persona and jive, but I was glad I had. Tom was one of my favorite people.

"It's great to see you, Tom! But I'm afraid you've caught me at something of a low point. One of my clients—and a new inhabitant of your establishment, I might add—has more of a record than I thought. And I've gotta join her up in intake in a few minutes."

"If anyone can spring her, it's you, Sugar," he said, moving toward the counter window with a stack of papers. "Drop by and visit when you get a chance."

I hit "print," jotted down a few details, waved to Tom, and headed upstairs to the courtroom.

The credo of the building: hurry up and wait. I'd for-gotten how annoying it could be. I had to be present in the courtroom when Kate's case was called—otherwise I might miss it—and that could take an hour or more. The one-page printout of her record and my sparse notes felt flimsy in my hand and didn't give me much to study as I marked time. And they were certainly unsettling.

Take a step back and look at this without emotion, I told my-self. Only three of the entries on the list were relevant to this court: Kate had been ticketed for drunk driving in 2005—not even a criminal offense in beer-loving Wisconsin—and had paid the fine. She'd been arrested again a year ago for the second OWI and, as I was too well aware, failed to show up for court, triggering an arrest warrant. To top it off, she'd been convicted of a misdemeanor for writing worthless checks in the spring of 2006. Not exactly the law-abiding citizen I'd thought her to be.

Then there were the several non-criminal cases. Civil judgments—probably for unpaid debts to creditors—and one case that looked to be an automobile repossession. *Must be a different Kathryn Daniels.* With the limited information I'd had time to print, I couldn't be sure.

When the judge left the bench for a ten-minute recess, I called my office. Though I was employed only part-time, today had been one of my scheduled workdays, and I should have been there a half-hour ago.

"Can you clear my calendar, Rosalee?" I asked my secre-tary after hastily explaining my absence. "And look up the number for the U.S. Clerk of Court, please?"

In an instant, Rosalee's equanimity and silky voice calmed me. "I brought in some mouth-watering butterscotch scones today," she said while I could hear her paging through the phone book. "I'll save one for you."

Having the phone number saved me from directory assistance but did little to further my quest for information about Kate's bigger case. My patience was no match for the automated answering system at the federal court, so I stabbed "0" on my phone and talked to a receptionist. She put me on hold and— after five minutes—I had to disconnect from the bland Muzak to rush back to the intake courtroom.

Kate's case was being called just as I walked in, and I joined her at the defense podium. Wearing a soiled orange jumpsuit with "County Jail" stenciled over the breast pocket, my friend looked on the verge of collapse and acknowledged my presence with only a slight tilt of her head.

The judge and ADA were new appointees whom I didn't know. But they knew their jobs. Without fanfare or argument, Kate's bail was set: five hundred dollars. I'd write a check before I left the building.

"I'll be over to the jail to see you in a few minutes," I said to Kate as she was led from the courtroom by the bailiffs.

I summoned yet another ounce of patience to wait in the ten-person line to post Kate's bail, pocketed the receipt, and gratefully left the courthouse. But the half-block, uphill walk to the jail felt like Mount Everest.

After passing yet another security screening, I waited with silent resignation and some self-consciousness in the fishbowl-like attorney-client visiting room. When—after fifteen minutes—the guards finally escorted Kate to meet me, I hugged her tightly and found myself reluctant to let go. *Who cares what they think?*

"What's happened to you, Kate?"

"I don't know," she said shaking her head. "I've been under so much pressure lately, I can't see straight. I'm not eating. I'm not sleeping. The research has stalled. You remember my mentor, Marty Braxton? He's been a Class A asshole, and I can't trust him or his judgment. Everyone around me is in crisis. There's just nothing going right. And now Yvonne." She sank into a chair and slumped forward, as though deflated by her expenditure of words.

I took a chair beside her. Where to begin? I wanted to know more about all of it. I wanted to help Kate sort through the distress and fix whatever was troubling her. But I needed to tackle today's biggest obstacle: getting her out from under a federal arrest warrant.

"What's this new prosecution all about?" I asked gently. "You must have some ideas."

"Not a clue, Caroline. I swear. But I wouldn't put it past Marty to have framed me."

As if on cue, the door was buzzed open and a disheveled auburn-haired woman wearing a too-tight tan pantsuit walked in. "Sorry to interrupt," she said while fumbling through a nylon briefcase for her credentials. "I'm Monica Smith-Kellor from the U.S. Pretrial Services office. We got word of Ms. Daniels' arrest, and I was hoping to be able to interview her for the bail investigation report. Would now be convenient?"

"Please slow down a bit," I said, glancing at her ID. "We don't know anything about this case and need some information before we agree."

"Okay." As she sat down across the table from us, I noticed the faint but distinct smell of Hall's cough drops, and she dabbed at the end of her nose with a Kleenex she had stored up her sleeve. "Sorry—a bit of a cold. I promise to keep my distance."

Monica handed me a copy of the two-page indictment, which charged Kate with three counts of theft of federal funds from a grant program at the university. She told us an initial court appearance would be held at one-thirty today, and it was her job to formulate a recommendation for the magistrate judge as to Kate's release. "Your client has the right to decline to answer any and all questions," Monica said to me.

Decline to answer any and all questions? Why would Kate elect not to answer questions if she wanted to get out of jail? I was feeling pretty befuddled, but, after all, these were white-collar crimes, and agreeing to the interview seemed like a no-brainer. I nodded to Kate to sign the consent for interview form.

Monica posed benign questions about Kate's family, education and employment history. When she began queries about criminal record and drug and alcohol use, though, I spoke up. "I'm sorry. I'm advising my client not to answer." The information I already had on those topics was too sketchy for me to know what to make of it. Monica simply nodded and forged ahead.

The questions about Kate's finances were a minefield, too, but it was too late to turn back once we'd started on them. Kate shook her head when asked if she had assets—savings, stocks, CDs, jewelry or collections. A second mortgage on her condo had eaten up virtually all her equity, she said, and her 2006 Audi was leased. And—to my surprise—Kate acknowledged having more debts than she could enumerate.

Monica was closing her file just as a jailer came to get Kate. "The marshals are here to pick you up," he said. "We gotta motor."

Without another word, Kate was gone.

Monica and I collected our things and walked together to the control center. "I'm not sure what our office's recommendation will be," she said. "I have to talk with my supervisor to see what he thinks. But stop by my office before court, and I'll give you a copy of the report."

"Do you happen to know who's prosecuting the case?" I asked, almost as an afterthought.

"Yes. George Cooper."

Ominous news: Cooper was a veteran prosecutor who handled a lot of high-profile cases.

"I spoke with him before I came over," Monica said, "and he told me he plans to recommend your client be detained pending trial."

Unable to trust my voice, I nodded, gave her a curt wave goodbye, and pretended to search for something in my briefcase. I couldn't let her see my frustration or my fear. *Detained pending trial. I can't let that happen to Kate.*

CHAPTER THREE

—w—

Wearing sunglasses and keeping my head down—I couldn't cope with small talk in the not-unlikely event I encountered someone I knew—I walked up to the capitol square. The breeze off Lake Monona smelled fresh and clean and renewed a bit of my energy.

There wasn't time for much of a meal, but an Asian food cart on the corner had always been a favorite of mine. I ordered a spring roll and a glass of lemonade to tide me over and sat to eat on one of the square's many benches. Large shade trees and plots of seasonal flowers provided a tranquil atmosphere, counterbalancing the government employees in sneakers power-walking through their lunch breaks. Finally, I gathered my courage and headed toward my destination.

I'd been in the contemporary navy blue U.S. District Courthouse—with its hanging neon sculpture that always reminded me of an instrument of torture—on only one previous occasion: when I'd been sworn into the federal bar. It was something all new lawyers did, whether or not you ever planned to practice in federal court.

The thorough security screening felt almost superfluous given the relative calm of the building, so different from the bustling and often chaotic county courthouse. I checked the building directory and headed for the marshals' office, hoping to meet with Kate before court. A pleasant-looking woman talked on the phone at the reception desk behind a bulletproof teller-type window. She glanced up at me but continued her conversation. *What is it with receptionists today?* Finally, she hung up. "Can I help you?"

"Yes. I'm here to see Kathryn Daniels. I'm her attorney."

"Let me check with the guys," she said and walked into a back room.

After another eternity, she returned. "They're processing her. It'll be about twenty-five minutes."

Processing. The word struck me oddly. *Just how do you process someone? Completely alter their texture and composition as in Velveeta cheese?* I knew from experience the deputies were taking her picture and fingerprints and gathering background information to use in case she skipped town. I somehow knew the *processing* would not be interrupted.

"Okay," I said. "I'll be back."

I almost bumped into Kate's prosecutor, George Cooper, as I walked into the hallway. Thankfully, he was talking with someone, and I didn't have to decide whether to approach him. Federal court felt like the big leagues to me, and my experience was in the minors.

I had seen Cooper once before at a symposium on criminal practice. A smaller, fifty-something Atticus Finch type with dark hair, graying at the temples, he wore obviously off-the-rack clothes that were several seasons old, and he was about two weeks past a needed haircut. But when he smiled and spoke, he was irresistible—apparently without knowing it. I suspected he charmed jurors—women and men alike—into guilty verdicts. I wasn't anxious to go up against him in court today, especially so ill prepared.

Yet another receptionist behind glass, this one at the pretrial services office, told me the bail report was still being typed but ushered me in to see Monica Smith-Kellor. Her desk displayed photographs of two bright-eyed children at various ages, and kids' art projects adorned the walls and bulletin board. I breathed a bit easier. We could connect.

"We've decided to recommend detention," Monica said without preface.

My hastily eaten lunch lurched in my stomach. "Why?"

"Well, first, Ms. Daniels is alleged to have embezzled a lot of money—about $150,000 from one grant program alone. Second, she's apparently said she would flee if arrested and recently renewed her passport. Then there's her arrest record, including the no-show on the last OWI. You have to admit she looks awful—I'm guessing a pretty serious alcohol problem. I don't believe we can trust her."

"I've known Kate Daniels for years," I said. "And this all sounds so unlike her."

"I understand. But I'm inclined to believe the court will want some assurances and pretty strict conditions to make sure she appears. You heard her say she doesn't have any money or property to post as bail, and I'm waiting for a call back from her family. Are you retained?"

"Uh, yes," I replied, caught totally off-guard by her inquiry.

This woman was asking a legitimate question: Was Kate paying me to be her lawyer? I'd been operating on autopilot since the early-morning phone call, as a friend who happened to be a lawyer, simply trying to handle the immediate crises. Kate needed a strong criminal defense attorney—one with experience in federal court. I decided in that instant that it would *not* be me. I'd cover today's hearing and pass the case off to someone qualified. Besides, I needed to get back to my family, my actual job, my real life—the life I'd recently chosen.

Willing myself to stand up, I moved toward the door. "Thanks for your time, Monica. Will you be in court?" I asked.

"Sure. I'll bring your copy of the bail report to the courtroom."

It was almost one o'clock when I got back to the mar- shals' office and learned they'd moved up the hearing. All the parties were available and a scheduling conflict had come up later for the judge. *A sunny fall afternoon—probably an impromptu golf match. What does it matter if defense counsel is beyond beleaguered?* Feeling like a pinball, I headed for the Magistrate's court.

The prosecutor strode into the courtroom behind me. "George Cooper," he said, extending his hand. "You must be Caroline Spencer. The clerk's office told me you were repre- senting Kathy Daniels."

"Kate," I said, pulling my hand away from his.

"Excuse me?" he replied with a puzzled expression.

"Kate. She uses 'Kate' or 'Kathryn.'" I felt compelled to make the point. When I was a prosecutor, we frequently gave defendants nicknames, many of which were unflattering. Somehow it rankled that this man would dare to use a diminutive nickname my friend detested.

"Oh, sorry. Look, I'll cut to the chase. I'm moving for detention based on the risk of flight," he said. "You're entitled to a detention hearing, which I'm prepared to have today. But if I were you, I'd ask for a continuance for a few days—you're allowed up to five—so you can put together a release plan. I really doubt Brillstein'll release her on P.R."

Stanley Brillstein was one of the magistrate judges who handled pretrial matters for the federal court. I'd appeared before him hundreds of times when I was an ADA and he was still a county judge, which was not much comfort here. Brillstein never seemed to give the defendant the benefit of the doubt, which had been just fine with me when I was a prosecutor. Now the tables were turned.

No way could I argue today for Kate's release on P.R.—personal recognizance or her own promise to appear. Not without knowing the facts and the ground rules.

Kate Daniels sat at the heavy oak defense table, flanked by two deputy marshals. She glanced up as I approached, her eyes empty.

Sliding into the chair next to her, I tried to engage her gaze. "This is the arraignment where they inform us of the charges and penalties," I said, hoping to convey an air of confidence. "We'll plead not guilty, and they'll talk about bail. It's not looking like we'll be able to get you released today. This judge is a hard-liner, and there are a lot of questions we need to clear up. Can you hold on for a day or two—two would be better—to put together a stronger case?"

Tears gathered in Kate's eyes and threatened to spill down her cheeks. She nodded wearily.

"All rise," said the clerk as U.S. Magistrate Stanley Brillstein walked through the door behind his bench. A short, moon-faced man with a recessed chin, he looked anything but ominous. But I knew way too many lawyers who'd misjudged him.

"Kathryn Daniels appears in person and by her attorney, Caroline Spencer," I said when prompted to enter my appearance.

Brillstein looked up over his reading glasses and half smiled in my direction. His respect for my previous work might carry some weight after all.

Kate flinched when Cooper finished his recitation of the charges and possible penalties: she faced up to ten years in prison on each of the three counts and hundreds of thousands of dollars in fines and restitution. She sat motionless, as I pleaded not guilty on her behalf.

The formalities finally accomplished, there came the inescapable question. "What is the government's position as to release or detention?" Judge Brillstein asked.

As he'd said he would, George Cooper requested the judge order Kate be kept in jail while awaiting her trial—an unusual move in white-collar cases like this. In federal court, detention can be ordered before trial only if the judge believes the defendant will flee or pose a danger to anyone in the community. No one was arguing Kate was dangerous, but

I'd have a tough time convincing Stan Brillstein she wouldn't flee.

"And your position on detention, Ms. Spencer?" Brillstein asked.

"Your Honor, I do not believe my client presents a risk of flight. However, I'm not prepared for a detention hearing today. We're requesting a two-day continuance."

"Very well. We'll schedule the detention hearing for three o'clock on Wednesday. Ms. Daniels, you'll remain in marshals' custody at the Dane County Jail at least until that time. We're adjourned." The judge rose, and we all followed suit.

The deputy marshals hurried over to usher Kate out the door. One of them nodded when I asked if I could see her at the lock-up. I almost wished he'd said no. I was so tired: tired from lack of sleep, tired of looking at a friend I no longer knew, and tired of David's words replaying in my mind, "We don't need Kate Daniels complicating our lives."

CHAPTER FOUR

The marshal's office interview rooms were all in use when I got to the lock-up. I sat alone in the sterile waiting area—where an annoying vent blew frigid air down my back—too keyed up and cold to doze. I wondered how Lily's day was going and what she'd decided to wear to school that morning. I wondered what Ida had packed her in her lunch bag. I reflected back on my decision to leave the criminal justice field and settle into more mundane, part-time work so I could spend more time as a mother.

When Lily had joined us, I had taken three months' maternity leave. But it hadn't been the storybook summer I'd hoped for. Lily was an easy-going baby, rarely insisting on attention. And David adored her and attended to her every desire—when he was home. His job was so demanding that summer that more often than not, I found myself alone with Lily. And more often than I cared to recognize, fear paralyzed me. Fear I'd have a heart attack, fear I'd slip in the shower and be knocked unconscious, fear I'd have an allergic reaction to a bee sting. I never feared Lily would succumb to crib death or choke on her formula: I had confidence in *her* ultimate health. Instead I worried I would somehow falter, and she'd be left alone with no one to depend on.

Not surprisingly, the panic attacks came back. What might start as free-floating anxiety or a fleeting worry could within seconds escalate into sheer terror: racing heart, narrowing field of vision with darkness clouding the periphery, certainty of imminent death or insanity. David was usually able to talk me down from the precipice and tried to be accessible to me by phone. But I hated feeling powerless and dependent.

My doctor prescribed an anti-anxiety medication and I resumed regular sessions with a psychologist. Both helped some: I had fewer and less severe attacks. But the attacks stubbornly refused to go away completely.

I didn't dare admit the relief I felt when it was time to return to my job as an ADA. The pressures of work—to file motions and briefs on time, to win convictions, to strike plea agreements when appropriate—were tangible and manageable. I had little time for introspection and even less time to be anxious. Lily thrived at her sitter, Eve's, where three other children provided hours of stimulation. Being a working mom felt right for me.

Inevitably, though, my responsibilities at work grew, and David's situation was no better than mine. An ex-Navy SEAL and former police officer, he'd joined an up-and-coming Chicago security-consulting firm. Although he could often work from their small Madison office, he couldn't completely avoid travel and, even when at home, was often on the phone or computer.

Lily had my undivided attention from the time I got home until her bedtime. Then, out came the briefcase and the homework. I felt like a blind juggler on a roller coaster, struggling to keep too many balls in the air while trying to anticipate the upcoming hills and curves. I became less tolerant of Lily's minor indiscretions—like begging for another story when it was time for lights out—and found myself snapping and nagging.

When Lily was in kindergarten, she began having nightmares and frequent stomach upsets, which her pediatrician attributed to "stress." It was as if I'd passed off my panic attacks to my daughter. Something had to give, and I would not let it be Lily.

With the help of a family counselor, we had gotten things back on track. David had negotiated a more workable schedule. I'd accepted a part-time position with a private law firm where my assignments were generally routine, non-criminal, and with predictable hours. I'd found a variety of lesser challenges to engage in: contested divorce cases, volunteering in Lily's classroom, and long-forgotten or never-learned homemaking tasks. While imperfect, my life had become, on balance, happy again.

I glanced up from my reverie as the receptionist knocked on the window and beckoned. An interview room was available.

The room was divided in half by a concrete block wall with a heavy screen-covered window. When I opened the door to enter, it banged against one of the two straight-backed

chairs that barely fit into my side of the room. A stainless
steel ledge at the base of the window was just wide enough to
write on. I sat down to wait. After a few minutes, the door to
the other room opened, and a deputy marshal ushered Kate
in. Though the screen obscured her facial expressions, I could
see her shoulders slump forward as she sank onto her chair.

I hesitated a moment before speaking, hoping Kate
would begin. She didn't.

"I'm so sorry, Kate. I've never practiced in federal court,
and I had no idea what we'd be up against today. I'll make
some calls when I leave here, and I'll recommend a good lawyer to represent you."

"I need you. I don't want anybody else to represent me,"
she said. "You know I'd do it for you."

A sick feeling overcame me. I didn't pause to consider
what it meant—I simply pushed it back. *Later*, I said to
myself.

"Let's take this a step at a time. I'll do some prep work
and research for the detention hearing, and then we'll decide
how to proceed."

No response.

I glanced through Monica Smith-Kellor's report and began to make notes. "I need to ask you some questions about
this bail report," I said, focusing not on my friend but on the
written page. "Tell me about the first OWI arrest. It says you
refused to take a Breathalyzer."

Kate sighed. "There was a reception to welcome the new
faculty members, and our department head insisted we all attend. Anyway, I had the flu and felt like shit. I had a couple
of drinks, thinking it'd help. I left early and got pulled over

a couple blocks away by a young cop. I started out being co-operative but couldn't handle it when he started coming on to me. So I refused to finish his silly sobriety tests or to blow into the machine. I'm sure I wasn't drunk."

"If you refuse to take a Breathalyzer, it's legally the same as being intoxicated," I said, looking up at her now. "Why didn't you call me when it happened?"

"You were with the prosecutor's office then. I didn't want to make things awkward for you."

"I could've referred you to a good attorney." But there was no sense belaboring the point. "Okay. What about the insufficient funds check charge?"

Kate shook her head. "What a comedy of errors," she said. "I was getting ready to attend a conference in Amsterdam, so I arranged for the university to directly deposit my travel advance into my bank account. The business office screwed it up and mailed the check. When I got home, I didn't get around to picking up my mail at the post office for several days—I'd stopped it while I was gone—and didn't discover the mistake right away. In the meantime, I wrote a few checks that bounced."

"Didn't your bank or the businesses contact you?"

"I was practically living in the lab at the time, Caroline. I guess I probably threw out the notices, assuming they were junk mail. I paid the fine and restitution, though. It's all resolved."

Throughout her responses, I tried in vain to read Kate's non-verbal cues. The security screen cast her in shadows, making it impossible to see whether her eyes were tear-filled or clear, whether she was scowling or impassive, whether her jaw was quivering or tight. Without subtle communication clues, her voice sounded disembodied and not particularly believable.

I forged ahead. "The biggest obstacle we have to overcome to get you released is your failure to appear on the second OWI. Tell me about that arrest."

"A cop pulled me over on West Wash about nine o'clock one night. Said I was driving erratically or some such nonsense. I'd just left the lab. One of the techs had brought in the stuff to make margaritas to celebrate the completion of our protocol. You know I hate margaritas. But I didn't want to dampen everyone's spirits, so I had one and then left. The cop said I failed the field sobriety tests, so he took me in to the station. This time I took the Breathalyzer, and they said the reading was just over the limit. I don't know how that could be with only one drink."

"Why didn't you go to court?" I asked.

"I did go to court. I pled not guilty. I wasn't driving erratically in the first place, so the officer had no cause to pull me over. Plus the field tests are subjective. This cop was a kid who had no clue what he was supposed to do, and I wasn't drunk. Obviously, he didn't operate the Breathalyzer correctly either. Caroline, you know I'm no drunk!"

It was true. Throughout college, Kate had been our designated driver. She drank only rarely, and I'd never seen her intoxicated. In recent years, we'd been together on a number of social occasions. Kate typically had one drink or a couple of glasses of wine, never showing any ill effects.

"But the failure to appear—"

"When I went to court and said I wanted a trial, they gave me a continuance. The ADA suggested I get a lawyer, but I got swamped at work and didn't get around to it. They never sent me a notice with a new court date. I just assumed it would be a while. You always hear about the backlogged judicial system. To tell you the truth, I'd pretty much forgotten about it until today. I've been so busy."

"What about the passport renewal and your threats to leave the country?"

"I'm scheduled to present a paper at a conference in London in December. My passport expired two months ago, so I got it renewed. I have *no* idea where they got the idea I said I'd flee. Caroline, that's ridiculous. It's probably some lie Marty Braxton made up. Please! You've got to get me out of here."

"Judge Brillstein's a tough one," I said, almost afraid to look at her. "He's probably going to want cash or a property bond to assure him you'll show." And, based on her answers during the bail interview, it was pretty clear she no longer had assets to be used for that purpose.

A deputy marshal knocked on my door and opened it a few inches. "Counselor, you've got about two minutes before we make the jail run," he said.

"Okay. Thanks."

I turned back to Kate. "They're going to be taking you back to the county jail in a couple minutes," I said. "I know it won't be pleasant, but the women's cell block is usually pretty quiet. You'll have your own cell, and you shouldn't be in any danger. I'll come see you tomorrow. In the meantime, is there anyone I can contact who'd be willing to post bail for you? Preferably someone here in Madison?"

Silence.

"Kate?"

"I heard you. And, no. There's no one."

The marshal opened Kate's door and motioned it was time for her to go.

"All right. I'll get in touch with your folks—"

"Don't. Don't you dare!" she said over her shoulder as she was led away.

Chapter Five

—⟋⟋\⟋—

The clock above the marshal's sign-out log read two-thirty. This had been the longest eleven-hour day I could ever recall. I decided to head home. The calls I needed to make could wait.

Two lanes of stalled traffic greeted me a half-mile onto the beltline. The third lane was moving at a crawl. I maneuvered into it and ignored the nonverbal pleas of the other motorists to cut in front of me. But that lane, too, came to a grinding halt. *Karma.*

I could've turned my cell phone back on—or the radio to find a traffic report—but the silence was alluring. My thoughts were not as simply silenced.

Why is Kate so adamant about me not calling her parents? I recalled the first weekend I had spent with her family. I had gone home with Kate for the brief Thanksgiving break during our freshman year and had one of my most memorable holiday experiences. The enormous estate of Corbett and Margaret Daniels had been brimming with people and conviviality. We stayed up late on Wednesday night, listening to music and discussing politics and current events. Corbett made sure our glasses were full and we each had a chance to speak our piece, and he showed an interest in every opinion.

Thanksgiving dinner was traditional, yet unlike any I'd ever partaken in—or have partaken in since. Three uniformed caterers served the meal in courses, each accompanied by an exquisite wine. The meal had been impeccably timed, yet leisurely, with room for toasts and jokes and laughter. Before he carved the turkey, Corbett stood, raised his wine glass, and told us all how grateful he was to be surrounded by friends and family.

I'd imagined with some chagrin the scene of my own family's dinner. The women would be buzzing around the cramped kitchen preparing the ordinary meal: coleslaw, overdone turkey, stuffing with too much sage, bland mashed potatoes and gravy, sweet potatoes topped with melted marshmallows, and cranberries fresh from the can. The meal would be devoured in fifteen minutes during the halftime of one of the important football games. My grandmother would interrupt and correct my grandfather's stories. My uncle, having had too much beer, would belch and tell a few off-color jokes, at which everyone would laugh in discomfort. And the men would return to the game while the women cleaned up.

I'd been in heaven being a part of the Daniels' festivities and told Kate so. She had responded that it was "a Hallmark Hall of Fame presentation." I hadn't gotten it then, and I still didn't get it.

Just as quickly as the traffic had come to a stop, the beltline began to move at its usual ten-miles-per-hour-over-the-speed-limit pace, and I made my way back to the here and now.

My relief when I pulled into the driveway was short-lived: As the garage door lifted, I saw David's car, and I was nowhere near ready for the confrontation his earlier call had portended. He stood in the kitchen listening to phone messages and turned toward me as I walked in.

"I didn't expect you till later," I said, dropping my briefcase and jacket next to his on the cluttered counter.

"I tried calling you several times this afternoon, but it went straight to voice mail," he said, taking me in his arms. "I wanted to get home before it's time to go pick up Lily so I could apologize. I was out of line, and I'm sorry."

With my face nestled against his chest—his starched oxford cloth shirt rumpled soft from the day's wear—I felt blessed consolation. And I began to sob.

While I'd explained many times the relief crying brought me, my tears make David as uncomfortable as his direct manner sometimes makes me. He turned off the answering system, gently took my hand, and led me to the soft leather couch in the family room. "I'm so sorry," he said again as we sat down. "Tell me what's wrong."

"Virtually everything about this day has been wrong," I said, "starting at three-thirty with the call from Kate. The phone rang in the middle of that recurring nightmare I've been having—I dreamed it was a fire alarm and I was trapped in a burning jail cell with the snitch. And then Kate told me she'd been detained by the cops and needed me to come. And

I didn't know what to do with Lily..." I was too choked up to continue.

David put his arm around my shoulder and murmured, "Easy, kiddo. Just take it a step at a time."

I took several breaths and continued more slowly. I related the circumstances of Kate's arrest and detention. David asked questions along the way, but remained dispassionate—until I mentioned the cash Kate had in her pocket at Yvonne Pritchard's.

He raised an eyebrow. "Are you sure she didn't go there to sell the girl some drugs?"

"How can you say that? You know Kate. You can't possibly think she's a drug dealer!" I said, shaking my head defensively.

"I didn't think she was a drunk driver, bad-check writer or embezzler either, but you said she's admitted to being two of them."

"Doug and Sam don't seem to think she's a dealer. And she gave them consent to test the bills for fingerprints and drug residue. I guess we'll just have to wait and see what they find, but I'm sure they won't find Yvonne's prints or any drugs on the money."

"So what's your next step?"

"Trying to line up a good lawyer to represent her in federal court. She says she wants me, but that's not gonna happen."

Another raised eyebrow.

"Seriously, David, I know it would be the exact wrong thing for our family at this point." *But can I really refuse her if she persists?* I thought to myself.

He glanced at his watch and got up off the couch. "More reality awaits," he said. "I didn't listen to all of them, but there are some messages you need to hear. Preferably with a glass of wine. I'll go get Lily and a pizza, and we can talk more after she goes to bed."

I uncorked a bottle of cabernet, poured a generous portion, and dialed the answering system. There were seven messages: one from Ida McKinley telling me Lily was safely ensconced at school that morning, one from Rosalee asking me to call her at the office, and five from Corbett Daniels, each more frantic—and demanding—than the last.

Corbett's first message said someone doing a bail investigation had contacted them, and he wanted to know what "this nonsense" was all about. The second said he'd called Monica Smith-Kellor after he was unable to reach me and she'd filled him in. Of course they'd post bail. They'd fight these "despicable bastards," apparently meaning the prosecutors, with everything they had. Then, should he and Margaret come for the detention hearing? Finally, "We'll be on the red-eye tonight. Make us a reservation at the Hilton, and call me back to let me know when we can meet."

With each message my resentment rose. *I'm your daughter's friend, not your slave.* I finished my glass of wine and stopped myself when I reached to pour another. *Quit being so petty,* I said to myself. *These are good people. They've had a huge shock and they're worried sick. It won't hurt you to be gracious.* I made the hotel reservation but, perhaps passive-aggressively, decided to wait a while before calling Corbett. And I was beginning to see why Kate hadn't wanted me to call her family. At least I could tell her I wasn't the one who'd initiated the contact.

—ᴍ—

Lily chattered her way through dinner: Mrs. McKinley was so nice. Mrs. McKinley made pancakes—in the shape of Mickey Mouse—for breakfast. Mrs. McKinley taught Lily a new song while brushing and French braiding her hair. Mrs. McKinley walked her into the classroom to see Lily's art project. Mrs. McKinley said Lily could come spend the night sometime soon and they'd bake cookies.

Covering his mouth with his napkin, David's eyes grinned at me. I was very happy to be home with my family.

By the time Lily finally fell asleep, I could barely hold my head up. The tension in my back and neck hadn't eased with three glasses of wine. David—in an effort, I sensed, to make further amends for his phone call—offered a massage. Without hesitation, I let him lead me to our bedroom.

My thoughts would not relax as easily as my aching muscles. "I've been indebted to Kate Daniels for almost half my life," I said, leaning up on one elbow.

"You haven't been indebted to her, you've *felt* indebted. There's a big difference," he said.

"But Lily—"

"That's been seven years, not seventeen."

"We've been over this before, David," I said, lying back down on the bed with exasperation.

It had been during our sophomore year in college when my symptoms had begun: chest pains, numbness in my hands and feet, difficulty swallowing, racing heart and loss of motor control. The symptoms hadn't always occurred together but all increased in frequency, and my efforts to ignore them were futile. I had convinced myself I was dying but, at the same time, was terrified to find out for sure.

I didn't even hear Kate come in one afternoon, as I sat on my bed absorbed in catastrophic thought. She badgered me until I told her what was wrong.

At Kate's insistence I went to an internist, who referred me to specialists for a multitude of tests. Each specialist reported the negative results with pleasure, expecting to see my relief. I would have been more relieved by an affirmative diagnosis—and with it a cure. Finally the internist sent me home with a prescription for Valium to take, as needed, for my "generalized anxiety." I had been skeptical at first, but the meds had resolved the symptoms and had eventually enabled me to learn about panic disorder and to experience some success in talk therapy.

"Yes, we've been over this before," David said, gently kneading fragrant cocoa butter into my shoulders. "But I still believe urging someone to get medical attention is a simple act of friendship—not a debt to be repaid. You've had this sense of obligation ever since I've known you, and I don't understand it. I can't help resenting Kate for whatever she does to foster those feelings."

It was the perfect time to tell David the rest of the story. But I couldn't bring myself to do it.

CHAPTER SIX

—ɯ—

Tuesday, September 11

I probably did sleep—between the mental list-making, tossing and turning, and glancing at the clock—but it certainly didn't feel like it come morning. About six, David woke up and found me staring at the ceiling.

"Why fight it?" he said. "Go ahead. Get up and get on with it. I'll get Lily off to school today."

So by seven o'clock, I was at my desk making lists on paper. Lost in thought—jotting down the positive and negative attributes of the many criminal defense attorneys I knew in the area—I startled when our managing partner, Frank Cleaver, walked in.

"Didn't mean to make you jump," he said, with his characteristic half-smile. In his late fifties, the paltry hair that remained on Frank's head was cut to short, white stubble. Tanned and fit, he believed people needed to play hard in order to be well rounded and productive, and I was sure he'd just come in from his morning racquetball game. But in the office, he was all business.

"I hope Rosalee explained why I wasn't in yesterday," I said, feeling a bit defensive about my unscheduled absence. "I got caught up in an unforeseen situation with a friend of mine and ended up handling her initial appearance on an indictment in federal court."

He nodded. "Your friend's the headline story in today's *State Journal*. 'University Prof Charged in Grant Fraud.' How do you know her?"

I shuddered. Publicity was another thing I hadn't considered.

"She was my best friend at Shenstone. After college, she went on to Stanford Med School, and I came here for law. Both our lives became pretty focused, and we kinda drifted apart. But we kept in touch. You know—weddings, reunions, that kind of thing. Several years ago, Kate moved here to work with her new mentor, Martin Braxton."

"Ah, yes. The esteemed Dr. Braxton!" said Frank.

"You know him?"

"I've been introduced to him at a few social occasions. He's very impressed with himself."

"You've gotta admit he's gorgeous," I said, grinning. "The first time I met him I almost mistook him for Tom Selleck. And Kate says he *is* brilliant."

"So you and Kate resumed your close friendship?" Frank asked.

"I'm not sure you could call it close—at least not like in college. We've gotten together for lunch or dinner or a party every few months. But we don't have much in common any-more." *Except one big thing*, I thought but didn't say.

Frank nodded. "Not unusual when you have a family and she doesn't."

"Yes, I've got a family. But Kate's got Marty Braxton. When she moved here, he advised her on everything: where she should live, what kind of car to buy, how to invest her money. He had her working ten hours a day and then ex-pected her to socialize with him in her off time. And she didn't seem bothered by it. I resented him for turning my friend into his shadow—especially since she'd always been so independent and strong. I never particularly liked Braxton and certainly never trusted him. Kate thinks he framed her."

"Oh?" Frank gave me a scrutinizing look. "What do you think?"

"At this point, I don't know what to think. But I do know Kate Daniels is incapable of having committed this crime."

As soon as the words left my mouth, I realized how naive they sounded. I'd had first-hand knowledge of cases where people were wrongly charged and even convicted, but those cases were few and far between. I felt my cheeks flush.

"So you're going to defend her?"

"No. We may not be able to find anyone to represent her in time for the detention hearing tomorrow. But I plan to refer her to someone else right afterward. And to be honest, I don't think the criminal guys in our office are up to the task." The firm had two young associates who handled crimi-nal matters—generally misdemeanors and low-level felonies in state court. But I'd seen both of them in action and wasn't impressed.

"No offense taken," Frank said. "And I agree with your decision not to take the case yourself. Your personal feelings would be bound to cloud your judgment."

I winced. He, too, must have recognized the absurdity of my statement about Kate's innocence.

When he got up to leave, I walked with him down the hall to the reception area and grabbed a copy of the morning paper off one of the coffee tables.

I strolled back to my desk and was a couple of paragraphs into the story when my private line rang. David, I assumed.

"Caroline, this is Margaret Daniels. We've just boarded a plane in Chicago and should be in Madison shortly. Can we visit Kathryn when we get there?"

I thought of the jail's claustrophobic visitation booths with the uncomfortable metal stools, the scarred Plexiglas windows, the grimy telephones you had to use to talk with the prisoners. Kate didn't need to be humiliated by visiting with her parents in those surroundings. Furthermore, Margaret was going to be appalled when she saw Kate's ghastly appearance. I decided to lie.

"The jail only allows family visitation on weekends," I said. "Plus, they go out of their way not to show favoritism to white collar inm—offenders." That much was true: I'd seen some of the jailers taking what I considered perverse pride in demeaning the inmates who were well to do.

"I think we can all do Kate a whole lot more good by working on a solid plan for her release," I said. "Could you come by my office early this afternoon to discuss it?"

"Certainly. What time?"

I checked my calendar. "How about one-thirty? I'll go see Kate later this morning and let her know you're in town and will be in court with her tomorrow."

My secretary walked in promptly at eight-fifteen and handed me a cup of Starbucks decaf. "How are you coping?" she asked.

Rosalee had just turned fifty but, unlike so many women I know, was completely unfazed by her age. With smooth, caramel-colored skin, her face resembled that of a toddler. She stood barely five feet tall and carried a bit too much weight for her doctor's liking, yet she was the picture of fashion. I rarely saw her without thinking "Wow!" Rosalee'd recently taken a demotion and cut back her hours in order to finish her college degree. Today was not one of her scheduled workdays, but here she was when I needed her.

I burst into tears.

"Oh, hon. I know things are a mess, but you'll sort it all out. Have a good cry, drink your coffee, and buzz me when you want to talk. I'll keep everyone out of your hair for now." Rosalee quietly shut the door behind her.

—✖—

My meeting with Kate that morning was pure torture—for both of us. Already seated in the visitation booth when I walked in, Kate hung her head and blinked repeatedly in a futile attempt to shut out the glaring lights. She wore the same hideous orange jumpsuit as before, the sleeve stained today with what looked like vomit. Her every movement set off uncontrollable shaking. Her pallor had worsened. Her eyes were swollen and red.

We visited in a more secure area of the jail today. I picked up the phone on my side of the booth and, after a moment, Kate followed suit. We struggled through the pleasantries, then I swallowed my reluctance and gave her the news. "Your parents are here in Madison."

"Oh, God, no..." Kate said, almost inaudibly. She grabbed the counter on her side of the booth as if to steady herself.

"It wasn't my choice. They got a call from Monica Smith-Kellor at pretrial services yesterday and booked the flight before I even had a chance to talk with them. But in truth, I think they can help a lot. I'm meeting with them this afternoon. I told them you couldn't have visitors here, so the first time you'll see them will be in court tomorrow. I'll probably ask them to testify on your behalf."

"No!"

Kate's intransigence both stunned and frustrated me. It took a concerted effort to keep my tone calm and even. "You have no choice—unless you want to stay in jail. Your parents' stability and reputations will go a long way with Judge Brillstein. You need them."

Kate's resolve deflated before my eyes. "Okay. Do what you have to do. I have a wicked headache and need to go back to my cell."

She stood and—with more energy than I would have expected she had—banged on the door with the heel of her fist. Within seconds a jailer appeared to escort her back to her quarters. Kate didn't look back at me as she left.

It had not been the enlightening interview I'd counted on. We'd had no opportunity to talk about finding her an attorney. And Kate had provided no ammunition for anyone to argue for her release. In fact, I had to agree with Monica Smith-Kellor. Kate didn't look trustworthy. I could only hope she'd get a reasonably good night's sleep and come into court appearing more like herself tomorrow.

—ɷ—

When I returned to my office, Rosalee was just coming back with two sacks from the deli. One contained her lunch and the other mine: a container of sliced fruit, a mineral water, and a toasted Asiago bagel with cream cheese. The bagel was still warm, and I knew the cream cheese would be softened to perfection. "You are truly an angel," I said with a grin.

On my desk sat a manila folder in which I found copies of Kate's rap sheet, a police report, and a few court papers pertaining to Kate's prior arrests. Rosalee walked in as I glanced through the pages.

"Oh, good. You saw them," she said. "Kenny was looking for something to do so I sent him over to the PD and the courthouse to get those records." Kenny—our paralegal—was more likely to look for a way out of an assignment than to seek extra work. I never understood why Frank Cleaver put up with him.

"Thanks, Rose. It would've taken me three weeks to get him to do it." Although she'd voluntarily gone from being our full-time office manager to a part-time secretary, Rosalee still carried a lot of clout within the firm.

I pointed to the reports. "Any surprises here?" I asked. Rosalee read—or at least skimmed—every piece of paper that came in for me. Her insights and synopses had often been life saving.

"Unfortunately, Kenny ran into a few stumbling blocks," she said, leaning against the doorframe. "He got the police report for the first OWI. But the other arrests were made by the sheriff's department, and they wouldn't release the reports to him without getting the sergeant's approval."

"I don't imagine he put up much of a stink, either?"

"No. And he says the clerk of court couldn't locate the file on the bad check charge. Not to worry, though. I'll ride Kenny 'til he gets everything."

Rosalee took a step toward her desk, then turned back to face me. "I hate to say it, Caroline," she said, "but I wonder if your friend's got more problems than this case."

"What do you mean?" I said, as my stomach did a little flip-flop.

"Well, each arrest by itself is no big deal. But it doesn't seem normal for a college professor to be in trouble like she's been."

"I know it seems odd," I said, "but I think her problems are related to the stress of her position. You know. Struggling for funding all the time, pressures to succeed with the research, pressures to publish. Then there are university politics to contend with, along with the everyday grind of teaching. Anyone would crack under the strain."

"Maybe you're right. But you and I have pressures too, and we don't get arrested for drunk driving, writing bad checks and grant fraud. And what's up with the dead student?"

She sounds just like David, I thought as I shrugged and absently stabbed a piece of cantaloupe with my fork.

After Rosalee went back to her workstation, I read through the documents. Kate was right about the cop who'd pulled her over on the first drunk driving ticket. He was the epitome of sleaze, and I'd cringed every time I had to prosecute his cases. While Kate had no legal defense for refusing to submit to the sobriety tests, I could see why she had.

The next item on my to-do list was to call a friend of a friend, now an assistant federal prosecutor, in hopes he'd give me some insight about detention hearings. He told me Magistrate Brillstein would rely heavily on the recommendation of the pretrial services officer. So, with some trepidation, I called Monica Smith-Kellor.

Kate's parents arrived at my office—precisely on time—just as I hung up. We exchanged perfunctory hugs and air kisses, and, though impeccably dressed and groomed as usual, their usual we-live-a-charmed-existence aura seemed less evident. Margaret took off her Armani sunglasses to reveal puffy red eyes. The ever-cool Corbett had a quiver in his voice. *Oh, to have a fifth of Scotch in my bottom desk drawer like lawyers in the movies*, I thought as they sat down together on my couch. The Danielses looked like they could use a shot or two.

"Did you see Kathryn today?" Margaret asked. "How is she?"

"Yes—briefly. She assured me she's safe and holding up okay," I said. I knew they would see Kate in court tomorrow, when there was a good chance she'd look even worse than today. *How do I put this?* "I should warn you, though, she's obviously been under a great deal of strain, and I doubt she's sleeping well. So she doesn't look great. Once we get her out, we can make sure she takes better care of herself."

"Can we assume she'll be released at the hearing tomorrow, then?" Corbett asked, sitting forward in his seat.

"I'm not assuming anything with this magistrate judge. But I do think it's likely." I shuffled through some papers on my desk to mask my discomfort. *I was just a kid when I knew these people*, I thought. *And now they're depending on me—looking to me as an expert when I'm in way over my head.*

"I just got off the phone with Monica Smith-Kellor," I said, "—the woman who called you for the bail investigation. She'll recommend release if the two of you will post $5,000 in cash and promise to forfeit $50,000 if Kate fails to appear. I'll need you to testify about why you believe Kate is a good bail risk. Then there would be routine conditions like Kate agreeing not to use drugs or alcohol and to report to Monica once a week."

"We agree and so will Kathryn," said Corbett without missing a beat. "I'll call my bank immediately for a cashier's check."

We decided Corbett would testify on Kate's behalf because Margaret was sure she'd break down on the stand. I went over the list of questions I had with him, jotting down the gist of his answers. His clear, concise responses assured me Corbett Daniels would be a strong witness.

Then came a moment of awkward silence. I had nothing further to discuss with them, but I sensed they had more on their minds.

"Has Kathryn made arrangements for your retainer?" Corbett asked.

"We haven't had a chance to talk about my fees yet, but the bill should be minimal since I won't be her lawyer much longer. I'll help her find someone to represent her after the detention hearing."

"Can't you do it?" Margaret asked, with a nervous edge to her voice.

"It's not advisable. It's difficult to be objective about a friend's case. And although I've been admitted to the federal bar, I've never practiced in federal court."

They exchanged a look that told me my rationale was falling on deaf ears. I needed to shore up my argument if I wanted to extricate myself from this mess without a boatload of guilt.

"It would be like Corbett performing surgery on a close friend or family member in an unfamiliar O.R. with all new staff. It's do-able, but not desirable," I said.

"But Corbett has done just that," Margaret said. "He performed a mastectomy for my sister in Corpus Christi two years ago. She was scared to death and didn't trust anyone else to do it. He was a godsend to her."

"Well—"

"Caroline, I made some calls today," said Corbett with a self-satisfied look. "I called an old fraternity brother of mine. Edward Benson—I understand you know him?"

"Yes. Yes, I do." Benson was one of Wisconsin's premier defense attorneys—flamboyant, arrogant and immensely talented.

"Ed says he defended a man you prosecuted for spousal abuse. He has high praise for your skills—and not just because you beat him. Says you had the best winning percentage in the whole DA's office."

True—but how would he know it?

Corbett laughed as if he could read the question on my face. "Ed's a bit anal—he's had some paralegal in his firm compiling statistics for years! But be that as it may, he knows his stuff. He says you're tough, organized and well respected. Says you could be earning two hundred and fifty grand doing criminal defense at any number of major firms here. So why are you wasting your skills practicing part-time as a generalist?"

Corbett has really done his homework. While proud of the kudos he'd listed, I couldn't help but resent his prying into something that was none of his business.

"My priorities have changed," I said, straightening the already perfectly aligned legal pad on my desk. "David and Lily mean more to me than any law practice. This firm allows me the flexibility to put them first. Ed Benson was one of the names I was going to suggest to Kate. Do you think he'd take the case?"

"Oh, the son-of-a-bitch would jump at the chance to get into the Daniels family's business," Corbett said. "But I couldn't stomach it!"

Margaret paled. I sensed we were on touchy ground.

"The bottom line is this." Corbett stood and brushed the wrinkles out of his trousers. "We want you to represent Kate. If you need to hire consultants to brief you on the specifics of federal practice, then do it. But we have every confidence you're the lawyer she needs, especially with your good reputation in this town."

"Let's take things one step at a time. After Kate is released, we can talk about her representation," I said. It wasn't the answer they wanted to hear, or the answer I truly wanted to give, but it would have to do. "I'll meet you in the hotel lobby around two tomorrow, and we'll all go over to the courthouse together."

After the Danielses left, I sat staring out my window, making a conscious effort to appreciate the crisp sky with its sparse wispy clouds. But Kate Daniels—my thirty-six-year-old, smart, professional friend—was stuck in a windowless gray cell and her dad was here calling the shots. I was far too uneasy to enjoy the view. Neither Corbett nor Kate Daniels would readily take "no" for an answer.

I thought back to the day in law school when one of my women professors had pulled me aside and recommended that I take an assertiveness training class. She had said I was one of her brightest students, but I needed to learn to stand up for my opinions. I'd followed her advice, and many times over the years—in conferences with other attorneys and in the courtroom—I had been grateful for it. My assertiveness skills would be sorely tested with Corbett and Kate.

Get on with it, I told myself and set about retrieving the voice messages I'd received during Kate's parents' visit. David's was the third: "Hi, dear. I'll be in a meeting for the rest of the day so we'll have to talk when we get home. But I wanted to let you know the social worker called: they found someone for us! Love you."

CHAPTER SEVEN

—Ⱳ—

My worn red leather wallet bulged with change, crumpled bills, receipts, long-expired credit cards, and business cards I'd collected for reasons I no longer remembered. The social worker's card had to be there too.

Linda Wordsworth had done the legally required home study for Lily's adoption seven-and-a-half years ago. A consummate professional, she'd delved artfully into our lives and psyches and had recommended the judge approve the adoption. She'd said it was a routine evaluation. But I'd been amazed at her ability to elicit answers to questions David and I had never even thought to ask ourselves: If we later had a biological child, would Lily become a second-class family member? Would our extended families accept Lily as one of their own? Would we treat Lily more leniently to compensate for her loss of her birth mother?

Now affiliated with an agency called Parenthood in Partnership, Linda facilitated surrogate-parenting arrangements, and we'd sought her out to explore that route to expanding our family. David and I laughed about the acronym PIP and joked we were hoping for a "little PIPsqueak."

With nervous excitement, I shuffled through the wallet and finally located Linda's card. I dialed the phone and held my breath 'til she answered—thankfully, on the first ring.

"Hi, Caroline," she said warmly. "I tried reaching you earlier but got your voice mail. Rather than leaving a message, I called David and gave him the news. What do you think?"

"I was in a meeting when he called, so he just left me a short message. Now he's in a meeting and can't tell me about it."

"Ah, the frustrations of phone tag. Let me fill you in. Last week we got an application from a woman in northern Wisconsin—Black River Falls—who says she wants to be a gestational carrier. She's thirty-two and has two kids, ages four and six. Hasn't worked outside the home since the oldest was born but was planning to go back to teaching when the youngest started school. Her husband was in the Army Reserves, deployed to Afghanistan."

I shuddered, afraid of where this was going.

"In July," Linda went on, "he ran into an IED and suffered massive injuries, including the loss of one leg. He'll recover, but she needs to be home to take care of him, and they're short on income."

"It sounds like she's already got enough troubles without dealing with someone else's pregnancy."

"Maybe—I'll be able to assess it better when and if I go to do the formal evaluation. But I talked with her and her husband on the phone for quite a while and was pretty impressed.

They said both of her pregnancies were easy, and she loved giving birth. There's only one thing that's troubling."

My heart sank. "What is it?"

"You know our agency recommends a gestational carrier charge between fifteen and twenty-five thousand dollars, but each one sets her own fee. This woman is asking forty-five thousand."

"Yikes—"

"Yes, it's a bit steep. Not unheard of, but steep."

"Do you have other intended parents who would pay that much? Will we be in a bidding war for her services?" I was startled to hear a bitchy edge to my own voice, but I felt so desperate to bring another child into our home, I couldn't seem to control my tone.

"No. You're the only couple whose criteria matched hers. And she says she hasn't applied to be a carrier with any other agency or private party. I'm inclined to believe her."

"What's the next step?" I asked.

"Talk to David and decide whether you want us to pursue this lead. You guys need to have a frank discussion about this. I hate to say it, but harsh financial realities sometimes help you clarify your real priorities. Be sure this is what you want."

"How long do we have to decide?" I chastised myself for feeling more than a little peevish toward the poor woman who would soon be contending with two young children *and* a disabled vet. The emotional baggage of my infertility often got the better of me.

"The applicant's got plenty on her plate. The husband will be coming home from the rehab facility next Monday, and they don't think they'd be ready to do the in vitro until at least December. So I told her we'd talk again in a few weeks."

"Okay. We'll be in touch."

—⟋⟍—

A half-hour later, Rosalee brought in some letters for me to sign. "What's up?" she asked. "You look miles away."

"I feel like I've been through hell and back with this Kate thing. And now I get a call, which should be good news, and instead it's opening up old wounds."

"Want to talk about it?"

I nodded, and Rosalee settled into a chair to listen.

"About eight months before we adopted Lily, I had an ectopic pregnancy—a bad one. The fetus had implanted in one of my fallopian tubes, which ruptured. We were camping up at the Apostle Islands when it happened, and things were pretty dicey by the time we got to the hospital." I paused, remembering how frightened and devastated David and I had been.

"Obviously they saved me," I said with a forced grin. "But they weren't able to save the tube. And it turned out my uterus was misshapen and the other tube wasn't connected. So, although we hadn't known it, the chances of a successful pregnancy were pretty slim. I was heartbroken, but David kept saying not to worry, we'd find a way to have kids."

I was always surprised when the pain of losing our baby came back to me. After all, I had only known of the pregnancy for a few weeks, had never felt its movement, hadn't seen any ultrasound pictures or picked out any names. We didn't even know if the child was a boy or a girl. A support group had helped us to acknowledge and deal with our loss, but I had never expected the persistent ache of grief could go on for years—or that, at times, it would be so excruciating.

I blinked back tears. Rosalee nodded and brushed at her own cheek.

"Then the opportunity to adopt Lily came up, and we jumped at the chance. She was the most wonderful baby I could ever imagine: sunny, bright, engaging. Since then, we've sometimes thought, why mess with success? But Lily wants a brother or sister, and David and I have always felt strongly she should have one.

"When she was three, we decided to try in vitro fertilization. The doctors said it was a long shot but were willing to give it a try. We put our lives on hold for months, we did all the tests, and I took the god-awful fertility meds. After the first procedure failed, I vowed never again: It was too emotionally draining. But six months later, at my mother's urging, I reconsidered, and we tried another round. Only to fail again."

"I'm so sorry, honey. I never knew," Rosalee said, shaking her head. "And to think of all the complaining I do about my kids."

"It's okay. If I weren't so insecure about it, I would have told you long ago."

"Insecure?"

"I know it sounds crazy, but I feel like less of a woman for not being able to have my own kids." I said, stifling a sob. "Maybe I took to heart all my mother's lamentations about 'When are you going to give us some grandchildren?' Maybe it's because I'll never be a part of the discussions about the joys of pregnancy and the horrors of childbirth. Maybe I'm afraid immortality only comes through your biological children. It's all irrational, but sometimes it's hard to turn off those thoughts—or the feelings that go along with them."

"Too true," Rosalee said, handing me a tissue from a box on the side table. "Why don't you tell me about the phone call that upset you again?"

I blew my nose and took a moment to collect my thoughts. "A few months ago," I said, "we applied to a local agency to find a surrogate to carry our child—they call it a gestational carrier. David and I would have to go through the medical procedures for harvest of the sperm and egg, but it would be our biological child carried by another woman. A woman who's already proven she can successfully carry a pregnancy to term."

I looked up to see Rosalee's reaction. She belonged to a somewhat conservative Christian church, and I wasn't entirely sure she'd approve of this new-age path to parenthood.

"I've read about this," she said. "What a blessing it would be if you could find the right person!"

The muscles in my face relaxed the instant I heard her comment—at least she'd be supportive if we could manage to afford to hire a surrogate. "Our social worker called today and said she had a potential candidate. But the woman would charge almost twice as much as we were expecting to pay in fees. Like forty-five thousand dollars. And that's just her fee, not any of the other expenses. We don't have that much in our budget."

"Honey, sometimes you just have to have faith things will work out the way they should. I'll keep you all in my prayers."

She stood, gave me a quick hug, and went out to answer her phone.

I sat at my desk, trying with little success to quiet my mind. I replayed several times Linda Wordsworth's little lecture about "harsh financial realities" helping to clarify priorities, becoming increasingly angry. *This is all so fucking unfair!*

—∞—

Since I was accomplishing nothing substantive at work, I left the office early enough to surprise Lily at school. She was delighted to skip out on her after-school program and grocery shop with me instead. And she apparently failed to notice her dad and I were preoccupied with our own thoughts during dinner.

With Lily finally asleep, David made a fire and poured two glasses of chilled Bailey's Irish Crème. I sank into the couch next to him and tucked my feet up under me.

"I was so excited when I got your message," I said. "But I felt like I'd been kicked in the stomach when Linda said the potential carrier wanted so much money. We don't live in California or New York. We're not movie stars, for God's sake! It all sounds so mercenary."

"I hear you," David said, getting up to tend the fire. He threw on a log and poked at it needlessly, clearly lost in thought. I was sure he'd say we needed to swallow our disappointment and hunker down again to wait for another possible surrogate.

"But I've been thinking," he said as he returned to the couch, "it's really only twenty thousand more than we'd planned. We can get a second mortgage. This is what you want, so let's go for it."

A twinge of defensiveness hit me. I sat forward, moving my feet to the floor. "What *I* want?"

"What I meant was, it means a lot to you to have our biological child, and I respect that."

"It doesn't mean a lot to you?" I asked, incredulous that we might not feel the same way about such an important issue. *Haven't we discussed this before?*

He met my eyes with undisguised tenderness. "I've been thinking a lot about it since Linda called. I have to be frank with you: it doesn't. I can't imagine loving a child more than I love Lily. So I'd be perfectly happy to adopt a sibling or two for her. But I think it's different for a man. And I don't have the pressure from my family that you have from yours."

My mother's words—uttered more than three years ago—still stung: "Why don't you try in vitro again? There's absolutely *nothing* more fulfilling than seeing yourself in your *own* children!"

"I honestly can't imagine I could love our biological child more than Lily either," I said. "But are you saying you want to pass on the surrogacy idea altogether? Or on this particular applicant?"

"Neither. I'm saying that one way or another, Lily should have a brother or sister before she's much older. We've already decided using a gestational carrier is the quickest way to achieve that. Now we just need to accept that it'll be more expensive than we'd hoped."

I nodded and snuggled next to him, relieved that he'd been able to "clarify our priorities." *Maybe Linda Wordsworth wasn't off base after all.*

We were silent for several minutes—the comfortable silence of two people who know one another intimately. Holding hands, mesmerized by the fire, and enveloped in the warmth of our love.

Finally, David spoke. "Do you want to call Linda and tell her our decision is to go forward, or do you want me to?"

"I'd appreciate it if you would. My day tomorrow is bound to be pretty hectic."

"Oh, yeah. In all the excitement, I forgot to ask you how the meeting with Kate's parents went."

"It was difficult," I said, lamenting the end of our personal interlude.

"In what way?"

There were so many ways I could have responded, but he deserved to know the truth. "They really want me to represent her."

The briefest glance at him told me what David thought: color drained from his face, and a prominent vein throbbed in his temple. "I can't help with this one, Caroline," he said in an incongruously calm voice. "The choice is completely up to you."

David stood up and nodded toward the fireplace. "The fire's under control," he said. "I'm heading to bed, and you don't need to stay up to tend it."

When he left the room, I noticed my hands were tightly clenched. *All the more reason to say no to the Daniels family.*

CHAPTER EIGHT

—⁓—

Wednesday, September 12

I'd always suspected I had a touch of ADD: I was never much good at multi-tasking and my thoughts often drifted off-course without warning. As a child, I'd gotten more than one report card with the comment, "Caroline is easily distracted."

So it was no small task for me to concentrate on Kate's detention hearing when I'd rather be thinking about our prospective gestational carrier, or traveling to Guatemala to adopt twins, or getting a call from a birth mom who just *knew* we were the right parents to raise her baby, or...

But my well-honed work ethic—and the thought of Kate in her vomit-stained orange attire—carried me through the morning. I formulated my arguments and bolstered them with some on-line research, outlining everything neatly on my legal pad with a purple felt-tipped pen.

I made a list of three criminal lawyers and their contact information to give to Kate, omitting "that son-of-a-bitch" Ed Benson in light of Corbett's caustic comments. But before I left my office, I added Benson's name. Kate needed the best, despite her father's thoughts on the matter.

When I arrived at the Hilton, Margaret and Corbett were just walking out of the hotel coffee shop, looking as disheveled as I'd ever seen them. Margaret absently wiped at a spot on her lapel with a linen handkerchief. Corbett's tie was askew and a lock of his salt-and-pepper hair fell awkwardly on his forehead.

"The courthouse is only about five blocks from here," I said. "I thought we'd walk over and get a bit of air."

They both nodded distractedly as I preceded them out the revolving door. It was a long walk, brimming with uncomfortable silence.

At the courthouse, I settled Kate's parents on a bench outside Judge Brillstein's courtroom and reluctantly went to meet her at the marshals' lockup.

The change in Kate astounded me. *Maybe all she did need was a good night's sleep. And maybe we taxpayers are springing for better jail mattresses than we know about.* In a clean orange uniform, she managed to look imperious and somewhat chic. Her thick wavy hair, always the envy of all her college friends, gleamed and elegantly framed her face. While I doubted make-up was allowed in the jail, Kate's lips and cheeks had the rosy glow of lipstick and blush. Her deep-brown eyes and white teeth sparkled.

"Hey, girlfriend!" she said with a grin. "Did you bring me a 'Get Out of Jail Free' card?"

"Well, not exactly free. But I think we've got the ticket." I summarized the proposed plan to win her release. To my surprise and relief, Kate raised no objection to her parents posting the bail.

As I got up to walk out, Kate blew me a kiss. "Thanks, Caroline. You're a real friend."

There's the Kathryn Daniels I know and love. Thank God she's back!

Before the proceeding began, I huddled in the courtroom with George Cooper and Monica Smith-Kellor and explained the release plan. Cooper nodded but didn't commit to supporting it. I hoped he'd at least give it strong consideration.

The marshals escorted Kate into the courtroom a minute later. She walked proudly—it brought to mind some political prisoner using body language to say "fuck you" to her captors. I fleetingly thought she should tone the pride down a notch. But, no matter: the judge didn't see her entrance, and her demeanor instantly alleviated her parents' fears. They watched in anticipation from the front row as Kate flashed them a smile and sat beside me at the table.

The interior of the courtroom matched the building's modernistic design: heavy light-oak furnishings, upholstered walls with silver accents and sleek oak trim. A small blue acrylic sign on the table read, "Please! Silence your cell phones." Thankful for the reminder, I powered mine down just as the judge took the bench.

After the formalities, Judge Brillstein said, "Okay, Mr. Cooper. You've moved for detention. It's your burden to convince me."

Cooper stood up. "Your Honor, based on a plan proposed by Pretrial Services and defense counsel, the government withdraws its motion to detain Ms. Daniels. We'll agree to the defendant's release on a $50,000 bond signed by her parents and secured with $5,000 cash. We'll want her to report for supervision, etcetera. Ms. Smith-Kellor has some suggestions for specific conditions, to which I understand the defendant agrees."

"Ms. Smith-Kellor?" the judge asked, nodding toward her.

"Yes, Your Honor," Monica said. "We believe the bond and conditions will ensure the defendant's future appearances." She went on to list the conditions: the defendant would report to her in person weekly, the defendant would refrain from any use of alcohol and illegal drugs, the defendant would give urine samples to prove she was drug-free, the defendant would surrender her passport...

I was struck by the tendency to refer to Kate as "the defendant"—it seemed almost calculated to depersonalize her. I glanced at Kate during the recitation. She seemed nonplussed by the terminology or any of the conditions. "Okay with you?" I whispered. Kate nodded.

The judge turned to me. "Ms. Spencer, your comments?"

"Your Honor, Ms. Daniels requests she be released on the terms described by Ms. Smith-Kellor," I said.

"Well, folks," the judge said, "this is all fine and dandy. But I'm the one who has to sign the release order, and I'm not convinced Ms. Daniels will come back to court. The bail report I read two days ago hasn't gone away. And for all I know $5,000—or even $50,000—may be a pittance to Ms.

Daniels' family. Maybe they'd gladly spend $50,000 to give her the opportunity to skip town. I want to hear from these people."

"Your Honor," I said with confidence, "since I hadn't anticipated Mr. Cooper would withdraw his motion to detain, I'm fully prepared to present evidence. Ms. Daniels' father, Dr. Corbett Daniels, is here to testify."

"Good. Good. Have him come forward."

Corbett took the stand, and we mechanically went through the preliminary questions: his name, address, and relationship to Kate.

"Dr. Daniels," I asked, "could you please describe the nature of your relationship to Kathryn. What I mean is, how do you get along? Do you have frequent contact? That kind of thing." I'd deliberately asked open-ended questions because I thought Corbett would be most comfortable giving an uninterrupted response.

Corbett's eyes filled with tears as he nodded almost imperceptibly in acknowledgment. I immediately regretted my approach. It would have been far easier for him to answer individual questions.

Leaning forward, he took a deep breath and began. "Kathryn is the youngest of our four children. She was a beautiful, mild-mannered baby—always smiling. From the beginning it was clear she was very bright, perhaps even smarter than her older siblings, who were straight-A students. Kathryn was always fascinated with my work—I'm a surgeon. Even as a young child, she'd come to my office to read my books and medical journals and ask questions of my staff and me. I was so proud when she decided to go to medical school and make surgery her career. I guess you could say Kathryn was—" Now he sobbed audibly, and the tears spilled down his cheeks.

I can't go through with this. This man should not have to be here justifying why his daughter should be released from jail.

Corbett inhaled deeply and dabbed at his eyes with a Kleenex proffered by the court clerk. "I'm sorry," he said. "Kathryn was and is the apple of my eye. She's been half a continent away from us physically since she moved to Wisconsin. But she's always kept in touch—calling at least a couple times a month. And she comes home for holidays and important family functions. She cares about her family."

I glanced over at Kate, who sat slumped in her chair, pointedly avoiding her father's eyes.

"Your Honor," Corbett squared his shoulders and continued, his voice stronger, "you question the extent of our fortune. I won't lie to you. Losing $50,000 would not break the bank, but it would not be a small matter either. I made a lot of money during my career, but I also put four children through graduate school, and—I'm ashamed to say—I've made some bad investments. But if necessary, I will pledge every penny I have to secure my daughter's release. You see, I know Kathryn, and I know she is not one to run from her problems. We are a law-abiding family. We will fight these unfounded charges with everything we've got, but within the law. I promise you she will appear in court for every proceeding."

I couldn't wait to excuse him from the witness stand, and I was confident the judge had heard enough. "Thank you, Dr. Daniels—" I began.

Corbett raised his hand to interrupt. "Excuse me. There's something more." He turned to face the judge. "Your Honor, my dear wife of forty-five years, Margaret Shenstone Daniels, is present in the courtroom. She's given me permission to speak for her, since she is very much afraid of public speaking. But if you wish to hear from her directly, she, too, will testify."

I looked over at Margaret who—her eyes glazed with tears and, I suspected, terror—nodded her head in agreement. "Thank you, Dr. Daniels," I said again. "I have no further questions."

"No questions, Your Honor," George Cooper said.

"Very well," Judge Brillstein said, pausing as if to collect his thoughts. "Dr. Daniels, you may step down." I said a brief, silent prayer that he would not ask me to call Margaret to the stand. I certainly didn't intend to offer her testimony without his request.

The judge waited respectfully while Corbett resumed his seat and my anxiety for Margaret grew. Finally he spoke. "I don't think it will be necessary to hear from Mrs. Daniels," he said, and I imagined everyone in the courtroom joined me in a sigh of relief. "I'm satisfied with Dr. Daniels' assurances, and I'm prepared to release the defendant on her father's $50,000 bond, with $5,000 to be posted in cash. I'm also ordering the conditions recommended by Ms. Smith-Kellor. The clerk will prepare the order."

I'd been entranced by Corbett's emotional statement and Margaret's anxious moment and hadn't been watching Kate's reaction. I reached over and squeezed her hand, expecting to sense in her the same satisfaction I was feeling. She smiled at me, but it felt false. It was as though she'd shut down emotionally and a robotic Kate Daniels had taken her place.

Magistrate Judge Stanley Brillstein looked straight at Kate. "You're a very fortunate woman, Ms. Daniels. Do you promise to appear at all times as scheduled and agree to comply with the terms we've discussed?"

"Yes, sir," she replied, and I was relieved she managed to sound engaged.

Kate's release didn't occur immediately. The U.S. Marshals had to take her back to the county jail, where—of course—there was more "processing." I, too, went to the jail. While waiting in the sparse, ground level lobby for her to be booked out, I puzzled over Kate's mood swings. She'd been so upbeat when I met with her in the morning and when she walked into the courtroom. Was it her father's moving testimony on the witness stand that deflated her mood? Or was her seemingly precarious mental state understandable given the circumstances?

Kate hugged me tightly as the jail door banged shut behind her. The distinctive sound of a three-hundred-pound steel door closing against a concrete and steel doorframe is one I'd gladly not hear again.

"Thanks," she said.

"You're welcome," I replied. "I'm just sorry it took so long. Your folks are waiting for us at the hotel. But first, we need to go over to pretrial services and get you signed up. I know you weren't really pleased with Monica before. But I've been more impressed with her during my recent conversations, and she did support your release. So please try—"

"I get it, Caroline," Kate interrupted wearily. "I promise to play nice. And though I'm not happy to be under her thumb, it sure beats the alternative. I don't know how long I would have lasted in jail."

The meeting with Monica Smith-Kellor went well. Kate maintained eye contact and nodded appropriately as Monica carefully outlined the requirements of her bail. While the conditions were somewhat inconvenient and demeaning—Kate would need to report once a week to prove she'd not left town and to give urine samples witnessed by Monica or one of her coworkers—they would not be difficult. Before we left, though, Monica asked Kate to give her first sample.

She explained, "If this sample were to test positive for any controlled substances, you would not be in violation, because it would reflect prior usage. But some drugs, like marijuana, stay in the system a long time. We need to send the urine to an off-site laboratory for a baseline reading of any drugs in your system on the day bail supervision begins."

While Kate went with her, I sat and waited in Monica's office. The whole notion of having to urinate in front of a stranger—or to *watch* a stranger urinating—made me shudder. I thought of how difficult it had sometimes been for me to give urine samples in the doctor's office, and that was only with a technician waiting but not watching. Kate and Monica returned surprisingly quickly and, even more surprisingly, both seemed unperturbed by the whole episode. I understood this was part of Monica's job, but how had Kate managed to remain nonplussed?

As we left the building, I turned to Kate. "I need to head back to my office and check on a few things. Your mom said they got a rental car and they'll give you a ride home from their hotel. Okay?"

Kate shook her head. "I can't face him alone, Caroline," she said, her voice faltering. "Come with me—please."

She looked unkempt—wearing the same clothes she'd had on when she was arrested—and I imagined what it would feel like for her to walk into the Hilton to join her elegantly attired parents. I nodded in tacit agreement and walked with her to the hotel.

In the lobby, Kate used the house phone to dial her parents' room. No answer. "That figures," she muttered. "They're probably in the bar."

They sat in a corner of the quiet, dimly lit bar—Corbett staring into his half-empty glass of amber liquid and Margaret running her forefinger around the rim of her coffee mug— and didn't see us at the doorway. Kate took a deep breath and walked toward them.

Margaret glanced up from the table as we approached and practically jumped from her chair. "Thank God," she said, taking Kate into her arms. "Thank God that's over."

Corbett remained seated and took a swig of his drink. "God had nothing to do with this, Margaret," he said caustically. "We owe our thanks to Caroline. And this is *far* from over."

I stood to the side, wanting nothing more than to extricate myself from this awkward reunion. Bless her heart, Margaret came to the rescue. "Of course—thank you, Caroline! Now, Kate, let's get you home and into some fresh clothes." She reached for her purse and turned to her husband. "We'll be back in time for dinner and can talk more then."

Corbett waved a hand in acknowledgement and promptly resumed his fixation with his drink.

"So that's how he's gonna play it," Kate said to her mother when we reached the lobby. "I've shamed him, so I get the cold shoulder."

Margaret shot her a look that seemed to say, "Not in front of Caroline," and fumbled in her bag for the car keys. "It's been a long, emotional day for all of us, dear," she said aloud.

"Yes, it has," I echoed. "And I've got to run. Kate, I'll be at home tomorrow. Give me a call around ten, okay?"

"Ten it is," Kate said. She and Margaret each gave me a quick hug, and I escaped through the revolving door, anxious to return to my normal life.

—⁙—

David had picked up Lily at school that day, and they were so engrossed in a game of "Who Am I?" that they barely nodded at me when I walked in. Seeing Lily's look of glee as she guessed his character washed away the trials of my day.

"We think a special treat's in order," David said to me when the round was over. "How does some dinner out and a trip to Vitense for mini-golf sound?"

"Divine!" I said. Although leftovers, a glass of wine, and a foot rub would have been my preference, I would gladly expend a little extra energy to prolong their sparkling mood.

But as we strolled through the golf course that evening, I found myself distracted, replaying in my mind the day's events. An inexplicable uneasiness overcame me as I thought of the equally inexplicable positive changes in Kate's appearance and demeanor in the marshal's lockup and in court that morning. *You're being silly. It's a good thing*, I told myself. But I couldn't shake the feeling.

A few minutes later, I flashed on the engraved sign that had been sitting on the courtroom table. *Shit! Did I turn my cell back on?* Reluctantly I pulled the phone from the pocket of my jeans. I pushed the power button and watched it come to life.

I had missed two calls, and there was one message, left at four o'clock: "It's Doug Connaboy. We're releasing your client's car—it's clean. But we need to talk to her again. Call me."

CHAPTER NINE

Thursday, September 13

Part-time professionals are always under pressure to make our schedules work. Trying to preserve both "off" and "on" time, to satisfy everyone on both fronts, and, often, to fit four or five days' work into two or three.

I wasn't scheduled to work today, but no way could Detective Connaboy's call go unreturned.

As soon as Lily was off to school, I poured myself a second cup of decaf, sat at the kitchen counter, and summoned the energy to make the call. "Sorry I didn't get back to you yesterday, Doug," I said when he answered. "What do you need to talk with Kate about?"

"Let's just say our investigation into Yvonne Pritchard's death has raised some new questions, and we hope your client will help clear them up."

My client. I gotta resolve this.

"Look," I said, "I sat in on Kate's interview with you the other night as a favor to her—as a friend who's also a lawyer. Right now I'm in the process of arranging other representation for her pending cases. So I need to know: Is she a suspect?" I held my breath, uncertain whether I really wanted to hear his response.

"Not at this point. But I think she may know more than she originally let on. Are you saying I can talk to her without you?"

"Oh man, Doug! I can't let you do that. You've got an unexplained death, and you tell me Kate might know something about it. Even a first year law student would realize Kate shouldn't talk to you without an attorney."

"I hear you, Caroline. But frankly I don't have time to wait until your friend finds another lawyer and brings him or her up to speed."

"Okay," I said, massaging my forehead with my free hand. "Kate's supposed to call me this morning. I'll see what she says and get back to you."

I didn't worry when Kate failed to call at ten o'clock. I'd never known her to wear a watch or concern herself with timeliness—which, over the years, had occasionally been hard for me to reconcile. I'd eventually learned not to let her upset my own schedule.

My to-do list today had "exercise" written in capital letters, and twinges of a stress headache told me now was the time. I arranged my cell phone and a cordless handset for the landline on the control panel of our treadmill, climbed on and began my workout.

By noon, I'd run three miles and done two loads of laundry, but I still hadn't heard from Kate. I sat on the couch in the family room, a basket of fresh smelling, folded clothing at my feet, and began placing calls.

There was no answer at Kate's home. Her cell phone went straight to voice mail. A secretary at her university office told me Kate had not been in yet and suggested I try the lab. That, too, met with negative results: the lab assistant said he'd been there all morning and hadn't seen her.

Finally I called my office, thinking perhaps Kate had tried to reach me there.

"It's odd," I told Rosalee, "Kate was supposed to call me this morning and didn't. And now I can't reach her. She's not at home, her office or the lab."

"Maybe she's in Mexico!"

"That's not funny!"

"I know I shouldn't tease you, hon. But you're overreacting. She just got out after three days in jail. She's probably got tons of errands to run and just forgot to call you."

"Maybe you're right," I said, but Rosalee's comments weren't totally convincing to me.

At two-thirty, Corbett Daniels called. "Have you heard from Kate?" he asked. "We slept in this morning, but Margaret tried to call her to get together for lunch and hasn't been able to reach her."

"No. I've tried too. I asked her to call this morning to set up an appointment, but she didn't." As soon as I said it, I could've kicked myself. I didn't want to give Corbett any more reason to be down on Kate. Moreover, I didn't want to worry Margaret.

"You don't think—"

"She just got out after spending three days in jail, Corbett. I'm sure she had a lot to catch up on—errands and the like. Don't worry."

"I suppose you're right. Well, in any event, Margaret and I would like to meet with you to settle the issue of representation."

"I appreciate your concern. But really, that's a matter for Kate to decide."

"I've posted $5,000 and promised $45,000 more. It seems to me I damn well have some say in the matter," Corbett said, his voice becoming increasingly forceful.

Whoa! He doesn't have to use that tone with me. Who the hell does he think he is?

"I got you involved in the bail process out of necessity," I said testily. "But Kate's out now, and she's a competent adult. So who she chooses as her lawyer—and paying the retainer— is her business."

But then I remembered Corbett crying on the witness stand and realized he *did* care about Kate. "Why don't you talk to her and ask if it's okay for you to be involved?" I asked. "With Kate's permission, I'd welcome your input."

"Okay. If you hear from Kate, please ask her to call. We're still at the Hilton and should be in all afternoon."

The question of Kate's whereabouts and my unfulfilled promise to call Doug Connaboy nagged at me as I tackled more mundane household tasks. Twice, I forced myself to sit down and practice yoga breathing to ward off the panicky thoughts bubbling up in my head. I cut my finger while slicing tomatoes for dinner and was cursing Kate for causing my carelessness when Lily bounded in the door.

"Is it okay if Anna comes over?" she asked as she deposited her backpack on the kitchen floor.

But Anna was at the door before I even had a chance to reply. I threw Lily a withering look: Anna was my least favorite of the neighborhood kids and Lily knew it. A tiny girl with ivory skin and white-blond hair, Anna looked and acted like an angel that is, in the presence of adults. But I'd overheard her making snotty comments and goading Lily into breaking our rules. David and I had begun referring to her as "Edie Haskell," after Wally's disingenuous friend on the old TV show "Leave it to Beaver." I didn't have the patience for her today.

"Hello, Anna," I said with as much restraint as I could muster. "You and Lily can play in the family room for half an hour; then it's time for her homework and chores."

Can this day get any worse?

Intent on applying pressure to the bloodstained paper towel I'd wrapped around my wounded finger, I jumped when my cell phone rang. *Finally!* But upon seeing the incoming number I let it go to voice mail. I'd always prided myself on taking rather than dodging calls, so I felt a stab of guilt at not answering this one from Doug Connaboy.

His terse message hit me right in the gut: "Please don't play defense-lawyer games with me, Caroline. You're better than that. Yvonne's parents are going through hell and they deserve some answers."

Chapter Ten

Friday, September 14

After a hectic and less-than-satisfying day at home, I welcomed the order of my office. Glancing through my messages, I was disappointed but not surprised to find none from Kate. Rosalee would have let me know if she'd heard from her yesterday.

Despite my many fears, I forced myself to wait until eight o'clock to begin making calls. Kate answered her home phone on the second ring.

A wave of relief washed over me: She hadn't fled the country. She hadn't committed suicide. She hadn't been killed by some unknown perpetrator who'd also killed Yvonne Pritchard. But in an instant, the wave receded, and I was left with unadulterated anger.

"Where the hell were you yesterday? I was worried sick when you didn't call and I couldn't reach you!"

"You and my parents!" Kate said, altogether too breezily for my liking. "They had the condo manager let them in about nine last night. I'm sure they expected to find me hanging from the shower rod. Instead they found me asleep. It was pretty embarrassing. I'd planned to read some research proposals for an hour or so and then call and meet them for dinner at the hotel. I read two pages and zonked out again—I only slept about three hours the night before last."

That doesn't explain where you were all day. Or why you didn't call like you promised you would. Or why you didn't answer your frickin' phone!

"I'm just glad you're okay," I heard myself say. *Oh, my God—she's making me schizophrenic.*

I took a sip of my chai tea and collected my thoughts. "Are your folks there?"

"Yes. They stayed at my place last night. They're going to check out of the hotel this morning and bring their stuff back here. They'll stay through early next week."

I guess Corbett quit with the cold shoulder routine. Thank God for that.

"I want to get together and talk," I said. "But before we do anything else, we need to have another meeting with Doug Connaboy and Sam Jacobs—"

"Can I get my car back?"

"Yes, you can," I replied, irritated at her self-centered interruption. "But the detectives want to ask you some more questions, and my inability to reach you yesterday isn't sitting too well with Doug."

"You told him you couldn't find me?" Kate asked incredulously.

"No. When I spoke with him yesterday morning, I told him I expected to hear from you soon and would call him back. When you didn't call, I didn't call back. He left me a message later in the day making it clear he didn't appreciate it. My credibility with these guys is on the line, Kate. Are you willing to meet with them this morning?"

"Of course, Caroline," she said. "I've got nothing to hide." Somehow I felt like I was talking to Lily's friend Anna.

"Hang on then. I'll put you on hold while I call Doug."

I consulted my schedule and hastily planned my appeal. "I apologize for not calling you back yesterday," I said when he finally answered his page. "Something came up—"

"I don't want apologies or excuses. Is she willing to talk with us?"

"Absolutely. Can you free up time this morning? Say about ten?"

"That works. Downtown—Detective Bureau. See you then." And he hung up.

Thankfully, Kate hadn't. "Okay, we're set," I told her. "You can ride back to the Hilton with your folks. I'll meet you in the lobby at nine forty-five. We'll go over a few ground rules and then go across the street to meet with the detectives at ten."

"It would be more convenient if we could make it later."

"No," I said, feeling my face flush. "If you want me there with you, it's gonna be at ten."

"Okay, okay. No need to get testy, Caroline. I'll meet you at the hotel."

—⁂—

I did a double take as Kate strode into the lobby. In the day and a half since I'd seen her, she'd regained her spark. The weight she'd lost wouldn't return as quickly, but we were well used to seeing—and admiring—rail-thin models. Wearing a short navy skirt, crisply tailored white blouse, and Hermes scarf, and shod in three-inch Ferragamo pumps, she looked stunning. *I'd kill to have those legs. She'll have the detectives drooling in their coffee.*

She hugged me warmly. "I've been an irresponsible bitch, and I'm sorry," she said.

Her simple yet seemingly heartfelt apology melted the top layers of my anger, and I could easily deal with the irritation that remained.

"It's okay. C'mon—let's sit a minute," I said, leading her toward an overstuffed couch.

"What do they want to know, Caroline?" she asked before we were even seated. "I've already told them everything."

"I don't know. But if I think there's anything you shouldn't answer I'll say so. And give me a signal—tap my knee under the table—if any of the questions raises concerns for you."

We walked to the police station and were ushered into an interview room promptly at ten.

Single-mindedly focused on the investigation, Doug Connaboy didn't take notice of Kate's appearance. Sam Jacobs sniffed appreciatively at her perfume, but went back to his notes without a second glance.

"Counselor. Ms. Daniels. Let's get right down to it," Doug said, gesturing to two chairs on one side of the Formica table. A tape recorder sat in the middle.

"I'm sure you won't mind if we record this conversation," he said to me. "And—just to cover all bases—I'd like to Mirandize Ms. Daniels before we begin."

"You told me she's not a suspect," I said with rising concern. "If that's true, why is this necessary? She's clearly not under arrest."

"I'm fine with waiving my rights, Caroline," Kate said, reaching for the pen and printed form on the table in front of Doug. "As I've said several times, I have nothing to hide."

"Thank you," Doug said. He slid the form to me to sign as witness and turned on the recorder.

"As you'll no doubt see on the news later today," Doug said, "the autopsy revealed Yvonne Pritchard died of cardiac arrest. She had no apparent cardiac risk factors: no congenital defects, enlargement, or anything like that. Toxicology results won't be in for a couple weeks, so we can't say for sure, but we have reason to believe she ingested cocaine.

"We also have reason to believe you, Ms. Daniels," he said, looking directly at Kate, "can tell us the source of that cocaine."

"I—"

"Wait," I said to Kate, glaring at her to ensure she stopped talking. I turned back to Doug. "If you want my client to answer this, I need to know why you're asking."

"Fair enough," he said, opening a manila folder and shuffling through it. "Pritchard's roommate—who's a pretty straight arrow, by the way—initially told us she didn't think Pritchard used controlled substances. Said they'd met one another at a religious retreat and were both into healthy lifestyles. We believed her, and a cursory examination of the death scene didn't reveal any drugs or paraphernalia."

"Just a minute," I said to Doug. "When I first talked with you that night, you said you were guessing the death was drug-related."

"A healthy twenty-three-year-old dies on Willy Street with no signs of violence?" he replied. "Naturally my first thought is O.D. But our interviews with your client and the roommate convinced us otherwise."

"So why are you back to the drug theory?"

"We sealed the apartment and took the roommate—Laquisha Abbott is her name—to stay with a friend. On Wednesday morning, Laquisha comes into the office with her pastor in tow. Says she wants to confess.

"As you might expect, we're all ears. But Laquisha's not confessing to murder—she's confessing to obstruction of justice." Doug handed me a typewritten report with a portion highlighted in yellow. "Why don't you both take a minute to read what I've marked?"

I slid the report onto the table between us, and Kate and I leaned in to read:

> Laquisha Abbott stated she returned to the apartment she shared with Pritchard around 0125 hours. She stated that Kathryn Daniels, whom she had previously met, was performing chest compressions on the unresponsive young woman. Abbott said she ascertained that Daniels had not called for help and immediately dialed 911.

Abbott reported Daniels said to her, "Clean up the coffee table. The cops can't find that shit." Abbott then noticed a *People* magazine with white powder and a rolled up advertising insert sitting on the table. She surmised Pritchard had snorted cocaine before becoming unconscious.

According to Abbott, she initially refused to get rid of the evidence. But Daniels yelled at her, "It'd kill her parents to know Yvonne's relapsed. Do it!" Abbott stated Daniels told her to flush the cocaine, rip up and flush the makeshift straw, and wipe off the magazine. She followed Daniels' instructions, putting the magazine in the recycling bin just as the paramedics arrived.

Laquisha Abbott admitted she had been untruthful to detectives during her initial interview. She stated Pritchard had previously been in drug treatment and had been clean for several years. However, about two months earlier, Pritchard confessed to her that she'd again started using cocaine. Abbott stated Pritchard did not name her source but stated he was a very attractive man that she'd met through her university advisor.

Kate and I looked up. "Laquisha Abbott is lying," she said firmly. "And I'm more than willing to take a polygraph to prove it."

I bent my head to whisper to Kate, but she shook me off.

"She may have disposed of cocaine before the EMTs arrived," Kate said. "I don't know—I was busy trying to save Yvonne's life. But she didn't do anything at my instruction except call 911."

"And you're not the 'university advisor' who introduced her to the dealer?" Sam Jacobs asked.

She shook her head. "No. Dr. Martin Braxton was Yvonne's primary advisor. But I think that part of Laquisha's story is probably a complete fabrication. She's far from the 'straight arrow' you think she is. Yvonne told me once she was reluctant to live with Laquisha because her older brother is a known coke dealer. Yvonne wanted to avoid any temptation to relapse."

She took a tissue out of her Coach bag and touched it to the corners of her eyes. "Yvonne was extremely intelligent, but she was also vulnerable. I got to know her pretty well this past couple years. Marty Braxton had her involved in lots of aspects of our research, and she spent hours in the lab. A research team becomes like a family—I came to love her like a daughter. She confided in me. Yeah, I knew she sometimes struggled not to relapse, and it worried me. Why do you think I went over there to check on her when I knew she was upset and depressed? We were *close.*"

Her face flushed and her cheeks wet with tears, Kate looked up at the detectives wearily. "I don't know any more than I've already told you," she said. "Can we go now?"

Doug switched off the recorder and nodded. "Sam, would you take Ms. Daniels to sign for her car, please?"

We stood awkwardly as Kate followed Jacobs out of the room. "I'll be in touch about that polygraph," he said to me.

"You don't believe her?"

Doug shrugged.

"Well, I do," I said vehemently, realizing at once it was true. Kate Daniels was sometimes tardy, inattentive to details, irritatingly self-centered, and arrogant. But I knew she was a good *person*, and clearly she'd cared about Yvonne. Like me, she took immense pride in her work. She'd do anything she could to keep her research on track—including making a late-night house call to a struggling graduate assistant.

I also realized my friend needed me to defend her—whatever it would entail.

CHAPTER ELEVEN

When I went to meet her, Kate stood in the hallway outside the detectives' bureau talking intently on her cell phone. She mouthed "ten minutes" to me. I nodded and walked out of the stuffy office building for some air—and to make a call of my own.

Leaning against a concrete planter, I searched through my briefcase to find a copy of our firm's fee schedule and then dialed the office.

"Hi, Frank," I said nervously when I reached the managing partner. I was fairly certain he wouldn't approve of what I had to say and decided to cut to the chase. "I've decided to represent Kathryn Daniels after all and wanted to talk with you about the arrangements."

He paused, I surmised to formulate a diplomatic response. "We're always happy for new business, Caroline. But I'm not sure this is a great idea for you personally. You know representing friends isn't recommended."

"I intend to set some ground rules before I formally sign on," I said with a twinge of defensiveness. "But I think this is something I need to do."

"Also, as I recall, you joined our firm to get *out* of criminal work."

"Only because of the horrendous hours, Frank. There's nothing more fascinating than criminal law—which I'm darn good at. And it's just one case." I noticed with some embarrassment the frustration in my voice. My tone sounded like that of a little kid trying to justify another bedtime story.

"One case that's likely to demand a lot of your time."

You're in this far, you might as well ask, I told myself. "Would you be willing to reassign some of my other work?"

Frank sighed. "I suppose. We've got a new associate coming on next month and I can shuffle some of it his way. I can't let you cut your friend any slack on the retainer or fees, though."

"Understood."

I made notes in the margins of the schedule as Frank and I discussed the contract Kate would need to sign to become—officially—my client. Engrossed in the conversation, I didn't hear her approach, but she was within earshot as I repeated to him the required dollar figures.

"Jesus," Kate said when I hung up. "You know I don't have that kind of money."

Might as well settle this, I thought as I took a seat on the edge of the planter. I waited while Kate did the same.

"Did you call the lawyers I suggested?"

"No. You know I want you."

"If you want me to take your case, that's what it'll cost. It's probably less than Ed Benson would charge. Or some high-powered firm from Milwaukee. Another alternative is for you to petition for court-appointed counsel. They have some good ones. But even though you're cash-poor, I doubt you'll qualify."

"I guess I have no choice but to ask my dad," she said, picking at some errant leaves in the dirt.

"How about one of your brothers?"

"No. I'd rather keep those relationships untainted. Things with my dad are already fucked up—you saw his 'shunning' routine at the hotel the other day. Asking him for money can't make it much worse."

"I thought he was over that. You know—being a guest in your home and all."

"Believe me, we don't have time today to get into my relationship with my dad," she said with a rueful half-smile.

"Speaking of relationships—my taking your case could put a major strain on our friendship. Are you willing to take that risk?" I was tired of confronting all these questions head-on, but it had to be done.

"You're underestimating me," she said. "I can take whatever professional advice you give without holding it against you as a friend. We can make it work."

"I need to know you'll not only respect my advice but follow my instructions," I persisted.

"You got it."

"That means calling when you say you will. And being straight with me."

"Caroline, I know I was in the wrong the other day. It won't happen again. You have my word."

"Okay."

We walked back to my office where Rosalee typed up the contract for Kate to sign. During a tense but brief phone call, Corbett agreed to pay the retainer, and within the hour he'd arranged for his bank to wire the funds. I sent Kate off with a promise to call her tomorrow.

Then, with carefully masked trepidation, I called David and asked him to meet me for a late lunch. Though I know intellectually that conflicts are a natural part of life, I'd spent a good deal of my own personal life avoiding them. Today, as if in the manic phase of a bipolar mood swing, I felt compelled to face all the confrontations head-on.

"To what do I owe the pleasure?" David asked when I walked into the aromatic little Italian restaurant just off the capitol square.

"You may not be so pleased when I tell you," I said uneasily as I squeezed past the table into the booth.

David dipped a torn piece of bread into the saucer of olive oil without looking up. "You took Kate's case, huh?"

"Yes."

His brow furrowed, and I sensed he was carefully considering his words. "It's your decision and I'll support you in it. But I'm not gonna lie and say I like it."

I collected my thoughts while the waiter served our Caesar salads, vaguely regretting having told David to order one for me. My stomach balked at the notion of tackling the crisp pile of greens, the steaming braised chicken, and—especially—the anchovies.

"I'm not sure I understand why you feel so strongly about this," I said.

"It's not the legal work that concerns me. I know you're up to that challenge. Hell, you'll probably even welcome it. But it's the emotional toll I'm worried about. When you're around Kate, I always get the sense you're trying to prove yourself—to justify that you're worthy of her attention. And it's worse with her father around. I resent that they have you wrapped around their fingers—"

"Oh, David," I said with exasperation.

"Let me finish, please. I'm also afraid this whole sordid mess will put a damper on the happiness and excitement we should be feeling about bringing another child into our home. The timing couldn't be worse."

"I disagree. The federal courts have a speedy trial law—this case will be over long before the baby arrives. And it will give me something worthwhile to focus on rather than worrying for months and months about whether we made the right decision in choosing to use a surrogate."

"And the meds and procedures necessary for harvesting the eggs?" he asked.

"I managed to go through it when I was working full-time. I can do it again now."

"As I said, it's your decision."

We ate in what was, for me, uncomfortable silence. David had no trouble finishing his salad—and the anchovies I maneuvered to the side of my plate. I managed only a few bites.

People sometimes assume my redheaded, green-eyed hulk of a husband has a fiery temper. Nothing could be further from the truth. But he does speak his mind, and not always diplomatically.

He pushed his plate forward, wiped his mouth, and set his linen napkin on the table. "I won't let you put our family on the back burner, Caroline. Especially not for a narcissistic part-time friend."

"What do you mean, part-time friend?" I demanded—loudly enough to startle the couple sitting next to us.

When he was sure the couple had gone back to their own conversation, David replied quietly. "You're always at Kate's beck and call. Like when she needs help packing and moving. Or when she needs someone to proofread an oh-so-important article or application. Or when she conjures up some social event and wants to be sure people will come. Or—on those rare occasions when she's bored—when she calls us at the last moment to wheedle an invitation for dinner. Does she ever reciprocate? The answer is no."

"You're being petty."

"I am not being petty, I'm just describing the way I see her treating you. You know I'm not one to hold a grudge, but there's another incident I never told you about that really pissed me off..."

"So tell me," I said petulantly.

"It was right after you miscarried from the second in vitro procedure. I had to fly to L.A. to set up that corporate security system and you were still home sick. I was so worried about you that I called Kate from the airport and asked if she'd go stay with you for a while. She said she was swamped at the lab but that after her four o'clock class she'd go surprise you and Lily with some dinner."

"I don't remember any of this."

"There's a reason you don't remember it. Lily answered the phone when I called home in the evening. I asked what Aunt Kate had brought for dinner, and she told me Kate hadn't been by—that you'd ordered Domino's pizza. I was livid. You might remember Glenda came over later with a bottle of wine and helped you talk things out. She dropped everything to be there for you when I called."

"I'm sure there was a good explanation why Kate didn't come."

"I don't know—I never asked her. But real friends keep their word. And you know the old saying: 'De Nile ain't just a river in Egypt.'"

I threw my napkin on my plate, stood up—setting the table askew as I caught it with my hip—and stormed out of the restaurant. *Fuck you, David. I don't need to hear any fucking clichés right now. And the hell you don't hold a grudge!*

CHAPTER TWELVE

I took a circuitous route back to my office, replaying in my mind our luncheon conversation. After the endorphins produced by my furiously paced walk kicked in, I sorted through David's comments. What had I found so vexatious? He'd said he didn't like the way Kate treated me, which seemed almost paternalistic—as if I couldn't look out for myself. It reminded me of how I felt during the height of my panic disorder, when I'd needed him to look out for me but railed at my own dependence. He'd called Kate narcissistic and a part-time friend. *Maybe she is, but how can he ignore what she's done for me?* And then the Libra-child in me—the one who's always balancing the scales—spoke to me in the third person. *You've never told him everything she's done.*

I had to clear the air. I sat at my desk, straightened my shoulders and called my husband for the second time that day. It went directly to voice mail. *Never mind*, I told myself. *Out with it.*

"David, I'm sorry," I said to the recorder. "I reacted defensively to what you said about Kate and about how you perceive me acting around her. I know she's often self-centered and that taking on her defense might be difficult, but I think I'm up to the task. I want you to tell me if you see me putting our family's well being behind Kate's, but I'll watch out for myself. Just like I needed to learn how to talk myself down from the ledge during panic attacks, I'm the one who needs to learn how to handle Kate."

I got home before David did that evening, and my eyes darted nervously toward the back door when I heard him drive into the garage.

He smiled as he walked into the kitchen. "Hey," he said, pecking me on the cheek. "I got your message just before I left the office. I'm sorry, too, for acting like a helicopter parent toward you. And I promise I'll hold my tongue about your friend. Are we good?"

I hugged him, drinking in his warmth and strength. "Yeah, we're good."

—w—

My first days as Kate Daniels' retained counsel were busy but passed without incident. George Cooper sent over the government's discovery materials, which all but filled the two cardboard boxes sitting prominently on my office credenza. There were hundreds of photocopied pages: FBI interview reports, correspondence, grant applications, accounting spreadsheets and telephone records. Reviewing all the materials was a daunting task, and I took a stack of photocopies with me every time I left the office.

Each night, I made it a point to spend "quality time"— a phrase I'd always abhorred—with Lily. But as soon as she was asleep, I delved into my briefcase full of the evidence the prosecutor claimed incriminated my friend. I pored over the documents, making notes in the margins and highlighting important points with a yellow marker.

"Their case is weak," I said to David one night, tapping my pen against my forehead. "I think Kate is right in thinking Marty Braxton is to blame."

"Remember when you were a prosecutor? You'd come home ragging about defense attorneys who made bad decisions for their clients because they'd failed to look at all sides of the cases. Are you falling into that trap?"

True to his word, David had been supportive of my decision to take on Kate's defense and had uttered nary a negative word about her since our uncomfortable lunch and ensuing truce. Though his question rankled me, I knew he was right: I had to pretend I was in George Cooper's shoes and view the evidence from his vantage point. Too bad so many of the reports were as confusing to me as a convoluted spy movie.

Monday, September 24

After two hours of struggling to interpret a spreadsheet the FBI had prepared in Kate's case, I needed a breather. I opened the manila file containing documents that our less-than-zealous paralegal Kenny—ten days after Rosalee began hounding him— had finally procured. I could decipher simple police reports and court records in my sleep.

I read the deputy sheriff's report of Kate's second arrest for driving while intoxicated, which didn't sound anything like what I remembered about Kate's account of the incident. Impatiently, I fished through my desk drawer to find the notes of my interview with her. She had told me she'd been pulled over for no apparent reason. Yet the deputy reported witnessing Kate run through a red light, narrowly missing another car in the intersection. Worse yet, I knew this deputy well, and he was neither inexperienced nor incompetent.

Kate had been honest about one thing: she'd blown .082 on the Breathalyzer, only slightly higher than the legal limit. But the deputy's description of her behavior led him—and me—to believe she was far more intoxicated. I didn't like where this was going.

The criminal complaint about the worthless checks charge was just as troubling. Kate had written over a thousand dollars worth of bad checks for an assortment of items: a leather jacket, an iPod, a TV and a VCR. Not exactly the ten-dollar-check-for-milk-and-bread scenario I'd envisioned after hearing Kate's version. And the stores, Kate's bank, and the DA's office had sent her a total of sixteen notices trying to collect on the checks.

These reports seemed to be about a different Kate Daniels than the one I had known for so many years. Or at least the Kate Daniels I had convinced myself I knew.

The day got even worse. After lunch Rosalee brought me a fax—a copy of a memorandum from the pretrial services officer to Magistrate Judge Brillstein—and watched in anticipation as I read it.

The short memo reported that laboratory tests of the urine specimen Kate provided on the day of her release were confirmed as positive for cocaine. The memo concluded: *"Ms. Daniels was questioned about the results and reiterated she had never used controlled substances, including cocaine. Since the drug ingestion clearly occurred prior to the defendant's release on bond, no action is requested of the Court. We will increase the frequency of urine testing and report any further positive results for judicial action."*

"Ms. Smith-Kellor called a few minutes ago while you were on the phone to tell you the fax was on its way," Rosalee said. "She was very apologetic. Said she was out sick last week and just saw the laboratory report this morning. She said to call her if you have any questions."

"Thanks, Rose," I said offhandedly. I suspected she wanted to talk about the memo, but I was in no mood for it.

I went over to my file cabinet and found some information I'd collected as a prosecutor—information about metabolic rates for various drugs of abuse.

"Impossible!" I said, slamming the papers to my desk.

"What's impossible?" Frank Cleaver asked, poking his head into my office.

"I just got a memo from pretrial services about Kate. They say the urine sample she gave on the day she was released from jail tested positive for coke. But this data shows that cocaine stays in your system for only a short time—like a couple of days at most. This would mean she used in jail. There's got to be some mistake."

"Caroline, you know drugs can sometimes be gotten in jails."

"Yes, I know," I said. "I once prosecuted a sheriff's deputy who smuggled marijuana in to the inmates for exorbitant fees. My point is, Kate wouldn't use drugs on the streets, much less have the means to procure them in jail."

"How can you be so sure she's not a user?"

"In college, most of us smoked pot. Kate was my only close friend who didn't. She knew we did but staunchly refused to try it. Said she had too much to lose."

"With all due respect, you've been out of college for a long time. People change. I assume you quit smoking pot?" he asked with a smile.

"Of course."

"Well, maybe Kate changed in the other direction."

"I can't see it. She's a doctor, for God's sake."

"Doctors are above the law?" Frank said, chuckling.

"No, but they know better than most people how dangerous drugs are. And I've seen Kate frequently enough in recent years to know she hasn't turned into a junkie."

"How goes the discovery?" he asked, obviously anxious to change the subject.

"It's slow and tedious going through the records. The FBI alleges several different means of embezzlement—reimbursement for travel that didn't occur, pocketing consulting fees that should've gone to the university. That kind of thing. There's paperwork showing a fictitious lab assistant was paid with grant funds, but I think it's a stretch to show Kate was responsible, and I don't see any proof she took the money. Marty Braxton had more opportunity in that instance. I think the travel reimbursements and consulting fees amount to accounting mix-ups—nothing more."

"Hmm. Well, hang in there. It'll all come together."

After Frank left, I re-read Monica's memo and was immediately troubled by another point: Kate hadn't called to tell me about the positive test result or of her conversation with the pretrial services officer.

Miraculously, Kate answered the phone in her office—the first place I tried. "Hang on a minute, Caroline," she said altogether too casually for my liking. I waited and listened as she finished a conversation with one of her students and asked him to pull the door shut on his way out. By the time she was free to talk, I'd worked myself into a tizzy of impatience and frustration, pacing behind my desk within the limits of my phone cord tether.

"I just got a memo from Monica about the positive UA," I began without preface. "Why didn't you call and tell me?"

"'Cause I didn't see it as a big deal," Kate said with an exaggerated sigh. "I haven't used cocaine, and I'm quite sure she believed me when I told her. Obviously there was a mistake in the testing—I'd just been released from jail for God's sake! The only aggravating thing is now I have to go down there three times a week to give samples. Is there anything you can do about it?"

Irritated with her nonchalance, I wanted nothing more than to hang up. Instead, I forged ahead, making a conscious effort to match my tone with my mood. "Well first of all, if Monica believed you, she wouldn't have increased the testing. Second, I can deal with things better if I hear them right away from you—it's not fair for me to get my information in memos from the court. Finally, you shouldn't be talking to *anybody* about *anything* to do with this case without me."

"Whoa! I'm sorry..."

Her hollow apology didn't fly. I waited a beat.

"You gotta remember, Caroline: I've got nothing to hide."

I'm getting pretty frickin' tired of hearing that. And I'm starting to believe it's not true.

Thursday, October 11

Despite the ups and downs of Kate's case, I'd successfully maintained a three-day-per-week work schedule, and this day off began blissfully. David and I got up early and enjoyed a rare fifteen minutes worth of adult conversation over the newspaper and coffee. Lily bounded out of bed when her alarm went off, uncharacteristically enthusiastic to start the day, and ran downstairs to greet us.

"Mom. You'd better get dressed. The field trip is this morning. What are you gonna wear?"

"I thought I'd wear my black corduroys and my red sweater."

"No! You'll look dorky. Please wear jeans like the other moms!"

"Okay, hon. Is a sweatshirt all right?"

"Only if it's a hoodie." Lily hurried off to her room.

"I sure hope there's a clean pair of jeans around here or I'm in trouble," I said, shaking my head.

"I did three loads of laundry last night," David said. "I'm sure I saw a pair of your jeans among them."

"You're the best!"

"Lily sure seems excited. Where's the field trip again?"

I grinned. "The children's museum. And you'd better not let Lily know you forgot or she'll take away your 'World's Best Dad' coffee mug. Remember—her class is putting on the puppet show there for the Head Start kids? And then we're touring the museum and having a catered lunch?"

David's face fell. "Oh, man. How *could* I forget?" he asked.

"Hey, cut yourself some slack. I know you've been distracted about those new accounts you're handling at work. And God knows I haven't been as communicative as I could be, what with Kate's case and all."

"There's no excuse. Lily hasn't stopped communicating with me; I just haven't been listening very carefully."

"David—"

"No," he said, grasping my hand and stroking it with his thumb. "Hear me out, Caroline. We've told ourselves over and over that family is our priority, and I'm afraid we're slipping back into our bad old habits."

Though I didn't want to admit it, the queasy feeling in my stomach told me he might be right. "Then we'll just have to be extra vigilant," I said. "Starting right now."

I got up from my stool and kissed the top of his head.

"Yes, we will," he murmured as I left to dress for my day.

The field trip had its trying moments: the noise level on the school bus was excruciating at times, and there were a few kids I'd have gladly medicated for ADHD. Nevertheless, the day was a welcome respite, and I kept the promise I'd made to myself to "be present." I chatted amiably with other parents, a couple of whom I was coming to know and feel close to. Best of all, Lily was clearly a part of a circle of nice kids that did not include Anna, a/k/a Edie Haskell. Anna and two other girls were too busy chatting up the handsome new male teacher to bother with Lily and her friends.

Lily and I went right from school to the supermarket to shop for the celebratory meal I suggested we plan for dinner. "What are we gonna celebrate?" she asked.

"Hmmm…how about that we're glad we're a family?"

Lily stopped the cart in the middle of the aisle, a puzzled look on her face.

"I know it sounds a little corny. But during the field trip today I was thinking how very blessed we are. A lot of the Head Start kids don't have two parents in their lives. A lot of them have to move all the time because they can't afford their apartments. Some of them don't even have enough food to eat. You and your dad and me have each other, a nice home, and plenty of the things we need. I think we need to celebrate that once in awhile."

Lily nodded thoughtfully. "We should probably get cheesecake for dessert," she said.

I couldn't argue with that idea.

With absolute delight, my daughter and I sang the songs from the day's puppet show as we cooked in the kitchen. The aroma of garlic and basil wafted from the pot of marinara sauce I stirred on the stove. Lily painstakingly tore the Romaine into bite-size pieces and poured most of a box of Caesar croutons into the salad bowl with them.

We were just wiping off the counters and waiting for the pasta water to boil when we heard David's car pull into the driveway.

"What's the occasion?" he asked as Lily led him—straight from the back door—into our seldom-used dining room, and she beamed at the carefully laid table, complete with candles and wine glasses.

"It's 'We're Glad We're a Family' Night!"

Dinner was heavenly. Lily proudly read us her favorite "Henry and Mudge" book before bedtime and went to sleep with a smile on her face.

It was nine o'clock before I wandered into the family room and noticed the voice mail message light blinking insistently. I hadn't bothered to pick up the phone in the kitchen to listen for messages—and probably wouldn't have cared that Kate had called at two-thirty and again at four, sounding frantic and cryptic. "Caroline, call me—it's urgent!" her last message said.

From nine o'clock until midnight I tried all of Kate's numbers, calling every few minutes to no avail.

Finally, at David's urging, I went to bed. I slept fitfully. My dreams were disturbing and I prayed not prophetic: Lily and I trapped in a car and sinking into a dark river, "bad guys" whom I'd previously sent to jail showing up at my door, and David unconscious in a hospital ICU.

CHAPTER THIRTEEN

—ɯ—

Friday, October 12

David's alarm woke me at six o'clock. He was leaving in half an hour to fly to Denver, so I had get-Lily-to-school duty. *It's a new day! Use this opportunity to chill out and enjoy your daughter*, I told myself.

My positive self-talk worked only to a point. I couldn't stop Kate's terse phone messages from playing over and over in my mind. Her tone and the word "urgent" gave me the dreadful feeling our next conversation wouldn't be a good one. Lily—the ever-keen observer—sensed my preoccupation. She grinned unabashedly when I reminded her Ida McKinley would be picking her up from school today for a long-awaited sleepover. With Ida, she'd receive undivided attention. Though happy for Lily, I couldn't help feeling guilty that I was neglecting her.

The slate gray sky was spitting rain as I dropped Lily off. I hated the thought of her waiting at the bus stop in the rain and had fallen prey to her pitiful plea, "Can you give me a ride?"

Running late, I opted for the beltline, usually the quickest route to my downtown office. When I found myself in the middle lane of a three-lane parking lot, boxed in by two semi-trucks, it was too late to turn back. My windshield wipers slapped at the now-steady rain, and I saw the flashing lights of emergency vehicles off in the distance.

The perfect storm for this panic attack sufferer: oppressively dark daytime weather, trapped in traffic, loud catastrophic thoughts that would not be silenced. *Kate's probably dead, and I wasn't there to help her!*

Before I could brace for it, the anxiety engulfed me. Heart racing, ears ringing, palms sweating cold, my fingers gripped the unmoving steering wheel with white knuckles.

Stop it! It's just a panic attack—no big deal. Predictable even, what with little sleep, the weather, David traveling, Kate's messages.

I remained paralyzed with terror for at least ten minutes, though it felt twice that long. Rather than helping, deep breathing made me more anxious. I stabbed at the preset radio buttons in a frantic effort to find a song I could sing to but found nothing but commercials and inanely yammering drive-time jocks. Finally—despite the deluge—I rolled down my window. The rain peppered my skin with almost instant, blessed relief. I looked to my left and saw a driver in the next lane staring incredulously. No matter—I'd broken the vicious, anxious cycle in my mind and had come back to the present reality.

Battling panic attacks is exhausting, and I arrived at my office looking like I'd been through a jungle war—or at least half of me had. I glanced at my wall mirror in disbelief: the left side of my hair was drenched, and mascara ran down my cheek. I looked down to see my left sleeve soaking wet and dripping on the floor. My right side, though sodden, was at least not drenched. I felt foolish, too, for two Kleenexes I'd grabbed from my purse during the elevator ride from the parking garage were no match for the water drizzling down my neck.

Rosalee walked in a moment later, took one look at me, and laughed. "What on earth? Did your umbrella blow inside out or something?"

I took off my blazer, pulled several more tissues from the box on my table, and blotted my neck. "I haven't been outside at all," I said ruefully. "But I did drive halfway to work with my window wide open."

"Because?"

"Because I had a horrific panic attack and needed wind and rain to pull me out of it." I'd shared little tidbits about my anxiety issues with her before, but she'd never seen me in a state like this.

"Oh, honey, I'm so sorry," she said without being overly solicitous. "Let me go get you a hot cup of tea and see if I can find you a towel." Her response was just what I needed—caring yet calm.

She came back in less than a minute, wielding a fluffy bath towel. "I had it in the gym bag I packed last week and never used," she said sheepishly. "The tea's brewing."

"Thanks, Rose." I closed the door and my window blinds, took off my wet clothes, and changed into a spare business suit I had hanging in my armoire for those occasions when

I needed to spruce up in a hurry. I toweled off my hair and finger-combed it, then shuffled through the message slips on my desk. Among them were requests to call Kate, Monica Smith-Kellor, and George Cooper. Each had called the previous afternoon, Kate three times.

Before I even had a chance to sit down another attorney, Julie Wutherspoon, knocked on my door and walked in, carrying a bag of PDQ donuts and a cup of coffee.

"I've been waiting for you," she said and, without ceremony, pushed the door shut with her foot, set the bag and coffee on my desk and settled herself into one of my chairs. Her visit took me aback: Julie and I were friendly but not friends, and she'd never set foot in my office before. Perhaps more surprising, she took no notice of my still-bedraggled state or the damp towel hanging over the back of her chair.

"Long story short," she said, reaching in for a powdered sugar donut and pushing the leftovers toward me, "would you and your husband be interested in adopting an infant?"

"What?" I asked, sinking into my chair with weak knees. "I think you're gonna need to make the short story longer." One of Julie's specialties, I knew, was adoption law, both international and domestic. But, since David and I had used another adoption attorney—one whom we trusted implicitly—I'd never discussed the subject with her.

"Fair enough."

Julie proceeded to explain: One of the firm's well-to-do clients had an eighteen-year-old daughter who'd just learned she was pregnant. Keeping the baby was out of the question for the family, since the father was a Mexican landscaper, far beneath their social strata. But the girl had adamantly refused to have an abortion and would agree to relinquish parental rights only if she and the father could select the adoptive parents. Julie was having a tough time finding a couple that met their criteria.

I felt my cheeks flush with embarrassment. "What made you think of us?" I asked. I didn't think our infertility was a topic of office-wide knowledge. I certainly hadn't talked about it with anyone but Rosalee, and she was the best keeper-of-secrets I'd ever known.

"I was talking to David at the Cleavers' anniversary party. When he found out adoption is one of my areas of specialty, he asked a ton of questions. What were the drawbacks to various international programs? How long does it take? Stuff like that. I just assumed you were considering it. Sorry if I misread things."

Though somewhat incredulous that David would speak at length with Julie about this at a *cocktail party*, I couldn't help being swept up by her proposal. "No, no," I stammered like a schoolgirl. "It's something we've certainly considered... what I meant was, what makes you think this couple would consider giving their baby to us?"

"I can't be sure, but based on the couples they've nixed, I think you're right on. They want people in their 30s with at least one other kid. Not too rich. Not too poor. 'Good marriage partnership.' In other words, a hands-on dad. Decent people but not 'right wing-nut Christians.' Does that fit you guys?"

I laughed. "I guess so."

"Plus, I'm guessing you wouldn't be opposed to having a Hispanic child. David was going on and on about the beautiful kids his sister adopted from El Salvador several years ago."

"True."

"Well, run it by him and let me know your initial reactions," she said, getting up to leave. "I'll put the search on hold until I hear from you, but let me know your tentative answer by early next week, okay?"

Dazed by this turn of events, I walked Julie out. "I'll get back to you on Monday," I said. Then—for good measure—I added, "I promise."

Sitting at her workstation outside my door, Rosalee raised an eyebrow and followed me back into my office.

"Pray tell, what's up!" she said, handing me the tea she'd brewed for me. "You're always turning down my homemade treats. Then Jules brings you cheap-ass donuts, and you've got crumbs on your face, and you're looking punch-drunk?"

I sank back onto my chair. "Julie just told me about an adoption lead for an infant. I gotta call David."

"By all means, call him," she said with excitement. "I'll keep the wolves at bay."

I looked at my watch. *Shit! He's probably in the air.*

But he answered on the first ring. "Hey! I was just going to call and let you know I'm stuck at O'Hare with weather delays. No way I'll make the Denver meeting, so—"

"Hush a minute," I said. "I've got some news: Julie Wutherspoon—you met her at Frank and Judy's party—just came in and asked if we'd be interested in adopting a baby. The mom is due in about seven months."

Silence.

"David, did you hear me?"

"I heard you," he said with a catch in his voice. "I don't know what to say... this could be an answer to our prayers. What do you think?"

The level of emotion in his voice caught me by surprise. "I don't know what to think," I said. "I was just wrapping my head around the surrogacy plan and this comes up. Julie needs an answer early next week."

"And Linda Wordsworth's scheduled to head up north to meet with our prospective surrogate next Friday."

"Maybe we need to reconsider our decision?" I asked, my stomach aflutter.

"I'd say so. Look, I'm gonna do this meeting by tele-conference and catch the two-thirty Van Galder bus back to Madison. I know Lily's going with Ida tonight. How 'bout I meet you at Paisan's at six and we'll talk over dinner?"

"It's a date."

Then—without warning—my office door burst open and in stormed a wild-eyed Kate. "They're trying to lock me up again," she yelled. "And my lawyer doesn't return my fuck-ing calls!"

Stunned and beyond words, I realized I still had the phone in my hand. "David—"

"I heard," he said tersely. And he hung up.

CHAPTER FOURTEEN

—⟋⟋⟋—

"Sit. Down. Kate," I said, with an eerie edge to my voice, clearly alarming Rosalee who had followed Kate into my office. "I can handle this, Rose. Shut the door on your way out, please."

Kate glared at me. "For chrissakes, Caroline, I don't need to sit down. I need you to keep me out of jail! Where the hell were you yesterday? I tried calling you all afternoon."

More resentment rose in my throat. *Remember your assertiveness techniques*, I told myself. *Don't let her rattle you!*

I watched Kate pace around my office, furiously rubbing the back of her neck. "I'm sorry you couldn't reach me," I said with an equanimity I didn't feel. Under my desk, my hands were clenched into fists. "I got your messages around nine and tried calling you at all your numbers. In fact, I tried until midnight."

Kate quit pacing.

"Please take a chair and tell me who wants to put you back in jail and why."

She sat with a huff. "They say I tested positive again."

My chest tightened. "Positive for what?" I asked, forcing myself to look straight at her.

"Cocaine."

"Cocaine?"

Kate nodded. "But it's all bullshit. Either their testing procedures are faulty or someone's out to get me."

"It's not bullshit," I said with a long, slow sigh. "And if I hadn't been personally involved with you as my client, I would've seen it right away. I could kick myself."

"You gotta believe me, Caroline. It's all a mistake."

I'd had little first-hand experience in dealing with substance abusers, but intuition told me there was no sense arguing with Kate. "Let me call Monica and see what she has to say. She called me yesterday and left a message."

Kate slumped in her chair with her ankles crossed, one foot tapping in a syncopated rhythm as if she were listening to her own private reggae band. She stared vacantly past me as I made the call.

The news from Monica Smith-Kellor was even worse than I'd expected. The retest of Kate's first urine sample again revealed cocaine. The next sample was also positive for cocaine and showed signs Kate had tried to dilute it. Monica had notified George Cooper, and they were petitioning the court to revoke bail. The only alternative Monica's office would support was inpatient treatment for at least twenty-one days.

"What about her job?" I asked.

"Didn't Kate tell you?"

Oh, man, what else?

"The Board of Regents voted on Wednesday to suspend her, pending the outcome of the case," Monica said. "She's not allowed to set foot on university property, including the lab."

I looked at Kate with growing animosity while her eyes remained fixated on a spot on the carpet.

"I see. Where do we go from here?" I asked Monica.

"I filed my violation report with Magistrate Brillstein this morning. I'll fax your copy over as soon as we get off the phone. George Cooper wants to schedule the bail revocation hearing for Monday morning. If you're going to get her into treatment, you'd better arrange it before then. Brillstein usually only approves treatment as an alternative to revocation if the defendant's already enrolled."

"Do you have any recommendation as to where the treatment should take place?"

"Not specifically. The local inpatient places are all pretty good—and pretty pricey. I presume Kate's still got insurance. You might want to check with her carrier first. If you've got a minute, I'll give you some names and phone numbers."

While I jotted down the information as Monica recited it to me, I eyed my friend who was again up and pacing.

"I don't need drug treatment," Kate said when I hung up the phone. "What I need is for these absurd fucking charges to be dropped so I can get on with my life and my work... and for all you busybodies to get off my case." She stalked toward the door.

"Kathryn Daniels, if you walk out that door, you can kiss our friendship good-bye. You can also give Rosalee the address where you want the retainer check mailed because I'll no longer be your lawyer." *Just go, please!* I thought but didn't have the wherewithal to say.

Kate stopped in her tracks—I could see her assessing whether I was serious—and then returned to her chair. I began to make some notes, planning my strategy but also giving her time to firm up her decision to stay. When I looked up, tears were streaming down Kate's face.

"What will my father say?" she said, hanging her head.

"Quite frankly, I don't care. Now let's get busy. We've got to get you enrolled in an inpatient drug program today. Sit tight a minute. I've got some things to go over with Rosalee."

When I returned, Kate had regained her composure and said she was ready to tackle the task at hand.

Kate didn't know much about her health care coverage but knew she belonged to an HMO. I called the health benefit coordinator and was pleased to learn they provided inpatient drug treatment at New Beginnings, one of the facilities suggested by Monica.

I gave Kate a thumbs-up and dialed the number. "Can I speak with an intake coordinator, please?"

A man identifying himself as Charles Sutton came on the line, speaking far too slowly for my current quotient of patience.

"Mr. Sutton, my name is Caroline Spencer. I have a friend who would like to be admitted to your inpatient program. She has a problem with cocaine. She's a member of Health Care Co-op. Could I bring her over in about an hour?"

"Hold on there, Ms.... What did you say your name was?"

"Spencer. Caroline Spencer."

"Well, Ms. Spencer, we don't admit everyone who drives up and says 'I want in.' We have to do a screening assessment. Having insurance helps, but it's not an automatic ticket. We currently have a waiting list of clients, and I don't expect an opening for about three weeks."

"Mr. Sutton, this is matter of some urgency. I wasn't anxious to bring it up, but my friend is on bail in a criminal case. Her bail will be revoked if we don't get her into a program this weekend."

"I can appreciate your problem. There are several people on the waiting list who have similar legal reasons for wanting in. I'd be happy to see your friend for an assessment so we can put her on the list if she qualifies. In fact, I've just had a cancellation and could see her at eleven o'clock today. But no way she's getting admitted today."

"Do you know if Health Care will pay for treatment at any other facility?"

"Sometimes they do if there's an urgent need and we're full. You'd still need an assessment from us and a letter saying there's no room in the inn."

"Okay. Please put her down for the eleven o'clock appointment. Her name is Kathryn Daniels. We'll see you then."

I called the other four treatment facilities and learned all but one had waiting lists. One private hospital, The Meadows, had immediate openings and, based on the information we provided, would admit Kate immediately—with a check for $10,000. More money would be due later. Rosalee was bringing my mail in as I looked at The Meadows' website, reading the program highlights to Kate.

"Excuse me," she said, "but I couldn't help overhearing. A woman from my church sent her son to The Meadows about a year ago, and I took her to visit him. It's a beautiful place—just a few miles south of the town of Oregon—rolling hills surrounded by trees. The program's great. Her son's been clean and sober ever since. I can call and ask if you could speak with him."

"Thanks, Rose, but I think it's out of Kate's price range. I'll keep it in mind if things change."

I looked at my watch: ten o'clock. I felt like the last horse out of the starting gate, running in a race that was way too short for me to make up ground. Fortunately, I found myself intensely focused rather than panicky. Kate's spirits, though, were deflating before my eyes. She sat slumped in her chair, her eyes vacant.

"C'mon. Let's get a bite of breakfast at Starbucks before we head over to see Mr. Sutton. It doesn't sound like we'll be able to convince him to take you today, but maybe he'll give us letters to satisfy the HMO and the court."

Service at the coffee shop was uncharacteristically slow, so we had our coffee and scones in the car. Kate nibbled and stared out the window as I drove. With any other client, I would have found the silence unbearable. With Kate, I couldn't bear to break it.

Finally she spoke. "I think my mother will loan me the money for The Meadows."

"Does she have it?" I asked.

"In her treatment fund."

"What?"

"It's a long story, but I guess we've got time. My mom's an alcoholic. It started about the time I was in elementary school—"

I choked on a sip of coffee. "But you told me you had no family history of substance abuse," I managed to sputter, with a sense of betrayal—and unease.

Kate continued as if she hadn't heard me or my tone. "I can remember overhearing arguments between my folks. Mom wanted to take a job at the Fine Arts Museum—you know she has a degree in art history—but dad wouldn't hear of it. 'No wife of mine is going to get a job!' She was supposed to be the supportive wife of the prominent surgeon and to do volunteer work and serve on committees.

"As she confided in me once, quite a bit later, it just wasn't enough. She began drinking more at cocktail time and at dinner. The only time we ever saw Mom happy was when she was drinking."

She paused and, before I managed to stop her, lit a cigarette. "Kate," I said with unmasked irritation, "not in the car." Unfazed, she took another drag, blew the smoke out the window, and tossed the cigarette after it.

"Well, as you can imagine," she continued, "Mom's drinking got out of hand. She was becoming an embarrassment to Dad at those ever-so-important social functions. He concocted a story about an illness in the family and spirited her away to dry out. Unfortunately, when Mom came home, Dad expected her to be a social drinker—to propose a toast at the hospital fundraiser, to share a cocktail with dinner guests. It wasn't long before she was back in the hospital. I think it happened three or four times altogether.

"After the last hospitalization, Mom was referred to a local psychologist who quickly saw how my father enabled her drinking. He wanted Dad to come to the sessions, which was never gonna happen. In fact, Dad forbade Mom from seeing the guy again and refused to pay any more of his bills."

I stopped for a red light and looked over at Kate. All I could think of was, *How am I ever going to tell David?*

"Anyway," Kate said, "my mom used money from an inheritance to set up her own account—that she would use to pay the psychologist of her choice. Corbett was pissed, but there was nothing he could do about it. And Mom's still sober."

"Why didn't you tell me?" I said. "Didn't you think it was relevant?"

"It's not exactly something I'm proud of. And besides, every family I know has a skeleton or two in their closets."

We fell back into silence, each lost in our own thoughts.

Something about this whole story didn't fit. "I was at your house quite frequently during college," I said, "and I don't remember your mother not drinking."

"I guess it was sort of a compromise my folks worked out. Mom would be served non-alcoholic beverages that looked like cocktails or wine or whatever, never drawing attention to the fact that she didn't drink. The household staff became adept at serving her when no one would notice. Plus, you know how the spotlight in a room is always focused on Corbett Daniels. No one ever paid any mind to what Margaret was or wasn't doing."

"I never noticed. Will it be awkward for you to call and ask her for the money?"

"Yeah. She was asking me a lot of questions when she was here—like she suspected me of being a drug addict. I kept assuring her I wasn't."

There was nothing to say. But I kept thinking this all could have been avoided if Kate had been truthful with me from the beginning.

"Honest, Caroline, I don't see myself as a drug addict. Yeah, I use coke once in a while. It helps me stay up when I'm working on projects. But I can stop any time. I'm not addicted."

"Well, at this juncture, whether you are or not is beside the point," I said wearily. "Going into inpatient treatment is the only way you can stay out of jail. Understand?"

"I do."

"I need you to be candid when you're having the assessment," I said. "Although, come to think of it, there may be no reason to go through with the assessment at New Beginnings if your mom can spare the money for The Meadows."

"My insurance may still pay for all or part of the treatment at The Meadows if New Beginnings says I need it and they're full, right?"

"That's my understanding."

"Then I can send Mom's money back. Who knows? She may need it again herself."

"Okay. Let's go see Sutton. But it might be a good idea to call your mom first. It may take her a while to transfer the money."

"Can I use your cell phone? Mine's dead."

"Sure, unless you want some privacy."

"Not necessary."

I handed her the phone and tried to fade into the background as Kate made her call.

"Mom, it's Kate... I'm fine... I know I've been difficult to reach. Something's come up, and I need your help. I wasn't completely honest with you when you were here—when you asked me about drugs," she said, hugging her knees to her chest and leaning away from me. "I've used cocaine, and some of my urine screens tested positive. Caroline thinks my only option is to go inpatient for treatment. I can get into a place today called The Meadows, which we hear good things about. But they need $10,000 up front..."

I regretted not pulling over somewhere so Kate could call her mom alone. She took a few hitching breaths and went on. "Can you do this without telling Dad? ...I know we should be honest with him, but I can't deal with it right now..."

From the corner of my eye, I watched Kate listening to her mother's response. After an excruciatingly long pause, she said, "It's First Federal... Wait, let me get the account number." Kate pulled out her wallet and read some numbers off a card. "Thanks, Mom. I love you."

She looked visibly relieved as she disconnected the call. "We're set."

I felt anything but relieved.

Ten minutes later, sitting in the waiting room while Kate was being interviewed, I said a silent prayer of thanks for my dull but stable background. Kate's family, whom I had envied for so many years, couldn't hold a candle to mine.

And, for the first time since Kate had barged into my office that morning, I had a moment to consider Julie Wutherspoon's out-of-the-blue offer of a baby to adopt.

Through our multiple-year odyssey with infertility, I'd learned not to get too excited about possibilities. Even thinking about this one felt risky. After all, hadn't Julie said the birth parents had already rejected other couples? *Don't get caught up in this now, I told myself. Focus on something you have some control over.*

I used my cell phone to call intake at The Meadows and, as expected, was told Kate could be admitted anytime that day. We were to bring a copy of Sutton's assessment if it was available.

I'd just hung up when Charles Sutton summoned me to his office, where Kate waited in sullen silence. "Your client signed a consent form authorizing me to speak with you," he said. "In my opinion, Ms. Daniels is psychologically dependent on cocaine and probably physiologically dependent as well. If you're willing to wait about fifteen minutes, I'll type up the letter you need which will explain my assessment. I think in-patient treatment is indicated, and I'll put her on our waiting list if you want."

"There's no way you could admit her here today?"

"I'm afraid not."

"Then we'll wait for the letter and take it with us to The Meadows. Hopefully her HMO will see its way clear to pay for treatment there."

Kate stalked out of Sutton's office, ignoring his outstretched hand. He waved me off as I started to apologize. "Goes with the territory," he said calmly. "Have a seat in the waiting room. It shouldn't take me too long—I'm a reasonably fast typist."

When I joined her in the crowded waiting room, Kate was already ensconced in the lone overstuffed chair. I sat on a straight-backed loveseat across the room, trying to stifle my resentment at her rude behavior. A half an hour later, when Charles Sutton brought me the written assessment, she was asleep in the chair, curled up like a toddler with her hands beneath her cheek. My mind couldn't even begin to process the incongruous picture.

She sat quietly as we drove to the bank and on to her home. Lulled into the comfort of the plan we'd made, I waited in the living room while Kate went into the master suite to pack her things, pondering the several turns my day had taken. I should've seen the next one coming. When Kate came out, I knew immediately she was higher than any proverbial kite. Her dark eyes—their pupils widened—flashed with enthusiasm. Her every movement was quick and jerky.

"I've been thinking this is all really unnecessary, Caroline," my friend said. "There's a hearing scheduled on Monday, right?"

I nodded in disbelief.

"Okay, then. We'll fight it," she said with relish. "I'm a respected member of the community. They can't lock me up like a common criminal. I'll get one of the pharmacology guys to come over and testify—he'll debunk their testing procedures—"

"You really don't get it, do you? George Cooper would like nothing more than to lock you up and may do it even if you're admitted to The Meadows. But it's your only choice: jail or The Meadows. What's it gonna be?"

She didn't answer. She strode back and forth across the room, then put some CDs in the changer and began straightening books and magazines, moving in sync with the music. I'd never seen anyone—much less someone I loved—under the influence of cocaine. I watched in a weird state of detachment, as if the circuits in my mind had blown from emotional overload, and I couldn't decide how to feel.

After about twenty minutes, Kate's euphoria ebbed and her movements slowed. She sat heavily on the couch next to me, her eyes brimming with tears. Realizing she'd come down, I asked again—more gently this time, "What's it gonna be?"

"Okay. You win. Let's get this over with."

I drove the narrow, winding country roads toward The Meadows in pouring rain, my hands affixed like vice grips to the steering wheel. Kate sat beside me, her shoulders hunched, staring absently out her side window. Neither of us said a word. My silence was rooted in anger—at Kate, yes, for falling prey to addiction and dragging me into her mess, but also at myself for failing to recognize the obvious warning signs.

A gravel driveway led up a hill to a nondescript brown building surrounded by trees. The rain persisted as we dashed to the door, and the admissions staff was no more welcoming than the weather. As angry as I was with Kate, I was still taken aback by the reception she received.

A sullen middle-aged woman, wearing a faded Nike warm-up suit and a nametag reading "Donna," came to get us at the front desk. Without a word, she led us to a stark examination room. When she turned to face us, I extended my hand. "Hello. I'm Caroline Spencer, and this is my friend Kathryn Daniels."

"I'm the intake worker," Donna said, half-heartedly shaking my hand. I recoiled at both her failure to identify herself and her stale breath.

Impervious to eye contact or questions, she vigorously pat-searched Kate and examined every inch of her belongings. I felt a visceral reaction to the harsh violation of Kate's privacy and was about to protest when Donna poked a finger under the rubber insole of one of Kate's running shoes and pulled out a plastic bag containing white powder. She expressed neither surprise nor appeasement and continued her search. As sheer panic registered on Kate's face, my anger at her melted into pity.

"I need to collect a urine sample," Donna said to us, pocketing the baggie of cocaine and a book of matches she'd taken from Kate's bag. "And, counselor, you need to wait in the hall." We followed her out of the examination room and watched as she locked the door, using a key that hung from a lanyard around her neck. I leaned against the wall, resisting the urge to slide down it and sit on the floor, and waited while Kate and Donna went to do their business. The hallway was deserted.

My stomach churned with indecision. I didn't understand why Rosalee had described The Meadows as beautiful. Everything about this place felt ominous: the brown intake building, the vacant hallway, the surly, all-business intake worker. I thought about the rare occasions when we'd needed to give Lily time-outs for bad behavior, and how we'd told ourselves that though it seemed harsh, it was necessary. Was *this* harsh place really necessary for Kate?

Probably.

I looked up to see Donna walking toward me, wearing rubber gloves and holding at arm's length a plastic cup full of urine. Kate trailed a few paces behind her. With her free hand, Donna unlocked the exam room door and motioned us inside. In our presence, she put a few drops of the yellow liquid onto a portable test kit and—triumphantly, I thought—held up the result.

"One last toot, huh?" she asked Kate. "Hope you enjoyed it."

I hoped that last toot wouldn't get her locked in jail come Monday.

CHAPTER FIFTEEN

—⚘—

David was seated at a window table when I arrived at the restaurant, an open bottle of Pinot Noir and two glasses in front of him. He stood and hugged me.

"I'm so glad to see you," I said, choking back a sob that had been building all day. "I started to worry you'd be so angry about my dealings with Kate that you wouldn't show up. I know it was totally irrational, but…"

He put his index finger to my lips and kissed the top of my head. "Hey, you don't ever have to worry about that. I promised I'd always be there: for better, for worse. And if there's one thing you should know about me, it's that I keep my word."

I nodded weakly as we sat down. "But you didn't vow not to say, 'I told you so.'"

"C'mon! You have to admit that's not my style," he said, pouring me a much-needed glass of wine. He was right—he wasn't into recrimination. *So why am I so uneasy?*

We sipped and looked out at Lake Monona, devoid of boaters in this evening's abysmal weather. The cruel white-capped waves lapped at the shore, and I suspected even the fish were hugging the weedy bottom for refuge from the wind and rain.

"I told the waiter to leave us alone with our Pinot and to bring a salad and two Garibaldis in half an hour. Let's get all the unpleasant news off the table before dinner," he said, refilling his own glass. "Tell me about Kate's histrionics."

"I guess that's as good a place to start as any," I said with a sigh. I really didn't want to talk about her, but Kate was the elephant in the room. "How much did you overhear?"

"Just that *they* were trying to lock her up, and she was pissed that you didn't call her back yesterday." He paused to clear his throat, and when he continued his voice quaked with emotion. "I was so angry about the way she talked to you... and more than a little angry that you took it. Sometimes I just want to jump in and defend you."

I reached over and put my hand atop his. "I'm angry at myself, too. For not being assertive enough with her. For ignoring the clear signs of her drug addiction."

David looked up from our hands in mild surprise.

"Yeah," I said wearily, "she tested positive for cocaine and apparently tried to dilute the urine sample. The pretrial services officer gave Kate the results yesterday and also told her George Cooper was filing a motion to revoke her bail. Of course, the officer called me, too, but I wasn't in the office to get the message. So... I spent today getting her assessed by a treatment specialist—who diagnosed her as dependent—and later getting her checked into treatment at a place near

Oregon. Even that may not be enough to satisfy the judge. We've got a hearing on Monday morning."

"Coke would explain a lot of her irascible behavior," he said, nodding slowly.

"Tell me about it," I said. And, after a fortifying sip of wine, I described how Kate had looked and acted while high and while crashing. I described the demeaning process of her admission to The Meadows and her desperate expression when the small stash was discovered in her shoe.

David leaned forward to listen and never shifted his gaze from me. "I'm sorry," he said. "It sounds like one hellacious day."

"If only I'd been prepared. I should've suspected."

"You know what they say about hindsight."

I fingered the stem of my wine glass, trying to summon enough courage to tell him what else was bothering me.

"Out with it," David said, gently pulling my hand away from the glass and caressing it.

"Do you remember when Kate came to talk with us about adopting her baby?"

"How could I forget?"

Kate had come to Madison to meet with Marty Braxton and iron out the details of joining his research team. She had—quite insistently—invited David and me to meet her at a campus bar one evening for drinks. Before we'd even been served, Kate had told us she was pregnant and hoped we'd adopt the child. A child it was "too late to abort."

The baby's father, a Moroccan doctor who was doing his residency with Kate at Stanford, knew nothing of the pregnancy and would shortly be returning home to his wife and children. Kate planned to tell people she was studying abroad during her last trimester and would give birth in Milwaukee. Then she'd move to Madison, and Marty Braxton would be none the wiser. Her parents did not and must never know. Kate's identity as the biological mother would be legally sealed until the child's eighteenth birthday. She had thought it all out and, moreover, had been confident we would accept.

"Remember how forthright she seemed?" I asked. "How she encouraged us to ask her any questions we could think of?"

David nodded.

"And do you remember I specifically asked whether there was any family history of mental illness or substance abuse?"

"Yeah. I remember."

"And how she said no?"

Another nod.

"Today, Kate told me her mother's an alcoholic. Not just a problem drinker—a hard-core alcoholic who's been in detox and treatment three or four times since Kate was a kid. Like that information wouldn't have been germane to our decision-making? Or like we wouldn't want to arm Lily with knowledge about a possible predisposition to alcoholism?"

I'd worked myself up into a furor, and David could hardly miss the tension in my voice.

"You confronted her, I take it?" he asked.

"Yes. And her lame response was she was ashamed. Plus, 'All families have skeletons in their closets.' She actually said that!"

"It's probably true."

"What? You're not defending her, are you?" I asked.

"No. Kate is a manipulator. She was then, and she is now. But I seriously doubt knowing about Margaret's alcoholism would've made much of a difference to us. We would've concluded a possible predisposition to addiction was no more a deal-breaker than a family history of cancer or heart disease. We wanted a healthy baby, which Kate gave us. And for which I'll always be grateful."

"You're saying I shouldn't be angry?"

"No. I'd never presume to tell you how to feel. I'm only suggesting you keep it in perspective."

He's right. It wouldn't have changed our minds.

With impeccable timing, the waiter brought our food, giving me time to compose myself. David and I always ordered Paisan's signature sandwich, the Garibaldi. Made with salami, ham, spicy cheese, tomatoes and peppers on a toasted roll, it was the best thing on the menu.

Over dinner, David and I chatted about his aborted business trip, about Lily's plans with Ida McKinley that evening, and about how we preferred the restaurant's old campus location to the current, modern space.

"There's still something bothering you, isn't there?" David asked after he'd finished his last bite of sandwich.

Sometimes it's so daunting being married to a mind reader. Especially one who believes you shouldn't stuff your emotions. I drained my wineglass.

"Uh-huh," I said. "And it clouds everything: I had a full-blown, monster of a panic attack on the way downtown this morning."

David moved to the chair next to me, slid close, and pulled my head onto his shoulder.

"I'm sorry, honey," he said.

"It's been forever since I had a bad one, and I was feeling so confident being off the Zoloft for a month. And, of course, I started thinking about how awful they were when Lily was a baby and I was home with her... and how I couldn't bear it if they came back like that again." I leaned against him, overcome by my negativity.

"But you've learned a lot in the past six years. You've learned to control them. You've got Dr. Brownhill," he said, gently stroking my arm. "And there's no shame in taking the meds if it comes to that. Go easy on yourself."

His words and his deep, soothing tone weren't quite enough to assuage my fears. "Yeah. But we've got these new, exciting baby opportunities to think about, and instead I'm concentrating on the albatross I've got around my neck and the specter of panic disorder stalking me."

"Just to be clear: Kate's the albatross, not me. Right?" he asked with a grin. I couldn't help but laugh. David went to the restroom and left me alone with my thoughts. I stopped to consciously focus on the joy Lily had brought to our lives. Yes, she was an anxious child, but she was also kind, sensitive, funny and breathtakingly beautiful. Kate had shown us a photograph of Lily's biological father, Fouad, and I could see why she'd fallen for him. And, not surprisingly, their child embodied their best physical attributes: Kate's long, lean frame and grace, Fouad's flawless butter-toffee skin and straight brown hair, and both Kate's and Fouad's ebony eyes. Lily looked nothing like David or me—something she occasionally lamented—yet I knew without question she felt securely a part of our family.

Would our having a biological child by a surrogate disturb Lily's sense of belonging? Would adopting the baby be fairer to her?

I looked up to see David approaching—followed by our waiter, carrying another bottle of wine.

"Did you think I got lost?" he asked with a grin.

"To be honest, I was lost in thought myself and didn't even realize you'd been gone so long. And if I have any more wine, no way can I drive home."

"Not to worry. I made some calls. Got us a room at the Hilton, and their shuttle will pick us up if it's still pouring. Called Ida and Lily, and they're happy as clams, all cozy with cookies and cocoa."

"But the money—"

"The Hilton is one of our clients. I got a great rate. We deserve a night out, Caroline." Warmed by wine, coffee and tiramisu, and especially by my husband's love, the day's disappointments and trials finally melted away. David chided me playfully when I pulled out a notebook and my purple pen to list the pros and cons of adoption and surrogacy. And I gloated when—coming back from the restroom—I saw him sneaking a peak at the notes.

By the time we left for the three-block walk to the hotel, the rain had stopped and we'd made our decision.

CHAPTER SIXTEEN

Saturday, October 13

I drifted awake Saturday morning in a luxurious down-comforter-covered bed, my husband snoring gently by my side. No abrasive alarm clocks. No looming appointments. My sleep had been undisturbed by nightmares and, for the first time in weeks, I felt rested.

Padding noiselessly across the plush carpet, I inched aside the drapes to reveal glorious sunshine. It was too inviting to be denied.

Collecting the clothing we'd hastily scattered on the floor the night before, I tiptoed to the bathroom for a shower, then left David a note on the counter: "8 a.m. – Off to the farmers' market. I have my cell. Love!"

Every Saturday morning from mid-April to early November, local area vendors gather around the Capitol Square to sell their seasonal produce, baked goods, honey, preserves, flowers and plants. Today I'd be somewhat out of place wearing yesterday's rumpled business attire, but that's part of the beauty of Madison: anything goes.

Stopping first for a cup of coffee and a flaky, fresh-baked scone, I strolled with the crowd. When breakfast was done, I bought a canvas bag and filled it with crisp apples, a pair of squash, and a half-dozen gourds for Lily. As I debated whether to lug a pumpkin back to the hotel, my cell phone chirped.

"G'morning, Mom! It's Lily," my one and only child said. I laughed: She'd certainly taken our phone etiquette lessons to heart.

"Hey, kiddo! I'm at the farmers' market—just trying to decide whether to buy you a pumpkin."

"You don't have to. Mrs. McKinley and I got three last night, and we've already carved them," she said. "Wait till you see 'em!"

"Great. I've already got a bagful of stuff and couldn't quite figure out how I was going to carry a pumpkin along with it. Your dad's still back at the hotel sleeping."

"What a lazy bones! Well—Mrs. McKinley and I are going to take Muffin for a walk. See you later, Alligator."

David and I enjoyed a leisurely lunch at the Hilton coffee shop, retrieved our cars and headed back to the suburbs.

After a relaxing start to the weekend, I didn't even mind doing homework. I spent a good part of Saturday and Sunday reading a book on cocaine addiction and studying case law I found on the Internet pertaining to federal bail revocation.

By late Sunday afternoon, I had my arguments well organized, but I knew there was still a very good chance that Judge Brillstein would order Kate to jail until her trial.

"How's it coming?" David asked when he walked in from raking leaves.

"I'm as prepared as I'm gonna be," I said, proudly showing him my outline. "But I'm afraid it might not be enough."

"Well, you worked on the opposite side when you were an ADA. You know the process and what arguments to make."

"That's not exactly true. In state court, we'd never consider detaining a white-collar crook. And the only way we'd revoke bail was if a defendant murdered a witness. It's a whole other game in federal court. Our crazy, reactionary Congress has passed laws making it way too easy for federal prosecutors to play hard ball."

David burst out laughing. "We need to get you a spot on 'Meet the Press!'"

He sat down beside me on the couch and jostled my shoulder. "But seriously, I'm curious about why this is so important to you. You've always said people need to be held responsible for the consequences of their own actions. And I know you're angry with Kate. You'd be justified in just letting the chips fall where they may."

"Excellent question—which I've been asking myself all day," I said, scratching at a rough patch on my hand. David reached over and stopped me.

"I've come to the conclusion I'm more competitive than I ever realized," I said. "I always loved the challenge of an adversarial court case: figuring out whodunit, how to find evidence to prove it, and how to convince a judge or jury. As a prosecutor, I thought I was motivated by a desire to protect the public from 'bad guys,' and I still think that's part of it. But, in all honesty, a big part of it is simply I want to win.

To show I'm better, smarter, more competent than opposing counsel. Maybe not so noble, huh?"

"I think honesty is always noble," David said. "And there's nothing inherently wrong with being competitive."

"Even if it's to defend someone who's in the wrong?"

"Isn't that the way our judicial system's set up?" he asked. "Everyone's got rights worth defending. I don't think there's anything wrong with mounting a vigorous defense for Kate. I only hope you'll be honest with yourself about your feelings toward her. And don't let her walk all over you out of some misguided notions about loyalty and obligation."

I nodded wordlessly as he went to the kitchen to make dinner. *He's right—Kate's rights are worthy of my best defense. And, despite my anger at her, my loyalty and obligation to her aren't misguided.*

—⚭—

Alone with my thoughts, my eyes were drawn to a black leather-bound album on the bookshelf: a scrapbook from my Shenstone College days. *I haven't looked at this in ages*, I thought as I pulled it off the shelf. *But I think I need to look at it now.*

Kate had given me the album for Christmas during our freshman year. I'd been embarrassed to receive the gift, its thick linen pages and embossed leather cover smelling of opulence, when my gift to her was a coffee mug I'd found at a local art fair. Noting my mortification, she assured me the album was a re-gift—something she'd been given by a relative and would never use. "You're the one who's always taking all those pictures, not me," she said. And the gifts had suited us: I filled the scrapbook with dozens of photographs, ticket stubs, newspaper clippings, and quotations, all memorializing the joys of college living, and Kate used the coffee mug every day until it fell off her desk during our senior year. I remembered her tears when she realized the shards of pottery could not be reassembled.

The pictures, depicting Kate and me and our other fresh-faced friends in various stages of dress and undress, brought back a flood of fond memories. I couldn't help but smile at the permed hair, the shoulder pads, the baggy sweatshirts. The photo of Kate and me in her brother's convertible, outfitted with sunglasses and headscarves, for our Thelma and Louise road trip. The picture of us in a campus bar, raising our wine glasses. I vividly remembered us singing along with UB40's "Red Red Wine."

Our college days had not been trouble-free. We'd lost one friend to suicide and another to a car accident; we'd suffered incredible emotional ups and downs. But there was something very special about the time we spent at Shenstone—and the bond my best friend Kate and I shared as we grew together into adulthood.

As I closed the cover, I closed my eyes and said a silent prayer. *God, please help me be as good an advocate for my friend as she was for me.*

CHAPTER SEVENTEEN

—◆—

Monday, October 15

Thankfully, Julie Wutherspoon was already at her desk when I arrived at eight. Stacks of paper, books, and at least five empty to-go cups covered the surface, and the screen of her computer monitor was almost obscured by dozens of crinkled post-it notes. She glanced up when I knocked on the doorframe.

"You talked with David?"

"Yes. We'd like to pursue this option," I heard myself say in an all-business tone. What I really wanted to do was jump up and shout, "Let's go for it!"

I'd always thought it odd Julie chose adoptions as an area of expertise. She had less-than-stellar social skills, was far from warm-and-fuzzy, and never seemed keen on eye contact. *Maybe detachment is a useful trait when you're dealing with something as emotionally charged as giving up or taking on a child?*

Today, though, she smiled at me. "Lemme text her," she said, reaching for her BlackBerry. "Miriam's an early riser."

I watched in admiration as, with lightning speed, Julie typed and sent her message. Within seconds, her phone rang.

"Hey—good morning. That couple I told you about?" Julie said. "They'd like to talk with you."

I realized I was holding my breath.

"Okay. Let me ask," she said. Then, turning to me, "Would you and David be available to meet with her and the baby's dad at two o'clock today?"

"It works for me," I said, "but give me a minute to check with him."

David's calendar, too, was clear.

Unable to stifle my smile, I all but ran back to my office, spinning Rosalee around in her chair as I passed it. She laughed like a five-year-old and came in to hear the news.

"We're meeting with the baby's parents this afternoon! Say a prayer they'll like us."

"Oh, honey. They'll adore you," Rosalee said, beaming. "I was hoping you'd choose this over the surrogacy thing. What tipped the scales for you?"

"It's difficult to put it into words. But we love Lily more than life itself, and this just feels like a better fit for her. It says to her that we prefer adoption to extraordinary methods to have a biological child. And it ensures she'll never have the sense that she's a second-class child."

Rosalee nodded thoughtfully. "You haven't told her yet, have you?"

"No. Not until we're a lot more confident it's actually gonna happen. But I have a pretty good feeling about it!"

I glanced at my clock. "Oh, shit, Rose. I wish I had a good feeling about Kate's revocation hearing—it's at ten. I need to review my notes."

—∞—

When I'd left Kate at The Meadows on Friday, I'd been told she could have no visitors or phone calls for three days. She could leave for court today only if escorted by a staff member, and I'd insisted the intake worker write orders in Kate's chart—in red pen—for the mandatory appearance. Sunday night, I'd left a message with the duty nurse saying Kate needed to meet me at the courthouse fifteen minutes before the hearing.

I must have checked my watch a hundred times between nine forty-five and nine fifty-five. Kate had still not appeared. I called The Meadows and learned Kate had signed out, but no one could decipher the time she left.

When Judge Brillstein's clerk called the case at ten o'clock sharp, I sat alone at the defense table, and George Cooper was ready to rumble.

"Your Honor," he said, "I request the Court order an arrest warrant for Kathryn Daniels. Against my better judgment, I issued a summons for her to appear today to show cause why bail should not be revoked. I should've asked for a warrant last week. Ms. Daniels, as the Court can see, is not present. A warrant is clearly indicated."

"Your comments, Ms. Spencer?" Judge Brillstein asked.

"Thank you, Your Honor. Last Friday afternoon, my client voluntarily entered a thirty-day inpatient drug treatment program at The Meadows. I personally took her there and sat through the intake process. I was informed Ms. Daniels would be allowed to leave The Meadows for her court appearance this morning but only with staff escort. I verified she signed out this morning and can only conclude they're on their way. I'd request the Court postpone the hearing for an hour. I'm sure Ms. Daniels will be here."

"I think your trust is misplaced," George Cooper said, glaring at me before turning to the judge. "I object. We all have busy calendars and don't have time for unnecessary delays."

"Ordinarily I'd agree with you, Mr. Cooper," Brillstein said, flipping the page of his calendar. "However, given the fact that Ms. Daniels is dependent on others to get her here, I'm willing to give her the benefit of the doubt. Are you available at two o'clock today?"

Two o'clock? No!

Cooper replied, "I don't like it, but I can be here."

"Your Honor," I said, my heart leaping into my throat, "I have a schedule conflict this afternoon. May we have a half-hour postponement instead? I'm sure my client will be here soon."

"Fifteen-minute recess. If the defendant is unavailable then, I'll grant the government's motion for a warrant." The judge stood and left the courtroom.

I dashed past Cooper into the hallway and pulled out my cell phone, while frantically looking around for Kate. I was in the middle of a conversation with The Meadows' treatment director when—at ten minutes after ten—Kate emerged from the elevator, accompanied by a young man and a middle-aged woman.

Kate's hair and clothes were clean and neat, but she looked pale and drawn. Her male escort, who introduced himself to me as Adam, apologized for being late. "I took the wrong turn when we got downtown. I'll explain to the judge if you want."

As it turned out, Adam had a lot of explaining to do. Judge Brillstein wanted testimony about the treatment program and Kate's admission. I left the defense table and whispered to Adam and his co-worker, who were seated in the front row, "Is either of you qualified to answer his questions?"

Adam nodded and proceeded to the witness stand.

"Sir, please state and spell your name and tell us your occupation," I said.

"Adam Larken, L-A-R-K-E-N. For the past five years I've been employed as a counselor at The Meadows treatment facility, located just outside Oregon, Wisconsin. I have a master's degree in social work from Columbia University, and I'm certified by the state as a chemical dependency counselor."

Adam answered all the questions I posed, as well as those of George Cooper and the judge. Kate sat impassively beside me as he described some of the withdrawal symptoms she'd suffered in the past two and a half days: night sweats, cocaine dreams, irritability. He also talked about the extent of her past drug use, and the fact that she was in denial of the seriousness of her problem. I was grateful he neglected to mention Kate was in possession of cocaine upon admission. The scales were already tipping perilously against her.

Adam went on to relate that if Judge Brillstein let Kate stay at The Meadows, she would be monitored and supervised for the next four weeks. He agreed to notify the court if she left without permission.

Even after this impressive, professional testimony, George Cooper persisted in his request to revoke Kate's bail. He argued her cocaine usage was criminal behavior, clearly occurring while she was on bail, and reported there was strong evidence she had also used cocaine in jail.

"Objection," I said, bolting to my feet to make my point. "Even if true, cocaine usage while in jail would not be subject to this court's jurisdiction."

"Hold on there, Ms. Spencer," Judge Brillstein replied. "I need to hear more about this. The statute clearly states I can consider the history and characteristics of the defendant in determining whether she can be released on conditions, and history of substance abuse *is* relevant."

I felt like a fourth grader who'd just volunteered the wrong answer to a math problem. *Why didn't I read the bail statutes more carefully?*

"Mr. Cooper, please tell me the basis for your statement," Brillstein said.

Cooper explained that the urine sample Kate gave at the time of her release on bail was positive for cocaine, both on initial testing and upon retest, indicating she'd used the drug during her three days in jail.

"Thank you," the judge said. "Any further argument, Mr. Cooper?"

Cooper paused a moment. "Yes. I think there's a strong likelihood cocaine usage caused the defendant to commit the grant fraud in the first place. This behavior should not be tolerated by the Court."

"I object, Your Honor," I said. "My client is presumed innocent of the crimes charged in the indictment. The purpose of this hearing is to determine whether there are conditions that will ensure her future appearances in court. Mr. Larken has described the program in which my client voluntarily enrolled. It's a sound and respected program that includes plenty of supervision. If she remains drug free, there is absolutely no risk she will flee."

"That's a big 'if,' Ms. Spencer," the judge said. We sat in silence while he considered the options—and while he reread the violation report and a brochure that had been proffered by Adam Larken.

Kate leaned toward me as if to whisper something, but I gestured for her to stop.

Finally, Judge Brillstein spoke. "I'm persuaded by your argument, Ms. Spencer, and by the merits of the treatment program. The conditions of release are modified to require Ms. Daniels to remain at The Meadows facility until the thirty-day program is completed. She'll need to sign an authorization for them to report her progress—and any illegal drug usage—to Ms. Smith-Kellor and me. We're adjourned." Again, he stood and left the courtroom.

I'd put out another fire. Kate, however, looked less than relieved. There was no time for us to chat—the counselors were in a hurry to get back to their appointments at The Meadows.

—⁓—

There had been several people seated in the courtroom when Kate's hearing began, I presumed for other appearances on the judge's calendar. With more pressing concerns on my mind, I hadn't paid much attention to them.

As I packed my briefcase to leave, I heard a voice from the back of the courtroom. "Do you have a few minutes, Caroline?"

I looked up in surprise to see Doug Connaboy approaching, wearing his going-to-court-or-a-funeral attire: a charcoal gray suit, white shirt and understated red tie. And I smelled his Old Spice.

"Wow! You clean up nicely," I said with a smile.

My attempt at levity fell flat. His stony expression—which I should have noticed—became more rather than less rigid, leaving me instantly uncomfortable.

"Sorry, Doug. I didn't mean to offend."

"I'm not offended. Just having a shitty day," he said, massaging his temples. "I've been subpoenaed in a trial in Judge Coburn's court, and they're running way behind schedule. When I saw your client's name on the court calendar, I thought I'd catch you. Hopefully make good use of otherwise wasted time."

"I've got a few minutes. What did you want to talk about?"

"Mind if we go down to second floor? I want to be available in the remote chance they call me to testify anytime soon."

We headed downstairs and sat on a padded bench outside the District Judges' courtrooms, overlooking the ultramodern lobby. I had to admit the interior of the courthouse was beautiful—sleek and soothing. Doug Connaboy, however, was clearly not soothed.

"Although it's not for publication yet, we got back the tox results on Yvonne Pritchard," he said, tugging at his tie. "She had very high levels of cocaine in her system, which almost certainly caused her cardiac arrest. I really want to nail whoever gave or sold her the drug." He paused, obviously inviting my response.

"And?" I asked warily, unwilling to go where I thought he was headed.

"And, I think your client knows who it was. I'd like you to persuade her to tell us. I'm prepared to ask Jerry Alexander to initiate prosecution against her for obstruction of justice, but I'd prefer not to have to go that route." Jerry Alexander was now the deputy district attorney. We'd worked closely together at the DA's office for almost eight years.

"And your evidence for the obstruction charge would be the roommate's claim that Kate told her to destroy evidence? A roommate who happens to have a coke dealer brother? It would come down to 'she said, she said,' and you'd never be able to make a case."

"I was upstairs in court for the whole revocation hearing, Caroline," Doug said caustically. "Despite her lofty position, your client's credibility with me is shot. She managed to get her hands on cocaine in the jail, for chrissakes! You'd better believe I'm gonna look into that, too."

I was spared from having to reply: a bailiff opened the door and summoned Doug to testify. He walked into the courtroom, glaring over his shoulder at me.

My chest tightened as I stood to leave the building.

CHAPTER EIGHTEEN

—⟋⟍—

The conversation with Doug Connaboy reverberated loudly in my mind, when what I really wanted to be thinking about was the afternoon's meeting with David, Julie and her client. How could I banish the unwelcome thoughts? A massage? A Bloody Mary?

Remember what Grandma Burnett always told you: You can't really escape from something unless you know what it is.

I walked out of the federal courthouse and dialed a number I knew by heart—the DA's office—and asked to speak with Jerry Alexander.

"You must have ESP," he said when he answered. "Tom Robbins is sitting here in my office, and we're discussing something we hope you can help with. Any chance you can come by?"

I looked at my watch: eleven-thirty. "I can be there in five minutes and can spare about an hour. Will that do?"

"Sure. See you soon."

—∿∿—

I had been back to the District Attorney's office several times since my resignation, usually for special occasions like baby showers and farewell parties. I'd had mixed emotions each time. The camaraderie I experienced during my tenure as a prosecutor was unparalleled. But so were the pressures.

Today, I received hugs and warm greetings from many of my old co-workers. It took me ten minutes to move from the reception area, past the lunchroom—smelling, as always, of burned coffee—and fifteen feet down the hall to Jerry's office.

It looked just as I remembered. Beige walls adorned with dozens of framed political cartoons. A nondescript desk buried under stacks and stacks of legal files and an empty pizza box. Tom Robbins occupied the only comfortable chair. He rose and engulfed me in his arms. "You're too thin, Miz Caroline! Ain't your husband makin' enough to feed you?" he said with a grin.

I laughed and turned to Jerry. His greeting, while warm, was decidedly less demonstrative. Shortly before I'd left the office, we had jointly prosecuted a major trial. We worked flawlessly together and presented a strong case. In my office, while waiting for the jury to deliberate, Jerry had put his hand on my shoulder. An innocent gesture—a platonic move made in offices everywhere every day. But this time it was different. I knew as well as I knew my own name he'd felt the same electricity I did. We had never spoken of it, but we had never again stood as closely to one another.

"It's good to see you, Jerry." I said.

"You, too," He moved his gym bag from another chair and motioned for me to sit. "Would you like a cup of coffee or anything?"

"No, thanks," I said. "Like I told you, I'm kind of pressed for time, and there's something I wanted to ask you about, too. How 'bout you go first?"

Jerry nodded. "I'll let Tom explain."

"As you know, Caroline, I'm in charge of investigating criminal conduct within the jail," Tom said. "I recently busted a deputy named Anita Jackson for bringing in coke. It's a damn shame, too, 'cause she was one of my better people. She'd been on the job about two years. A sister. Single mom, supporting herself and her two kids. Always glad to work overtime.

"Last week we did a shake down of the women's cell block and found two eight-balls of coke. The inmates snitched on Anita in a heartbeat. They'll roll on anybody to save their own asses. Once the administration had her name, they insisted on setting her up. She was caught on video making a delivery."

I knew where this was going—and I didn't like it.

"Anita broke down immediately and gave a full confession," Tom said. "She said the first time she brought in coke was several weeks ago—for your client, Dr. Daniels."

"Oh, man—" I started to protest.

"Hold on," said Jerry. "We don't think Kathryn Daniels set it up or even suggested it. Her pusher friend did that."

"Who's 'her pusher friend'?" I asked.

"Joe Ames."

Joe Ames? I had a vague recollection of seeing that name somewhere in the discovery materials from George Cooper and struggled to recall in what context. It wasn't coming to me.

"I presume from your reaction the name is familiar to you?" Jerry asked.

I shrugged.

Tom shifted in his chair and continued. "As we've reconstructed it, Joe Ames, claiming to be your client's brother, visited her on her first night in jail. We don't believe she'd made any outgoing phone calls, so he must have decided to visit on his own. We presume he asked her if she'd like him to get her some cocaine and she said yes. But their conversation wasn't one of the ones being monitored that evening."

"Why's that?" I asked, though it didn't matter to me. In reality, I was stalling. I needed time to digest what I was hearing.

"Lack of manpower and equipment," Tom said with a sigh. "Our visiting room officers have to focus on the folks they think are most suspicious. Ames walked in looking like a businessman visiting his college professor sister, and the officers figured they should concentrate on the gang-bangers in the next booth instead. Ninety percent of the time they would've been right."

"Ames is slick one," Jerry said. "He and his wife have a catering and cleaning business—mostly a front—through which he runs his drug money. He even takes phone orders and accepts credit card payments. Meaning Kate could charge her cocaine by phone from the jail. From the volume of credit card receipts we've looked at, a number of professional people regularly availed themselves of the 'catering' and 'cleaning' services."

"But how did he hook up with Anita Jackson?" I asked.

"We're not sure why he targeted her," said Jerry. "He started grooming Anita some time ago. Somehow he found out where she lived. At any rate, he followed her when she walked her kids to school one morning. Struck up a conversation about how she was smart to see them to school. So many bad things can happen to kids these days. Then he started talking about how much it costs to raise kids. How they're always needing braces or shoes. Anita told us she wanted to run away from this guy but felt she needed to see what he was getting at."

My stomach felt queasy. "Ames used her kids to get her to comply?" I asked.

"You got it," Tom said. "Eventually he made it clear: he'd pay her to smuggle drugs into specific prisoners at the jail. But the bigger perk was his implicit agreement not to hurt her kids. He gave her a couple grams of coke to deliver to your client, and Anita reluctantly agreed."

"Why didn't she come to you for help, Tom?"

"I wish she had. But she wasn't confident the cops would be able to protect her kids. A couple years ago, one of her cousins agreed to testify against her gangster boyfriend— with the understanding, of course, that she'd receive protection—and ended up bludgeoned to death with a brick."

"I remember that case," I said, grimacing. "The detective assigned to the case got fired, didn't he?"

"Yeah," Jerry said, "but three months too late for the victim."

Tom continued, "Since Anita's agreed to testify against Joe Ames, we've moved her and her mother and the kids. It's pretty disruptive, but I think we can keep 'em safe."

"Kate was only in jail a few days. How did Ames get other buyers there?" I asked.

"You know the inmate grapevine," Jerry said. "Before long, five other inmates were placing phone-in orders."

Jerry ran his hand through his hair. "We'd like your client to testify against Ames. Anita's testimony might not be enough by itself, and your client could seal our case."

"I'll talk with Kate about it as soon as I can."

Tom got up to leave. "It's important, Caroline. We need to put this asshole away." He gave me a quick peck on the cheek and was out the door.

Jerry shifted in his chair and loosened his tie. "What did you want to talk to me about?" he asked.

"Doug Connaboy is threatening that you'll prosecute Kate Daniels for obstruction of evidence in the Yvonne Pritchard case."

"Yeah. I talked with him the other day. He thinks she's protecting someone."

"My client swears she's not. And has volunteered to take a polygraph," I said.

"You know we don't have the resources to hook someone up to the machine every time we think they're lying. Doug has an uncanny ability to see through bullshit. And frankly, I think your client's handing you a load of it. Has it occurred to you that Pritchard's dealer and Joe Ames might be one and the same?"

To my own consternation, none of this had occurred to me. But Jerry didn't need to know that. "I'll consider what you've said," I said. "What happens now?"

"I don't have the time or inclination to prosecute Kate Daniels for possessing cocaine in jail. I just want her testimony about it. But more than anything, I want whoever sold drugs to that poor dead girl. If your client knows who it was and doesn't come clean, I won't hesitate to go after her with everything I've got."

"Thanks for your candor," I said, though I didn't like his message. "I'll be in touch." There was no electricity and no warmth when I shook Jerry's hand to leave. Yet another example of how Kate Daniels was driving a wedge between me and the "good guys" who'd known and respected me for years.

—⁓—

The walk back to my office calmed me some, but my nerves were still raw when I walked in. Rosalee was off this afternoon, and without her I felt suddenly rudderless—and famished. I grabbed a granola bar from my desk drawer and inhaled it, taking the edge off and enabling me to think.

David met me in my office a few minutes before two o'clock. I told him the judge had allowed Kate to remain at the treatment center; David told me briefly about his morning. And then it was time for our meeting.

"Is this what it's like when you're in a trial?" he asked. "I feel like I'm going to be judged by a jury."

"I'm a lot more confident in a courtroom," I whispered as we walked into the conference room where Julie Wutherspoon and the young couple were waiting.

I couldn't help but stare: the child of these two kids would be a knockout.

Miriam, a tiny girl with cherub cheeks, ice blue eyes and picture-perfect teeth, spoke with a confidence beyond her eighteen years. "Thank you so much for seeing us. This is the most important decision we'll ever make, and we don't believe we can do so without personally meeting the prospective parents."

Antonio, her boyfriend, was quieter but equally impressive. His deep, dark eyes were warm and welcoming, and when he smiled, a disarming dimple appeared in his cheek. "I'm very pleased to meet you," he said in flawless, unaccented English.

Handshakes and introductions complete, Julie motioned for us all to take our seats. Miriam and Antonio sat next to one another, holding hands. Julie sat to Miriam's right, and David and I sat across the table from them.

"Why don't you tell the Spencers a little about yourselves?" Julie said.

"Sure," Miriam said. "I'm a senior at Edgewood High School. I've already got enough credits to graduate, so I won't have to attend this coming spring if the pregnancy gets too rough. My parents want me to do the Ivy League thing, and my grades and SATs should be good enough for that. But," she said, looking at her boyfriend with adoration, "I'm leaning toward somewhere closer to home. Antonio graduated from West High School last year, and he's been going to tech school part-time while working with his father. We struck up a friendship about a year ago when they were doing a landscape project at my parents' house." She nodded for him to chime in.

"I knew right away I wanted us to be more than friends," Antonio said—and there was that dimple. "But we took it slow and didn't really become a couple until last spring. My family loves Miriam, but, unfortunately, her parents don't feel the same way about me. They went ballistic when they found out about the pregnancy. And rightly so: we should've been more careful."

"We love each other," Miriam said. "But we're smart enough to know we're unprepared for a family at this point. We want this child to have the best possible chance for happiness."

"Do you want to remain involved in the child's life?" I asked before I could censor myself.

Antonio looked at Miriam, whose eyes instantly welled with tears. "We've thought a lot about that question," he said. "We think it would be too confusing for the child— and too hard on everyone. So… no. No contact, no pictures, no updates."

I sighed silently with relief. A complicated relationship with one birth parent was more than enough for us to handle.

They talked of their future plans. Antonio intended to get a degree in landscape architecture and to take over his father's business, which currently had twenty employees. Miriam leaned toward a career in social work. They told us they'd never used drugs, rarely drank alcohol, and Miriam hadn't touched a drop since the EPT stick read "yes."

And then it was our turn. Miriam and Antonio asked David and me more questions than I could have imagined: about our marriage, our careers, our child-rearing philosophies, and Lily's adjustment. We smiled through it all, though my facial muscles grew tired from the tension I felt.

"Beatles or Stones?" Miriam finally asked, then giggled at the puzzled look on my face. "Sorry—we had a bet on it."

When I replied, "Beatles. Definitely!" she pumped her fist with glee.

I glanced at Julie, who pursed her lips and scowled. Giggling and fist pumping were definitely not in her repertoire of behaviors, and I doubted she had a position on the 'Beatles versus Stones' question. She looked at David and me. "I think we're finished here, but why don't you two give us a few minutes so I can confer with my clients. I just want to make sure we've covered all the bases."

"Okay," I said. "We'll wait in the reception area while you talk. Come get us when you're ready." David and I pushed our chairs from the table, got up and walked into the hallway. If felt awkward to me. *Should we have said something on the way out?* It wasn't clear to me whether we'd have another chance to talk with Miriam and Antonio.

David and I sat next to one another on a couch in the waiting area. "These are great kids," I said, grabbing his hand. "I sure hope they like us."

"I think they like us." We sat in silence, periodically looking at the wall clock and crossing and uncrossing our legs. When Julie came out to see us ten minutes later, I could read nothing in her facial expression. She folded her arms across her chest and shook her head in irritation. "Before they decide," she said, "they want to meet Lily and ask her some questions."

My heart jumped into my throat. I looked over at David as he pulled his hand from mine. He stood up abruptly and turned to walk toward my office. "No," he said. "That's not gonna happen."

CHAPTER NINETEEN

—⁓—

My husband always reminds me to keep an even keel, and we had both managed to do so during our long interview with Miriam and Antonio. But as we headed back to my office, his brisk pace and steely eyes told me he was way off kilter.

"If they wanted to talk with our daughter, why didn't they tell us from the get-go?" he asked, kicking at the carpet in front of my desk with the toe of his shoe. "We could've told them no right away and saved ourselves a lot of time and energy."

In that instant I realized he'd allowed himself to be more swept up in the excitement about adopting Miriam and Antonio's baby than he'd let on. I looked away, his suffering too painful to watch. My eyes stung with tears.

I closed my office door, grabbed a Kleenex and sat on the couch, waiting for our emotions to settle a bit. David remained standing, staring out the window.

Five minutes later, after one unanswered knock, Julie stormed in. "You know this is a deal-breaker, don't you?"

she said sharply. She heaved herself into my spare chair and glared at me. "We were so close. Can't you talk him into this, Caroline?"

Her dismissive attitude toward my husband rankled me and was more than I could take. I blew my nose, wiped my eyes with a soggy, mascara-stained tissue, and sat up straighter.

"First of all, I don't appreciate your tone or talking about David as if he weren't standing here in the room with us. Second, I don't intend to 'talk him into it.' I agree with him completely."

Her jaw dropped.

"We have a solemn obligation to protect our daughter, Julie," I said, rising to stand over her and astonishing myself with my heartfelt fervor. "We can't put her in the position to be the deal-maker or deal-breaker here. She doesn't even *know* we were considering adopting this baby, for God's sake. And how do you think she'd feel if she learned we were and the deal was nixed because of something she said or didn't say? Please convey *our* decision to your clients. And it's non-negotiable."

Julie shook her head. Without a word, she got up from the chair and marched out the door, letting it slam behind her.

David and I exchanged a glance—conveying in a nano-second our solidarity—and suddenly I was okay again. We could handle anything, as long as we faced it together.

"Thanks for putting it so eloquently," David said. "I would've been much less diplomatic!"

"You're welcome," I said. "And, please promise me we'll never become so desperate to have a child that we stop thinking rationally."

"You got it."

I walked to my desk to shut down my computer. "Let's get out of here. I need a glass of wine and a hefty dose of seven-year-old-girl chatter."

—⁓—

Lily was at once delighted by simultaneous undivided attention from two parents and mindful of our deflated moods. She passed out more compliments and endearments than we could count and hung on our every word. *She certainly didn't inherit her considerate nature from her biological mom.*

After a cobbled-together stir-fry dinner, which Lily proclaimed the best she'd ever tasted, we all sat together on the couch for an "I Love Lucy" festival. We'd received the whole video series of the black-and-white TV show as a gift and treasured every episode. I never tired of watching Lily laughing 'til she cried at the antics of Lucy and Ethel. Sit-com friendships are beyond enviable.

For a while, at least, I was able to forget the day's disappointments. Neither David nor I put up any resistance to our daughter's plea for "just one more episode" before bedtime.

I let Lily soak an extra ten minutes in her cloyingly sweet Bubbleberry Mr. Bubble bath and reveled in her warmth as I wrapped her in a large soft towel. "Thanks, Mom. You're the best!"

Tuesday, October 16

The foul-smelling inmate snitch lurked behind a cement pillar in the basement-parking garage of my office building and, as I approached my car, sprang out and shoved me to the ground. Sitting astride me, pressing my face against dank concrete, he bound my hands and feet and then my mouth with duct tape. With the strength of a madman, he yanked me up and threw me into the trunk, striking my head against the frame.

The next thing I knew, I was seated at my kitchen counter—still bound but no longer gagged—watching in horror as he rummaged through the cutlery drawer. "Please," I said quietly, hoping to find a way to reason with him.

"Shut the fuck up," he yelled.

Lily bounded in the back door and stopped in her tracks, unable to comprehend the scene. "What—"

With a beefy, tattooed and filthy arm, he grabbed her around the neck, wielding a carving knife in the other hand.

"No!" I screamed, bolting upright in bed. My shoulders heaved with sobs. I shook my head in a futile effort to banish the horrific scene and felt David's arms envelope me.

His heart raced against mine as he held me close, tenderly stroking my back.

Without warning, Lily burst through our bedroom door, slamming it against the wall as she barreled toward the bed. "What's wrong?" she shrieked, renewing my terror.

My hysteria had to have been as terrifying to David and Lily as my nightmare—with the recurring evil character— had been to me.

"Climb in, honey," David said, scooting over to make room for her in the bed between us. "Your mom just had a very scary dream. That's all."

My scream must've exorcised the demons—at least temporarily—for I was able to sleep in peace the rest of the night.

But Lily's alarm clock—usually muffled by our closed door—startled me awake at six forty-five. Her raggedy and less-than-sweet-smelling blanket sat on my pillow and confused me, until I looked over to see her nestled against her dad's back, both oblivious to the annoying beep.

I shook her shoulder. "You slept with us last night, Pumpkin. Go shut off your alarm and get moving."

Lily padded out—thankfully without complaint. Sinking back against the pillows, I stared at the ceiling, unprepared to face the day and harboring a nagging sense of trepidation.

David sat up slowly and reached for the long-sleeved t-shirt he kept at the foot of the bed. I tilted my head and absently watched as he poked his head and arms through the shirt.

He walked to the door, shut it silently, then came back to sit next to me on the edge of the bed.

"I'm worried about you," he said. "You've got stress written all over your face, you're not sleeping well, and now your nightmare's scaring the bejesus out of Lily and me. Don't you think it's time you called Dr. Brownhill?"

"You're probably right," I said without conviction. I thought the world of my therapist, but it felt a little like defeat to go back to her.

"You'll call her today?" he asked and pointedly waited for my reply.

"Okay."

—∽∿∿—

Dr. Clarice Brownhill had been the psychologist assigned by the court to evaluate David and me as prospective adoptive parents before Lily's birth. I'd made an instant connection with her, and I later sought her out for therapy for my panic attacks. A compact woman with short, silver-gray hair, she wore classically stylish clothes woven from natural fibers, Native American jewelry, and the most loving smile imaginable.

I called the clinic as soon as it opened and was grateful to learn Dr. Brownhill had had a cancellation and could see me later in the morning. Much as I hated to admit it, David was right: I needed her help.

Dr. Brownhill's office always set me at ease. Sunlight streamed through the slats of the wooden window shutters, lush green plants contributed oxygen and life, and the buttery-soft overstuffed furniture soothed raw nerves and muscles. Redolent with the ever-present fresh flowers on her desk and spiced tea brewing in a pot in the corner, the room whispered sanctuary. Here, I felt truly cared for.

"Tell me what brings you here today," Dr. Brownhill said when she'd seated herself in a massive club chair, her bare feet tucked under her.

I tried to swallow the lump in my throat and grabbed a tissue from the box sitting next to me. "Last night I woke up screaming from the worst conceivable nightmare and scared David and Lily half to death."

Dr. Brownhill listened as I recounted the details. "It does sound terrifying."

"And it was so vivid and realistic—not like some dreams where everything's jumbled together." I said. "That scared me even more."

"Dream analysis isn't my area of expertise." She scratched her head with her pen. "But perhaps the dream's intensity was your subconscious mind's way of forcing you to confront a critical issue you might otherwise try to ignore. Does that sound plausible to you?"

I nodded. "Yes, but I'm not sure which issue. There seem to be plenty." I told her about my recent panic attack, about the adoption and surrogacy options we'd been considering, and about Kate's multiple legal problems and her unwillingness to cooperate with the cops. Dr. Brownhill was one of only a handful of people who knew Lily was Kate's biological child.

"I find it interesting the bad guy in your dream is, as you call him, 'a snitch,' and your law enforcement friends are asking Kate to testify against her source. It's also interesting that you're helpless to stop the snitch from hurting Lily."

"So you think my defending Kate is the biggest source of my stress?"

"You know you're the only one who can answer that," she replied with a smile.

"I didn't want to take this case in the first place but didn't feel I had any choice."

"A lack of choices is always problematic," she said. "Why did you feel you didn't have a choice?"

"I told you how helpful Kate was to me when I started having the panic attacks in college. If she hadn't made me see a doctor to get on medication, I don't know what would have happened. And then she gave us Lily…"

Dr. Brownhill gave me her "go on" nod.

"I felt obligated to represent her."

"Hmmm. Did Kate say as much to you?"

"Not in so many words. Just a few comments like 'I'd do it for you.'"

"Let's take this point by point," Dr. Brownhill said. "It seems to me that suggesting a friend see a doctor is pretty innocuous. An appropriate response might be a thank-you note or a nice bottle of wine—not a life-long sense of indebtedness." ·

She looked at me expectantly, and my stomach did a little flip-flop. I couldn't bring myself to answer.

"Okay. Then we'll move on to 'she gave us Lily.' The gift of a child is immeasurable, for sure, but you and David gave Kate a gift in return: a positive solution for what could otherwise have been a life-changing problem."

"Kate could have elected to terminate the pregnancy and no one would have been the wiser," I said. "Although she initially claimed it was too late for an abortion, that turned out not to be true."

"But Kate was morally opposed to abortion and was afraid of the guilt she would feel if she chose that route."

"What?" I asked. "Where'd you get that idea?"

"You told me."

"When?"

"If you remember, before the adoption, you and David had access to Kate's medical records and her psych evaluation, and you talked to me about what you'd read. I'm somewhat ashamed to admit it, but after I saw the article in the paper about her arrest, I went back and reviewed my notes from those old sessions. That's how I recall what you told me at the time."

Dr. Brownhill must've read the puzzled look on my face.

"What I'm saying is this," she said, "Kate did you a favor by giving you her child, but you did *her* a favor by saving her from hell and damnation—at least in her mind."

"Why don't I remember that?" I asked, shaking my head. *Didn't Kate recently tell me she planned to give Yvonne Pritchard money for an abortion? Something she once found morally reprehensible?* I was confused by the conflicting information but didn't have the energy to pursue the train of thought. "That's a side of her I just can't see."

"You've had a lot of other things on your mind since the day you signed on to become Lily's mom. But you also need to keep in mind addiction is a progressive disease. Kate has progressively morphed into someone different than the friend you once knew. And addiction also alters one's moral compass—as evidenced by all the addicts who steal from their families to support their habits."

"Maybe you're right," I said, not wanting to face what I already knew. "But what do I do?"

"Could you give up Kate's case?"

—⟋⟍—

Tuesday evening, while Lily was at a Brownie meeting, David and I sat bundled up in front of a fire on the patio, a bottle of wine on the table between us. The cool air reminded me of the all-too-quickly-coming winter.

We stared in silence for a while, mesmerized by the tongues of flame dancing among the logs.

"Did the session with Dr. Brownhill help?" he finally asked.

I nodded. "It always helps me to talk to her."

"I get the sense there's still a lot on your mind," he said, reaching over to take my hand. "You feel miles away from me."

I swallowed a few times, unsure I could trust my voice not to break. "Talking with Dr. Brownhill didn't change the fact that there's way too much emotional stuff going on, and it's all out of our control."

The wind shifted, and a pillar of smoke wafted David's way. He moved his chair close to the other side of mine, took my hand again, and looked at me with concern.

"My worlds are colliding," I said, "after all my efforts to keep them separate. It feels like one of those apocalypse movies with invaders on every side and the clock ticking away."

He shifted in his chair. "Did she have any suggestions?"

I paused for a moment over a sip of wine and collected my thoughts. No way was I going to tell him she'd suggested I consider giving up Kate's case. I didn't feel like rehashing why I'd taken the case to begin with. Moreover, I didn't want to field any more questions about my sense of obligation to Kate. "She says I should take each problem by itself, examine it, and try to recognize how I feel about it," I replied.

"And?"

"Well... take the adoption, for example. We agonized about whether to choose Linda Wordsworth's surrogacy candidate or Miriam and Antonio's baby. We made the choice to go for the adoption, felt confident and enthusiastic about it, and then got shot down. It's just so fucking frustrating. Thank heaven we didn't call Linda off—though it'll take me a while to gear back up emotionally for surrogacy."

David was silent for a moment, then said quietly, "Linda called me today."

Instantly on edge, I sat forward in my chair. "When were you going to tell me? What did she say?"

Letting go of my hand, he took his time refilling our glasses.

"She said our potential surrogate is thinking of contracting with another couple."

My heart sank. "A bidding war?"

"No..." he said slowly. "More like she's pressing for an immediate answer—and Linda hasn't even had the opportunity to interview her on our behalf."

"Oh, no, David. I don't think I can bear it if we lose another option. What did you tell her?"

He got up and put another log on the fire as my impatience grew by the second.

I shook my head in dismay. "Don't tell me you burned this bridge, too."

"Wait just a minute," he shot back, spinning around to face me. "I thought we were on the same page in thinking Miriam and Antonio's request to interview Lily was out of line. We both agreed to say no. And now you're implying I 'burned the bridge.'"

"I'm sorry, David. We are on the same page about it. It's just..." I thought for a moment. "My emotions feel raw... It's like all the wounds from the miscarriages and years of infertility have been ripped open again. I didn't mean to take it out on you."

He nodded and poked at the fire.

"So what did you tell Linda?" I asked.

"I thought about our conversation yesterday—you know, about being desperate? Giving in to the surrogate's demand for an immediate answer and acquiescing to her financial demands felt like acts of desperation."

"So you told her no."

"Caroline, I really believe we need to let this percolate for a while. Being turned down by Miriam and Antonio was a big deal, and we deserve time to make the right decision," he said. "I told her we wouldn't be able to give her an answer until Friday."

"And her response?"

"She wasn't optimistic that the surrogate would wait."

As if to ward off the cold, I hugged myself and began rocking back and forth in my chair. Yes, I'd told David we shouldn't act out of desperation—but maybe I'd been wrong.

CHAPTER TWENTY

—m—

Wednesday, October 17

"Joe Ames," I said to Kate when we were alone in the counselor's office.

I had called The Meadows for permission to see her. Adam Larken had agreed I could visit for half an hour before a mandatory nine o'clock group meeting, but he'd taken up twenty minutes of my allotted time reporting on Kate's progress. The positive news was she hadn't used drugs or absconded. On a less-than-positive note, she was moody and withdrawn during counseling sessions and not "invested in the program."

I found it difficult to hear him criticize her, especially in her presence. I didn't exactly feel defensive for my friend, and—lord knows—I'd been muttering under my breath about her for weeks. But his direct and blunt manner made me uncomfortable. Like my husband, Adam didn't mince words or apologize for the truth. *Maybe Kate needs me to be more blunt with her*, I thought as he walked out of the office, closing the door behind him.

After my conversations with Doug Connaboy, Jerry Alexander and Tom Robbins, I had gone back through the investigative reports looking for specific references to Joe Ames. There were more than I cared to admit, and I'd been remiss in not noticing them during the first go-rounds. "I know a couple of things about Ames," I said to Kate. "First, he supplied the coke you used in jail. Second, you put him on the university payroll, I assume in exchange for drugs."

Kate didn't look at me, sitting motionless and glaring past me out the window.

"The feds and the local cops haven't yet interfaced on Ames. I'm not even sure the feds know he's a dealer," I said. "But the locals want him bad. They suspect he sold the drugs that killed your student, and I think you'd be able to confirm or deny those suspicions. You need to tell them the truth."

Her face twisted in anger. "Whose side are you on?"

"What's that supposed to mean?"

"Just what I said, Caroline." She sprang to her feet, crossed the room, and leaned on the windowsill, stretching her back. "You're not working with the cops anymore. Your job is to defend me. And Joe Ames is off limits. I won't inform on him."

"Not even to give Yvonne's family some closure?"

She turned to me. "'Closure' is a crock of shit. And, no— not even for that. The cops can play connect-the-dots without my help."

"May I ask why?"

Silence, then a tear trickled down her cheek. "Remember when you first met David? You told me you knew you'd found your soul mate."

I nodded.

"Joe Ames is like that for me. I love him."

—⁓—

I drove back to the city in stunned silence. In fact, when I pulled into the parking lot, I had one of those frightening how-on-earth-did-I-get-here? moments.

Maybe I should give up this case. The thought of calling Doug Connaboy and telling him Kate wouldn't cooperate tied my stomach in knots. And yet the notion of letting Kate down was unthinkable—I couldn't wrap my head around it.

"Jerry Alexander called earlier," Rosalee said as I walked into my office to a ringing phone. "I suspect this is him again. Do you want to take it?"

"Might as well," I sighed, flinging my briefcase and purse on the side chair.

"Did you talk to your client?" Jerry barked through the phone, making no effort at small talk—or to hide his impatience.

"Yeah. She's unwilling to meet with Doug Connaboy or Tom Robbins about anything to do with Joe Ames. I'm sorry—"

"Not as sorry as she's gonna be when we come down on her for obstructing justice."

"C'mon, Jerr. We both know that'd be a loser case for you."

I heard him shuffling papers and then drop the phone; I recalled the many times I'd seen his failed attempts at multi-tasking.

"You could learn how to use your speaker phone," I said with a half-hearted chuckle when he picked up again.

"No cajoling, Caroline. I'm pissed. We're all frustrated at the lack of progress on this Pritchard thing. And I know in my heart Joe Ames is one bad motherfucker."

"I wish I could help, but it's out of my hands."

"Is she afraid of him?"

"I can't answer that."

"Can't or won't?"

Good question. "Doesn't matter, Jerr," I said with brusqueness I didn't feel. "I'll call you if anything changes. And I trust you'll pass on our regrets to Doug and Tom." My hand was shaking as I put down the phone. My friend was in the wrong here, and it felt wrong for me to be defending her.

—⁓—

"Wanna go to lunch, Rosalee?" I asked when she brought in the mail late that morning. I'd managed to suppress the residual guilt from my conversation with Jerry and had finished writing a brief in a complicated property dispute case. "I'm starved, and I have a taste for Mexican."

"Not that food cart on the Square."

"No, I'm thinking La Hacienda on Park Street. I want to be waited on. And to avoid cops and lawyers."

She grinned. "Let me get my purse."

We arrived just before the lunch crowd and took a table by the window at the back of the large dining room. I pushed aside the colorful serape drape to let in more sunshine and dived into the basket of tortilla chips, dripping salsa on my plastic menu.

"Make yourself at home," Rosalee said, laughing as she settled herself into the chair across from me.

"I suppose I should stick to Jarrito's," I told our waiter. But when he came back to report they'd run out of my favor ite flavor—lime—I caved. "A Dos Equis sounds divine!"

The quick service wasn't conducive to leisurely conversation, but between bites I brought Rosalee up to speed on the soap opera my life had become.

"I'm sorry the adoption didn't work out," she said, searching through her purse for her always-elusive lipstick. "Maybe Julie will come up with some other good leads."

"Doubtful. She barely nodded when I said hi to her in the coffee room this morning. We pissed her off when we refused to allow her clients to interview Lily."

"For what it's worth, I think you did the right thing."

Talking with Rosalee always relaxed me, and the beer didn't hurt either. I felt a sense of almost-normalcy as we boarded the elevator in the parking garage to return to work.

When the door began to open on the first floor, I glanced up in mild irritation—I'd never been a fan of elevators, especially when they stopped and started. I turned back to Rosalee and said, "Let's add a reference to the case the Court of Appeals decided last week..."

My breath caught in my throat. Miriam and Antonio stood in the lobby waiting to ride up.

"You mean Evers versus Mitchum?" Rosalee asked, oblivious to my shock and discomfort. "You're right—I think that's on point."

Miriam smiled and looked down as they walked in. Smelling her light, airy perfume I cringed, certain that I, myself, smelled of beer. I nodded, mumbled a "hello" and proceeded to study my feet. Rosalee continued our conversation, though I contributed nothing but a series of nods.

When the elevator finally opened on our floor and we stepped out, Miriam waited. "We're headed over to see Ms. Wutherspoon," she said to me. "But if you've got a minute, we'd like to talk to you first."

Rosalee did a double take, and a look of recognition registered on her face. She smiled, patted my elbow and walked down the corridor.

"Okay," I said with hesitation, not in the least bit anxious to irritate the raw wound of my disappointment. "Do you want to come in my office?"

"Here is good," Miriam said as we moved away from the bank of elevators.

Antonio stared at a spot on the carpet, then glanced up at me with apparent embarrassment. "We wanted to apologize for being out of line," he said.

I stifled a gasp. *Could this be happening?*

Miriam nodded. "We've done a lot of thinking over the past two days," she said. "We really admire how you and your husband stood up for your daughter. We came to tell Ms. Wutherspoon we'd like to proceed with plans for you to adopt our baby—that is, if you're still interested."

Chapter Twenty-one

—ɯ—

"We're back in the running," I said to Rosalee as I floated past her desk. "I gotta call David. I'm so nervous I can hardly see straight."

I couldn't imagine him saying no to the adoption, but he *had* said we needed to let decisions percolate. After the letdown, we'd talked about how Miriam and Antonio might have been too young and conflicted for us to deal with in the first place. Maybe that was pure rationalization, but, still, I knew I had to talk with him before giving them an answer now. I pushed the speed dial for David's office.

His secretary said he was out doing a security evaluation and wouldn't be back in the office this afternoon. His cell phone went straight to voice mail, and I impatiently disconnected without leaving a message. With oafish fingers, I struggled with the tiny keyboard on my cell phone to text, "Call me ASAP," and waited for a response that would not come. When my desk phone rang a minute later, I jumped.

I glanced at the caller ID. Julie. *I can't give her an answer without talking to David, can I? Of course not.*

I picked up. "Hello, Julie."

"My clients said they talked with you in the lobby, so I'll cut to the chase: Do you want to go ahead with this?"

"Much as I'd like to give you an immediate answer, I need to speak with David first. And he's not available this afternoon."

I held my breath.

"Oh, for chrissakes," she muttered. "This is dragging on far too long. Miriam and Antonio are sitting here. Can I put you on speaker?"

I wasn't a fan of the disembodied, hollow quality of calls on speakerphone, but I could hardly refuse. "Okay."

Julie's speaker clicked on. "Please repeat what you just told me for my clients' benefit."

Feeling the sudden compulsion to have my hands free, I pushed the speaker button on my own phone. "Hello, again," I said nervously. "When I got back to my office, I tried reaching my husband but I won't be able to speak with him until this evening. May I give you an answer tomorrow morning?"

"But you both seemed so sure when we met you on Monday—that is before we asked you to talk with Lily," Miriam said with a trace of impatience—maybe Julie's attitude was contagious. "Why do you think he'd say no now?"

Excellent question.

"I'm not sure what he'll say. We were very disappointed when we left here on Monday. We thought this door was closed permanently, and we had a tough time coming to grips with the loss. Now it looks like the door's open again, but I can't agree to walk through it by myself."

"Well…" Miriam said.

"Please, let me finish. We've suffered through a lot in our quest to have other children: an ectopic pregnancy, a miscarriage, and months filled with sorrow over failed fertility treatments. But through it all, we've learned how important it is to handle things together. David and I are a team, every step of the way."

"That's fine," Antonio said with authority. "We can wait until tomorrow for your answer."

I unclenched the fists I hadn't realize I'd clenched and felt a wave of relief flood my body.

"All right, then," Julie said. "I guess it's settled. Call me first thing, Caroline."

—⟶⟵—

The temptation to leave work for the day was great, but it was only two o'clock. Instead I chose the classical playlist on my iPod and forced myself to concentrate on the investigative reports in Kate's case. It was like an unfinished jigsaw puzzle: George Cooper was required by law to give me all the pieces but didn't have to put it together for me. That was my job. I could already see some of the university's research money had gone where it shouldn't have gone. But I could not see how Cooper could prove beyond a reasonable doubt Kate was responsible.

About an hour later, Rosalee buzzed me on the intercom. "Ms. Spencer, there's a Martin Braxton here, asking to see you," she said in her haughtiest tone. "I explained you were very busy, and it would be best if he were to make an appointment. Nevertheless, he asks if you can spare a few minutes to see him."

Clearly Kate's colleague, the pompous Dr. Braxton, had rubbed Rosalee the wrong way, and she was intent on putting him in his place.

"It's okay, Rose," I said. "You can show him in."

I pulled at my right ear while Braxton took his seat—my signal for Rosalee to interrupt us in ten minutes, announcing my "next client."

"Caroline, please forgive my intrusion," he said, settling into his chair with his shoulders back and legs spread wide. "But I was in the area and thought I'd stop by to see how things are going for Kathryn. I'm quite concerned about her."

"I'm sure you are. The thing is, Kate hasn't given me permission to share the details of her case with you. I can only discuss what's public record." *But there's no reason I can't get information from you*, I thought with a teaspoonful of glee. *No one's in a better position to help me put the jigsaw puzzle together than you—you were right there when it all went down!*

"I suppose you've heard Kate's at The Meadows as a condition of her bail?" I asked.

"Yes. Yes, I've heard. At first it surprised me, but the more I thought about it, drug usage would explain some of Kathryn's behavior over the years."

"Dr. Braxton, may I ask you some questions that might help me put some things into perspective?"

"Of course. I'll do anything to help Kathryn. And please call me Marty."

"All right. Tell me about your working relationship with Kate on this grant, Marty. How did it evolve?"

As soon as he opened his mouth, I knew I should've asked a more specific question. Marty had the same look on his face as my grandfather when someone asked him about living through the Depression. We could be here for hours.

"When I first met Kathryn, she was a surgical resident at Stanford," he said, leaning back in the chair with his hands behind his head. "I was there visiting a surgeon friend of mine. A group of us got together for drinks one evening, and I had the opportunity to chat with her. She confided she was unhappy in surgery."

"Yes, I remember Kate telling me that."

"I inquired whether she'd ever considered research," he said. "Told her I'd be delighted to have someone of her caliber on my team."

Or someone with her looks.

"She elected to pursue a Ph.D. while working as my re-search assistant. Kathryn is, as you know, a very bright wom-an. The university was delighted to hire her to teach once she'd finished."

My irritation at him was growing. He had to know I knew all of this.

"For the past five years, we've been co-applicants on all of the grants for our research, sharing equal responsibility in the planning, administration and work. Quite frankly, I've been struggling without her. She's much better at dealing with the research assistants than I am. She has incredible intuition about what will or will not work in the lab. Caroline, we need her. Can you win an acquittal?"

"Oh, it's far too early to tell," I replied, determined to remain vague. "Maybe you can answer a few questions for me about the case. I know the alleged fraud was first discovered during an audit by the university. Was it a routine audit or had they been tipped off to potential problems?"

"Officially, I can't say. But one of the auditors told me in confidence they were looking for problems. It seems a student who'd applied to be a lab assistant became disgruntled when she was rejected. She told the university about the person Kathryn put on the payroll who did not actually work for us."

Joe Ames. "Was it common knowledge?"

"Oh, no. *I* should've known, because I co-signed the paperwork. But I simply signed the forms Kathryn presented to me. I hold myself personally responsible for the mess: I should've paid more attention to the details. But I trusted Kathryn."

"Back to the disgruntled student," I said. "How did she find out about the fictitious employee?"

"I believe one of her friends worked for us and had seen the payroll."

"Was there only one fictitious research assistant?" I asked.

"I think so, but he was paid for three years."

"Tell me about—"

The intercom buzzed.

I picked up the phone, rather than leaving it on the speaker. "Rosalee, Dr. Braxton and I still have a few things to discuss. Could you please take a message and then hold my calls? Thanks."

"I'm sorry," I said, returning to Marty. "What can you tell me about how the rest of the fraud was accomplished? Let's start with the consulting fees."

"Sure. Kathryn and I are well-known researchers—you might say we're ahead of the field. When other scientists seek to replicate or expand on our research, they often call on us as consultants. We help set up protocols, explain our findings, that kind of thing. Any fees we're paid for such consulting are supposed to go back to the university. Apparently, Kathryn kept some of the fees."

"I see. I guess the rest was pretty simple: submitting phony expense vouchers for travel not taken or padding the actual expenses?"

"Yes, that's basically it. Kathryn rarely traveled—she said she didn't like to be away—but she submitted travel vouchers pretty regularly."

The information he was providing wasn't new to me, but I was fascinated to see how he couched his answers about what he did and did not know. "Marty, you said drug usage might explain some of Kate's behavior. Can you give me a few specifics?"

"Well, let me think. Her mood. She'd go for long stretches being upbeat and energetic. Then she'd suddenly turn sullen and testy, especially to me. I chalked it up to PMS at first, but her moodiness didn't really seem to fit a regular pattern."

He tracked her periods?

"She became prone to making mistakes, usually clerical in nature," he said, shifting in his chair. "And she sometimes missed meetings and other appointments without notice.

Some of the staff complained about her, which would have been unheard of a few years ago."

"Okay, that's helpful. Can I call you if I have other questions as I'm preparing for trial?"

"Certainly." Braxton leaned forward and put his hands on his knees. "Do you think the case will go to trial?"

"That's my assumption at this point," I said off-handedly. "What are the chances of Kate being reinstated at the university?"

"If she's acquitted, the Board of Regents is required to reinstate. If she's found guilty, slim to none."

I thanked Braxton for his time and ushered him out to the lobby.

"That man is an officious misogynist," Rosalee sputtered as I walked past her desk on the way to my office. "If I worked for him, I'd probably use drugs too!"

I laughed. "Unfortunately, working for a jerk is not a legal defense for fraud."

Back at my desk, I leaned back in my chair and consciously adopted Braxton's hands-behind-the-head pose. I closed my eyes and thought about what he'd said, trying to remember my visceral reactions to his answers and non-answers. *Something's fishy here.*

I got up and rushed to the conference room, where I could spread several reports over the table to compare them. All of a sudden it became clear. "Holy shit!" I said aloud. "They're both guilty."

CHAPTER TWENTY-TWO

—∞—

"What's wrong?" David asked in a panic when I answered my cell phone on the drive home. "I just got your text."

Oh, shit...what was I thinking? I never text him—he must've been frantic with worry.

"I'm sorry, David. I didn't mean to scare you. Nothing's wrong. I should've left a voice message explaining: Miriam and Antonio changed their minds about meeting Lily and want us to adopt their baby. And I couldn't give Julie Wutherspoon an answer without talking to you."

Just then, the young kid driving in the next lane swerved to avoid a shredded truck tire and came within inches of my car. Jerking the wheel in a reflexive move, I dropped my phone and had to yell to David, "I'll call you back in a minute when I can pull over."

I hastily took the next exit off the beltline and pulled into a parking lot. My limbs felt like Jell-O as the rush of adrenaline subsided. *Small wonder driving contributes to my panic attacks—it's a minefield out there.*

I dialed David again. "Sorry. Traffic was a bitch, and a kid almost ran into me."

"Thank heaven everything's okay," he said. "I'm in my car, too, so let's talk when we get home. I'll pick up Lily." He hung up.

I knew David hated to talk while driving, but I would've liked a quick "Yes!" to the adoption question. *What's he thinking?*

The suspense was short-lived. Five minutes after I got home and before I even got through the day's mail, I heard the garage door open and David drove in.

"Hi, Pumpkin," I said, tousling Lily's hair as she trudged past me through the kitchen. "How was your day?"

"It was okay. Dad said you guys have something to talk about, so I'm gonna go to my room and do my homework." She looked as apprehensive as I felt.

David walked in, dropped his briefcase on the counter, gave me a quick hug, and reached into the fridge for a beer. "Want one?"

"Oh, yeah."

We headed for the family room, put our feet up on the coffee table and looked at each other. "Do you want to tell me about your day?" I asked.

"Later. First tell me about Miriam and Antonio."

So I did.

"Ah. The roller coaster ride continues," he said when I finished. "Did you get the sense they're really set on us now?"

"I did. The most encouraging thing for me was Antonio speaking up, first to apologize for 'being out of line' and then to say we could give them an answer tomorrow. I felt like he heard me when I described our emotional excursion in search of parenthood."

"Shall we go for it?" he asked, then laughed. "This really feels like déjà vu all over again."

"Yes, it does. And yes, I think we should."

"That's my vote too."

"I think it's time to tell Lily what's going on," I said.

I returned to the family room with two more beers, this time in mugs so frosty the handles bit my skin, just as David led a tearful Lily to the couch.

She sat between us hugging her knees.

"Why are you crying, honey?" I asked.

"I think those are tears of relief," David said, putting his arm around her shoulder.

Lily nodded. "When Dad said you needed to talk, I got worried. I thought you were gonna get a divorce. Then, when he said to come down for good news, I just started crying."

The good news was instantly banished from my mind. "Divorce? What would make you think that?" I asked.

"You and Dad yell at each other a lot. And so do Anna's mom and dad—and they're getting a divorce. She might have to move to an apartment or go to a different school."

"We don't yell—"

"Caroline," David said, "I think our conversations, especially when we disagree, might sound pretty loud to seven-year-old ears. Huh, Lily?"

She nodded again.

"You don't have to be afraid when people speak their minds. Your mom and I love each other very much and always will. We don't ever plan to get a divorce. But to keep our marriage healthy, we vowed to always say what we feel, even if the other person doesn't like hearing it. Do you understand?"

"I guess so," she said without conviction.

"The good news we have to tell you just might convince you we're not getting divorced," he said, shaking her gently by the elbow. "And if you say 'pretty please,' we just might tell you."

Lily couldn't help herself: the corners of her mouth slid into a reasonable facsimile of a smile. "Pretty please."

"Okay. Since you asked nicely—"

"Dad—"

"Your mom and I heard about a young woman who's pregnant and isn't able to raise the baby herself. It looks like we may be able to adopt it. What do you think?"

"A baby?" she asked tentatively.

Not exactly the reaction I'd expected—or hoped for.

"Yes. Due in about seven months," I said, ever the cheerer-upper, grinning like an idiot in an effort to lift her mood.

But Lily was miles away, lost in her own thoughts. And neither David nor I could read them. We exchanged a questioning look, and I nodded toward him as if to say, "You try."

"Honey, look at me."

She hung her head.

He leaned forward, lifted her chin and faced her straight on. "Lily, a few minutes ago we talked about how important it is in a family to say what you feel. Mom and I just told you something we thought you'd be very happy about. You've always said you wanted a brother or sister. But we can see you're not happy. Please tell us what you're thinking."

More tears.

"C'mon. Out with it."

"I *thought* I wanted a little sister or brother," she said, wiping her tears with the back of her hand. "But I'm scared."

"Scared? Of what?" I asked, puzzled and aching with her obvious distress.

"I don't know. Maybe that you won't love me as much. Maybe that the baby will look like you. Things will be so different."

I choked back a sob.

"Yes, Lily," David said, "things will be very different. Babies demand a lot of attention, and we'll need your help to care for him or her. But I promise you we have more than enough love to go around, for you and twelve more kids."

I waited for him to tackle Lily's other concern—namely the baby might physically resemble David and me, while she did not. But he just hugged her.

What to say? I can't ignore this, and I have to do it just right.

"Honey," I forged ahead with weighted words, "you said you were worried, too, that the baby might look like us?"

"Yeah," she said tentatively, pulling away from her dad's embrace.

"We can't predict for sure what it'll look like. The mom is white—she has blonde hair and blue eyes—and looks a bit like me. The dad is Mexican. His skin is about the same color as yours. He's very handsome and has a wonderful dimple in his cheek. So the baby will probably have darker skin than your dad and me and may look a lot like you. We'll just have to wait and see."

"You met them? The real parents?"

"Yes, we did," I said.

"I didn't know you could do that," she said.

"Sometimes," David replied. "There's lots of ways to do adoptions these days."

"So will this kid get to see its real parents, too?"

I cringed inside at the "real parents" thing—for oh so many reasons. But this wasn't the time to tackle that issue.

"No. They don't plan to keep in contact with us or the child," I said. "That's often too difficult for everyone."

Lily got up and headed toward the kitchen. "I wish I could've met my real mom."

I bit my lip to stop it from trembling and stared after her, unable to reply.

CHAPTER TWENTY-THREE

Sunday, October 28

I had spoken with Kate at The Meadows a few times by phone but, aside from my short, futile meeting to convince her to snitch on Joe Ames, I hadn't visited her there. Both she and Adam Larken said she needed time to work on "her program." Today, however, was a family day—when family members and close friends were invited to sit in. Kate had called on Tuesday and, in an uncharacteristically timid voice, asked me to come for lunch and the early afternoon meeting. Although Sundays were usually reserved for David and Lily, I felt compelled to say yes. This was clearly important to Kate.

David and Lily sailed out the door, hand-in-hand, Lily on Cloud Nine because she had a brunch and matinee date with Dad. I felt a stab of jealousy, at both of them, as I watched them leave.

Even my favorite music failed to lift my mood as I drove the deserted back roads to the treatment center.

This meeting would take place not in the intake unit—where we'd had our initial meeting with stone-faced Donna—but in The Meadows' main lodge. A pleasant gray-haired woman at the information desk checked my name against a list on her clipboard and handed me a form to sign. By doing so, I agreed to keep in confidence the personal information revealed by the patients. I scribbled my name and set off for the dining room.

Walking down the gleaming hallways, I marveled at the difference between The Meadows and the dark, dingy hospital in the movie "Clean and Sober." Kate was lucky her mom could afford this place.

She waited for me outside the dining room, looking much like Lily waiting to be picked up after her first day of school. *Did they think I wouldn't show up?*

"How ya doin'?" I asked, after a quick hug.

"Better. I think I'm finally doing better."

Indeed, she looked better: some of the luster had returned to her hair, and her skin had the healthy glow of someone who'd spent time outside. Although tense, she appeared well rested.

"Thanks for coming," Kate said. "You're the closest thing to family I have around here, and I feel a lot closer to you than my family."

"Hey! I'm glad to be here."

"One more thing, Caroline. Just for today, can we pretend you're not my lawyer?"

"Sure. Let's do that."

Kate and I sat at a round lunch table with a young male patient—I judged him to be about nineteen years old—and his parents and younger sister. We discussed the weather for about two minutes and then fell into awkward silence.

But Adam Larken worked the room like a bride at her wedding, moving from table to table, welcoming the visitors and easing the patients' nerves with his light-hearted comments and laughter. Everyone seemed more relaxed as about twenty of us, including six patients, left the dining room for the meeting.

The conference room with its plush carpeting, soft lighting and reasonably comfortable upholstered chairs, was decorated in mauve and soft grays, the walls adorned with tasteful watercolors. A coffee service sat on a sideboard. At first glance, the room was welcoming and calming—that is until we realized the chairs were arranged in a circle and we'd all be face-to-face with strangers and demons being confronted.

We hovered around the coffee area making small talk, postponing the inevitable. Finally, Adam asked us all to take seats.

"Your presence means a lot to us," Adam said with his engaging smile. "Our program is based on the twelve steps of A.A. and N.A. We're all working on step one: we're admitting we're powerless over alcohol or other drugs and our lives have become unmanageable. Some of us are already working on other steps as well.

"This afternoon, we're going to have a kind of open meeting. Each of us will share a few experiences of powerlessness so you have a frame of reference for our treatment. Then we'll go on to share some positive strides we've made in the program. You've all agreed in writing not to discuss confidential information about the patients outside of the facility. As in

A.A., our participants are to remain anonymous. Please honor this pledge."

We all nodded.

"I'll start," he said. "I'm Adam. And I'm a cocaine addict."

I hoped my gasp was inaudible. *This articulate, together counselor was addicted to cocaine?* I noticed some of the other guests fidgeting uncomfortably in their seats.

"I can tell some of you are surprised or shocked," Adam said, "but I suspect you'll be even more taken aback when you hear my story.

"I came from a wealthy family in Whitefish Bay, with every material thing I ever wanted. I was loved, but I didn't know it. As a teenager I started hanging with an older, faster crowd. We did every drug imaginable, but cocaine was my favorite. It gave me a sense of invincibility and well-being I'd never experienced before."

He paused and sipped his coffee, glancing at the wide-eyed audience around him. "At first it was easy to get coke. We all had plenty of spending money and shared our stashes. But before too long, I didn't want to share with anyone, and I didn't have enough money to buy as much as I was using.

"Some of my friends began dealing coke in order to support their own habits but that never occurred to me. Instead, I sold things: my stereo, jewelry, sporting equipment. Eventually my car. My parents never noticed many of my things were gone, but I did have to explain why my car was missing. I said it'd been stolen when I was in downtown Milwaukee. Naturally, my father called the police and the insurance company, so I had to make sure the guy I sold it to kept the car away from our neighborhood."

Adam shook his head. "When I stole some of my mother's diamond jewelry and pawned it to buy coke, I got caught. My father gave me an ultimatum: either enter treatment or move out. He had me admitted here—at The Meadows. I lasted two days before I split—on a mission to score some cocaine.

"When I went home three days later, all the locks had been changed. I found an envelope and a letter from my father where the house key had been hidden. It said my treatment at The Meadows was paid for and I could return here when I was ready. But I wasn't welcome at home until I was clean and sober."

For the first time during his recitation, Adam's voice quivered. "I felt so angry and rejected. I spent a year and a half living on the streets of New York City—hustling to keep myself supplied with cocaine. One day I looked at myself and saw with horror what I'd become, and I hitched a ride back here. True to his word, my dad had guaranteed my readmission.

"It wasn't easy, but I completed treatment and high school. With God's help—and my family's—I went on to college and graduate school to become a counselor. I've been clean and sober for nine years, four months and twenty-one days."

We sat flabbergasted for a moment, then burst into spontaneous applause.

The young man who had been at our lunch table went next. "My name is Robert, and I'm an alcoholic."

Robert's story, though less sordid than Adam's, was no less moving. He'd been sober for sixteen days.

And then it was Kate's turn.

"I'm Kathryn. I'm a cocaine addict."

The naked reality of her statement stunned me, even though it wasn't news.

"A lot of kids experiment with drugs in high school or college," she said. "Not me. I didn't want anything to stand in the way of my plan to become a doctor, like my father. But even after reaching my goals, I still felt inadequate. When someone finally convinced me to try cocaine, I couldn't believe how good I felt. It was the most uplifting feeling I'd ever experienced.

"Like Adam, I had enough money to buy my cocaine at first. But the more I used, the more I needed. I gave up everything for cocaine."

Kate glanced over at me. As her lawyer, I couldn't allow her to make admissions of criminal wrongdoing in front of this group. I put my forefinger to my lips. I don't know whether Kate caught the gesture or the panicked look in my eyes.

"I can't really go into what happened from there," she said. "But I can tell you I ended up in jail and did not come here voluntarily. Since I've been here, I can see how powerless I was... am... over cocaine. Now I want to stay and finish the program. I've been clean and sober for fifteen days."

The stories of the four other patients reflected the same self-destructive patterns. One middle-aged woman was hooked on tranquilizers, prescribed by her physicians. A young man described himself as "addicted to everything"—inhalants, cocaine, speed and alcohol. The other two, a woman in her mid-thirties and a man of about seventy, were alcoholics.

After the patients finished their individual stories, Adam began a discussion and invited our questions. I was amazed at how much I learned and amazed at how comfortable I was with the hugs and warm handshakes we exchanged when the meeting broke up.

"There's one more thing," Adam said to us as we were standing around the room getting ready to leave. "Each of the group members has earned a twenty-four-hour pass this week. The only restriction is the pass must be spent at the home of a family member or close friend. They'll be tested for drug and alcohol use when they get back here. Please be as supportive as you can if the patient spends a pass with you."

Kate looked as relieved and exhausted as I felt as we walked toward the main entrance.

"You know you're welcome to come stay with us on your pass," I said to her.

"I'd really appreciate it," she said. "I can't imagine who else I could ask, and I was even reluctant to ask you."

"I wouldn't have offered if I didn't mean it. When would you like to come?"

"I dunno. What would be convenient for you and David?"

I stopped and faced her. "I'm not concerned about any inconvenience. I just need to know what you'd like to do while on pass. Do you have business to take care of? Do you want to discuss the case with me? Or do you want to just relax and do fun stuff?"

A look of pure bewilderment crossed her eyes.

"Gee, I hadn't thought that far," Kate said.

"Do you want to think about it and call me?"

"No," she blurted—as if afraid I'd withdraw the offer. "Maybe you could pick me up one morning and drop me off to get my car. I could do some errands and meet you in the afternoon to talk about court. Then we could just have dinner with David and Lily and watch TV or something."

"Sounds fine. How about Thursday? I'm off that day and none of us has anything planned Thursday evening."

"Great! Thanks. I'll let Adam know."

"Okay," I said. "About nine-thirty?"

"Yeah. That's perfect. Caroline, thanks for everything," she said, abruptly turning and walking back toward the residential wing.

It wasn't the picture-perfect farewell I'd had in mind—especially after the emotionally charged afternoon—but I headed for the front door.

Just as I reached the reception desk, I heard Kate's voice behind me. "Wait, Caroline! There's something I want to give you."

She handed me a long, white business envelope, bulging at the seams.

"Please read this, and you'll understand better what I've been going through. Wait till tomorrow morning though. You've already had enough of this place for one day."

She was gone again before I could respond. The envelope felt both physically and emotionally heavy in my hand.

CHAPTER TWENTY-FOUR

Monday, October 29

I punched the snooze button on the alarm clock, not once but three times, throwing our morning ritual into a tailspin. David and I rushed around to get showered and dressed, while Lily sat in the kitchen ready to leave for school.

I darted into the McDonald's drive-through for coffee and a breakfast biscuit. And it was eight forty-five before I was seated at my desk, massaging my throbbing temples—not exactly a stellar start to the week.

Rosalee walked in with a stack of paperwork. "Headache?" she asked.

"Uh-huh. I'm afraid David and I had a little too much wine last night. It felt great going down but not so great this morning."

"Poor child!" Rosalee said with mock sympathy. "You want some aspirin?"

"Thanks. I already took some. It'll pass as I move around."

"How was the visit to The Meadows yesterday?"

"Enlightening. Exhausting. I think that's why I over-indulged when I got home—it was heavenly just to relax with my family." I thought about the envelope Kate had given me and was glad I'd ignored it—even after David asked what it was.

Rosalee shot me a questioning look, but the phone rang before I could finish my synopsis. She closed the door on her way out of the office.

"Hello. This is Caroline Spencer."

"Corbett Daniels. We need to talk."

Oh, great—this is just what I need. "Sure. What's up?" I asked.

"I got a call from Kathryn last night, and she's talking nonsense."

"What sort of nonsense?"

"She's buying into this drug treatment thing hook, line, and sinker. Claims she's a junkie. It's absurd."

"You don't believe her?"

"Oh, I don't doubt she experimented with some things she shouldn't have. I'm told cocaine is quite prevalent in university settings—especially among research types. But my Kathryn addicted? Never! She's far too bright."

"Well—"

"And another thing: she says she wants to plead guilty. I told you before, I'll not have it!"

"I—"

"Listen to me, Caroline. You've got to talk some sense into her. She can't give in to this frivolous prosecution. What will people think? Her career will be ruined."

"I'll be sure to pass on your concerns to Kate when we next speak."

"I'm sure you can convince her to go to trial. Margaret and I are counting on you." He hung up.

Not two seconds later, my intercom buzzed.

"I have George Cooper on the line," Rosalee said. "Do you want to take it?"

"Yes. Put him through," I said with a sigh.

"Good morning, George. I hope you're calling to tell me you're dismissing the case against Kate Daniels."

"Not likely."

In the past couple of weeks, I'd spoken with Cooper a few times by phone. He had taken me by surprise with his quick sense of humor and easygoing manner. There was no mistaking his serious dedication to his work, but his conversations were peppered with witticisms. I'd found myself enjoying our conversations.

"Seriously," he said, "I think I have some good news for both of us."

"Do tell."

"It seems my case agent, Carter Ellingson, was networking with his friends over at County and caught wind of an investigation regarding a bad guy named Joe Ames. We're thinking, what an odd coincidence: that's the name of your client's research assistant!"

"Go on."

"So Carter, being the astute agent he is, runs the name by some FBI guys who handle drugs. Lo and behold, there's serious interest in Ames. In fact, a lot more interest than we have in trying to cobble together a case against him for his part in the grant fraud."

"Ellingson didn't know before that Ames sold coke?"

"Nope. Carter suspected Kate Daniels did some blow, but it never dawned on him she had her source on the payroll. He works white collar cases, not dopers."

"So?"

"What I'm getting at," he said, "is a possible 5K motion if Kate gives us Joe Ames."

"5K?"

"Caroline, Caroline. You've got to read the sentencing guidelines. A 5K motion allows the judge to give a lower-than-usual sentence based on a defendant's cooperation. It can mean a lot less time."

"George, we're six weeks away from trial, and you're on me about sentencing guidelines?"

"I'm serious. Sentencing in federal court is complicated, and Kate Daniels is likely to get a pretty stiff sentence."

"If she's convicted."

"Right," he said with a chuckle.

"I know you feds are handing down harsh sentences for drug cases, but remember, this isn't a drug case."

"Nevertheless, if your client goes to trial and loses, she's facing thirty to thirty-seven months. In prison. Not probation. If she pleads guilty, she's looking at twenty-one to twenty-seven months. With truthful testimony against Ames, we could get it down to somewhere in the range of twelve to eighteen. If you want, we can get together and crunch the numbers. But there's no denying her cooperation would be a big help—to both of us."

I didn't like hearing the numbers he was talking about. "What, specifically, would you want Kate to do?"

"First, we'd want what Jerry Alexander and Tom Robbins have already been asking for: a truthful statement about Yvonne Pritchard's death and about Ames smuggling coke into the jail. Then info about how much coke your client bought from him on the university's dime. We'd need her testimony at the grand jury and later, if Ames goes to trial."

"A pretty tall order. I'll talk to Kate. When do you need an answer?"

"I'd like to know now. But how 'bout by tomorrow afternoon? I'd like to set up an interview for late this week."

My throbbing head throbbed harder. "Wait a minute!" I said. "This is all presuming we'd agree to plead guilty. We're nowhere close to that. Brillstein hasn't even ruled on my motions."

"Kate doesn't have to plead guilty in order to benefit from cooperating. It can't hurt her. I'll fax you an immunity letter. Nothing she says can be used against her in her own case."

"I need to know more about Joe Ames and his connections. Would Kate be putting herself in danger by rolling over on him?"

"At this point, I think Kate can answer that better than we can. But I'll have Carter put the drug agents in touch with you."

"I'll talk to Kate and get back to you."

"By tomorrow?"

"I'll do my best, George. Thanks for the call."

The notion of Dr. Kathryn Daniels testifying before a grand jury about a drug dealer boggled my mind. And Corbett Daniels would be appalled.

I needed to move around. I got up, did a few yoga stretches, and walked out to Rosalee's desk.

She looked up at me. "Headache better?"

I shook my head and immediately regretted it. "Nope. And these phone calls sure haven't helped. Rose, I ordered a copy of the federal sentencing guidelines last week. Did it come in yet, by any chance?"

"I'll let your impertinence slide this morning because I know you're under pressure. You know I always bring in your books as soon as they arrive," Rosalee said. "The mail should be here in about twenty minutes."

"Thanks. I'm going to wander down and see if Frank's around."

The managing partner's door was open, and he was just hanging up the phone. I knocked on the doorjamb and asked, "Frank, do you have a minute?"

"I do if you're willing to walk with me to Starbucks. I'm starved."

We sat at a corner table in the coffee shop. I ordered another cup of coffee while Frank chose juice, a scone and a fruit cup.

"What's on your mind?" he asked.

"Kathryn Daniels' case. What else? It's gotten way more sordid than I'd ever thought possible. Kate's grant fraud—and I'm almost sure she committed it—included putting her cocaine dealer on the university payroll. The same guy intimidated a jail guard into smuggling coke in to Kate while she was detained. The feds and county guys want to nail him. They want to interview her and then they want her grand jury and trial testimony to seal the case against him. What do you think?"

"I think your case is a helluva lot more interesting than most of the stuff this firm is working on!" he said, grinning.

"Frank! I'm serious. I had no scruples about using C.I.s when I was a prosecutor. But having my client work as one is another story."

"C.I.s?"

"Confidential informants," I said. "They're usually the lowest of the low."

"You know I don't do criminal work. But it seems to me you have to get past your biases and decide whether it's in the best interest of your client to participate. What does she have to gain or lose from doing so?"

"It sounds like her cooperation would buy a much lower sentence if she's convicted."

"What's the down side of Kate cooperating with the cops?"

"I'm not sure. The danger, I guess. Although no one can tell me much about the dealer."

"Kate can tell you. And she's certainly old enough and smart enough to make an informed decision."

When I got back to my office, a copy of the sentencing guidelines manual sat prominently in the middle of my desk, adorned with a smiley face on a Post-It note. Rosalee knew I detested smiley faces. But I could see how the temptation had been too much to resist.

I spent the next hour poring through the manual, which was very specific and beyond technical. I swallowed two more aspirin with some lukewarm coffee. Even a cursory review of the guidelines told me Kate needed to "snitch." If not, she'd be in prison for longer than I cared to imagine.

I called Adam Larken and made an appointment to see Kate late that afternoon. He said she could miss the scheduled recreation period: her volleyball team wouldn't miss her.

—⚬⚬—

Wearing a grey sweat suit and running shoes, her hair pulled up into a saucy ponytail, Kate looked younger than when I'd first met her at Shenstone. But the apprehensive expression on her face was new.

"We can go into the TV lounge. Everyone's at group."

"That works for me."

"Did you read it?" Kate asked before we even sat down.

"What?"

"Did you read my letter?"

"No," I said, "sorry. Things were pretty hectic this morning, and I didn't get time—"

"Oh, shit, Caroline! It would've been so much easier for us to talk if you'd read it."

"I'm really sorry. I didn't know. Can you tell me what was in the letter?"

She sat in silence for a moment, reminding me of Lily when she'd learned the truth about Santa Claus. "I don't have the energy. Just please, please read it as soon as you can."

"Sure. I promise," I said, feeling like an utter jerk. "There's something important I need to ask you."

I explained what I'd learned about the sentencing guidelines and the amount of time she might face if she didn't cooperate against Joe Ames.

"I can't," she said.

"What do you mean you can't? Are you afraid of him? Or of his associates?"

"I already told you why: I love him."

"Oh, don't say that! He's used you just like he used that poor jail guard—what's her name?"

"Anita."

"Yes. Anita. Surely you can see that. Plus, he's married," I said.

"I know."

As I frantically tried to formulate more arguments, Adam Larken tapped at the door. Kate motioned him in.

"Hi, Caroline. Kate's told me she wants to plead guilty, and I wanted to talk to you about when that might occur. Do you have time to discuss it?"

Unable to hide my frustration, I looked at Kate and snapped, "Adam is the second person today to tell me you plan to plead guilty—your father being the first. I'm more than a little irritated that I'm the last to know."

"If you'd read my letter you wouldn't be the last to know."

Her pointed reply deflated my anger, but not enough to induce me to apologize yet again.

I glanced at Kate. "Do you mind if I share our dilemma with Adam?" I asked.

"It's fine," she said caustically.

"I have no problem with the notion of Kate pleading guilty," I said. "In fact, I can see some real advantages to doing so. The trouble is, even with a plea agreement, I think the sentence could be as high as twenty-seven months in prison. The only way to cut that time is for Kate to cooperate with authorities and testify against her source. Unless he's likely to retaliate, I think it's a good move. Kate disagrees."

Adam turned to Kate. "Why?" he asked.

"I love him."

"You love the cocaine he provides," he said.

"The twelve steps say we're to make amends unless making amends would injure others," she said, glaring at Adam. "Snitching on Joe sure seems to me to be injurious."

"I think you're reading it wrong," Adam said. "From what you've shared in group, it sounds like he's messed up a lot of people's lives. There's nothing in the twelve steps saying you can't give information to the police. In fact, it's the responsible thing to do. It's hard, but the community—and that's you—needs to get involved in all kinds of ways to solve this drug problem. Do you want your dealer going out and manipulating other people the way he's done you?"

"No."

"Are you afraid of him?" I asked Kate again. "Would he hurt you if you testified?"

"No, he wouldn't. He fancies himself a businessman, not a crook."

Some businessman, I thought. Intimidating a single mother into smuggling cocaine into a jail?

"Well, will you at least think about it?" I asked. "I need to let George Cooper know our answer tomorrow."

"Okay, I'll think about it. I'll call you tomorrow morning around ten. Will you be at home?"

"No. I need to go in to the office and study up on this."

"I want to plead guilty, Caroline—and soon."

I put on my coat and gathered my purse and scarf. "I'll have Cooper send over a proposed plea agreement. But it'll take me at least a week to go over the guidelines and make sure we'd be doing the right thing."

"Pleading guilty is the right thing," she said.

"And helping the cops lock up your source isn't?" I said as I walked out the door.

—⁓—

Thankfully, I hadn't planned to return to my office. Lily was happy I picked her up from her after-school program while there was still plenty of daylight. Kate's letter to me—still in its sealed envelope—sat on the kitchen counter where I had left it. I sent Lily outside to play with friends, made myself a vodka gimlet, and sat down in the family room to read.

> *Dear Caroline,*
>
> *Adam assigned us each to write a letter to someone we're close to, disclosing something about the addiction. You were the first (and only) person who came to my mind. You may be surprised to know you're still the best friend I have in this world. It seems odd because we haven't seen much of each other these past several years.*
>
> *He also asked us to try to reconstruct or identify the forces that contributed to our addictions, so we can "plug*

up the holes" in our lives and try to avoid problems in the future. Well, you know me (at least as well as anyone does). I started making an outline, with arrows leading here and there. Imagine trying to organize this task! I'm typing so I can't draw arrows, make lists, etc., and so you don't have to put up with my stereotypical doctor-scrawl. Please bear with me.

How did Kathryn Shenstone Daniels, of the Daniels family, get in this mess? The short answer: Corbett Fucking Daniels. Caroline (and Adam, because you'll read this, too), I'm trying to take responsibility for my own actions. (And I will take responsibility for my adult actions.) But my father both made and ruined me, and I can't help how angry I am for that ruin.

My father wasn't home a lot when I was a kid, but his presence dominated the household, even in his absence. It was so bizarre how we all anticipated his every whim all the time. My mother especially tried to get us all to do things my father would like. She was the queen of enablers.

I was luckier in some ways than my brothers and sister because I was smarter. It was a piece of cake for me to make A's. I remember I brought home a report card in second grade that had all A's and one lousy B (in math). Based on my father's reaction, you would have thought I'd flunked out. He ranted and raved about how I hadn't worked up to my potential and how disappointed he was in me. The fucker didn't talk to me for two days afterward.

Suddenly and inexplicably nauseous, I set down the letter, closed my eyes and massaged my temples. *Please, God, I can't deal with a panic attack right now.*

I remembered a suggestion of Dr. Brownhill's: Pay attention to your body's cues and try to discern what's triggering them. After a few cleansing breaths, I realized what was making me anxious. Kate and I had had similar experiences when we'd brought home less-than-perfect report cards, only my critique came from my mother and was much more subtle— just a raised eyebrow and a deflated "Oh…" for a B-minus in fourth grade science class. I'd read her loud and clear. I vowed never to disappoint her again, and I'd never allowed myself to achieve less than an A again. Perfectionism, according to Dr. Brownhill, contributed to my panic attacks.

Acknowledging this bitter memory did help. And with another sip of my gimlet, the nausea subsided. I could read on.

> *My siblings seemed to have thicker skin and let Dad's criticism roll off their backs. I couldn't. I kept trying harder and harder to please him. My mother never stood up to him. (I'm like her, I guess. We both just tried in vain to win his approval.) (And we both eventually cracked!)*
>
> *Don't get me wrong. There were days (and sometimes weeks) without his criticism. But looking back on it, everything I did was for my father. There were things I remember liking to do (like bowling and painting-by-numbers, to name a few) that he discouraged or flat-out forbid because they weren't suitable for a Daniels. After*

a while, I couldn't distinguish between the things I really
liked and the things he expected me to like.

I looked up as David came through the door with Lily on his shoulders, both giggling and singing "Heigh Ho, Heigh Ho, It's Home From Work We Go!" With a glance in my direction, David realized I was in no mood for frivolity. "Run along, Snow White," he said to Lily, shooing her upstairs toward her room. "We'll call you when it's time to wash up for dinner."

"I thought we'd order pizza. Okay?" I asked.

"Sure, hon. What's up?" he asked.

"Things have just happened so fast today—things I was totally unprepared for. First of all, I hear from Corbett Daniels that Kate wants to plead guilty—"

"I doubt that went over too well with him, did it?"

I shook my head.

"Well, what do you think about it?" David asked.

"Oh, it's probably inevitable. I have no factual defense because she's guilty of most everything they're alleging. And I sure wasn't having any luck coming up with a legal defense. Prosecuting cases was a snap compared to defending them. It's hard to pull rabbits out of a hat."

"Especially if you've got scruples," David said with a smile.

"Yeah."

He sat down next to me on the couch. "So what else is bothering you? I'm getting the distinct impression I haven't heard the half of it."

"George Cooper called to tell me the feds want Kate to roll over on her coke supplier. Consent to an interview, testify at the grand jury and trial—the whole nine yards. So I went out to meet with Kate again to try to convince her."

"Do you think she should do it?"

"It's the only way she can buy a reasonable sentence. I'm not sure I can bear to watch her go away for a long time. She agreed to think about it overnight—that's all the time Cooper is giving us—and her counselor Adam supports the idea. I guess I'll just have to wait and see."

"I see you're reading the contents of the mystery envelope?"

"Yes. And I think this is the hardest part of the day. I don't know why I assumed she had given me copies of articles or something to read. Kate was really hurt today when she realized I hadn't read this letter, and I can see why. She invested so much time and emotion into it."

"What's it say?"

"So far—and I'm only about a quarter of the way through it—it's about her childhood and her father. It's only recently I've seen glimpses of it, but apparently he's a domineering, demanding ass of a man."

"I'm not surprised."

"Really? I spent quite a bit of time with her family when I was in college and always thought Corbett was the perfect father."

"That's precisely what he wanted you to think, but he always struck me as disingenuous. There are plenty of men like him in the business world."

"I'm sure you're right. Lily and I are very lucky you're a nice, for-real guy." I leaned back against his shoulder. Suddenly, I'd had enough of Kate and Corbett Daniels for one day. "Hey! What do you say we go out to eat? I need a break."

"It's fine with me. Give me ten minutes to change."

I carefully folded Kate's letter, put it back in the envelope and returned it to the kitchen counter. *It'll keep.*

We let Lily pick the restaurant—she had discriminating taste for a seven-year-old. The smallish neighborhood place had limited seating but a mouth-watering menu. The hot, savory soup and fresh-from-the oven bread combined with the attention of my husband and daughter filled me up and warmed my soul.

"I expect this is what it feels like to be in heaven," I said.

David nodded.

We headed home from the restaurant, and—it being hair-washing night—I helped Lily bathe and get ready for bed. "Can we snuggle a while?" she asked when I tucked her in.

Reading the rest of Kate's letter could wait fifteen minutes. "You bet!" I said. Her room was a little chilly, so I climbed under the covers while we talked. Lily told me about the new girl in her class and her awesome silver sneakers. As she recited and spelled several words from the new spelling list, I drifted off to sleep in comfortable communion with my daughter. I didn't wake until the sun shone through the blinds.

CHAPTER TWENTY-FIVE

—w—

Tuesday, October 30

I went into the kitchen, started the coffee, and held a mug under the dripping filter basket. After half a cup of the ultra-strong brew, my head felt clear enough to resume reading Kate's letter.

> *I was particularly tuned into my father's emotions during Mom's more marked binges and when she was hospitalized. My father seemed so vulnerable. (Can you believe it? I was worried about HIM???) Anyway, he was often more affectionate (if you can call it that) and complimentary to me during those times. He would say things like, "I'm so proud of you Kate. You're so much stronger than HER."*
>
> *One weekend when I was about thirteen, while my father was away at a conference, I had such terrible chest pains and heart palpitations that my mother rushed me*

to the emergency room. When the doctors told her it was anxiety, she specifically asked that they not tell my father. She said he had enough on his mind and it would be better not to worry him. She knew and I knew that he would think less of me if he learned of this weakness. In one way, it helped knowing that I wasn't having a heart attack. In another, it was awful facing the realization my father would only accept me if I was perfect.

I graduated first in my high school class and made my father proud. He allowed me to go to Shenstone (although it wasn't an Ivy League school), because they had such a strong science program. (It probably didn't hurt the place was founded by Mom's grandfather!) Also, it was close to home, and my father needed to have me around once in a while to show me off to his friends.

Strangely enough, I liked to go home pretty frequently too. But only if I took you along or if one of my brothers was going to be home with a friend. Corbett Daniels was the perfect host, always gregarious and welcoming to our friends. He was much more likely to show warmth toward us with company around. I think we all longed for those times because it made us feel like we were a normal family. Even as small children, we looked forward to company. We would have to mind our manners and make sure we didn't do anything foolish or rowdy, but that stuff was easy. We never had to worry about what kind of mood our father would be in or whether he'd berate us. If we had company, he'd be Ward Cleaver.

As I got up to pour another cup of coffee, I remembered one specific weekend at the Daniels' residence. On Sunday afternoon, I had gone with Kate and her father to their country club, where he'd arranged for them to play in a tennis tournament. I remembered how envious I'd been of their relationship as they strolled off the court companionably, having won the hard-fought match. Kate had looked so happy, so strong, confident and vital. *How could I have missed the truth?*

My thoughts were interrupted by the distant sounds of Lily's Mickey Mouse alarm clock and David showering upstairs. Time to get moving. I folded Kate's letter and put it in my briefcase to finish at the office.

—∿∿—

I skipped the usual morning chitchat and made my way straight back to my office. Rosalee was off today. I browsed through my e-mail and found only one that wouldn't wait: a message from Julie Wutherspoon with three large files attached. My heart skipped a beat. *Please let this be good news.*

But Julie, in her usual straightforward manner, was simply sending documents for our review: the tentative adoption agreement, the court papers appointing a guardian ad litem—or impartial lawyer—for the unborn child, and the report of Miriam's most recent medical exam. I scrolled down to open the attachments and noticed a P.S. "Spoiler alert: Miriam is fine and the pregnancy is on track, but don't read the medical records if you want to remain in suspense!!"

I hit "print" and dialed David.

"What's up?" he asked.

"Julie sent Miriam's medical records. Do you want to know whether it's a boy or a girl?"

"Hmmm. That wasn't an option with Lily, was it?"

"No. Kate didn't have an amnio and the only ultrasound she had was inconclusive."

Silence.

"No, I don't think I want to know," he said slowly. "But can I call you later? I've got a client due in five minutes."

I stifled my disappointment. "Sure."

Not for the first time, I rued the day our law firm opted for ultra-bright white copy paper. The pages in my printer mocked me. Like a flashing neon sign, they were impossible to ignore. "Read me, READ ME," they seemed to say.

Where's Rosalee when I need her? She could hold onto these reports for me. And if she peeked, she'd keep her mouth shut.

I wandered down to the lunchroom and bought a bag of M&Ms from the vending machine, hoping that succumbing to one temptation could distract me from another. At least for a while. And, sure enough, by the time I got back to my office, I was able to pull the pages out of the printer, seal them—unread—in a brown manila envelope, and put them in the back of my file cabinet.

I leaned back in my desk chair, popped a few more melt-in-your-mouth morsels, and stared at Kate's letter. After reading and rereading the first three paragraphs, my comprehension kicked in.

I wonder if you remember how I sweated out being accepted to med school at Stanford. I was pretty sure I could get in to some school, but if I weren't accepted into

Dad's alma mater, he'd be so disappointed. Fortunately (I think), I was accepted.

You can't believe how difficult medical school was. EVERYONE was so smart. I wasn't the brightest or even close. And I knew I would be in competition with all my classmates for the best residencies. During the spring of my first year of medical school, a guy offered me cocaine. It was after a particularly tough exam. I really don't know why I agreed. It was so contrary to everything I'd ever done. But something inside me said fuck it.

I can't describe to you how wonderful it was. For the first time in my life, I felt invincible. I was energized and alert. So began my love affair with cocaine. The affair that has gotten me into the fix I'm in.

A chill overcame me. I rocked forward in my chair and stared at the pages. I'd assumed Kate began using cocaine after Lily's birth, not years before. I forced myself to read on.

At first, I used cocaine mainly on weekends. It was easy to get, and my father's allowance and my trust funds payments were more than enough to cover the expense. During my third year of med school, I used coke almost daily, always for some legitimate reason like needing to stay up late to study or needing an "edge" for a presentation or an exam. I could no longer afford my habit. Unbeknownst to my parents, I took out LOANS, ostensibly to help pay tuition and expenses during my third and fourth years. In med school, you can get student loans in a heartbeat. The banks had no way of knowing Corbett

Daniels was paying all my expenses and their loans were going up my nose.

During fourth year, I had to nail down my choices for residency programs. My father expected me to go into surgery, and I continued to do what he expected. Although in my heart of hearts, I knew I had no business being anywhere near a scalpel, I didn't have the courage to admit it.

My first half-year of residency was torture. Believe it or not, Caroline, I used cocaine before some procedures because I thought it HELPED me function. Sometimes I vowed to stay straight but couldn't do it because I was shaking so hard. To this day, I can't believe my mentors didn't know or suspect. I began drinking and using Valium to ease the transition between high and straight.

My trembling hands caused the words to jump on the page. Kate had gotten pregnant with Lily during her surgical residency—and she hadn't told us she was an addict. Anger coursed through my veins, my blood pressure rose perceptibly. Without thinking, I speed-dialed David's office, only to learn, again, he was with a client. I left a message asking for him to call me. I got up and paced, then paced some more. *You've got to read on*, I told myself. Slowing my strides, I walked around my office and read.

Caroline, I'm sorry but I could never bring myself to tell you. But this is the truth. I rarely used cocaine when I began seeing Fouad. Aside from being a philanderer, he was pretty straight and didn't approve of drugs or alcohol. He was also great for my ego; I didn't feel as compelled to get high when I was around him. When I found out I was pregnant, I went back and counted. Maybe I'd used cocaine eight or ten times altogether, and I'd only taken Valium a few times. I convinced myself I didn't need to tell you as long as I stayed clean for the rest of the pregnancy. And I succeeded. I guess I'm one of those people who being pregnant agrees with. I felt great the whole time and hardly craved drugs or booze.

Still, it was worrisome not knowing whether the baby would be affected by my early cocaine and Valium use. So when Lily came out with ten fingers and ten toes and got a ten on her APGAR tests, I was very relieved. And again, I'm so very, very sorry for having put her at risk.

I slumped on the couch, my chest tight, my mind racing with "What ifs?" My phone rang, but I let it go to voice mail.

After I ignored three more phone calls, the intercom buzzed. "I'm sorry to bother you, Ms. Spencer," said the receptionist, "but your husband said to tell you he'll meet you here for lunch. Also, Kate Daniels is on the line... says it's urgent. May I put her through?"

"Okay," I said, moving through my mental fog toward the desk to pick up the phone.

"I'll do it, Caroline."

"What?"

"Rat on Joe."

I couldn't bring myself to care—or to respond.

"You read it, didn't you?" Kate said. "You finally read my letter."

"Uh-huh."

"And?"

"And I don't know. I just don't know."

—⁓—

When David knocked and came into my office shortly after eleven o'clock, he found me lying on my couch, an ice pack covering my eyes. I hadn't been able to do anything but cry since I hung up on Kate.

He knelt down beside me and stroked my arm. "There's something wrong with the baby, isn't there?"

Perplexed, I sat up and saw the pain on his face. "Oh, no. It's not that."

"Then what—"

I reached for Kate's letter on the coffee table and handed it to him. "Read this," I said. "You can skip down to when she starts her residency at Stanford."

David sat next to me, pulled his glasses out of his pocket and read intently.

"I saw this coming," he said when he'd finished.

"You knew?"

"I suspected."

"Before we adopted Lily?" I asked, my pitch rising to heights that frightened me.

"No, not then. After Kate went into treatment. I started wondering how long she'd been a user, and I started thinking about what signs we might have missed."

"And?"

"I remembered the first time I met her—at that Shenstone Homecoming. She was wide-eyed and hyper, and she and her slickster boyfriend kept disappearing. If memory serves, I voiced my suspicion they might be getting high, but you assured me she wasn't a user."

I tried to picture the reunion weekend but drew a blank.

"Then in the past several years, I had some uneasy feelings about her—especially before I left the police force. She never looked me in the eye. And last year, there was a guy at one of her parties who I'd once busted for possession. But I didn't have strong evidence, so I never said anything to you."

I stood up and resumed pacing.

"I'm so angry, David. She used cocaine and Valium while pregnant with our child, for God's sake, and then she didn't tell us. I was pissed when I found out she lied about her mom's alcoholism, but this is so much worse."

"Is it?"

I felt my face flush. "What the fuck are you saying?"

"Calm down, Caroline, and let's be honest about this. Have you forgotten we thought of adopting the baby whose mother was an admitted, hard-core crack addict?"

I shook my head. "I haven't forgotten. That other couple stepped up, though, before we ever gave it serious consideration."

"But if they hadn't stepped up, we would have had to weigh the pros and cons, and there's a very real chance we would've said no."

"What's your point, David?"

"My point is Kate did us a favor: She saved us from agonizing over whether we should or shouldn't adopt Lily—who's perfect, by the way, despite her prenatal exposure to drugs. And what if we'd known and declined to adopt her?" he asked, his voice breaking. "I can't bear to think of life without her."

The truth of his words cut the legs off my anger. I collapsed back onto the couch, too emotionally spent to feel even the relief.

David took my face in his hands. "We need some air," he said. "Get your coat and walk with me."

Arm in arm, for I needed his steady physical support, we made our way toward James Madison Park. Huddled together against the wicked northerly wind off Lake Mendota, we sat on a bench, staring at—but not seeing—the white capped waves.

"One foot in front of the other, kiddo," he finally said, squeezing my shoulder. It had been our credo during the long, anguishing months of infertility treatments: a reminder to keep plodding.

"You're right again," I said, forcing a brief smile. "And, as usual, Kate's predicament needs my attention."

"What's next?"

"She called this morning, right after I'd read the part about using drugs during her pregnancy. Said she wanted to testify against her dealer."

"Good news. What made her change her mind?"

"I have no idea. I was so upset about Lily, I hung up on her. Before you got to the office, I was planning to withdraw from her case. And to divorce myself from her life."

"And now?"

"I'm seeing her more as a pathetic, screwed-up lost soul who's trying to get back on the right path. Trying to be honest and make amends."

"What kind of toll will it take on you to see this case through?"

"Since she wants to plead guilty—and since we'll be back on the good guys' team when she cooperates with them—I think I can handle it."

"What about your personal feelings toward her?"

"That's a tougher question. I went from sympathetic to livid to beholden in the course of one morning. I think I need to try detachment. Isn't that what they suggest in Al-Anon?"

"Seems like I read that somewhere," he said, pushing an errant lock of hair out of my eyes.

"Are you still okay with having her stay with us Thursday night?"

"Uh-huh. Remember, I skipped the livid phase."

I punched him lightly in the arm and stood up. "I've got calls to make."

"What about lunch?"

"Oh, yeah. I forgot. Could we just do quick sandwiches at the sub shop down the street?"

"As long as we don't get 'em to go," he said with a smile. "We deserve a half-hour or so for a sit-down lunch." He was right, of course, but I would have been fine with eating at my desk.

Back at the office I phoned The Meadows and left a message for Kate to call me. I needed to be sure she was on board with the cooperation thing before telling George Cooper.

While I waited for her call, I picked up Kate's letter, determined to finish it. The worst had to be behind me now.

I was almost five months pregnant when Marty Braxton convinced me to come work with him and get my Ph.D. It was a godsend. I could leave Stanford before anyone realized I was pregnant, and I could get the hell out of surgery. My dad was furious, but at least he could save face by playing up the fact that an eminent researcher had recruited me for his team. And no one seemed to think it odd that I took a five-month vacation before I got here.

I'd vowed to stay clean and sober after the baby was born, but post-partum depression hit me like you can't believe. And the research and graduate studies were more difficult than I could have imagined. So before long, I'd relapsed. I told myself I could quit again when I felt stronger, but somehow that day never came.

By the time I completed my Ph.D. and got hired as an instructor, I was badly in debt. My salary was sufficient to meet my living expenses and loan payments. But there wasn't a lot left over for coke.

I petitioned to use my trust fund for the down payment on my condo. (Someone of my stature needs a prestigious residence.) Eventually, I maxed out my credit cards, took second and third mortgages, and began borrowing from Peter to pay Paul. All to buy cocaine.

I told you in the past about my affair with Marty Braxton. It didn't last long; he's too much of a womanizer to remain faithful, even to his mistress! My self-esteem was low, but even I didn't need to put up with his philandering. (Plus, he was far less intoxicating than cocaine.) But I was always able to see his brilliance as a researcher, and we managed a decent working relationship.

About five years ago, I met Joe Ames. You've seen him at a couple of parties at my house over the years, and I think I introduced you once. In addition to being breathtakingly beautiful, Joe is very smart. I think he was kind of a "bad boy" version of Marty Braxton. We went to bed together the first night we met, after doing lines of his incredible cocaine. But he didn't agree to sell me coke until he knew a lot about me and what I did. Eventually, though, he was my most consistent and best source.

Joe would make subtle suggestions about how I could pay for cocaine if money was short. I'd write bad checks for things he'd like or could sell (C.D.s, clothing, etc.). He would take them in trade. Usually I was able to make good on the checks when I got paid.

As time went on, and he learned more about the grant programs, Joe suggested padding my expense accounts to come up with extra cash. He eventually convinced me to put him on the payroll. Marty knew I was seeing Joe but didn't know he was selling me coke. When Marty discovered the payroll thing, he was furious. Ostensibly, that is. I later found out he did the same thing with his mistress. That was okay with me, because he would no longer be able to turn me in.

The phone rang. Seeing The Meadows' number on my caller ID unsettled me: I wasn't nearly as detached as I wanted or needed to be. But I had to answer it.

"It's Kate," she said. "Are we good?"

"I'm sorry I hung up on you," I said, knowing full well I wasn't answering her question. "David helped me think things through, and I've calmed down. Were you serious about cooperating with the cops?"

"Completely."

I breathed a sigh of relief. "Can I ask what made you change your mind?"

"I talked it over in group last night. They made me see my reluctance to rat on Joe was simply reluctance to give up coke. If he gets arrested, my last—and now only—source is gone. It was a reality I didn't want to acknowledge. But if I'm really serious about staying drug free, which I am, I have to put my money where my mouth is."

"I agree. I'll call George Cooper and set something up."

"Let's do it Thursday while I'm on pass. I want to get this over with."

"Okay. I'll try for Thursday. Am I still picking you up at nine-thirty?"

"Yes. That's perfect."

I put in a call to the prosecutor who was "in conference," and, settling down to wait for yet another return call, I continued reading Kate's missive.

I can't describe how stupid and shameful I feel for doing what I did. It's inexcusable. It's irresponsible. And yes, it's criminal. I am a criminal. What's worse than taking the money, though, is I set our research back by months (maybe even years). Marty and I could have made a lot more progress if I wasn't always focused on cocaine, and God knows I was higher than a kite a LOT of the time. Marty will have to find new funding.

Which brings me to my next point: I will plead guilty, but I refuse to implicate Marty in ANY of the fraud. That includes his putting Barbara on the payroll and some of his questionable travel claims. THIS IS NOT NEGOTIABLE. Caroline, you must NEVER disclose his wrongdoing to anyone. I will pay restitution and accept any blame for all of the fraud.

I'm not being a martyr here. Marty Braxton's contributions to the field of medicine have been and will continue to be invaluable. There is nothing to be gained by taking him down with me. (In fact, much would be lost if I did.)

The university will fire me when I plead guilty, but that's okay. I have a few prospective buyers for the condo and don't think it will take long to sell, so I'll be without major expenses. I'd like to do this soon and get on with my probation or jail or whatever so I can begin putting my life back together.

Caroline, I'm sorry I manipulated you into defending me. When I first got arrested, I was really in denial (as these treatment people LOVE to say). Denial of the extent of my drug problem and my fraud. I hoped you (my very bright friend) could wave some magic wand and get me out of it. At the very least, I hoped you could be manipulated into not looking for the skeletons in my closet. I was wrong.

I've read the stacks and stacks of discovery materials you've given me (often at three a.m. when I can't sleep anyway). They've got a strong case against me. I also know my positive urine samples didn't help my case. My God, I even got coke IN JAIL!

I love you, Caroline. At least as much as I'm capable of loving anyone. I'm glad you're in my corner.

I sat at my desk for the next half-hour, unable to focus through the tears. I managed to stifle the sobs that threatened to erupt from my core, but I could not stop crying. Not to answer the telephone, which rang twice. Not to answer the person who knocked at my door. Not to answer my computer's insistent alerts about new e-mail messages. My tears finally spent, I got up, left the office and drove to the welcoming refuge of my home.

George Cooper reached me there that evening and agreed to set up Kate's debriefing for Thursday afternoon at the FBI office. We would meet Tom Robbins, Detectives Connaboy and Jacobs, a state drug investigator, and Special Agent Carter Ellingson. Cooper would be out of town for several days and could not be there himself. "Don't worry about it," he said when I questioned whether we should proceed without him. "They can handle it on their own."

CHAPTER TWENTY-SIX

—⚏—

Wednesday, October 31

"Feel free to dunk 'em," Dr. Brownhill said, handing me a mug of tea and nodding to a plate of cookies on the table. "My ninety-year-old mother made them. They're tasty but a tad dry, and I don't have the heart to tell her she's lost her touch."

A mental image of an elderly woman baking cookies for her daughter brought tears to my eyes.

"Oh, my dear," Dr. Brownhill said, sitting forward in her chair. "It looks like you've got stuff bubbling right there under the surface. Tell me."

She nodded and prodded until I brought her up to date on my life and finished telling her my mixed emotions toward Kate. "Let's start with the anger," she said. "Are you ready to let it go?"

"I thought so when I talked with David. You know, he's right about Kate saving us from worry and informed

cision-making. But I'm still angry she risked Lily's health
sing drugs."

Do you believe her when she says she didn't use after
learning she was pregnant?"

"Yes…"

I sat in silence for a minute, my thoughts meandering
every which way, then hung my head and sobbed.

"What is it, Caroline?"

"I just realized: I was taking anti-anxiety meds and using
alcohol when I had my ectopic pregnancy. We hadn't planned
it; it just happened. Just like Kate. And I've been so judg-
mental about her when I was guilty of the same thing. How
can I be such a hypocrite?"

"Go easy on yourself. You're a mother, and anything that
threatened or threatens Lily causes you to be ultra-sensitive
and protective. And remember, we have defense mechanisms
for a reason."

"But I hate being in the wrong."

"You're human, just like the rest of us. And it's human
nature to make mistakes—sometimes even hurtful ones. If
it would make you feel better, you could apologize to Kate."

"I'm still angry…"

"About what?"

"That she'd throw away her life and important work for
cocaine. That she cares more about cocaine than us. And that
if Lily someday chooses to learn the identity of her biological
mother—which I'm almost sure she will—the story will be
way more complicated than we ever imagined."

"Unfortunately, addictions are incredibly powerful and very often destructive. Have you thought about going to Al-Anon to help you get some perspective on this?"

"Interesting you should ask. I've read some of their stuff, and I was just telling David I probably needed to practice some of their detachment."

"A worthy goal, but maybe more difficult in your case since you're her defense attorney."

"Yeah. I was going to withdraw, but now that she's decided to plead guilty, I think I can handle it. And I'm relieved she's going to do the right thing and inform on her dealer."

"Because?"

"I guess because criminal defense isn't my niche," I said, shaking my head. "Because I still identify with the prosecution, despite my intellectual understanding that crooks have the right to due process."

"You've got a lot on your plate: an addicted friend with a boatload of legal issues, a prospective adoption and a seven-year-old child who's ambivalent about a new sibling, keeping your panic attacks at bay..."

I smiled. "Is this supposed to make me feel better?"

"I'm only pointing out what your subconscious already knows," she said gently. "Just be sure to give yourself time to breathe, relax and laugh."

"I'll try to fit it in," I said. But it was a hollow promise.

CHAPTER TWENTY-SEVEN

—⟋⟍—

Thursday, November 1

The morning's cold, suffocating fog threatened to send me into a tailspin. My headlights reflected off the mist, and the incessant wipers, while necessary to keep the windshield clear of humidity, distracted and riled me. My hands, as clammy as the weather, gripped the steering wheel as I took what felt like an interminable trip to The Meadows.

Kate waited under an overhang at the door to the residential building, an overnight bag slung over her shoulder. She dashed to the car and climbed in. "Thanks," she said, somewhat warily, I thought.

"I'm glad to see you," I said. And it was true: having someone else in the car eased my panicky feelings.

By the time we got back to Madison, the fog had lifted, and our small talk had taken the edge off our tension.

"I need to stop off at home to pick up my car and some paperwork," Kate said. "Then I'm off to meet with the realtor. Can we have lunch before the pow-wow?"

"Sure."

Assuming Kate would want time to herself, I'd planned to simply drop her off at her condo. But as we neared her home, Kate grew more and more agitated. Her speech quickened, and her eyes became darker and almost glassy. My unease returned.

By the time we arrived at her building, I was beside myself. "Do you have any coffee? I've only had time for half a cup this morning and another sure would hit the spot."

It sounded phony, even to me. I realized what I feared was a replay of our last visit to Kate's apartment—when she'd gone in the bathroom and used cocaine.

"I'd be happy to make you some coffee, Caroline, but you don't have to feel compelled to come in. I promise you there's no coke left."

"I just—"

"I know why you're suspicious. I'm feeling pretty weird. Adam told me to expect it, and I should've warned you, too. You see, our bodies react just like Pavlov's dogs. Remember, they salivated at early cues that food was on the way? Well, my body is having a physical reaction in anticipation of cocaine—I used to use it here a lot—and I probably look like I'm high already."

"Yeah. You do."

"I never recognized this when it happened to me before. I'm glad Adam prepared me. Otherwise I might have been more tempted to use."

"More tempted?"

"Yes, Caroline. I'm still tempted. C'mon in."

Kate made a pot of coffee and toasted some English muffins she found in the back of her freezer. When I left about forty-five minutes later, she looked calm and in control.

"I'll see you at Fridays' at quarter to one," she said.

It was a working lunch. We reviewed George Cooper's immunity letter, which promised any self-incriminating statements Kate made would not be used against her. We talked about telling the truth and making sure she understood each question before answering.

Finally, the question I'd been waiting to ask: "Do you know who sold drugs to Yvonne Pritchard?"

Kate nodded. "Joe Ames."

"You'll have to tell them that."

She nodded again and her eyes glistened with tears. "I really liked Yvonne. And I feel like shit for keeping her family in the dark so long."

The waiter was slow with our food and later with the check. Kate got up to use the restroom. "I'll meet you in the parking lot," she said.

We were already late for our appointment when I finally got change from the check, but I decided to use the bathroom myself. *Better here than at the FBI office*, I thought, entering the back hallway. Kate leaned against the wall with her back to me, talking on the phone.

"...one. I'll meet you at five. Usual place," she said. "Thanks, Jo-Jo."

My rage was instantaneous.

"What in the hell do you think you're doing?" I demanded.

Kate turned to face me. "What do you mean, sneaking up on me like that?"

"No, Kate. This is not about me or about sneaking. I'm on my way to a public restroom, and I hear you talking, in public, to the last person in the world you should be talking to right now."

"It's not what you think—"

"Bullshit!" I said. Then, at a more moderate volume, "'Jo-Jo' Ames is your fucking coke dealer, and you were setting up another deal. Shut up and come with me. We've got a meeting to attend." I grabbed her elbow and steered her out of the restaurant to my car.

"We'll pick up your car later," I said.

Kate slumped in the seat, her body convulsing with sobs. "I'm sorry, Caroline," she said between gulps of air. "I don't know what came over me. I'm so nervous. I'm so scared..."

I regained my composure, and it hit me, perhaps for the first time, how truly powerless my friend was over this insidious chemical. Oh yes, I'd read and believed Kate's written words. But this was clear evidence I could see with my own eyes. My anger dissipated as quickly as it had come, and an overwhelming sadness took its place. I tried to swallow the painful lump in my throat and wiped the tears from my cheeks, determined to soldier through the emotional minefields of the rest of the day.

"It's okay," I said, turning the ignition key. "We'll work it out."

—⚉—

"I was afraid you'd decided not to come," said Carter Ellingson as he escorted us into a small conference room at the FBI's office.

"I called from the car to say we'd be late," I said. "I guess the receptionist didn't get the message to you."

I greeted Tom Robbins warmly and introduced him to Kate. Doug Connaboy and Sam Jacobs walked in as we were getting situated and nodded to us. Then came a scruffy-looking man of about thirty, dressed in torn, filthy jeans, a denim jacket and a New York Yankees baseball cap. His dirty-blond hair was long and unkempt, and he had a faded, untrimmed beard. Were it not for his cocky demeanor, I would have thought him a street person.

"Caroline, this is Rick Shelton, from state narcotics," Tom said.

"We've had the pleasure," Shelton said after a quick glance my way. He turned to Kate and extended his hand. "And this must be Kathryn Daniels."

She nodded and shook his hand.

"Forgive me, but I can't place you, Mr. Shelton," I said.

"I'm crushed," he said with undisguised insincerity. "It was almost exactly five years ago. I'd just started working as a narc after transferring from the Rhinelander PD. You were an ADA and threw out my first bust because I hadn't properly Mirandized the bad guy."

The recognition must have flashed across my face.

"Don't worry. I hold no grudges. You made me a better cop," he said.

I remembered Shelton as a younger, clean-shaven drug agent. He had been working the university area and had arrested the president of one of the fraternities for selling marijuana. After reading the arrest reports and the defendant's confession, I called Shelton's supervisor and told him I declined to prosecute because the defendant had clearly not been advised of his rights.

Later, Rick Shelton had come storming into my office demanding to know why I'd rejected his case. I told him every fifth grader who'd ever watched cop shows knew about Miranda, and we didn't have time to waste on losing cases.

Perhaps I should have been more diplomatic, I thought, seated across the conference table from him.

Carter Ellingson, a consummate professional, re-introduced everyone for the record and went over the ground rules. Kate was expected to tell the truth, but nothing she said could be used against her. Then he sat back and let the others ask their questions.

Doug Connaboy went first. "The DA's agreed not to prosecute you for obstruction of justice if you tell us what you know about Yvonne Pritchard's death."

"I know Joe Ames sold her the cocaine she used that night," Kate said in a barely audible voice. "I was going to her place to buy drugs from him myself, but I was delayed and he left before I got there."

"She didn't use the cocaine in your presence?"

"No, that part of my earlier statement was true: Yvonne was unconscious on the floor when I arrived."

"Did you tell the roommate, Laquisha Abbott, to flush the remaining cocaine?"

"Yes."

"Did Ames give you any instructions about removing evidence?"

"No. I never spoke to him about Yvonne's death."

"Do you know how Yvonne met Joe Ames in the first place?" Connaboy asked.

"I introduced them to one another, at a party at my house, a couple of months before she died. We all used cocaine together at that party."

I could feel Kate's shame as she related this to the detectives. And I could not help feeling some of it reflected on me. These guys knew she'd been my friend before she became my client. *Do they think I knew she was a user?*

Rick Shelton asked the next set of questions and, perhaps because of his arrogant manner, Kate responded with more confidence. She admitted she and Ames had had a sexual relationship for more than a year.

"Why did you stop sleeping with him?" Shelton asked.

Kate looked down at her feet. "I found out he was married," she said.

"How did you find that out?" Shelton asked.

"I don't really see the relevance of these questions," I said. I got the strong impression Shelton was just being nosy and couldn't see how this related to his investigation.

"It's okay, Caroline," Kate said. "I want to tell them everything. I learned Joe was married after I hired him, ostensibly as a research assistant—I guess it was about a year and a half ago. Personnel sent over some forms that Joe had completed incorrectly and needed to be re-done. I noticed he'd listed Jolene, his wife, as next of kin. 'Joe and Jolene.' It's almost too cute. I confronted him, and he admitted it. He said Jolene knew all about us and didn't mind. I minded, though."

"But you continued to buy cocaine from him?" Ellingson asked.

"At first I wasn't going to. But after all, he was already on the payroll and had agreed to provide coke in return. I decided not to let my personal hurt get in the way."

They asked Kate how much cocaine she'd purchased from Ames over various periods of time, how and where they'd arranged the deliveries, and who had been with him. Kate was able to provide many details of her deals but she didn't know any of his associates. And he never discussed his sources.

"Tell us about how Ames got coke to you at the jail," Tom Robbins said.

"Okay," Kate said, taking a deep breath. "It was the first night I was there. Joe showed up to see me during visiting hours."

"Had you called to ask him to come?" Robbins asked.

"No. In fact I was surprised he knew I was there. He laughed and said it was all over the news. How could he not know? Anyway, we chatted a while. Pretty soon he asked me in our code if I wanted him to get me some coke."

"Describe your code, please," Robbins said.

"Sure," Kate said. "When we talked on the phone we never used the word cocaine. We'd talk as if I were ordering catering. For example, I would say I was having a dinner party for twenty-eight if I wanted a whole ounce of coke. You know—twenty-eight grams. Half an ounce would be 'dinner for fourteen.' If I just needed a gram, I'd order 'dessert' for a few friends."

"So, specifically, what did he say to you at the jail?" Robbins asked.

"He said, 'Would you like me to arrange for some dessert while you're here?' I was pretty stunned, because I had no idea he could get it in to me. I said sure, and he said he'd put it on my Visa bill. He already knew my card number."

"Did he say how he'd get it to you?"

"He said I shouldn't worry about that part. He'd work it out."

"Tell us how the delivery was made," Robbins said.

"The next afternoon, when Anita came on duty, she called me out of the cell block. I thought I had a visitor or something. But she motioned for me to come near the control room and I noticed none of the other officers were around. Anita handed me a Bic pen from her pants pocket, which she said my 'friend' had given her. She looked just miserable. I took it back to my cell. There was about a gram of coke inside the pen tube. I was glad to get it, but I felt really bad for Anita because I sensed she wasn't doing this willingly. I know how persuasive Joe can be."

"Did you share the cocaine with any other inmates?"

"No. I wanted it to last as long as possible since I wasn't sure when I'd get out. There was a little left, hidden in a slit in the mattress, when I left."

"Did you talk to Ames about it after you got out?" Robbins asked.

"Yes. Joe said he'd been thinking about establishing a jail connection because a number of his customers had gotten arrested over the years. He said he had the names of several guards who might be in a position to smuggle stuff into the jail. He'd investigated some of their backgrounds. He selected Anita when I got arrested. I feel just awful about what's happened to her."

"When did you last see Joe Ames?" Shelton asked.

"About a week before I went into treatment. He delivered some 'dessert for an intimate dinner party.'"

"A gram?" Shelton asked.

"Yes. A gram."

"And when did you last talk to Ames?" Ellingson asked.

Kate glanced at me and then at her watch. "About two hours ago."

"Two hours ago?" Shelton asked, his eyes wide with renewed interest.

"Yes," Kate said.

"How and why did this conversation take place?" he asked.

"I called him from the restaurant where we were having lunch and told him I needed dessert for a few friends tonight at five o'clock. It was stupid, and I'm sorry I did it. Obviously, I've thought better of it in the past couple hours, and I won't pick it up."

"Was he at all suspicious of you?" Shelton asked.

"No. I'm sure he wasn't. He sounded glad to hear from me. After all, I'm a good customer." Kate smiled ruefully. "He'd be happy to sell to me regardless of how much trouble it could get me in."

"Ladies, we need a short break," Rick Shelton said, standing abruptly. "Gentlemen, may I have a word with you?"

The men left the conference room.

"You did very well, Kate," I said, and I meant it.

"I probably got myself in more hot water by telling them about today's call, huh?"

"No. You didn't. The immunity letter took care of that. They can't use what you've said against you."

As we sat in silence for a few moments, I reviewed in my mind the answers Kate had given. She'd been forthright and appropriately apologetic for her behavior, making it clear she wanted to be on the right side of the law. I felt no small measure of relief at the message she'd conveyed.

"They've been gone a while," Kate finally said. "What do you think they're being so secretive about?"

She was right: they were being secretive. "I'm not sure," I said, biting my lip, "but my guess is they're going to ask you to take delivery of the coke you ordered and trap Joe in the process." The whole idea made me nervous. I wished George Cooper had been able to attend the meeting: his presence would have set my mind at ease. After all, he was the one who'd granted Kate immunity for her cooperation.

"Do I have to?" Kate asked.

"No," I said. "You don't have to do anything."

"Should I do it?"

"It depends. The more help you're able to give them, the more consideration you'll get when you're sentenced. But it's not worth risking your sobriety or your safety."

"I'm not worried about my safety. It might really help me to see him arrested. It might bring some closure to my stupid, fucking relationship with Joe Ames."

Ten minutes later, the guys returned. Tom Robbins told us his part in the investigation was finished. He shook Kate's hand, gave me a brotherly hug, and left.

Rick Shelton took charge. He spoke directly to Kate, as if I weren't even present. "It's about four o'clock—only an hour from your planned meet with Ames. We can't get authorization in time for you to do a 'controlled buy' of the coke. Can you call him and arrange a later time?"

"Excuse me," I said caustically. I wasn't about to let him steamroll Kate—or forget he needed to work through me. "Please slow down and explain to my client and me exactly what you're proposing." I thought I saw the corner of Doug Connaboy's lip approaching a smile. Rick Shelton was not his kind of cop.

"You're right, counselor. I'm sorry," Shelton said, though his tone belied his words. "Kate, what we're proposing is that you help us further by setting up Joe Ames. We'd like you to call him and let us record the conversation. We'd like you to postpone your transaction, possibly until late tomorrow. Then we'd like you to wear a wire when you pick up the coke from him. We'll arrest him as soon as you give us an agreed upon signal. He's got the money, you've got the dope. We test the dope. We put Ames in jail."

Kate turned to me. "What's your opinion?"

"It's a pretty standard arrangement. But he left out a bit: Before you're fitted with the body wire, they thoroughly search you so they can make sure you don't have any dope before the buy. They do the same afterward to make sure you don't keep any. Also, I'm concerned about the wire. Has Joe Ames ever frisked you or asked you to lift your shirt before dealing with you before?"

"No. Never. Remember, I've dealt with him for years. And about the searches: it can't be any worse than the strip search in jail, can it?"

I shook my head.

"One more thing," Shelton said. "You ordered a gram, right?"

Kate nodded.

"We'd need you to buy at least an ounce. Two would be better. Can you make that plausible?"

"He'd never believe it if I ordered two ounces to pick up tonight or tomorrow. Saturday, maybe," Kate said.

"I need to remind you all that Kate is due back at The Meadows tomorrow morning," I said.

"I'll be eligible for another five-hour pass on Saturday afternoon," she said. "Could we do it then?"

Shelton and Ellingson looked at each other and nodded their agreement.

Carter Ellingson handed me a paper. "Your client will need to sign this form authorizing us to monitor and tape her phone call to Ames today."

—ᴧᴧᴧ—

At four thirty-five that afternoon, Kate texted Joe Ames with the message: "Call K.D. ASAP." She gave the number to the FBI's undercover line, which was equipped with a speaker and recording device.

We waited in silence, absurdly watching the phone, and startled when it finally rang a minute later.

Kate answered. "K.D. here."

"Hey. What's up? I'm fifteen minutes out."

"Look, Jo-Jo. I'm jammed up and can't make it. My lawyer won't let me out of her sight. I was only able to slip away for a few minutes to call you."

"Too bad."

"I'm getting out of The Meadows Saturday morning. I'll be leaving on an extended vacation the next day. I want to have an informal party to say goodbye to my friends and co-workers on Saturday night. Could you handle a party of, say, fifty-six on such short notice?"

"Ooh, baby. That's a tall order. We'd have to charge you top dollar, say twelve per head. But yeah, I think we could handle it. Informal, you say? Like an appetizer buffet, I'm thinking?" We could almost hear the smile in his voice.

"Yes. Sounds perfect. You know I trust your judgment."

"We'd need to get into your kitchen by three on Saturday, okay?"

"Sure. See you then." She hung up.

"Beautiful, Kate," Shelton said. "You did great!"

"Translation, please," Ellingson said. "I want to make sure we're all clear on what's happening."

"Kate just ordered two ounces—roughly fifty-six grams—of coke for twelve-hundred dollars an ounce," Shelton said. "Right, Kate?"

"Right."

"And where will delivery take place?" I asked. "Surely not at your place?"

"No," Kate said. "The kitchen is our code word for the union terrace. Over at the university. Joe likes to do all of his deliveries outdoors—even in winter. I'm to meet him at three o'clock."

CHAPTER TWENTY-EIGHT

—m—

By the time we got home, David and Lily had conjured up a feast: salad, baked potatoes, steak, and a fresh apple pie from Scott's Pastry Shoppe for dessert. Although I hadn't discussed it with him, David had stashed the wine and liquor somewhere out of sight.

Kate and I were drained—both mentally and physically—from our odyssey of a day, and we enjoyed being pampered.

Watching Lily and Kate interact, I thought about their relationship over the years. Kate had always tried to keep her distance, being polite and generous but not demonstrative toward Lily, I assumed out of deference to David and me. Lily had never been put out by Kate's manner as she was by other standoffish friends of ours. Instead, she'd been attracted to Kate—as if she could no more resist Kate than Newton's apple could resist the earth's gravitational pull. Could it be Lily felt connected to Kate—that she subconsciously knew her as her birth mother?

While David grilled the steaks, Lily cuddled up on the sofa between Kate and me, and Kate looked as happy as I'd ever seen her. *Maybe being clean and sober awakened her to feelings she never knew she had? Or was it the relief in knowing her secrets were out, and we were still in her corner?*

At dinner, Lily charmed us with stories of her classmates' antics and showed off her math skills by reciting her times tables. Basking in the attention of three spellbound adults, her insecurities over the coming sibling had apparently been banished, at least for now.

We were almost done eating when Lily looked up from her plate and noticed a break in the conversation. As if she'd been waiting for just this moment, she asked with obvious glee, "Aunt Kate, did Mom tell you we're going to adopt a baby?"

David coughed, choking on a sip of water. Stunned and pleased by Lily's changed attitude, yet embarrassed that I'd kept the news from Kate, I couldn't find words.

Kate glanced from me to David to Lily, then burst into a grin. "That's so cool, honey! You'll be a great big sister."

Lily chattered on for a while, oblivious to the fact that Kate hadn't answered her question: No, your mom hasn't told me about the adoption.

"I'm sorry I didn't tell you," I said to Kate when Lily paused for a bite of potato. "We just found out and haven't shared our news with anyone outside the family yet."

"But Aunt Kate's part of the family," Lily mumbled with a mouthful.

"I meant—"

"It's okay, Caroline. I understand," Kate said. "Lily, I think your mom and dad meant your real family—and you know I'm not really your aunt, right?"

With a puzzled expression, Lily looked down at her lap. "I know you're not my real aunt. I've only got three of those. But it still seems like you're part of my real family."

Uneasiness rose in my throat. This felt like dangerous ground.

"Honey, it's fine that you told Kate about the baby," David said. "It feels like she's part of our family, and that's what's important. Remember when we talked about having enough love for more kids?"

Lily raised her head. "Sure."

"Well, it's the same thing: We have enough love to include other adults in our family, too."

The discomfort passed as swiftly as it had come. David got up to clear the table and serve the pie, and Lily, announcing she was too full for dessert, trotted off to watch TV.

"Do you know whether it's a boy or girl?" Kate asked when David sat down again.

I looked at him. "Oh my God. How could I have forgotten?"

He laughed. "Your ADD kicking in again?"

"The report of the mom's most recent medical exam was faxed to me two days ago, but I didn't look at it," I explained to Kate. "The attorney said not to look if we wanted to remain in suspense, David said he didn't want to know, and I never got around to deciding whether I want to or not. I can't believe I forgot—"

"Did my bombshells have something to do with that?" she asked.

"Oh, yeah," I said, surprised by my own candor.

"You can't know how sorry I am for throwing a monkey wrench into your lives," she said, "especially when you guys have happy stuff to be thinking about."

"It's—"

"No, Caroline. You're going to say it's okay, but it's not. And I intend to make amends, however long it takes."

Kate and I put away the leftovers and loaded the dishwasher while David helped Lily with her homework. We all watched a couple more "Lucy" episodes and headed upstairs early. It had been a long day.

"Thank you for saying that—about having enough love for Kate in our family," I said to David when we were in bed. "I know you don't care for her—"

"Honey—"

"Let me finish. You don't have to pretend you like her. It was still a great thing you did for Lily and me, because, for whatever reason, we love Kate. And it hurts us to see her hurting."

"My feelings toward Kate Daniels are way too complex to discuss in depth this late at night," he said with a sigh. "But let me give you the abbreviated version: I love her for the gift of our child. I hate her for using and aggravating you. I wish I'd known her before the addiction took hold, because then I could better see what you see in her. But I have to say I caught glimpses of it tonight, which was good. That's why I said what I said, and I meant it. Her apology to us later was another positive sign."

I curled up under his arm, resting my head on his chest, and took solace in his steady heartbeat. "You're a good man, David Spencer."

It was one of my favorite things: lying in the darkened bedroom and talking in hushed tones with my husband. The crisp, cool sheets warmed by our down comforter. The soft whirring of the ceiling fan we kept running winter, summer, spring, and fall. The hazy outline of the now bare maple trees outside our window. But more than that: a time to depressurize and communicate with the person I respected more than anyone in the world.

"So you really don't want to know the gender of our child-to-be?" I asked.

"No, I don't. But you can look if you want."

"I'm not sure I could keep it secret. I guess I'll think about it for a while."

Then I told him about my day, beginning with Kate's call to Joe Ames.

"After all this trouble, she called him to buy more cocaine?" he asked.

"And probably would have gone to pick it up if I hadn't overheard the conversation. I was so pissed. Then she crumbled like a stale cookie—she started sobbing and looked completely defeated and ashamed. I couldn't be pissed anymore, I felt so sorry for her. Do you think she was playing me?"

"What did your gut say?"

"That it wasn't an act."

"You have good instincts, you've just gotta trust them," he said.

"Kate redeemed herself during the debriefing. She told them Ames was Yvonne Pritchard's dealer and corroborated what they knew about his smuggling coke into the jail. She also answered truthfully when they asked when she'd last spoken to Ames. We've got a controlled buy set up for Saturday."

"They're gonna wait until then to arrest him?"

"Yeah. They want an airtight case."

"I hope it sticks," he said.

CHAPTER TWENTY-NINE

—ɯɯ—

Saturday, November 3

A small spitfire of a woman, Special Agent Robards stood about five feet tall and had short carrot-colored hair and a face full of freckles. Wearing tight jeans—about a size four—and a black turtleneck sweater, she could've been a college student. But she was all business.

"Ms. Daniels. Ms. Spencer. I'm Nancy Robards from DCI. Wisconsin Division of Criminal Investigation, that is. I'm here to provide technical support for the controlled buy. Shall we get started?"

We nodded.

"Counselor, you're free to come in while I search your client and put on the wire. In fact, I'd appreciate it if you would. You can help out."

We followed her down the hallway into a large restroom. "Ms. Daniels—" Nancy said.

"You can call me Kate."

"Okay. Kate. I'll need you to remove your clothing to do the search. You can leave your underwear on."

"Agent Shelton told me not to wear a bra. And to wear a tight t-shirt."

"Ah! His old 'get the bad-guy to think with his dick so he forgets to look for the wire' ploy," she said with a scowl.

"Do they teach you that in narc school?" I asked.

"No—Shelton thought it up on his own. And as much as I hate to say it, he has a pretty good record of busting folks with wires. Doesn't make him any less of a pig, though."

She turned to Kate. "I'm sorry for the embarrassment. You can leave your shirt on and I'll pat search you through it."

Nancy explained she would be using a mini transmitter with a very small flat microphone. She cut off pieces of thin, almost transparent, surgical tape to secure the wires. At Nancy's instruction, Kate held the microphone in place where her breast met her armpit. I applied the tape Nancy handed to me, to hold it and the thin wire in place. As Nancy predicted, the slim profile of the microphone was hidden in the folds where the sleeve joined the body of the shirt. She assured us the microphone was sensitive enough to pick up conversations through the layers of fabric. The transmitter itself was to go on the inside of Kate's thigh. The wire ran under her arm and along the elastic of her underpants.

"Only a real letch would find this. Since you'll be going outside, put your hoodie back on but leave it unzipped."

We went back to the conference room and met Rick Shelton and Carter Ellingson, who was counting bills—hundreds, fifties, and twenties. He turned to Shelton. "It checks out," he said. "Twenty-five hundred dollars."

Shelton asked Kate for her purse and searched it. He took all the bills out of her wallet and handed them to me. "Please hold this, counselor, so it doesn't get mixed with the buy money." Then he handed Kate the envelope in which Carter Ellingson had placed the money. "Here, Kate. There's an extra hundred just in case. We've recorded all the serial numbers of the bills. I need you to walk outside with Agent Robards so we can do a sound check."

We heard them loud and clear through the transmitter's receiver.

After Ellingson, Shelton, and two other officers searched Kate's car, she got in. Shelton motioned for her to roll down the window. "Okay. We're set. We'll be a car-length or two behind you. Keep the radio off."

Ellingson turned to me. "I've got your cell phone number," he said. "We'll call you as soon as the bust comes down, and you can meet us back here."

—⁂—

It was the longest two hours I've ever spent. I wandered around the nearby shopping mall, absently looking at the merchandise. After an hour and a half, I pulled out my cell phone and dialed our home number. No answer. No answering machine. *Maybe there's something about the mall that interferes with the phone signals. Maybe the agents have been trying to reach me and couldn't.*

In desperation, I called Ida McKinley who, without asking any questions, called me right back. The phone worked flawlessly—the reception was fine.

Naturally I jumped when Carter Ellingson called, and his terse communication did nothing to calm my nerves. "The bust went down," he said. "We're heading back to the office."

"How—" I started to ask, but he'd already hung up.

It took me only five minutes to get from the shopping mall to the parking lot at the FBI office. In fact, I arrived just before Kate and the surveillance team.

Something was amiss. Kate stumbled as she got out of her car and shook off the hand Ellingson offered to steady her. Both of them pointedly avoided my eye contact. Nancy Robards hurried ahead of us toward the building.

"Where's Rick Shelton?" I called to her.

She paused with her hand on the doorknob and turned to me. "He and another agent are transporting Ames to the jail."

That's good news.

"How did it go?" I asked Ellingson when he could no longer avoid me.

"There were a few snags, but the buy went down. We got him."

"What kind of snags?"

"I'll tell you when we get inside. Nancy needs to get the wire off. They need it on another case downtown."

While Kate and Nancy Robards went to remove the microphone and transmitter, I followed Ellingson into the conference room.

"Please tell me what's going on, Carter."

"Let's listen to the tape. I think it'll explain a lot." He put a cassette into a tape player on a table next to the wall. "Ames was late and he was obviously suspicious. When he met your client at the union, Ames said they needed to go for a ride—in his car. We had a tough time maintaining surveillance and almost missed the arrest signal. He made the trade at the McDonald's on Regent Street. Lots of people around. Lots of traffic."

I sank into a chair, and Ellingson started the tape. It was surprisingly clear.

"Hey, Jo-Jo. It's good to see you!" Kate said.

"You too, babe. Look, we gotta take a ride. My car's up on Langdon Street. C'mon."

They apparently walked in silence to Ames' car. Then we heard the sounds of the car doors shutting, the ignition, and the radio.

"I need a hug, Kate," Ames said.

"Jo-Jo! What are you doing?" Kate asked, sounding alarmed.

"Can't be too careful, babe. Lift up your t-shirt."

"Nice," Ames said. "I never figured you for the braless type, Professor."

"I'm not. Someone swiped my sports bra out of the laundry room. All us junkies do our wash together, you know."

"Take your sweatshirt off."

"What?"

"I said, 'take your sweatshirt off.'"

"Why?"

"Your tits look nice in a t-shirt. And I expect you see the importance of making me happy."

A moment of silence. "So why do you want two O.Z.'s?" Ames asked.

"I get out of the treatment center on Monday. I'm booked on a flight from O'Hare to Costa Rica on Monday night. I want a supply to tide me over until I establish some connections there. I don't plan to return."

"I thought they took your passport," Ames said.

"They did. One of my foreign colleagues at the university was able to procure some new documents."

"Aren't you worried about customs?"

"Get real, Jo-Jo. Who smuggles drugs out of the country?"

Ames laughed. "I guess you're right. But this all seems so unlike you. You'd probably get probation if you stuck around."

"I thought so too, until my lawyer starting figuring the sentencing guidelines. I'm looking at more like two or three years. I can't do it. My career is shot. What's the point of sticking around here?"

"What'll you do in Costa Rica?"

"I've been there. I speak Spanish. Maybe I can get some more phony papers and actually practice medicine. Maybe I'll move on to another country. I don't know for sure—I just want to get out of here."

They drove without talking for several minutes. We could hear someone tapping along with the rhythm of the radio.

"Why are we stopping here?" Kate asked.

"For some privacy. Surely you want a sample?"

"I can't, Joe. I've gotta pee in a bottle in about an hour."

"What do you care? You're leaving the country on Monday. They can't get you locked up that fast."

"If I'm dirty today, I won't get out Monday."

"Is the place locked?"

"No."

"Then you can walk out on Monday. I'm beginning to wonder if you're trying to set me up."

"You know I wouldn't do that, Jo-Jo. I love you."

"You haven't let me make love to you in ages."

"No. And I won't as long as you're married. But I've always loved you. And I wouldn't set you up," Kate said.

"Prove it. Do a line. Here."

I gripped the arms of my chair, listening in horror. Three seconds of silence.

"Whoa!" Kate exclaimed in exhilaration.

"Go ahead," Ames said. "Have another."

"Thanks—don't mind if I do," Kate replied.

We heard the car start and the two laughing with glee. Ellingson and I exchanged mournful glances: Kate's obvious use of cocaine might undermine both his case and mine.

"McDonald's?" Kate asked.

"It's just a parking lot," Ames said. "Show me the money."

"Twenty-four, right?"

"Yep. Thanks, babe. Reach into the glove box. It's in the black sunglasses case."

Kate and Nancy Robards walked into the room, just as we heard the sound of the glove compartment opening and closing. Then another moment of silence.

"Bueno, José. Gracias!" Kate said on the tape. Those words were the signal to surveillance officers that the transaction had taken place and they should arrest Ames.

Ellingson shut off the tape.

"Unfortunately," he said, "we were a block away when Kate gave the signal. We got there in time to block the driveway so Ames couldn't leave. Fortunately, he was too dumbfounded to do anything stupid—like grab Kate or run."

Kate was shaking as she sank down into the chair next to me. "I'm sorry, Caroline. I didn't want to use, but I didn't know what else to do."

I reached over and held her hand but couldn't meet her eyes. *I shouldn't have allowed her to do this.*

"It was unavoidable," Ellingson said. "I'm really sorry it came down that way, Kate. But your cooperation made the case. We won't let it go unnoticed."

Ellingson and Robards asked Kate a number of questions to clarify the details of her encounter with Joe Ames.

"We'll file the complaint against Ames with the federal magistrate judge tomorrow," Ellingson said. "The state agents think we'll get more time there than in local court. We'll need your testimony at the grand jury a week from Monday."

"What about the charge for providing cocaine to Yvonne Pritchard?" I asked.

"It'll bring more time as a penalty enhancer in federal court than as a separate local charge. I think the county will still pursue their case against Ames for smuggling into the jail, just to have another kick at him. But there's no rush to file that charge."

"Okay," I said.

"George Cooper or I will call Ms. Spencer with the details about the grand jury," he said to Kate. "Thanks for your help today. You did great."

—w—

I got us back to The Meadows by five o'clock, as required by the terms of Kate's pass, without incurring a speeding ticket, though I had to apply my brakes and pretend to be driving prudently when I saw a sheriff's squad at one of the intersections on the way. I'd promised Kate I would go in with her to meet the counselor on duty.

Her hooded sweatshirt now zipped up to the neck and her shoulders slumped in defeat, she signed in at the desk of the main lodge. My feet felt heavy as we walked down the long, deserted corridor to the counselor's office. The carpet muffled our steps, and all I could hear was my pulse throbbing in my ears.

The counselor looked up from her newspaper as Kate knocked on the doorjamb. "Rene, this is my friend and lawyer, Caroline Spencer," she said, without hesitation. "I'm positive for coke. I used this afternoon."

"Oh?" Rene replied.

"Actually, I'm to blame," I said to her, my words rushing together. "At my recommendation, Kate has been working with some drug agents who are investigating her source. They set up a buy this afternoon. Kate wore a wire, and I listened to the conversation. She had to use cocaine so he wouldn't suspect."

Rene's look told me my excuse had fallen on deaf ears. "Well, let's get the UA and you can talk about it with Adam on Monday," she said to Kate. "I'm afraid you need to go now," she said to me.

I reached out to touch Kate's elbow, but she hurried past me and disappeared into the bathroom across the hall, Rene trailing behind.

I knew the overwhelming helplessness I felt as I walked numbly down the corridor would follow me home.

CHAPTER THIRTY

Monday, November 5

I had phoned The Meadows on Sunday afternoon, but the receptionist had said Kate was in a meeting and couldn't be disturbed. Although I'd specifically asked her to do so, Kate hadn't returned my call.

Kate didn't call Monday morning either. But Adam Larken did.

"What in hell were you thinking?" he demanded.

"What do you mean?" I said, although, in truth, I knew full well what he meant. His question was the same one I'd been asking myself for thirty-six hours.

"When you asked my opinion about Kate providing information against her source, you mentioned testimony. You never mentioned a set-up. You never mentioned she'd be expected to be around or handle cocaine. That was completely irresponsible!"

"When I discussed it with you, we never intended for Kate to do anything but talk. Things just developed."

"Whatever. I called Monica Smith-Kellor this morning to report the positive urine sample, just as I promised the judge I would. You can sort it all out with her. But you need to know this has been a big set-back for your friend."

His words stung. I'm my own most strident critic, but I come undone when an outsider judges me harshly. *Let it go*, I told myself—without success. My stomach knotted. The light-headed, almost out-of-body feeling that often accompanies my panic attacks overcame me. *Let. It. Go. Do not let this derail you. Breathe.*

Without knowing it, Rosalee saved me with a stack of mail. "It's early today," she said, breezing into my office. "And no surprises, which is always good news on a Monday."

That little human connection—and a whiff of her Clinique Happy perfume—brought me out of myself and gave me the confidence to move forward. *Bless you, Rose*, I said to myself after she'd gone.

I had no desire to discuss Saturday's fiasco with Kate's pretrial services officer, but it was inevitable. I dialed her office. "Ms. Smith-Kellor is in court," the receptionist said. "I expect her back in a couple of hours."

I left her a voice message and went to find a newspaper. Not surprisingly, there had been nothing in the Sunday *State Journal* about Joe Ames' arrest, but I hoped to find an article today. Again, nothing. I called George Cooper's office and learned he, too, was out. *Hopefully Monica and George are together, locking up that son-of-a-bitch.*

After lunch I found an e-mail from Julie Wutherspoon which read, "Important—Call me ASAP." There was also a note from Rosalee that Monica had called back, with "bad news" written on the bottom. I kept my door open, listening for Rosalee to return to her desk, and dialed Julie's extension. Voice mail.

"Rose, what does 'bad news' mean?" I asked when she got back a few minutes later.

"Ms. Smith-Kellor said she'd be in the rest of the afternoon so you should be able to reach her. But she also said she'd be faxing over a violation report and a petition to revoke Kate's bail. Judge Brillstein's secretary told her he wants the hearing tomorrow afternoon."

What next? "Is it—"

"No, the fax isn't here yet. I was just down the hall checking it when you came in. Sheila knows it's important, and she'll bring it over as soon as it rolls in."

"Thanks," I said. "I'm sorry I'm grumpy. This has been a pretty shitty few days."

I tried George Cooper again—he'd gotten us into this mess, and he'd damn well better have the key to keeping Kate out of jail. His secretary responded with unmasked pique. "I told you I'd give him your message as soon as he returned. Which he hasn't."

"I'm sorry to bother you again," I replied, feeling like a third-grader caught talking in class. "It's a matter of some urgency."

"I'll have him call you when he gets back."

Rosalee brought in the fax from Monica Smith-Kellor just as I put down the phone. Only three paragraphs, the memo reported Kate gave a urine sample to The Meadows staff on Saturday, which tested positive for cocaine. The pretrial services officer recommended revocation of her bail.

Magistrate Judge Brillstein's signature was scrawled across the bottom of the petition for the hearing, along with a notation that it had been scheduled for four o'clock tomorrow afternoon. Nowhere was it mentioned *why* Kate had used cocaine.

George Cooper called a few minutes later. "Sorry I'm out of breath," he said. "My secretary said it was urgent. What's up?"

"What's up is Pretrial Services is petitioning to revoke my client's bail for using cocaine."

"Oh, shit!"

"Oh, shit, is right. I'm counting on your help with this."

"Just because she's cooperating with us doesn't give her license to use coke. The judge has every right to revoke."

"You haven't listened to the tape?"

"What tape?"

"The tape-recording of the controlled buy on Saturday—"

"Controlled buy?" Cooper said. "Last I heard, the guys were debriefing your client on Thursday. Who set up the buy, and who did they buy from?"

My internal alarms blared. *How could he not know about this?*

"Carter Ellingson was in on it, but Rick Shelton seemed to be in charge and his coworker wired Kate up. She bought two ounces of coke from Joe Ames—after he made her sample it. Carter said you'd be filing a federal complaint against Ames yesterday or today."

"Shelton. That fucking cowboy. He knows federal defendants aren't allowed to do controlled buys without specific permission from the judge. He took advantage of the fact that Ellingson's new and doesn't work drug cases."

Can this situation get any worse? "George, if you didn't know about the buy or about Ames' arrest, did anyone actually file the complaint against him?"

"Hold on."

For five minutes I sat, irritated beyond words, as Cooper left the phone to seek an answer. I bit at a hangnail, drawing blood, and fumbled through my purse for a tissue to blot it. Finding none, I used the hem of my blazer and chastised myself for doing so.

Vowing to give Cooper ten more minutes before I hung up, I watched the digital clock tick away. He came back in the nick of time.

"Sorry. My wife and I were out of town for a long weekend, and our flight last night got cancelled. We just got back this morning, so I wasn't up to speed. Turns out the on-call attorney, Victoria Sanchez, pulled things together and filed the complaint against Ames yesterday. I spoke to her a minute ago, right after Ames' initial appearance in court."

I sensed there was worse news to come. "And?"

"The complaint charged him with the sale of cocaine to an 'unnamed' confidential informant. Victoria said Rick Shelton wrote the affidavit to support the complaint, but he didn't specify Kate was the informant, and Victoria didn't ask for the name. Carter Ellingson was there when they did the paperwork, too. He told her Ames was believed to be the supplier of the drugs that killed Yvonne Pritchard, but

Detective Connaboy wanted another corroborating witness before he made his case."

"So the criminal complaint charged Ames with only one small deal, namely the two ounces he sold Kate on Saturday? And it didn't mention the very important fact that Ames sold coke to the dead girl?" I asked, trying to control my temper.

"Yeah. We'll indict him with the more aggravating facts, but the grand jury doesn't convene until next Monday."

"Please don't tell me the magistrate released him today."

"No, he didn't. Victoria moved for detention and a three-day continuance for the detention hearing. But Magistrate Brillstein only agreed to set it over until tomorrow afternoon because defense counsel pitched a bitch. We've gotta get our ducks in a row on this one."

"So what happens to Kate?" I asked.

He paused before answering. A pregnant pause, filled with foreboding. "That's another thing I'm sorry about," he said. "Victoria Sanchez got the call about the petition to re-voke your client's bail and saw the judge set it for a hearing tomorrow. She looked at the docket sheet, realized this was your client's second revocation hearing, and—"

"George, tell me she didn't get an arrest warrant."

"She did—it's office policy. If I'd been here, I would've made an exception. But she didn't know Kate was cooperating. While I had you on hold, I tried to recall the warrant, but the marshals just served it. I'm sorry."

"They arrested her?"

"A few minutes ago. At the treatment center."

I wanted to scream and cry. My friend would be spending another night at the Dane County Jail. And she'd come to court tomorrow wearing the hideous orange jumpsuit that made her look guiltier than hell. And I'd been powerless to stop any of this.

"Caroline, you've got my promise: I'll oppose revocation with everything I've got. And if it's any consolation, I'll be in as much trouble with Judge Brillstein as Kate."

I'm frickin' tired of being powerless. It's time to get control of this situation. "I'll need a copy of the tape to prepare for tomorrow's hearing," I said to Cooper.

"Okay. I'll call Ellingson and have him dub you a copy. I'll have them get it over to you by ten o'clock tomorrow. Okay?"

"No. I need it before then. I'll have a messenger at Ellingson's office at four this afternoon to pick it up."

"You got it—I'll get them right on it. And I really am sorry about all of this. It was irresponsible of Shelton to set up the buy, and I should've given stricter instructions about the investigation."

Carter Ellingson called frantically a few minutes later. He'd been ordered by George Cooper to copy the tape, but it was in DCI custody. Rick Shelton was out of his office, so Ellingson couldn't access the tape.

"I happen to know Shelton is never incommunicado," I said with more authority than I felt. "Call him. Page him. I don't care how you do it. But by three-fifteen today, I expect a call telling me where my messenger should pick up the tape at four."

Rick Shelton personally delivered a copy of the tape to me at four-fifteen. "Sorry I'm a bit late," he said with a smug grin as he handed me the cassette. "Street construction, you know."

More like you're a passive-aggressive asshole. "Whatever." I'd made my point, and it was better to have the tape today than tomorrow. Rosalee had agreed to stay late to transcribe it.

I stopped by the jail to see Kate before heading home, but she was still in the booking area and couldn't have visitors.

Lily was playing at a neighbor's and David sat at the kitchen counter reading the newspaper when I walked in.

"What's wrong?" he asked as I collapsed onto the stool beside him.

"Am I that transparent?"

"'Fraid so."

I told him about the petition to revoke Kate's bail, about her arrest and tomorrow's hearing. "On top of that, I had a message to call Julie and I haven't been able to reach her. I tried several times."

"Any idea what it's about?" he asked with a look of alarm.

"She said it was important but nothing more. I've had an uneasy feeling about it all afternoon."

—⚏—

The phone rang while I was peeling potatoes for dinner. Lily answered in the family room and yelled, "Mom—it's for you."

Drying my hands on a dishtowel, I grabbed for the handset in the kitchen.

"It's Julie. Sorry I couldn't get back to you earlier. I was in trial on a messy custody case. Is David home?"

"Yes," I said warily. *This doesn't sound like good news.* "Why?"

"It's a decision you both need to make, so I thought it'd be easier to explain it once," she said. I heard her shuffling papers in the background.

I called to him, my heart racing, "David, pick up the extension, please." I sat heavily on a stool and reached for the glass of wine I'd poured earlier.

"I'm gathering you didn't read the medical report," Julie said when David picked up.

"No," he said. "We decided we didn't want to know the baby's gender."

"Gender?" she asked. "Oh. You thought that's what I meant about keeping you in suspense. No—Miriam's not far enough along for that."

"Julie," I said with exasperation, silently cursing her limited social skills. "What's going on?"

"At the last exam, the doc was suspicious she might be carrying more than one infant. The ultrasound exam this morning confirmed it: It's twins."

"Twins!" I said, and, with the sudden realization I held a cordless phone, walked into the family room.

"And everything's okay?" David asked.

"Yes and yes," Julie said. "Miriam's pretty small, so it may get dicey further along. But everything looks good so far. My question is, do you still want to proceed with the adoption?"

David and I looked at each other, grinning.

"Yes," we said simultaneously.

Lily, who'd been watching us with her usual concern and curiosity, ran over to me and tugged at my elbow. "What's going on?" she asked.

"The baby is two babies—we're going to have twins," I said to her. Then back to Julie, "I'll call you tomorrow. We need to celebrate."

Lily expressed none of the fears she'd had earlier about being displaced in our hearts by a baby, which I found surprising. Two infants would certainly take more time and attention. Perhaps she realized she'd be an integral part of their caregiving and her place in the family was secure. At any rate, the dinner I finally managed to put on the table was a festive one, filled with speculation about whether we'd have a boy and a girl or two boys or two girls, chatter about possible names, and discussion about how we'd convert the guest room into quarters for two.

My mind would not be easily silenced as I tried to sleep. While excited about mothering twins, I was also apprehensive. Haunting memories of being at home with baby Lily and struggling with panic attacks kept nagging at me. And then came the thoughts about Kate and her revocation hearing. Could I convince the judge to release her to The Meadows? Had my irresponsibility in allowing her to be around cocaine caused her to relapse?

About midnight, I bolted up in bed.

"What is it?" David asked with alarm. "Another dream?"

"No, I'm wide awake. I've got to call George Cooper. Kate and Joe Ames are both scheduled for hearings tomorrow afternoon. They'll be in the U.S. Marshal's lock-up at the same time, and I can't let that happen."

CHAPTER THIRTY-ONE

Tuesday, November 6

I sat at my desk reading over the transcript of Kate and Joe Ames' encounter when George Cooper returned my frantic message.

"I got your voice mail, and I'll make sure the deputies keep your client separated from Ames," he said.

"With all due respect, George, I'd like to talk with someone myself. Kate told the cops he's responsible for Yvonne Pritchard's death. She also set him up to get busted. I can't have them anywhere near one another. Can you ring the marshal in on a three-way?"

"I'll try. Hold on."

Within a minute, Cooper connected the conference call, and we got it resolved. Kate would be kept in a holding cell on a different floor from the lock-up. The marshal agreed to have a deputy with her at all times. *Thank you, God.*

In addition to the offensive jumpsuit, Kate wore a grim expression when I visited her at the jail that morning. "What the fuck happened?" she asked. "I cooperate, tell them everything I know, set up the guy I love, and get arrested in return? No wonder the government's losing the war on drugs."

"This is your second bail revocation hearing, and it's the U.S. Attorney's policy to issue arrest warrants after more than one violation. George Cooper wasn't around to authorize a waiver."

"I would've shown up for the hearing."

"I know."

"So how does it look?" Kate asked, her voice barely audible through the visitor's telephone.

"I haven't a clue," I said. "Cooper's promised to argue vigorously against revocation. But, as you already know, Stan Brillstein has a mind of his own. This may be a battle rather than a skirmish."

The wretched look in Kate's eyes told me she hadn't wanted to hear the truth any more than I'd wanted to say it.

"Let's talk about your testimony," I said.

"Testimony?" she asked, her voice quivering. What a different Kate Daniels than the one I had known a year or two ago. Gone was the poise and self-confidence that, cocaine-induced or otherwise, she had always exuded.

"I don't think I can do it," she said.

"Yes, you can. I'm not going to put you on the stand unless I have to. But it may be necessary for you to describe how much you feared for your safety when Ames became suspicious of you."

She inclined her head backward and closed her eyes. "You're so naive, Caroline. I wasn't afraid for my safety. I was fearful of losing my freedom for a dirty UA, and I could honestly protest a bit on some level. I knew if I didn't sample it Joe wouldn't sell to me and the bust wouldn't go down. And I *wanted* to use the cocaine. I wanted to escape to Costa Rica, or even to the McDonald's restroom, with the whole two ounces. There's only one thing that brought me to my senses and made me say the arrest signal. While I was looking at the coke, Joe started feeling me up."

I felt like the wind had been knocked out of me. *How many times do I need to be reminded about her powerlessness over cocaine before I finally get it?* "Okay, Kate, I won't put you on the stand. Let me go get ahold of Adam and see if he'll testify on your behalf."

Now she looked down at her lap.

"Another thing," I said, "Joe Ames has a detention hearing at three today, so you'll be at the federal courthouse at the same time. They're making arrangements to transport and hold you separately. But if you see him, don't say anything."

No response.

"Kate, it's important. Not a word to him, okay?"

"Okay."

When Kate left the visiting booth, I sat for a moment, rolling my neck and doodling on my legal pad. *What in God's name do I do?* I had planned to argue in court that Kate had used cocaine out of fear, but it wasn't true. I had never intentionally lied to a judge before, and I didn't want to start now. But I had to try not to incriminate my client.

—⁂—

At four o'clock, George Cooper was still absent from the courtroom. I'd hoped to catch him in the hallway to hear what had happened at Joe Ames' detention hearing, but he was nowhere to be found.

"My schedule is tight," Judge Brillstein said as he took the bench, looking up to see Cooper rushing in. "I'm glad everyone was able to make it. When I released Ms. Daniels to the treatment program less than a month ago, I made it clear I would not tolerate illegal drug use, and I'm not about to delay dealing with it. Ms. Smith-Kellor has submitted a report indicating the defendant in fact used cocaine three days ago. Ms. Spencer, does your client dispute that?"

"No, Your Honor."

"I'll tell you flat out I'm inclined to revoke her bail. Unfortunately, I'm required to hear argument," he said sardonically. "Mr. Cooper, your position?"

"Your Honor," Cooper said hurriedly, as if to get it over with, "the government recommends Ms. Daniels be continued on pretrial release. There are some circumstances of which the Court is not aware: Ms. Daniels was cooperating with law enforcement authorities when the cocaine usage occurred."

The judge glared at him. "What?"

Carter Ellingson and George Cooper sat together at the prosecution table wearing hangdog expressions that would have been funny if not for the circumstances.

"Judge," Cooper said, "last week I approached Ms. Spencer and asked whether her client would be willing to cooperate in the investigation of a suspected cocaine dealer with whom we had reason to believe she was acquainted. She consented. I arranged for Ms. Daniels to be interviewed by Special Agent Ellingson here, along with DCI Agent Richard Shelton, Lieutenant Tom Robbins from the county sheriff's department, and a couple of detectives from the Madison PD. I regret I did not make the time to attend myself."

At the mention of Shelton's name, Judge Brillstein shook his head several times. But he held his tongue while Cooper continued.

"During the course of the interview, it was suggested that Ms. Daniels contact the suspect on a monitored telephone to arrange for the purchase of—"

"Mr. Cooper," the judge said, "you and all of your agents are well aware of this court's prohibition against using defendants as active informants. Just how did such a suggestion come to be posed to Ms. Daniels?"

I cringed inside. Kate's telephone call from T.G.I. Friday's to Joe Ames was a clear violation of her bail conditions. If George Cooper mentioned it, it would be obvious to the judge that Kate had been trying to buy cocaine while on pass from The Meadows.

"Your Honor, as I said, I was not present at the interview nor have I seen written reports from those who were. But Agent Ellingson informs me Agent Shelton inquired whether the suspect would still be willing to sell the defendant cocaine. When Ms. Daniels said she thought he would, Agent Shelton suggested they set him up. Unfortunately, neither

Agent Ellingson nor Ms. Spencer was aware of the Court's order against defendants' participating in such investigations."

"How is this possible?" Brillstein barked.

"With all due respect, Your Honor," Cooper continued, "the order is somewhat unique to this district—although courts in some other districts are adopting similar policies. In any event, Agent Ellingson is relatively new to this area and was not informed of the prohibition when he came here. You may not be aware of it, but he does not generally work drug crimes, where informants are typically used. And, as for Ms. Spencer, she—"

"...doesn't practice in federal court," Brillstein said. "So she can't be expected to know the rules. It's the old 'I didn't know' defense. Well, you all should have known. And there's no question Agent Shelton knew. I've had him in my courtroom before and made it abundantly clear. I don't see him here today. I've half a mind to hold him in contempt for his blatant disregard of our policy. Nevertheless, I've no desire to prolong the discomfiture of this defendant and her counsel, so let's get on with this. Suffice it to say, Mr. Cooper, I hold you personally responsible for losing control of this investigation.

"Ms. Spencer," the judge went on, "why don't you tell me what happened from there?"

"Yes, Your Honor. Before I begin, I'd like to point out the government promised my client immunity in return for her information and cooperation. I submit anything relative to that cooperation cannot be used against her."

I looked to George Cooper, who nodded and said, "Ms. Spencer's representation is accurate, Your Honor."

"Very well," Brillstein said. "But keep in mind an immunity promise does not give one grounds to use controlled substances. Please proceed."

"On the same afternoon as the interview," I continued, "this past Thursday, my client agreed to make a telephone call to the suspect. The call was monitored and recorded by the agents. She ordered a quantity of cocaine to be picked up on Saturday afternoon, while she was on a five-hour pass from The Meadows. The suspect agreed.

"On Saturday," I said, "we went to the FBI office where an agent fitted my client with a body wire. They searched her car and her person. They found absolutely no contraband. My client met the suspect as arranged, while under the surveillance of the officers. Your Honor, I have a transcript of the conversation, marked 'Defense Exhibit One,' which I'd like to present to the Court."

"No objection," George Cooper said as I handed him and the judge their copies.

"As you can see, the suspect, Ames, was suspicious of my client—"

"Hold on a minute," Brillstein said. "Are you referring to Joseph Ames, the defendant in the case I just heard?"

Oh, shit! I thought. *I shouldn't have mentioned his name.* But there were no spectators in the courtroom, so I took a deep breath and quit berating myself. "Yes, Your Honor," I said.

"All right. That raises more questions, but you may proceed."

"Ames was suspicious," I repeated. "Although my client made excuses not to use cocaine, Ames continued to insist she do so. I submit her refusal to use the drug would have jeopardized the investigation and perhaps her personal safety."

I hurried on so the judge didn't have time to comment.

"My client admitted the use of cocaine immediately when she returned to The Meadows a few hours later. I stood right next to her at the time and can attest to it. She didn't wait for the results of the mandatory urine test. Further, her primary counselor, Adam Larken, is here in court today. He's prepared to testify, if Your Honor wishes to hear directly from him."

"Yes, Ms. Spencer, let's hear from him," Brillstein said. "As I recall, he provided some impressive testimony last time he was here."

I had hoped the judge would simply let me proffer, or summarize, what Adam would say if called to testify. We hadn't had time to rehearse any questions, and I took very seriously the old adage that a lawyer should never ask a witness *any* question without knowing the answer. I hated being unprepared. My stomach churned as I approached the stand and said a silent prayer that Adam's responses would help rather than hurt us.

"Mr. Larken," I said after the standard questions about his identity, "please tell me your initial reaction when you learned about Saturday's events."

"I was furious. Not at Kate, but at you and the cops for allowing her to be in a situation where she would be expected to touch and possibly use cocaine. I considered it very irresponsible of you."

"In hindsight, I agree with you, Mr. Larken. And I know Mr. Cooper does as well. How did Ms. Daniels act when she told you she'd used cocaine?"

"Defeated. She thought it was a major setback. In my opinion, she was genuinely remorseful and very ashamed. I would prefer not to get into our discussions of her thoughts and feelings. But I will give you another opinion: Kathryn Daniels learned something important as a result of this encounter with cocaine. I believe she'll be stronger in recovery as a result. Without prompting from me, Kate volunteered to remain in the program two weeks longer than planned, to solidify her progress. There is space available for her to stay, and it's a move I recommend to virtually any patient who can afford it."

Recalling Kate had used cocaine hours before her admission to The Meadows—which the judge didn't know—I had to carefully word my next question.

"Mr. Larken, have any of my client's other urine samples tested positive for drug usage during her stay at your facility?"

"No."

"Do you believe she's making a sincere effort to recover from her addiction?"

"Yes, I do."

"Thank you," I said to Adam. "Your Honor, I have no further questions."

"Mr. Cooper," Judge Brillstein said, indicating it was the prosecutor's turn to examine the witness.

"No questions, Your Honor."

"Very well," Brillstein said, "I have a few questions of my own. Mr. Larken, what are the chances Ms. Daniels will be able to remain drug free?"

"I'm sorry, sir. I can't answer that."

"Can't or won't?"

"Can't, sir. I have no way of predicting. There are far too many variables. Statistical studies aren't very useful in forecasting behavior for the individual. I do know Ms. Daniels is motivated, bright, has excellent social skills and has positive ties in the community. In my experience, all of those things enhance someone's chances for long-term recovery from addiction. And her willingness to commit to an extended stay at our facility is a good sign."

"Thank you."

George Cooper, having recovered his usual eloquence, argued Kate's cocaine use was situational in nature and unintentional. He urged the Court not to hold my client responsible for his own negligence. He praised Kate's willingness to cooperate with authorities and suggested it was a true sign of her desire to turn her life around. How different, I thought, than when he'd argued for her detention several weeks ago.

When Cooper finished, I stood up to begin my argument.

"Ms. Spencer," Brillstein said, "I don't need to hear anymore. Ms. Daniels, your pretrial release conditions are continued. Please don't make me regret it. I'll be issuing an order as to Mr. Shelton."

Without further comment, he stood and left the courtroom.

Kate turned and hugged me tightly. It was the most spontaneous demonstration of affection I'd ever seen from her. That alone gave me hope for her future.

Kate had to go back to the county jail with the marshals to be booked out. They approached her just as I turned to George Cooper to ask the outcome of Joe Ames' detention hearing.

"Judge Brillstein ordered his release on a property bond," he said, looking down at his shoes. "I expect the sonuvabitch'll be back on the streets tomorrow morning."

Kate couldn't help but hear, and her look of alarm heightened my own aggravation. I threw my pen on the table. "How in the *hell* can this be happening?"

Chapter Thirty-Two

"If you've got time to stop by my office," George Cooper said after the marshals had left the courtroom with Kate, "I'll fill you in on Ames."

I glanced at my watch. "I guess so." Lily had a basketball game after school, and she and David would be home late. Adam Larken had agreed to wait for Kate and give her a ride back to the treatment center.

Cooper's office was disheveled but nonetheless welcoming, like an island of warmth in this otherwise sleek, impersonal sea of a building. The desk chair creaked as he settled into it and rested his feet on the battle-scarred oak desk. "Coke?" he asked.

I sat in his weathered leather club chair in bewildered silence until he handed me a cold can of Coca Cola from the mini-fridge behind his desk. "I thought you were referring to the drug," I said, with a nervous laugh of relief.

He grinned. "There's been altogether too much talk about drugs today. I wish I could offer you a beer. You look like you need one, and I know I do."

I nodded. "So tell me how it is that an asshole like Ames gets released when I've gotta swim against a tidal wave to keep Kate in drug treatment."

"Ed Benson—"

"Ed Benson's representing him?" I sputtered.

"Oh, yeah. And he's worth every penny Ames' wife spent to hire him. He put on a wonderful dog and pony show."

"Meaning?"

"First of all, Ames manages to make jail garb look like something out of fucking GQ. I don't know how he did it, but he's clean-shaven, the jumpsuit looks like it's fresh from the laundry, every hair on his head is neatly trimmed. He's bright-eyed, attentive to the judge, polite beyond words."

He shook his head and took a sip from his can. "Benson's got Ames' wife and mother—in a wheelchair with an oxygen tank, by the way—sitting in the front row, looking like a Grant Wood painting. Salt of the earth folks, not flashy."

"Even if he's got Jesus Christ in his corner, I still don't see how they get beyond the fact that Ames sold the drugs that killed a young woman," I said with exasperation.

Cooper rubbed his forehead with one hand and set his Coke on the desk. "That's the dicey part," he said. "I couldn't give the court any direct evidence about it; all I could do was proffer what our 'unnamed witness' told the cops. Benson argued the judge should disregard the statements because he couldn't cross-examine someone we wouldn't identify. Since Kate hasn't even been before the grand jury yet, and her statement wasn't given under oath, I couldn't argue much about the reliability of our witness."

"Did Benson offer any testimony?"

"Oh, yeah. The mother, between coughing fits, testified she has congestive heart failure and a limited life expectancy. And, of course, her son is one of her primary caregivers. Then the wife testified she needs him to help with the catering business."

"I thought the business was a sham."

"Turns out it is partly legit. Jolene Ames is a graduate of some fancy culinary institute and has a fair number of actual clients."

"And she risks her livelihood to let her husband launder drug proceeds?"

"I think the guy is a sociopath who's able to convince anyone—particularly women—to do whatever he wants. I did manage to get the judge to order a property bond, secured by the ailing mother's house, and a curfew with an electronic ankle bracelet. He'll have to be home by seven o'clock every night. It's not much, but it's better than nothing. And when we indict him on the more serious stuff, maybe we can get the judge to reconsider."

"You need Kate to testify next Monday?"

"Yes. We'll send a subpoena with the exact time, but she should plan on being there the better part of the day. You can come with her and sit in the hall, but you know you can't go into the grand jury room with her, right?"

"Yes, Professor Cooper, I remember that from law school."

"I didn't mean to be condescending. You can't imagine how many lawyers I have to argue with about it. Let me find the report from her interview so you can prep her—make sure we have everything on paper the way she remembers it."

"Okay. I've got an appointment to see her on Friday, and I'll go over it with her."

He shuffled through a stack of papers on the cluttered desk.

"By the way, thanks for your help in court today," I said. I was grateful to have a not-entirely-adversarial relationship with someone working on the other side of the aisle.

"It was the least I could do. I hate getting chewed out by Brillstein—it gives me flashbacks to my Catholic school days—but I had it coming. I should have known Shelton would fuck things up. He crosses the line way too often."

"I threw out a case of his five years ago for failure to Mirandize. I was wondering if he held a grudge."

"Oh, I wouldn't put it past him. But I doubt if his grudge against you had anything to do with his decision-making in this case. Shelton's too myopic. He saw a quick way to make a case against Joe Ames and jumped at it. My only problem now will be arguing against an order of contempt if Brillstein follows through on his threat. Hell, I agree with Brillstein!"

"George, you don't think Shelton would've told Ed Benson that Kate set up the bust, do you?"

My question clearly caught him unawares. "I… I can't imagine that."

I dropped the subject but couldn't help worrying about his less than emphatic answer.

We chatted a while about cops, agents, and lawyers we both knew and about trends in the law. It was an amiable conversation and reminded me how much I missed the camaraderie of the district attorney's office.

"Gee, this has been nice—almost like we're not on opposing teams," I said lightly. "But I've gotta get home."

"Sure. Before you go, though, I've got a couple questions. First, do we have a plea agreement?"

"Plain and simple: yes. Kate doesn't even want me to argue with your loss figures. We need to meet again and sign it, but I'll bring it back to you on Monday. Okay?"

"Great. That answers all my questions. I'm surprised you agree with the numbers, though. I probably shouldn't say it, but I thought our proof on some of the losses was mushy. Like the $18,500 in salary that went to Barbara Hughes and some of the travel vouchers."

"Kate accepts responsibility for all of it."

"How noble. Off the record?" he asked.

"My response is the same both on and off the record."

"Also noble," he said with a knowing chuckle.

"Are you planning to charge Joe Ames with the grant fraud?" I asked.

"We could do it with Kate's help," he said. "But the documentary evidence to back up her testimony is pretty ambiguous. Ames was savvy: He used the account to which the payroll checks were deposited only for that income. He used a debit card to make all the withdrawals, never any written checks. And his signature card on the account doesn't look anything like his known handwriting. I think Ed Benson could make a case he was framed and never personally got any of the proceeds of the fraud."

"Did he report the income on his tax returns?" I asked.

"Yes. There is that, but IRS agents aren't always a big hit with jurors. And the university isn't anxious for any more adverse publicity. We've got an airtight case on the cocaine charges, and the penalty for causing a death is hefty. Plus, the state is prosecuting him for bringing drugs into the jail. He's in deep doo-doo."

"Just so he goes away for a long time," I said, as Cooper walked me to the door.

—∿—

I pulled into the driveway just behind David and Lily. She ran out of his car and bounced up to meet me, her eyes and cheeks flushed with excitement, her body smelling of little-girl sweat.

"Mom! I scored four baskets! Plus the last one made us win the game! It was so cool... you shoulda been there."

"That's wonderful, honey. I'm really proud of you. And I'm sorry I wasn't there to see it."

"Oh, that's okay. Dad says he got it on video. It was just so cool with everybody jumping up and down and hugging me and stuff. Let's go watch it!"

David was no cinematographer, and he'd barely captured the ball reaching the basket. The videotape did depict Lily's exuberance as she celebrated with her teammates, and my heart hurt for not being there to see it in person.

After one replay, Lily hurried over to share the news with Ida McKinley. David and I beamed at each other.

"Can your day top that?" he asked.

"Not a chance. Thank heaven for our simple life in the 'burbs!"

Chapter Thirty-three

—⚒—

Thursday, November 8

"Call nine-one-one," David yelled to me as he burst through our kitchen door around three-thirty, an ashen-faced Lily and her friend Megan in tow. "Tell them it's an attempted child abduction."

I sat at the counter concentrating on a Sudoku puzzle, and I couldn't make sense of what was happening. "What—"

"Do it!" he shouted, bringing me out of my befuddlement. "I'll explain in a minute."

As I reached for the phone, my adrenaline rising precipitously, David knelt in front of Lily, looked her straight in the eye and said in a calm, sure voice, "You're safe, honey. We'll get him."

Gulping air between sobs, she collapsed in his arms.

"Caroline," David said, with almost scary composure, "tell them the suspect's vehicle has Wisconsin plates, number 4769-BYX. It's a late model gray Honda Accord."

I followed his instructions as he rocked Lily back and forth, murmuring in her ear, "It's okay, Pumpkin. It's okay."

When I hung up, David told me in a nutshell what had happened. And before the surreal scene fully became real to me, the cops drove up, sirens blaring. Wide-eyed, Megan jumped up and down with excitement. "They're here already. Cool!"

I shot her a scathing look, which fazed her not at all.

Carrying leggy Lily on one hip, David answered the front door. "Thanks for your quick response, guys. C'mon in."

He ushered the two fresh-faced sheriff's deputies, one blond and the other Latino, into the living room and introduced them to the girls. "They're second grade classmates and were walking home from the bus stop, which is three blocks down—at the entrance to our cul-de-sac," he said. "The incident occurred about half a block from our house. The suspect was driving toward me as I drove onto the street, and I took note of the car because there are rarely vehicles here we don't recognize."

Thank heaven for David, I thought, and I sensed the deputies did too. They were clearly in over their heads. Deputy Rodriguez's hands trembled as he fumbled for his pen and notebook. But I felt a wave of gratitude toward him as he regarded Lily with kindness and respect. She was plastered to her father's side and still hadn't uttered a word.

"Lily, honey," David said, taking her hand in his, "please tell these officers what happened—"

"I'll tell it," Megan said, squirming on the couch beside me.

"There'll be plenty of questions for you, too," David said to her. "But let's hear from Lily first."

Lily swallowed hard. "I saw the car when we came around the corner," she said, repeatedly twisting a lock of hair around her finger. "As we got closer, I realized it was a strange car, but then I saw the man looking at a map and talking on the phone. So I thought maybe he was just lost..."

I watched, paralyzed, as she buried her face against David's side.

"You're doing fine, Lily," Deputy Rodriguez said. "Please tell us what happened next."

She half-turned in his direction and said in a whisper, "He... he was parked across the street from us. He rolled down the window and called to me."

Another pause.

"I know it's not easy," David said, "but we need you to tell us what he said."

Unable to control herself anymore, Megan finished the story. "He asked her, 'Are you Lily Spencer?' Then he said, 'I don't want to hurt you. I just want to give you this note for your mom.' He tried to hand Lily the note, but she wouldn't go near the car. So I did. He gave me the note and drove away. I was reading it to her when her dad came home."

"Lily, is that how you remember it, too?" Deputy Rodriguez asked.

She nodded. "I was so scared!"

"You were right not to go near the car," he said to her. "And where's the note?"

"It's on the kitchen counter," David said. "Caroline will show you."

Apparently relieved to have a task, Deputy Johnson jumped up to accompany me.

I hadn't noticed the note before. In stark black lettering on a half sheet of plain white copy paper was scrawled, "I know where Lily lives and I know her REAL mommy is a snitch."

My knees threatened to give way. I put my hands on the counter to steady myself.

Deputy Johnson reached for the note.

"No—don't touch it!" I shrieked.

Above his starched uniform collar, his still-pimply neck flushed with embarrassment, and I felt a pang of guilt for calling him out.

"I'm sorry for yelling," I said in a more moderate tone. "It's just that I really want to catch this fucker."

"No, you're right," he stammered. "I'm going to run out to the car for an evidence bag. I'll be right back."

When I was satisfied the evidence was secure, I headed back into the living room. "We need to call Detective Connaboy and George Cooper," I said to David. "I think I know who did this."

The girls and I sat in the living room while the officers talked with David behind closed doors in the dining room: They didn't want Lily and Megan to be influenced by his description of the perpetrator.

Megan swung her legs back and forth, repeatedly kicking the bottom of the couch with her heels. Annoyed, I put my hand on her knees to stop her.

"What's a snitch, Mom?" Lily asked a minute or so later.

"A tattletale," Megan said with an I-know-something-you-don't-know look. "But what did the note mean about your 'real' mommy?"

Stunned by her forthright question, neither Lily nor I answered. We were literally saved by the bell when Megan's mother, alarmed to see the squad car in our driveway, rang the doorbell and stormed in the front door.

I gave her the abbreviated version of what had transpired, and, to my great relief, she kept Megan in check.

Despite her bluster, Megan was unable to give many details of "the man." She knew he was white and thought he wore a black shirt. In contrast, Lily described his dark-brown hair, green eyes, gleaming white teeth, and the deep, smooth voice with which he'd called to her. Lily said he sat tall enough in the seat for her to see he wore a black, silky shirt. I had no doubt she could identify the bad guy in a police line-up, but I prayed it wouldn't come to that.

Lily was less anxious by the time Detective Doug Connaboy arrived and assuaged our fears: Joe Ames, driving the vehicle described by David, had been spotted and apprehended in Madison, only ten minutes after our nine-one-one call. He'd immediately invoked his right to remain silent, but Doug expressed confidence they had enough evidence to hold him and, at the very least, to revoke his bail. He took detailed statements from David, Lily and Megan, closed his notebook with satisfaction, and stood up to leave.

I leaned against the wall in the foyer as we said goodbye, relieved beyond words that Ames was back in jail and trusting that Doug would do everything in his power to keep him there.

—∽∽—

After dinner David, Lily and I lingered at the table, each of us drained and distracted by our own thoughts.

Lily looked up from her plate, her lower lip trembling. "How can my real mom be a tattletale?" she asked. "She's dead."

David and I exchanged looks of astonishment.

We had told Lily she was adopted as soon as she was old enough to understand. She knew her birth mother had been unable to care for her but had loved her enough to arrange for her placement with our "forever family," where she would grow up safe, happy and loved. She knew David and I believed God meant for her to be our daughter. She didn't know we knew her birth mother—and wouldn't know that for several years.

"What makes you say that?" I asked with equanimity I did not feel.

Silence.

"Honey," David said, "Mom asked you a question we really need you to answer. What makes you say your birth mom is dead?"

"Well... I saw this movie at Anna's house..."

Frickin' Anna. This is all we need.

"Go on, honey," David said. "Tell us about the movie."

"Well... this woman who wasn't married was gonna have a baby, and she found out she had cancer. And she wouldn't let the doctors give her medicine to cure it because it would hurt the baby. And she knew she was gonna die so she found a family to adopt the baby. And Anna said that's probably what happened with my real mom."

I had no idea what to say. Although clearly stunned, David found words. "Anna's wrong, honey. Your biological mom wasn't sick when she arranged for your adoption. She couldn't care for you because she was single and immature. Do you know what immature means?"

Lily nodded.

"Do you have more questions?" he asked.

"If she's alive, why hasn't she come to meet me?"

Her forlorn look cut me to the quick.

David sniffed back tears. "The adoption rules in your case don't allow that to happen until you're older—and then only if you both want to meet each other. Mom and I will help you do that, if you want, when the time comes."

"It doesn't seem fair," Lily said, looking down at the dinner she'd barely touched.

"Maybe not," David said. "But the social workers and the judge who made the rules thought it would be best for everybody."

She picked up her fork and poked at her cold mac and cheese.

"What else, Lily?" I asked.

"That man, Mr. Ames... How does he know you're not my real mom? And how does he know she tattles?"

I gasped. *She's right! How does he know?*

CHAPTER THIRTY-FOUR

Friday, November 9

I didn't know David when he was a SEAL, and he'd shared next to nothing with me about those bygone missions. But when I met him in the kitchen that morning, I caught a glimpse of what he must have been like.

Every trace of softness was gone, every emotion set aside, replaced by steely determination to accomplish his mission—to protect Lily.

"Caroline," he said, "We can't trust anyone else with our daughter's physical safety and emotional well-being. I was awake most of last night, making mental lists of what you and I need to do today to keep her safe and sound."

I nodded. "Tell me."

"First, we meet with Kate to determine what information she's disclosed to Ames about this family and how that might impact the situation. Second, we meet with Doug Connaboy and any other local cops who can help us gather and present evidence of witness intimidation. Finally, we meet with George Cooper and any involved agents to get Ames' federal bail revoked. We don't do this by phone or fax or e-mail. We do it in person."

His dispassionate yet impassioned recitation of the plan sent shivers through my body. I admired his ability to remain calm and rational in a time of crisis, especially since I'd tossed and turned all night in fruitless thought. I'd follow him through hell on this undertaking.

"I agree completely," I said. "I already have an appointment to see Kate at The Meadows at nine-thirty. Can you make it then?"

"Absolutely. That will give us time to take Lily to school and talk with the principal before we go."

"She's up and rolling," I said, reaching to pour a cup of coffee. "She's acting like nothing's happened."

"One foot in front of the other," he said, with a hint of his non-SEAL persona.

"Want some?" I asked, inclining my head toward the coffee.

But the commando was back. "No, thank you. While I'm in the shower, please get me Connaboy and Cooper's phone numbers. I want to make sure they're available to see us."

Morning was never Lily's finest hour, and her demeanor today was much like usual. She stared into her cereal bowl, occasionally lifting a spoonful to her mouth. She spilled milk on the counter and whined for a second glass of OJ. But even she took note when David appeared, dressed for the day.

"Wow, Dad. You look... different."

The tailored navy wool suit he'd gotten on a trip to Rome, the pale blue shirt, and the muted silk tie combined to say, "I mean business."

He kissed Lily on the head. "Almost ready, kiddo? Your mom and I will drive you to school today so we can talk with the principal about what happened yesterday."

"Why, Daddy?" I could hear the concern in her voice. Lily hated to make waves, and a conference with the principal was bound to churn up her stomach.

"I'm sure Megan and the other kids will be talking about it, and Mr. Wendig will want to hear it from us."

"But that man's in jail, right?" she said, her eyes welling with tears.

No soft platitudes or hugs of condolence today.

"Yes, Lily," he said. "He's in jail. And your mom and I intend to make sure that's where he stays."

His unwavering assurance quelled her tears.

—⁂—

The color drained from Kate's face as we walked into the conference room. Her gaze flashed between me and David and she sat forward on the edge of her chair. "What's wrong?"

David and I took chairs across the table from her.

"Lily's safe, no thanks to you," David said, his stony gaze pinning her to the wall. "Joe Ames is in jail, where he belongs. Now tell us how he knows about her."

"I don't—"

"No bullshit, Kate," I said, adopting David's unyielding tone. "For God's sake, tell us what you told him about Lily."

She hung her head and ran her hands through her hair. "You've got to believe how sorry I am," she said.

David and I exchanged a look—a look that said, "Let's be quiet and wait for *her* to talk."

Eventually she did. "It happened one night, a couple years ago. Joe was at my place. We'd polished off a bottle of wine and done some lines of coke. He said we should have unprotected sex so we could truly experience the sensations."

Her eyes drifted off, as if she was replaying the scene in her mind, and then she went on. "And I said something like 'I won't make that mistake again.' He got all curious and convinced me when you really love someone you don't keep secrets from them."

"So you told him you'd had a baby?" I asked, my patience having long since abandoned me.

"Uh-huh. I said I'd had a baby about five years earlier and placed her for adoption. I knew right away I shouldn't have said it. In fact, I made him leave—and didn't even go to bed with him."

A vein in David's temple throbbed. "We don't give a rat's ass about your sex life," he said with undisguised rancor. "What else did you tell him?"

Kate sobbed. "He kept pressing me for information. I finally told him her name was Lily and that she'd been adopted by friends, but I wouldn't say who or where. Then, at a party at my house about a year ago, Joe overheard you talking about Lily and put two and two together."

"And then you told him where we live," David said with a quiet and terrible grimace. "We've always had unlisted numbers and, for obvious reasons, religiously guard our privacy. And you fuckin' told him."

Her head shot up. "He knows where you live? I swear, I never told him that. Is that what this is about? Did he come to your house? Did he hurt Lily?"

Kate's distress, which I knew in my heart was genuine, neutralized much of my anger.

David paused to regard her, and I sensed he, too, believed her. With newfound calm, he told her about Ames' contact with Lily and Megan, the note, and the subsequent apprehension only a few miles from our house. With each detail, Kate became more and more agitated.

"The motherfucker..." she yelled, tears streaming down her reddened cheeks. "Why is he doing this? The cops pretended to arrest me when they arrested him so he wouldn't know I was wearing a wire. And then I did end up in jail that night—he had to have heard about it."

"It's pretty clear to me he doesn't want you testifying before the federal grand jury," I said. "He knows you can link him to way more cocaine than he was busted for. And worst of all, he knows you can link him to Yvonne Pritchard's death."

"How would he know I've agreed to testify? That's supposed to be a secret, isn't it?"

"It doesn't take a rocket scientist to figure out who they're calling as witnesses," I said. "And he sent you a crystal clear warning to say no to their call."

"The cops can take the subpoena and stick it up their asses. I'm not testifying if it puts Lily at risk. I'd rather serve the thirty-year maximum sentence than do that," she said, shaking her head. "I deserve it. I'm the one who brought her into this."

David stood up and walked slowly around the room, his hands clasped loosely behind his back. I could tell he was weighing his words. "No, Kate. We need you to testify to put this arrogant prick in prison. He's operated with impunity for a long time and thinks he's invincible. But he's gotten careless lately, first with the jail guard, and now trying to get at you through Lily. He didn't do his homework nearly well enough when he picked us to fuck with."

"But Lily—"

"We'll keep her safe. You just need to do your part to bring him down. Okay?"

She blotted her tears with the sleeve of her t-shirt and nodded. "Okay."

The original purpose of my scheduled meeting with Kate was to have her review and sign the plea agreement. David went out to the car to make some phone calls while we accomplished that task.

Kate did not meet my eyes as I explained the written document. She scrawled her name in the signature block, and left the room with a mumbled goodbye. I sensed her shame, but felt no compulsion to alleviate it.

I got to the parking lot to find David sitting on the hood of our car, his cell phone propped between his shoulder and his ear, jotting notes on a legal pad. "Do you mind driving?" he asked when he hung up. "I need to make a few more calls."

When he finished his calls, I pulled over onto the shoulder of the country road, by happenstance in front of a red brick farmhouse surrounded by lush evergreens. *How incongruous, I thought, dealing with life and death issues in the midst of idyllic Americana.*

My heart was in my throat. I put the car in park and turned to David. "We have to tell Lily, don't we?" I asked.

"Yes, we do."

"Do you think she's prepared to hear the truth?"

"It wouldn't be my choice to do this now. But there could very well be testimony in open court about the note Ames gave her and his attempt to intimidate the 'real mommy.' If the public's going to hear it, Lily deserves to hear it first. And we'll just have to prepare her."

I nodded numbly and pulled back onto the highway. We had a lot to accomplish in the hours ahead.

Thankfully, the judicial system worked like clockwork. David and Megan's mom went with a sheriff's investigator to the kids' school, and both girls picked Joe Ames out of a photo line-up. With that ammunition, along with David's positive identification and the arresting officer's report, Deputy District Attorney Jerry Alexander filed a criminal complaint in Dane County Circuit Court charging Ames with intimidation of a witness.

We met with George Cooper, who got another arrest warrant for Ames—mostly as a precaution in the unlikely event the county released him—and filed a motion to revoke the federal bail.

At the end of the day, even I felt confident Ames would remain behind bars.

It was almost six o'clock when we picked Lily up at the after school program, and she deserved a treat. "What say we head to Perkins and get breakfast for dinner?" I said with a smile she clearly recognized as false. But it wasn't often we sanctioned pancakes and syrup this late in the day, and, despite her precociousness, she was, at heart, a seven-year-old kid.

We sat in a booth, and David and I watched with distracted pleasure as she poured on the gooey maple-flavored nectar, enjoying every bite. I'd ordered a patty melt and had to force myself to eat half.

On a sugar high, Lily jabbered the whole way home, stopping only to sing along with some songs she recognized on the oldies station. I spent the ride ringing my hands and silently rehearsing the conversation to come.

"C'mon in the family room," I said to her when we got home. "There's something we need to talk about."

"But I've got math homework."

"I'll write a note to your teacher if you don't get it done."

Perhaps exhausted from his take-charge day, David passed me the baton, nodding to me over Lily's head as she sat between us on the couch. She smelled of maple syrup, and I could see two or three sticky strands in her hair, which, for some odd reason, warmed me.

She squirmed a minute, then gave me a puzzled look, as if to say, "What's up?"

"Lily, you asked us some questions yesterday about your biological mom, and we put you off. That wasn't fair—"

"It's okay—"

"Honey, please let me finish. Your dad and I were very angry with the man—Mr. Ames—who came to our street and scared you and Megan. He wasn't there to hurt you or kidnap you. He was there because of a court case I'm working on—"

"Aunt Kate's case, right?"

I nodded. Oh, how I wished we could avoid this talk for about ten years. There was no easy way to go at the truth. *Out with it.*

"Lily, Kate is your biological mom," I said.

Her eyes grew wide and bright. And she grinned. "I knew it!"

CHAPTER THIRTY-FIVE

Monday, November 12

"She said she knew it and smiled a big Cheshire cat smile," I told Dr. Brownhill. "I don't know what to make of it."

"Some pretty well respected psychologists and physicians believe a child learns everything there is to know about its mother in utero: her voice, her smell, her mannerisms, her expressions. Lily's had periodic contact with Kate all these years, so it doesn't surprise me she kept those memories alive. And, when told her birth mother's identity, she had an 'I knew it' feeling."

"And what of her apparent happiness about it, especially in light of all Kate's troubles?"

"Validation perhaps? The pleasure of a mystery solved? I can't say for sure. But feel free to ask her how she felt, and why. It'll help her sort it all out."

"I will."

"I presume you told Lily about Kate's addiction?"

"Yes. We said Kate began using drugs after I knew her in college, while she was in medical school, and continued until she got pregnant. We told Lily Kate's drug usage was one sign of her immaturity, a quality Kate herself recognized, and it made her realize it would be best to place Lily for adoption."

"Do you think she understood?"

"At least to some degree. But I confessed to Lily that I can't really understand why Kate went back to using after her birth or how someone could love drugs more than their family, and their job, and their freedom. I was going to tell her addiction is a disease—like cancer or pneumonia—that, left untreated, will get worse. But since I can't even wrap my head around that notion, I decided not to go there. At least not yet."

I paused to take a sip of tea and leaned my head back against the oversized chair cushion.

"You don't buy into the disease model?"

"I have a tough time with it. Sometimes I think it's an excuse to justify bad behavior and lack of personal responsibility. You know, 'I'm an addict and I can't help myself.'"

"Sounds like you've got some unresolved anger toward your friend."

"Oh, yeah. More than a little. But at the same time, I love her, I feel sorry for her, and I feel indebted to her." I regretted the words as soon as they rolled off my tongue.

"Ah, the debt…" Dr. Brownhill said, shifting in her chair.

"I really don't want to rehash it again," I said, with a too quick smile. I could feel tension in my facial muscles and made a conscious effort to relax. *Let's just move on—please!*

"Your choice," she said evenly. "Does Kate know you told Lily the truth?"

"Uh-huh. I called her last night after Lily went to bed. She understood. Amazingly, she focused most on the practicalities of it all: whether we'd still let her see Lily, what Lily would call her, whether we'd tell our parents and hers."

"Do you think those are unreasonable questions?"

"No, but not the most important questions. I told her I didn't foresee any changes: she'll still see Lily, who, by the way, told us she wants to continue referring to her as Aunt Kate. I told her I didn't see the need for any of the grandparents, biological or adoptive, to know about it, since they're all miles away. I also told her my primary focus is on making Lily feel secure—to know she can tell us or ask us anything, and we'll always love her."

"How are you feeling now that Lily and Kate know about one another?"

"To be honest, I'm feeling a lot more pressure. The realization hit me in the middle of the night: the stakes involved with my legal defense of Kate have been ratcheted up. The harsher the sentence she receives, the harder it will be on Lily."

"Do you really think that's true?"

"I know it's true. We told Lily that Kate stole money from the university to buy drugs, that she'll have to go to court soon to face the consequences, and that my job is to help her get a fair sentence. When we got done, she looked at me and said, 'Mommy, I hope you can convince the judge not to send Aunt Kate to prison.' I'd say the stakes have gone up."

CHAPTER THIRTY-SIX

—∞—

Friday, November 23

Kate left The Meadows on a sunny, cool afternoon. I went to her farewell ceremony—a joyous yet tearful event called the Rites of Passage—a group meeting of past and current patients and staff, focusing on Kate's progress and the tasks she'd faced.

The intense emotional attachment these people had with one another rankled me at first, and I didn't know why. Then I realized I was jealous—jealous of their bond and jealous that these people could do more for Kate than I, her close friend and lawyer.

Kate's eyes glimmered with tears and pride as she listened.

A sixty-something, heavyset black woman named Bernice, who'd been discharged about a week earlier, described her own homecoming.

"Child, it was hard," she said, shaking her head so hard her chins waggled. "I felt pretty confident when I walked out the door here. But when I walked in the door at home and saw the mess Walter had left and the bills piled up and the refrigerator empty and the answering machine blinking, I said 'Lord help me! I am not prepared for this!'"

Her throaty chuckle touched me. "Then I sat down, took a deep breath, closed my eyes and imagined myself back here in group. Walter thought I'd lost my marbles, but I didn't care. I remembered something you said to me one day, Katie. You said I had a remarkable way of cutting through the crap, and I was one of the strongest people you knew. Well, that got me through the day. And honey, it takes one to know one! I know you'll have the strength too."

"Did it get easier?" Kate asked.

"Sure it did. Day by day, child," Bernice said. "The second day home I panicked when I stumbled onto a bottle of vodka I'd hidden months ago. Had to call my daughter to help me pour it out. But yesterday, when I found an old bottle of Valium, I was able to laugh and flush 'em all by myself! You can do it, too."

Denise, an anorexic-thin, pale woman of about twenty, spoke up next. "Kate, I just want you to know how you've helped me these past few days. You're so strong and cool. I know I'll never be where you are… I mean with your education and career and all. But you helped me see what I've been doing to my body and all. I vowed to learn from my mistakes just like you have."

Kate looked down at her feet. "Thanks, Denise," she said. "But don't ever put me up on a pedestal. I've made some major mistakes. In fact, I'm going in to federal court Monday to plead guilty to stealing a bunch of money, which I used to feed my coke habit. And in about two months I'll be going to prison. I hope for not too long."

"Wow. I didn't know," Denise said. The group—almost as one—fidgeted in their seats.

"Hey, it's okay. Adam is the only one here who knew." She nodded toward me and said, "Caroline is my lawyer as well as my friend. She asked me not to talk about it until we decided what to do.

"Let me tell you, it'll be a relief to get it all out in the open. This place and, more importantly, you people have given me the tools and support to face it all. I love you and thank you for that!"

Each member of the group spoke, some awkwardly, some eloquently. Jake, with the sunken eyes and unkempt beard of a burned-out aging rocker, read a poem he'd written for the occasion. His insight and compassion, and the beauty of the poem, surprised me.

Adam Larken spoke last. He mentioned Kate's many strengths: her intelligence, perceptiveness, sense of humor, candor and drive. He reminded her of her weaknesses—her tendencies toward self-criticism and allowing men to control her—and encouraged her to love and honor herself.

"It's been a pleasure to work with you, Kate," Adam said in closing. "Your outpatient counselor Sharon and all the wise folks in N.A. and A.A. will take over from here. But I hope you'll remember to call on me, too. I'll always be there for you."

—m—

"Do you want to come in?" Kate asked as we pulled up in front of her building. I couldn't read her mood.

"Do you want me to?"

"Not particularly," she said, without a trace of discourtesy. "But I know you, Caroline, and I can see you're uneasy about my being alone."

"I guess you're right. After what Bernice said at the meeting, I worry about you being overwhelmed at your own homecoming."

"Bernice went home to a no-account husband who only came to one family session the whole time she was at The Meadows, and then he left early. I have no Walter to contend with. And, I swear, no hidden stashes of coke or booze or pills. I'm feeling strong enough to be alone. Honest."

"Okay. But call me if you need anything. You've got my cell phone number."

"Caroline, chill!" Kate said. "I'm not worried about getting in touch with someone if I need to. I have all three of your numbers. I've got three for Adam, two for Sharon, and one for Bernice and almost everyone else in the group. I can reach Jake telepathically if all the world's phone systems crash."

The image brought me an involuntary but very welcome giggle. "Okay, then! Meet me at my office at ten Monday morning?"

"You got it. Thanks, friend."

I watched in admiration as Kate practically leaped up her front steps, her duffle bag and backpack slung over one shoulder as if they were weightless. She turned to wave and wink as

I drove away. She could've been off to a college tennis match fifteen years earlier.

Monday, November 26

Kate appeared in my office promptly on Monday morning, wearing a classic navy blue suit, a simple cream-colored blouse and small gold hoop earrings. Looking nothing like the cocaine addict who'd been arrested weeks earlier, she was the picture of conservative respectability—perfect for an appearance before Judge Hugh Coburn.

"Hey, you look great," I said as she sat down.

"Thanks!"

"How did the weekend go?"

"It was fine, Caroline. Just fine. About seven o'clock Friday night I recorded a new message for the answering machine because my well-wishers wouldn't—or couldn't—leave me alone. It said, 'Hi, this is Kate. I'm neither drunk nor stoned. I promise you'll be the first person I call if I feel a relapse coming on. But I need some quiet time. Thanks for your understanding and concern.' I set the machine to pick up on the first ring and took a long soak in the Jacuzzi. There were probably ten sheepish hang-ups before I went to bed at nine-thirty. I slept like a baby, took a run Saturday morning, had a huge breakfast, and I felt like I could handle anything. Yesterday I started packing and had coffee with Luann, my N.A. sponsor. Caught up on some TV. It was heavenly."

"I'm glad," I said with heartfelt relief.

"So tell me what to expect."

I explained what would happen at the plea hearing from start to finish. A good deal of time would be spent reviewing the rights Kate would be forfeiting by pleading guilty, including the right to ever own or possess a firearm.

"You mean I won't be able to participate in the annual fox hunt anymore?" she asked.

Is she being facetious?

"Fox hunt?"

"I'm just kidding, but it does sound like the kind of pretentious sport my dad would get into!"

We had no time for another discussion about Corbett Daniels, so I forged ahead in preparation for the hearing.

George Cooper had told me about the timetable: the judge would order the probation department to conduct a presentence investigation and to calculate tentative sentencing guidelines. Their report would be due in five weeks. Then, we'd have up to five additional weeks—including time to respond to the report—before the sentencing hearing. We could waive our right to five weeks if we wanted the sentencing to take place sooner.

"We'll waive, Caroline," Kate said.

"Are you sure? You've got your condo up for sale. The extra time might come in handy."

"Do you need five weeks to prepare?" she asked.

"No. Two weeks should be enough time for me," I said without thinking.

"Then let's ask for two weeks. Caroline, I want to get this over and get on with my real life."

I paused for a moment, wondering if I'd been too hasty. But I was as anxious as Kate to put this case behind us. "Okay, two weeks it is. The judge will ask you a lot of routine questions. Always pay attention and answer, 'Yes, Your Honor,' or 'No, Your Honor.' If you don't understand something, ask if you can talk with me—"

"Piece of cake, Caroline. I've watched every lawyer show from 'Perry Mason' to 'Boston Legal.'"

"At some point, Judge Coburn will ask you to tell in your own words what you did. Keep it simple—no details. We'll provide details to the probation officer. Be contrite but don't belabor it."

"Okay. No problem," Kate said with an air of supreme confidence.

I, too, was confident. Plea hearings were often tedious but rarely did anything surprising happen there.

Rosalee knocked on the door at ten-thirty and brought in two cups of her aromatic secret-blend coffee and two gigantic maple walnut muffins.

"You're an angel. How'd you know I didn't have time for breakfast?" I asked.

"I can hear your stomach growling all the way out here!" she said, laughing. "Seriously, I tried a new recipe yesterday and my gentleman friend was unimpressed. I decided to bring them here rather than eat them all myself."

Kate and I sat quietly sipping and nibbling while we read over some reports George Cooper had sent me that morning. When she got up to stretch, her repeated glances in my direction told me she wanted to talk.

"What's on your mind?" I asked.

"Did you tell my father about the hearing today?"

"No. The last time I talked to him, he made it pretty clear a guilty plea would be unacceptable to him. But more than anything, I decided it wasn't his business unless you wanted it to be."

"But I seem to recall your promising to keep him informed," Kate said.

"I promised to keep him informed of anything that might jeopardize the bail he posted. Pleading guilty doesn't fit the bill."

"How 'bout when we got called back to court after I used coke with Joe Ames?" she asked, resuming her seat. "That certainly jeopardized his bail."

I'd never considered calling Corbett during that tenuous situation which, in retrospect, wasn't really fair to him. I brushed some crumbs from my desk into the wastebasket while wracking my brain for an answer. "No, I didn't call him," I said finally. "There's no precedent for taking bail money for technical violations like drug use. Your dad's money would only be forfeited if you fled."

"I almost left the country."

I choked on a sip of coffee. "What?"

She nodded. "It's true. The night before the controlled buy, I concocted a plan. I was going to call Joe, have him pick me up early at The Meadows and go with him to get my two ounces. He would've done it. He also would've driven me to the airport to catch a flight. Joe relished any opportunity to beat the system. I wasn't totally bullshitting when I told him on the tape I planned to go to Costa Rica."

"Were you lying when you told him you had new identification documents?" I asked, afraid to hear the answer.

"No. I wasn't lying."

"Oh, Kate. How—"

"It's kind of a long story. Do you really want to hear it?"

God, no! But I guess I'd better. "Uh-huh."

"Joe Ames loved the union terrace. I think he always regretted not going to college, and he'd hang out there engaging in all kinds of intellectual and philosophical discussions with whoever would listen, which made him feel smart. And, as you might expect, he recruited customers and sexual partners."

She paused to take a bite of her muffin and became lost in thought.

"Earth to Kate."

"I'm sorry, Caroline," she said with a trace of sadness. "Even after all this time, it's difficult for me to think about him. There was a lot I loved about Joe, although Adam Larken insists it was really his cocaine I loved.

"Well anyway, even before I found out Joe was married, I knew he cheated on me. I'd see him around campus arm-in-arm with other women, and he often stood me up. I don't know why I put up with it, but I did.

"One day—I guess it was a few months before my arrest—I was waiting for Joe at the terrace, and he didn't show. I was sitting there morosely drinking my beer when this big black guy with a British accent came up and asked if he could sit down. I said yes, mostly in hopes Joe would show up and find him there. Thorpe was his name."

Kate took another bite and washed it down with a sip of coffee. "Long story short, Joe never did come," she said. "But Thorpe was a pretty interesting guy, a graduate student in business administration from Nigeria, maybe thirty-five years old. We went out several times, but there was no physical chemistry, maybe because I was still too hung up on Joe. Thorpe and I remained friends. We'd do a few lines or have a few drinks together. Occasionally go to a movie."

"Did Joe ever find out?" I asked.

"Sure. But it didn't enrage him like I'd hoped. He'd make a few caustic, racist comments, but he didn't care enough about me to work up any anger."

Is she ever going to get to the point? Yet a part of me was fascinated by the details.

"A couple days after I got out of jail, Thorpe came by my apartment. He was leaving the next day to return to Nigeria, an unexpected trip because his mother was ill. He said he'd seen the news accounts about my arrest and had brought me a 'care package.'"

"A 'care package?'" I asked.

"Yeah. He handed me a box containing about two thousand dollars in cash, a certified birth certificate for a girl born in London in 1970, and a British passport in the same name. There was no photograph on the passport. He told me after I had a picture taken I should take the passport to a guy he knew to have it laminated and sealed. Thorpe gave me the guy's first name, number, and a code to use."

I couldn't even imagine her in the scene, which reminded me of something out of a spy movie. "You didn't do it, did you?"

"Yes, Caroline. I did. That very afternoon. It was somewhat disconcerting calling and meeting the guy, but it all worked smoothly."

"What were you thinking?"

"I guess I wasn't thinking. Being in jail where I was forced to withdraw from cocaine scared me to death. And just knowing I could flee if I needed to or wanted to gave me some comfort for a while. Plus, I'd begun using cocaine again as soon as I got out of jail, so my judgment was obviously not the best."

"You mean it wasn't just one time?" I asked.

"I wish I could say it was. But, no, I used pretty regularly. In jail I learned all about how to beat drug tests."

Oh, my God—can this get any more sordid? "How's that?"

"Well, for example, you can use right after you drop a sample. The PO almost never calls you back for a test the next day or even the day after. You know—budget constraints. You can flush your system with water or juices or certain health food supplements. I confess, I learned none of this stuff in med school."

"Does it work?"

"Not very well," she said, "since it wasn't long before I got caught. Ergo my hasty admission to The Meadows."

I laughed nervously. "Back to the documents."

"Oh, yeah. Sorry for the digression," Kate said dispassionately. "I locked the passport and birth certificate in my safe for a couple days. Then I took things a step further. I went to Milwaukee and got a state photo I.D. card, using the birth certificate and passport for documentation. I used a mail box service center for my address."

The matter-of-fact manner in which she related the events set off Klaxons in my head, but I forged ahead, purposely silencing the alarms. "Were you seriously considering leaving the country?"

She nodded.

"What stopped you?"

"At first it was because I couldn't come up with the cash. Most of the money Thorpe had given me was as counterfeit as the passport."

"Please don't tell me you spent some of it."

"I tried. I gave two hundred to Joe for some coke, but he took one look at the bills and knew they were phony. He accused me of trying to fuck with him, but I convinced him I hadn't known the money was fake. He accepted the money in payment for coke—only at twice the cost. I'm sure he passed it on." She shrugged.

"Anyway," Kate said, "I kept the fake I.D. and became more conflicted about my plans to split. The more involved I got in treatment, the less inclined I was to leave. Until the night before I set up Joe. Then I started feeling completely panicky about everything: wearing the wire, being around cocaine again, seeing Joe, going to prison. It gave me real relief to plan my escape."

"But you didn't go. Why not?" I asked almost absently, focused instead on a placid watercolor on my wall—one that had always helped to center me. I had to get my bearings.

"Because of you and Lily," she said, her voice softening. "You've been so steadfast in your support, and I knew Lily would think less of me. But more than that, the thought of never being able to see or talk with you or watch Lily grow up was more than I could handle."

I looked at Kate. She brushed back a lock of hair, then wiped the corner of her eye with the heel of her hand. *Don't be sidetracked by her tears*, I told myself.

"So I decided to stay," Kate said. "My resolve lasted until I got in Joe's car and saw the coke. It's a miracle I came to my senses again and was able to give the arrest signal."

I paused to collect my thoughts. "Do you still have the false documents?" I asked.

"Yes, although I had the foresight to put them in my safety deposit box where I couldn't get to them in the middle of the night. We can stop at the bank after court. Maybe have a bonfire tonight?"

"I'd like you to get them out, but we won't be burning them just yet," I said. George Cooper might be very interested in Kate's friend Thorpe. And possessing some concrete evidence couldn't hurt, could it?

CHAPTER THIRTY-SEVEN

—ᘏ—

We arrived at the courthouse with five minutes to spare and used the time to stop in the restroom, apparently to the discomfiture of George Cooper. I saw him at counsel table, his eyes caught in a battle between his watch and the door, as Kate and I walked into the courtroom.

Fortunately, we'd gone over everything beforehand, because just as we took our seats Judge Coburn appeared on the bench. I stifled a "Wow!" The black-and-white newspaper photos hadn't done him justice. Judge Coburn was at least six-five and looked even more imposing as he stood with perfect posture on the raised dais of the bench. I knew from what I'd read that he was sixty-seven years old, but the only evidence of age was his pure white hair. His deep tan offset vivid sky blue eyes, which sparkled as he greeted us. This guy did not look and sound at all like the "hanging judge" he was reputed to be.

"We've got about half an hour's worth of questions and answers to get through," the judge said in a melodious baritone voice. "So please remain seated when you respond."

Coburn informed Kate of her rights and asked a list of questions designed to ensure she was competent to enter an informed guilty plea. When he described her loss of privileges—including the right to bear arms—Kate adopted a solemn demeanor and said she understood. At the same time, she surreptitiously drew a frowny face on the legal pad in front of me, forcing me to suppress a giggle.

When called upon, George Cooper recited the terms of the plea agreement: Kate would plead guilty to one count of embezzling money from the government grant program, all of her illegal behavior would be used to determine the appropriate sentencing range, and the prosecutor would recommend a lower sentence because of her cooperation in another investigation. Finally, he summarized the evidence of Kate's crime.

"Ms. Daniels," Judge Coburn said, "please tell me in your own words what you did."

"I was co-administrator of a research grant at the university from National Institutes of Health. Through various means, I stole money from the grant and used it for my own purposes."

"And those purposes were?" the judge asked.

"Well actually, Your Honor, I guess I misspoke," Kate said. "There was really only one purpose—to buy cocaine to feed my addiction."

"You were addicted to cocaine?"

"Yes, Your Honor, I was and I am," Kate said.

"You're addicted now?" the judge asked, with a hint of annoyance. "When I asked you earlier if you were under the influence of alcohol or drugs, I believe you said no."

"I'm sorry, Judge," Kate said. "I didn't mean to be confusing. Although I am a cocaine addict, I have been able to remain drug free for some time and, God willing, I will continue to. I'm completely sober as we speak."

Good answer, Kate.

"Very well," the judge said, pausing to look down at his notes. "You said you stole money through various means. Please describe some of those means."

"At first it was by padding my expense account or applying for reimbursement for business trips I hadn't taken. Later, I hired my cocaine supplier, supposedly as a research assistant. The salary was paid by the grant. He never did any work and was in fact unqualified to do research, but he gave me cocaine in return for the paychecks. That's basically it, Your Honor."

"And do you agree with Mr. Cooper that the total loss to the grant program was approximately $147,682?"

"Yes, Your Honor."

"Then, Ms. Daniels, how do you plead to Count One of the indictment: guilty or not guilty?" the judge asked.

"Guilty."

Judge Coburn ordered the probation department to conduct a presentence investigation and submit its report by the end of December. He looked up from his calendar and said, "Ms. Spencer, you're entitled to five weeks to respond to the report."

"We'll waive the five weeks, Your Honor. If possible, we'd like sentencing to take place two weeks after the presentence report is completed."

"Fine, but you'll have only one week to file any objections, and I don't tolerate late filings."

"Understood, Your Honor," I said. "Thank you."

"Okay. We'll schedule sentencing for the soonest date I have open, the eighteenth of January. Ms. Garrety from the probation office is here," the judge said, nodding to a small table on the side of the courtroom, where a petite blonde woman sat. Until the judge pointed her out, I hadn't noticed her. "She'll meet with you immediately after the hearing to begin the investigation. Is there any reason to reconsider bail?"

"None, Your Honor," George Cooper said.

Judge Coburn tipped his head toward me.

"None, Your Honor," I said.

"Very well. We're adjourned."

I shook hands with Cooper and chatted with him as we stood up to leave. Ms. Garrety approached our cluster with purpose. Cooper stopped talking mid-sentence and folded his arms across his chest, which struck me as odd and somewhat rude. *What's up with this? He gets us to plead guilty and then we're personas non grata?*

"Hello, Helen," he said stiffly. "Kate Daniels, Caroline Spencer—this is Helen Garrety from the probation office. I assume you're assigned to this case, Helen?"

She nodded and shook hands with us. "George, when can I pick up your file?"

"Is tomorrow soon enough?" he asked in reply.

"That'll be fine. I'll come by around ten." With that, Ms. Garrety turned to Kate and me as if to dismiss Cooper. After an awkward pause, he smiled and waved to us behind her shoulder before striding out of the courtroom.

"I need to meet with you now, Ms. Daniels, to begin the process. Ms. Spencer, you're welcome to sit in on this and all meetings," Ms. Garrety said.

I looked at my watch and realized my plans to pick up Lily and to prepare dinner at a leisurely pace were about to disintegrate. I couldn't help but resent the intrusion on my time.

"I intend to be present for all your meetings with my client," I said. "But we didn't know one would be scheduled after the plea hearing. It wasn't on the notice we received from the court."

"It's standard procedure," she said, "as I guess you could tell from the judge's comments."

"Nevertheless," I said, somewhat peevishly, "it would have helped if you'd called to inform us ahead of time. This is Ms. Daniels' first plea hearing, and I don't routinely practice in federal court, so we have no way of knowing about unwritten standard procedures."

"I understand, and you're right," she replied evenly. "I should have called you ahead of time. Unfortunately, I just received the assignment late this morning. Can you spare an hour?"

My knee-jerk reaction would have been to say no. But something told me it would not behoove my client or me to squabble with this woman, who could be very influential with the judge. "Sure," I said, and we followed her out of the courtroom.

Helen Garrety was very slight with long straight hair and iridescent skin. She wore a pale pink suit—the skirt falling just below her knees—and off-white pumps, her only jewelry a pair of pearl earrings. I realized how disconcerting I found her—an ethereal-looking creature who was all business and would not be put off.

Her office was equally disconcerting and offered few clues about her personal life—no photographs of family members or pets or vacation spots, no cartoons tacked to the bulletin board, no diplomas, no whimsical posters or bric-a-brac. Her walls were adorned only with a few art prints in modest frames. Her reference books sat neatly aligned on the shelves and the desk bore only a computer and a notepad.

While I was an ADA, I had once attended a safety seminar where we were told to rid our offices of family photos and items that might identify us to the criminals we met with there. I remembered we'd all nodded in agreement: It made sense to keep your personal life private so you and your family would be less vulnerable. But when it came right down to it, few of us took the precautionary step to remove those things from our work domains. Perhaps we were simply too busy or thought ourselves invincible. Helen Garrety, it seemed, had taken the safety seminar to heart, which made her seem a bit of a goody two shoes to me. *Or maybe she has no life.*

"I want to explain the presentence process to you," she said, looking at Kate.

"Excuse me," I said, drawing her attention to me. "I've gone over this at some length with my client. Maybe we could save some time and move on to the specifics."

"I'm sure you've gone over things from your perspective," Helen said calmly, "but it's important that you both understand mine."

I found myself oddly placated by her response. She had just told me to buzz off and let her do her job the way she wanted to, but she said it in a manner that diffused any hint of conflict.

Kate, too, appeared lulled by this rather peculiar woman. "It's okay, Caroline. I'd like to hear what Ms. Garrety has to add."

"Please. I'd prefer for you both to call me Helen. We'll be spending quite a bit of time together, and it's easier if we can be less formal."

Kate listened to Helen's description of what would be accomplished in the next several weeks. None of it was new to me or, I thought, to Kate. But, as if hearing it for the first time, she nodded in understanding and asked several questions as Helen proceeded.

Helen would review George Cooper's file, which contained all of the investigators' reports and documents. She would ask Kate and me to comment and provide our view of what had transpired. It was her job to provide information to the judge as impartially as possible—she wasn't on either "side."

"It's critically important that everything you say to me be truthful," Helen told Kate. My ears perked up. "If you prefer not to answer a question, please say so. Or if you don't remember or don't know, please say so. The sentencing guidelines can be unforgiving if you provide false information during the course of my investigation."

"I appreciate your concern, but I assure you I fully intend to make a clean breast of things," Kate said. "That's why I decided to plead guilty."

"Okay, I promised I'd only take an hour today," Helen said, reaching into her top desk drawer for her calendar, "so let's schedule our next meetings. Caroline, did I hear you say you'll want to be present for all of my interviews?"

"Oh, I don't think that will be necessary," Kate said. "I've got nothing to hide."

"You and I will certainly talk about it, Kate, but let's plan on my attending. And I don't intend to keep you quiet. It's more to keep me informed and prepared for the sentencing. Plus I need to make sure Helen doesn't stick bamboo shoots under your fingernails to induce you to reveal your darkest secrets," I said smiling, hoping to inject some levity into the conversation. My attempt fell flat—Helen pursed her lips and went back to her calendar.

The dates set, Helen escorted us out of the probation office without fanfare or small talk.

"That was weird," I said to Kate as we walked to the car.

"What do you mean?"

"I dunno. She was so businesslike or something. I can't quite put my finger on it."

"You're just miffed because she didn't laugh at your lame joke," Kate said. "I thought she was nice."

"She was nice. And she has this almost hypnotic manner—it's disarming. She can probably get people to tell her the most intimate details of their lives. I'm just not sure we can trust her."

"Well, she flat out told us she's not on my side," Kate said. "I don't imagine you can expect much more candor."

"She also said she's not on George Cooper's side. And I'm not sure I believe that."

"I don't know about that, Caroline. She was pretty curt with him, and he didn't seem thrilled to see her."

"Yeah. Like I said—she's weird!" *And maybe dangerous.*

CHAPTER THIRTY-EIGHT

—⟋ɯ⟍—

Tuesday, November 27

I sat at my desk doodling and staring out the window, waiting for a return call from George Cooper, obsessed with telling him about Kate's friend Thorpe. A dark sedan driving by the building somehow caught my attention, reminding me of the FBI. Carter Ellingson could talk with me about the potential value of Kate's information. I rifled through my file, found his number, and was pleased to hear him pick up on the second ring.

"Hello, Carter. It's Caroline Spencer, Kate Daniels's attorney," I said, somewhat uncertain as to how to proceed.

"What can I do for you?"

"Actually, I was hoping we could do something for you. I'm not sure you're aware of it, but my client pled guilty yesterday—"

"Yes. George Cooper told me it was scheduled, but I didn't have time to come to the hearing."

"Cooper agreed to recommend a downward adjustment in the sentence in return for her help with Joe Ames. But I've just learned she may also be able to provide some information on a Nigerian she met at the university—somebody named Thorpe something-or-other. I just wondered if you could give me a tentative idea about your level of interest."

Ellingson didn't hesitate a second, and I could almost feel his excitement through the receiver.

"I can't speak for the U.S. Attorney's Office, but if the 'Thorpe' your client knows is the one I'm thinking of, I would be very interested in talking with her. As I'm sure you know," Ellingson went on, "Nigerian fraud schemes have developed all over the country. At my last post, New York City, I worked almost exclusively on those scams. This Thorpe is a major player, and I'd love to get something on him."

"Kate tells me he went back to Nigeria."

"Not likely. How much does she know about him?"

"I'd better check with George before filling you in. I need to make sure Kate's immunity agreement will extend to anything she tells you about Thorpe. But I can tell you Thorpe handed her some items that may have his prints on them."

"Where are these 'items' currently?"

"In a safety deposit box."

"Please! Tell your client not to touch them until after we talk. I could meet with you both this afternoon."

"I'll call you as soon as I talk to George."

I was shutting down my computer and packing my briefcase to go home when Cooper finally returned my call. The day had been a waste—I'd found it impossible to concentrate on anything but Kate's new treasure trove of information, especially not the tedious deposition about a disputed property settlement in a divorce case that sat on my desk. My regularly assigned work was backing up and getting short shrift.

"Sorry it's taken me so long to get back to you," Cooper said. "I was in grand jury most of the day."

"I understand. When I couldn't reach you, I called Carter."

"Yeah," Cooper said acerbically. "He was one of my witnesses this afternoon. While we were on break, he told me Kate has some more info. He's pushing for a quick meeting."

"I'd like something in writing, extending her immunity agreement to this other pattern of conduct."

"Can you give me some idea what we're talking about here? Was she on the grassy knoll in Dallas, or did she jaywalk across rush hour traffic on University Avenue?"

"Kate wasn't even born in 1963!"

"I keep dating myself. And you weren't alive in 1963 either. I'm impressed you caught my reference."

"I'm a big Oliver Stone fan. At any rate, this was a bit more serious than jaywalking. In a nutshell, Kate met and befriended a Nigerian who was either attending or hanging around the university. They did some coke together and briefly saw each other socially. Shortly after Kate's release from jail, this guy approached her with some counterfeit I.D. documents."

"Ellingson says she's got them in a safety deposit box?"

"I shouldn't have been so quick to mention that to him," I said.

"Oh, don't worry. I'm not anxious to give your client— and my star witness against Joe Ames—any more grief. Is it safe to surmise Kate is in possession of some things she shouldn't have?"

"Yes, I guess that's it in a nutshell."

"Has she used any of this identification?"

"I'd need to do some research to determine what laws she's actually broken," I said.

"Hmmm. Well, if they're not readily apparent to you, I suspect they're not the kind of thing we'd be intent on prosecuting her for. Why don't you send me a proffer, and I'll run it by the U.S. Attorney. I'm pretty sure he'd be willing to extend the immunity."

"You don't have that authority yourself?"

"Everyone's got their channels."

I laughed. "Okay. Can we tentatively schedule a debriefing?"

"How about day after tomorrow? Ellingson'll have my head if we don't do it this week."

"That's the day Kate and I are scheduled to meet Helen Garrety. But I suppose I could call her and ask to postpone."

"I wouldn't recommend that," George said.

"Oh?" I asked in my best leading-question tone.

"Let's just say Ms. Garrety has a tendency to be opinionated, and I would urge you to be completely cooperative with her. Don't make any waves. She has an uncanny way of influencing the judges—not so much by what she says but how she says it. Could you free up some time later tomorrow afternoon? Say three o'clock? After the last fiasco with Shelton, I can't very well let Ellingson interview her alone."

I dug my appointment book out of the bottom of my briefcase and paged through it until I found the date: "18 cookies" was noted in red pen. I'd volunteered to bake cookies for Lily's Brownie troop meeting tomorrow night and had promised her they'd be gingerbread people. Not exactly the kind of schedule conflict I could share with George Cooper.

"I can spare two hours if we start promptly at three," I said. "And of course I'll have to clear this with Kate."

"I understand. Can you fax me the proffer of her testimony by noon?"

"I'll do my best. One o'clock at the latest."

"Okay. Call me in the a.m. if Kate doesn't agree. Otherwise fax the proffer, and I'll have the immunity letter for her signature when we meet at three." He hung up.

I pulled the depositions out of my briefcase and replaced them with the federal criminal codebook, grabbed the laptop I'd planned to leave at the office, and headed out the door.

Once on the freeway, I speed-dialed Ida McKinley on my cell phone to let her know I'd be late getting home. Since Lily had early dismissal from school, she'd cajoled me into letting her go to Ida's for the afternoon.

"I'm glad you called, dear," she said. "Lily just took Muffin out in the yard, and I wanted to talk with you out of her earshot."

"Oh?"

"When I picked Lily up at school, I asked her if she'd like to do anything special. She didn't hesitate a minute before asking me if I would teach her to make gingerbread cookies. So we stopped at the store and bought ingredients. It was only as we were getting ready to decorate the cookies that Lily confessed you had volunteered to make them but she wasn't sure you knew how."

"If the truth be told," I said with chagrin, "I haven't made gingerbread cookies since about fourth grade. I have my grandmother's old cookie cutter and her recipe, but as I remember, they were tricky. I don't think I told Lily that, though."

"Who knows how kids come up with their ideas," Ida said. "Anyway, I suggested you might have wanted this to be a mother-daughter project, and we agreed the two of you should frost them together."

"I don't know how to thank you. As it is, something's come up and this evening will be busier than I'd planned."

As I hung up, feelings of guilt and inadequacy rushed over me. Totally self-absorbed, I changed lanes without signaling and was startled back to reality when the man in the next car honked and flipped me off. I mouthed, "I'm sorry," and felt all the more deficient.

A mile or so later, when traffic thinned, I dialed Kate's number. Her machine answered, "Hi. I'm out taking care of business—legitimate business, I assure you! So please leave your name and number and I'll call you later." The whimsical message and tone were so out of character for the Kate I had known and not entirely apropos, I thought, for the situation in which she found herself. I made a mental note to talk with her about it. After all, what would Helen Garrety think if she heard it?

I left a message explaining I needed to meet with her in the morning, and, if she agreed, we'd meet tomorrow afternoon with Cooper and Ellingson. "Call me as soon as you get in, no matter what time," I said before ringing off.

My thoughts were still racing as I arrived at home. But sweet, competent and caring Ida—with her measured speech and her faintly Southern accent—had an instantly calming effect. And Lily beamed with pride as she showed me the gingerbread cookies Ida had taught her to make.

After dinner, David, Lily, and I squeezed colored frosting onto her creations. We giggled and had a contest to see who could draw the most outrageous shirt. David won hands down.

As I helped Lily get ready for bed, untangling and brushing her long hair as gently as possible, I said, "I'm happy you made the cookies with Ida today. It was very thoughtful of you."

"You're welcome, Mommy."

"Ida tells me you were a little concerned I wouldn't know how to make them."

"Well, not exactly. Megan told me it took her mom three batches before she got twelve that didn't break. And I know how busy you've been."

"You are a wonderful child, Lily, and I love you so much. But I don't want you to have to worry about me or my time. I'm old enough to do that myself!"

"I know, Mom, but I can't help it."

—⁊⁊—

When Kate finally called around midnight, I was wide awake in bed, reading and re-reading, without comprehending, the first five pages of the new John Grisham, at my wit's end with worry. "Where have you been?" I asked. David, in the bathroom brushing his teeth, looked up at me in alarm.

"Excuse me," Kate said, laughing. "I already have one mother and don't need another. You remember Jake from The Meadows? He graduated today, and we went out for dinner and a movie to celebrate."

I remembered his faded t-shirt and scruffy beard and hair. "Do you think that was wise?" I asked.

"Wise?" Kate asked, her voice losing all trace of levity. "Jake McEdwards is the most decent, kind, and sensible person I've ever met. And if you'd get past your rigid, middle-class mindset, you'd see it too. Without Jake's help and friendship, I never would have made it through that incredibly tough program. And if I want to see him in the outside world, I damned well will!"

"You'd better make sure you're not in violation of your bail conditions by doing so."

"Meaning what?"

"Meaning he'd better not have a criminal record—"

"Fuck you, Caroline. For your information, Jake has never been arrested—not even for OWI. His reasons for entering treatment were far nobler than mine: he'd lost his wife and children due to his alcoholism and wanted to save his job. He's been a high school Spanish teacher for fifteen years."

"I'm sorry. I—"

"Drop it. I got your message, and I'll meet you at your office at ten." She hung up.

I burst into tears and was shaking uncontrollably as I put down the phone by our bedside. Without a word, David rinsed his mouth, set his toothbrush on the bathroom counter, and came to hug me.

"I'm such an idiot," I said. "My life is so out of control my seven-year-old daughter is protecting me. I was so immersed in my thoughts that I drove like a fool and almost killed another driver. And I pissed off my friend by insulting a good person and judging him by his appearance. In one day, I've managed to do several of the things I hate."

"Calm down, honey. Self-flagellation doesn't become you—and it's certainly not useful. You're seeing today what most of us see about ourselves everyday: we're fallible. As I remember from your treatment, one of the causes of panic attacks is striving for perfection, right?"

"Right."

"And trying to control the uncontrollable?"

"Yes," I said, but with little conviction.

"Well, you can't control the fact that Lily is super-sensitive and a lot like you. You can only share with her the techniques you've learned over the years to deal with it. And you—of all people—should know you can't control Kate."

But it sure as hell feels like she's controlling me.

CHAPTER THIRTY-NINE

Wednesday, November 28

I hadn't taken notes when Kate first told me about her relationship with Thorpe. Now, I had her repeat her story and asked for details along the way. She knew more about him than she'd originally let on: she knew his last name, she knew the street name of his cocaine source, and she'd recently seen the man who had finished her counterfeit passport.

"This is the kind of stuff the FBI wants, Kate. They need snitch information to get to guys like Thorpe, and George Cooper and I recognize your willingness to help in investigations is 'doing the right thing.' But you have to know it's a double-edged sword: In the back of our minds, we're saying, 'My God, she was involved in more illegal behavior?'"

"Caroline," Kate said with a long slow sigh, "I understand what you're saying. Sometimes I can't believe it myself. How did the daughter of a prominent family—herself a respected, educated professional—sink so low as to steal and consort with drug dealers and con men?

"I'm not sure how I got so far off-track, but I know my road to recovery will involve making amends. I believe in the laws of this country, and I don't want to go on disrespecting them. I'm not doing this to get a reduced sentence, although I can't deny that would be a nice benefit. Go ahead and prepare your proffer. I'll tell Ellingson everything I know."

Rosalee was off today. Kate read over my shoulder as I typed our statement into the computer, correcting errors and commenting as she saw the need. We worked well together, as we had in college. During one all-nighter, while smoking cigarettes and consuming pot after pot of black coffee, we had written a one-act play set during World War II. Our imaginations had been better then, but we were certainly better writers today.

We finished with a flourish. I signed the document and took it down the hall to the fax machine. When I returned, Kate sat staring at my watercolor.

"About last night," I said, looking down at my shoes.

Kate turned to me. "We don't need to rehash it. I said what was on my mind and I let it go. Honestly. I've gotten better at that lately."

"But I didn't say what I want to say—namely, I'm sorry. I was dead wrong. I'm your friend and your lawyer, but I'm not your keeper. And I certainly wasn't demonstrating much confidence in your judgment."

"Ah, Caroline. You were wrong to judge Jake by his appearance. But God knows I've given you a multitude of reasons to question my judgment. Don't kick yourself for that.

It will take a long time before anyone else will have confidence in my judgment."

She got up, grabbed her purse off the floor and headed for the door. "I need to go meet with my realtor. I'll see you at the U.S. Attorney's office at three. Don't be late!"

That day's debriefing with Carter Ellingson and George Cooper went off without a hitch, and Ellingson was beyond grateful for the leads Kate provided. The interviews with Helen Garrety were another story altogether.

Thursday, November 29

Helen Garrety rang the doorbell of Kate's condo ten minutes ahead of the appointed time. Kate and I put aside the college yearbook we'd been studying for the past hour and wiped the smiles from reminiscing about days gone by off our faces. Back to reality.

Helen Garrety looked less waif-like in tailored charcoal slacks, a softly patterned silk shirt, and flats. She declined a cup of coffee as Kate poured another for herself and one for me.

"If you don't mind, I'd like to get started right away," Garrety said, easing onto a stool at the breakfast bar. "We have quite a bit of ground to cover today."

Her interviewing skills were masterful, among the best I'd ever seen. With nods, faint smiles, and remarkably few questions, Garrety elicited information I'd never known about my long-time friend: That an older sister had drowned in the family's swimming pool. That Kate had been diagnosed as dyslexic in the second grade. That her father—when

Kate was ten—had left the family and lived for a year with a woman much younger than Margaret. While I found this both startling and fascinating, it was nonetheless innocuous information when it came to Kate's sentencing. We'd agreed to discuss the important matter—her criminal behavior—during our next meeting at Garrety's office.

"Tell me about your research," Garrety said, turning to a blank page in her notepad. I stretched in my chair and followed her lead. This might provide some strong ammunition for my sentencing arguments.

Who among us doesn't enjoy talking about our work? That is, when someone's truly listening. My modest, self-effacing husband glows when asked to share stories of his clients, their security issues, and his solutions for them. I imagine even a sixteen-year-old goes home from his job at McDonald's and regales his family with tales of broken French-fryers, rude customers, and bossy bosses.

Kate Daniels was no different. And Helen Garrety truly listened while she described with pride the ongoing research and the progress she and her colleagues had made.

Finished with this line of inquiry, Garrety consulted her watch. "We haven't gotten as far as I planned today," she said, "but I've got another appointment. Let's leave discussion of your substance abuse until next week."

I nodded in assent.

"The only thing left on my agenda today," Garrety said to Kate, "is a quick tour of your home."

Kate showed her around the spacious condo while I lingered in the kitchen, jotting notes for my sentencing arguments. She escorted the probation officer out and returned with a look of exhaustion on her face.

"Good Lord! What took you guys so long?" I asked.

"The woman's thorough, that's for sure," Kate said with a hint of a smile. I realized she'd been smiling a lot lately—and not always effortlessly. "She asked questions about everything in every room. Who painted that picture? Where did you get that vase? Is that armoire antique or a reproduction? How long ago did you redecorate the powder room? She took down my every answer."

"Did—"

"Yes, I told her the truth!"

Thursday, December 6

Our initial interview with Helen Garrety niggled at me—so much so that I called a defense lawyer I knew for some advice. A former hippie from New York, Jim Corcoran had come here for law school in the late '60s and never left. He'd shed his beard and long hair but retained his civil libertarian bent. He also knew the ins and outs of federal court.

Over a burger and beer at a dive near the county courthouse—his favorite lunch spot—I explained to Jim the situation: Kate had pleaded guilty, cooperated with the cops, and was working on selling her assets to pay full restitution. But I got funny vibes about Helen Garrety's exhaustive questioning. Should I limit her questions at our upcoming session?

"I've got one single piece of advice on the issue," Jim said. "Don't let your client talk to the PO about her crime." He resumed the attack on his cheeseburger.

"But don't we risk the three-point credit for her acceptance of responsibility if she doesn't agree to be interviewed about it?" I asked.

He washed down his bite with a swig of beer. "Which judge did you draw?" he asked.

"Hugh Coburn."

"At the plea hearing, he questioned her about what she'd done, right?"

I nodded.

"Did she hedge?"

"Not at all," I said. "She was very forthright."

"Then the potential pitfalls of the interview outweigh anything you'd hope to gain. If you absolutely feel you have to say something, submit a written statement outlining her conduct. But make sure George Cooper reads it first and agrees with your facts. Then have your client write a personal letter to the judge—okayed by you, of course—admitting and apologizing for her crime. She can describe her cocaine addiction—the court already knows all about that. But don't let her come off like a victim."

"Right."

"Do your best to have a check ready to pay full restitution on the day of sentencing," he added, "and I'm sure the judge will give her the three-point credit."

Even Jim's confident assessment of the situation failed to reassure me. "Won't it piss off Helen Garrety if we decline the interview at this late date?"

"I haven't personally worked with her yet—she's only been on the job about a year. I hear she's a real devotee of the sentencing guidelines, though. Which is all the more reason to decline the interview."

"I guess we could still meet with her and let her ask questions in person about Kate's prior record and drug use."

"Even that's risky, since they're all intertwined with this crime," he said, wiping ketchup from the corner of his mouth with a crumpled paper napkin. "But that's your call."

"One more thing, Jim," I said. "George Cooper's agreed to file a 5K motion for downward departure based on her cooperation in two cases. One is her coke dealer—the guy she put on the university payroll as a fictitious research assistant. The other case is unrelated, a Nigerian con man who gave her a phony passport and some funny money."

Jim raised an eyebrow then drained his beer mug. "I hope she's not a typical university professor. As a taxpayer, I'd be pissed if she was."

"Me, too. Anyway, Cooper says she could probably expect more benefit if he waited to file the motion for reduction of sentence after those two cases are settled."

"That's been my experience," he said. "Your client would be in suspense longer, but the wait is usually worth it. She might get a one- or two-level downward departure if he files early, but a three- or four-level reduction in sentence later, once the judge can see the real value of her help."

"Let me make sure I understand. You recommend we have Cooper delay filing the motion for reduction, and Kate gets sentenced without it. Then, when the dealer and the con man are charged, and hopefully convicted, Cooper files a motion to bring Kate back to have her sentence modified—presumably much lower?"

"You got it."

I left the bar and drove directly to Kate's, relieved to find her at home, amid piles of packing boxes, books, and papers.

"To what do I owe this honor?" she asked, handing me a Diet Pepsi from the refrigerator.

I explained my concerns about our upcoming interview. "I agree with Jim Corcoran," I said. "I think we should cancel."

"C'mon, Caroline! You can't be serious!" Kate said. "It'd look like I've got something to hide. Which I don't!"

It's just like the drug couriers on the interstate, stopped by state troopers. They'd get pulled over for speeding, or a broken taillight, or a cracked windshield. The cop would casually ask if they were carrying any drugs—to which the answer would always be no. Then the cop would ask permission to search the car. More often than most people could imagine, the couriers would consent to the search, knowing full well there was a kilo of cocaine, or marijuana, or methamphetamine hidden not well enough to remain undetected by the trooper or the drug dog that would be summoned to help. They wouldn't refuse, because then the cop would think they were guilty.

I relayed this all to Kate.

"It's not the same thing at all," she said.

"Even when I worked for the DA, smack dab on the side of law and order," I said, "I would never give someone consent to search my car. You can't be sure someone's not trying to set you up. And you don't know what they're looking for. You can't be sure of those things now either."

"You're being paranoid, Caroline. I don't know why you have a bad feeling about Helen Garrety. I think she likes me, and I believe we have a pretty good rapport."

"It's not a question of her liking or disliking you. It's how she perceives what you've done. And as for rapport—she's gotten you to disclose everything about yourself while revealing nothing of herself."

"But we've been over and over the sentencing guidelines. It seems like a pretty objective system to me, and I don't see how talking to her can hurt me."

"I agree with you to a point," I said. "But Helen Garrety makes a confidential recommendation to Judge Coburn for a specific sentence. If the range is twelve to eighteen months in prison and she recommends eighteen because of some personal judgment she's made, there's nothing we can do about it. It's safer to present your side of the story on paper. That way we can choose our words carefully and read it over and over to make sure we won't be misinterpreted."

I paused, overwhelmed by feelings I hadn't seen coming on. "I know I sound overly cautious, but I don't want you to spend one more day in prison than necessary. Because part of me will be there with you."

Kate finally sat to rest on top of a packing crate. "Okay," she said. "We'll do it your way about the crime. But I would like to talk with her about my addiction in person. I'll be sure not to make excuses."

She got up and started putting more books in a box.

"You know Caroline, sometimes you analyze things too much," Kate said. "Sometimes you just have to go with your gut."

"Maybe... but I've got a queasy feeling in my gut."

"That's because your head's spinning from looking at things from three-hundred and sixty different angles."

I called Helen Garrety and told her of our change in plans. Not surprisingly, I could read nothing in her equable response. "I appreciate your telling me ahead of time. It'll shorten our interview and free up my afternoon a bit," she said as I rang off.

"Before I go," I said to Kate, "we need to talk about the motion for a lower sentence based on your cooperation. Jim Corcoran recommends we have George Cooper wait until after you're sentenced to request a reduction. He thinks we may get more bang for your buck."

As I explained Jim's rationale, Kate became more and more agitated, no longer packing boxes but pacing the room.

"I already got Joe Ames busted and testified before the grand jury to get him indicted, and then I gave them a boatload of evidence against Thorpe Akani," she said.

"But they might need you to testify if Ames goes to trial, and they're not even ready to indict Akani—that could take six months."

"I don't want to wait. I want my reward when I'm sentenced. I know you're gonna argue for probation or work release. But if the judge gives me prison time, I want to know right then and there how long I'll have to serve. It's the only way I'll be able to cope with it."

"Even if you could get a bigger sentence reduction by waiting?" I asked, exasperated by her failure to see reason.

"Even then." She put a cigarette in her mouth and lit it as she paced.

"I think you're making a hasty decision," I said, miffed by both her attitude and her smoking.

"It's my call, Caroline. And I've made it. End of discussion."

Friday, December 7

I felt compelled to take charge when we met at Garrety's still-sterile office several days later. "My client wants to talk with you personally about the offense and her prior record," I said. "But, as you know, I've asked her not to. We'll submit a written statement instead. She'll talk with you about her substance abuse today."

Garrety nodded and got down to business—no idle chatter for her.

My heart ached for Kate as she repeated the story: her mother's addiction to alcohol, her father's contributions to the problem, her own insecurities and the invincibility she felt when using cocaine. She did more than recite empty facts and figures. Kate bared her soul yet again.

Helen Garrety nodded from time to time and made almost constant eye contact with Kate—encouraging her ever so subtly. When Kate paused in her recitation, Garrety inquired about another aspect of the problem.

"Please tell me about how your cocaine usage affected your work," she said, leaning a bit closer to Kate. I felt like I was in one of the hypnotic trances I'd learned to self-induce to relieve my panic attacks—a comfortable state I was reluctant to disturb. Now Helen Garrety asked my friend for potentially damning information and I sat immobilized, listening without hearing.

Kate stretched in her chair. "That's a tough question," she said. "I took pride in my research and always wanted to do my best. Sometimes the cocaine gave me the boost I needed or the extra energy to do the work. It may have helped me concentrate."

"You went to the lab when you were high?" Garrety asked. As her voice rose in surprise, I realized Kate had taken the earlier question more literally than Garrety had intended it. She'd meant, "Tell me how your cocaine habit affected your career." Candid Kate had incriminated herself once more. There was nothing I could do but hold my breath and hope she could acquit herself.

"Sometimes, but not often," Kate said. "There were lab assistants to monitor things on a routine basis. If I used coke when I was working, it was more often while I was collating data or writing."

"Wasn't your attention to detail impaired?"

"Well, at the time, I'd swear it wasn't. But in retrospect, it had to be. It's like the drunk who insists he's fully capable of driving a car. He thinks he's okay, but objective measures of reflexes, perception, and the like would show it's just not true."

"Could you have made mistakes in copying or interpreting your data when you were using?" Garrety asked.

"I hope not. But since I've been sober, I've gone over the work I did then, trying to be sure. So far, things have checked out okay."

It was a good answer—one that partially alleviated my concerns.

Garrety switched gears: She asked about The Meadows program and how Kate felt about her progress, and the interview ended on a positive note.

"Did I do okay, counselor?" Kate asked—as if she had nary a care in the world—while we walked toward the parking lot.

I saw nothing to be gained by sharing my earlier alarm.

CHAPTER FORTY

—⚏—

I saw very little of Kate in the weeks following our last interview with Helen Garrety. I had plenty to keep me busy: playing catch-up on the work I'd pushed to the back burner while focusing on Kate's case, researching federal sentencing procedures, and end-of-the-year tax planning for a few clients, not to mention shopping for Christmas.

Kate called and e-mailed periodically, reportedly busy with the sale and packing of her belongings, and with attending counseling and N.A. meetings. I was happy to keep things with her on a superficial level and lived by the mantra: no news is good news.

In some respects, though, I was in a state of purgatory. I struggled constantly to avoid getting excited about the babies—knowing enough to know the adoption wasn't a done deal. And speculation about the sentence Kate might receive when she returned to court in January was always in the back of my mind.

Friday, December 21

Closing on the sale of Kate's condo was set for this afternoon. Her bail conditions required her to let the pretrial services officer know in advance where she'd be moving, a requirement that weighed far more heavily on me than Kate.

I'd asked her about it several times. On the last occasion, about a week earlier, she'd suggested she might move in with her friend Jake McEdwards or perhaps go stay with her family in California until the sentencing hearing.

"Kate, you can't leave the state without the Court's permission, and it takes time to get permission," I had said with exasperation.

I'd invited Kate to stay with us. After all, we wouldn't be turning our guest room into a nursery for a few months yet. Her hesitation puzzled me: I had found Lily's exuberant "Please say yes, Aunt Kate, puh-leeze!" irresistible. Kate had simply replied, "Thanks, but no."

I sat at my desk, scratching my head with my purple pen and staring out the window. *How can she pack up and leave her home without knowing where she's going to sleep tonight?*

I left three messages for Kate before she finally returned my call—at three o'clock in the afternoon—and I answered with thinly veiled anger. "Why am I the only one who's the least bit concerned about your remaining out of jail?"

"Whoa, Caroline!" she said. "I told you I'd get back to you by today and let you know my plans. I will take you up on the offer to stay with you after all. I'll call Monica Smith-Kellor in a couple minutes and let her know."

"If she's not in, don't just leave a voice message. Make sure to talk with someone else—"

But she'd already hung up.

I rushed home, emptied four drawers and half a closet rack, and hastily dusted the furniture in the guest room. I needn't have hurried, though. We'd long since put away the dinner dishes and Lily was freshly bathed and climbing into bed when Kate finally pulled in the driveway.

Great start to a holiday weekend. What in God's name was I thinking when I invited her here?

—⁕—

Our Christmas celebration was quiet. David's parents came to visit but, as was their habit, stayed at a hotel. Kate joined us for church on Christmas Eve but had dinner the next day with Marty Braxton and his wife, leaving us some family-alone time. Although reluctant to admit it—even to myself—I felt relieved to have time away from her. And it was refreshing to be able to serve wine with our meal. David and his dad bundled up and had brandy and cigars on the deck after dinner. For the day, at least, the overriding tension of Kate's case was banished from my consciousness.

Wednesday, December 26

The room was eerily quiet when I woke from yet another nightmare—a chase dream in which a masked gunman had shot me in the chest. My left arm and shoulder ached. My pulse raced. My nightgown clung to my skin, adhered with cold sweat. *Oh, God, I'm having a heart attack.*

Should I wake David? Maybe it's just a panic attack. But what if it's not? Why does my left arm hurt? I prayed. I tried every relaxation technique I could remember.

You've got to get help, I told myself, almost out loud. I turned on my bedside lamp, my peripheral vision clouding.

I nudged David. "Honey, please wake up," I heard my disembodied voice say.

Bless his heart, my rock-solid partner roused himself out of an apparently deep sleep without complaint.

"What's wrong?" he asked, putting his arm around my shoulder.

By that point it was a struggle to speak. "A heart attack, I think. I think I need to go to the hospital."

"Sit tight," he said, rushing into the bathroom. He returned in seconds with a pill and a cup of water. "Take this—it's an aspirin. I'll go get Kate."

I gulped down the pill. "Why? We don't need to wake her."

"A—she's a doctor. And, B—someone needs to stay with Lily. I'd rather not take her with us." He pulled a robe out of the closet and threw it on as he headed down the hall.

A minute later, Kate followed him back into the room.

"The aspirin was a good call, David," she said. She reached for my wrist to get a pulse while watching the bedside clock, then put her ear against my back and listened for a moment. "Do you guys happen to have a blood pressure cuff?"

I'm betting ninety-nine percent of panic attack sufferers have them.

Kate stroked my hair while David went to fetch it. Then she applied the cuff to my arm, watching in silence until the digital reading was final.

"I'm no cardiologist, but I doubt you're having a heart attack," she said.

Kate's confident manner, her quick exam, and several deep breaths helped me realize the episode was only panic. And, as always, sharing my fears reduced their power to scare me. Still, I wasn't relieved. The thought of returning to the hell of frequent attacks frightened me almost as much as death. It had been so long since I'd suffered a full-blown, we've-got-to-go-to-the-hospital episode.

"Thanks, Kate," I said slumping back against the pillows in defeat.

"No biggie," she said, walking out the door.

I finally summoned the energy to get up and change into a fresh nightgown. "I feel so foolish for waking you guys," I said to David.

He climbed back into bed. "You only woke one of us," he said.

"What do you mean?" I asked, switching off the lamp and crawling in beside him.

"When I went down the hall to get her, I saw light coming from under Kate's door. I knocked and called her name, and she responded right away. Said something like, 'Just a sec.' Then I heard some shuffling around, and she fumbled to unlock the door and open it."

I felt an ache in the back of my throat and had to swallow a few times before I spoke. "Why would she have her door locked? Do you think she's using?"

David reached for my hand and intertwined his fingers in mine. "I don't know. She seemed pretty appropriate when she was checking you out. But truth be told, I was so worried about you that I didn't pay much attention to how she was acting."

"I guess we're gonna have to pay a little more attention."

"I think so."

CHAPTER FORTY-ONE

Monday, December 31

"Mom, there's a message," said Lily, as she ran past the phone in the family room to retrieve her ballet slippers. We'd had a perfect day: lunch at Ella's Deli, professional manicures, and shopping for a new tutu for her dance class.

I retrieved the message with disinterest and groaned to myself when I heard Kate's voice. "You're not answering your cell. Call me!"

She'd left the message three hours ago. I went back in the kitchen, fumbled through my purse, and I found my cell phone set to silent—as requested by our nail salon. I'd missed two calls from Kate.

I wanted to read a magazine and relax before making our New Year's Eve dinner, not call a client. In fact, a regular client wouldn't have my home or cell phone number. And she wouldn't be living in my guest room.

Kate stormed in the back door just as I began to dial her number. "Have you seen it?" she asked.

"What?"

"The fucking presentence report."

"No. You know I wasn't in my office today."

"Well, I wish to hell you had been," she said. She reached into her backpack, withdrew a manila envelope and slammed it onto the counter. "Then you could explain to me how this could happen. That goddamn bitch is recommending I do three and a half years in prison—and maybe more. That's not what you told me I'd be looking at!"

"Hold on a minute, Kate," I said, my voice cracking and rising to match hers. "You're out of line."

She raised her head to glare at me, and I saw her eyes—bloodshot, with pupils dilated to the max. Instantaneous rage sent a dose of adrenaline coursing through my body. "And you're high, too, aren't you?" I virtually screamed. "I can't believe you have the audacity to come in here yelling at me for not doing my job when you're doing everything in your power to sabotage me."

"Get off my fucking back," she shot back. "You don't know the first thing about it."

I spun around to leave the room, and there was Lily, standing in the kitchen doorway wearing her new ballet out-fit. No question she'd heard it all. Her eyes darted between Kate and me, and with trembling lips she ran to my side. "Are you okay, Mommy?"

"I'm sorry for scaring you, Lily," Kate said quickly. "It wasn't right for me to yell like that." She crouched down and reached over as if to pat Lily on the back.

But my daughter would have none of the apology. She moved her shoulder to avoid Kate's touch, leaned against my hip, and crossed her arms in defiance. Then, looking Kate straight in the eye, she said, "I'm glad you're not my mommy anymore. I hate you!"

Lily turned her back to Kate and hugged me, her warm face pressed against my stomach. I knew what I had to do.

"Pack your things, Kate. You're no longer welcome in this house." I needed a few minutes to collect myself before saying any more.

Kate didn't reply. She seemed unable to focus, and I vaguely wondered whether she'd heard me. But I'd deal with that after I made sure Lily was okay.

With every ounce of willpower in my body, I managed to slow my heartbeat and summon a calm tone. "C'mon, honey," I said to Lily. "Let's go talk in your room."

We walked arm in arm upstairs and sat together on her bed, her bare arms goose-pimply in the cool air. I drew the comforter up around her. "Tell me what you're thinking, Lily. It's important to get it out."

She sniffed back tears. "How can she be so mean? After how hard you worked on her case? It's not right. I really, really don't like her."

I buried my nose in her hair and inhaled its sweet scent, trying to get my own bearings. "For a long time, I've had mixed feelings about your Aunt Kate. Sometimes I've loved her. Sometimes—right now for instance—I've been so angry at things she's done that I've hated her. Sometimes I've felt sorry for her..."

"Me, too."

"There's one thing that will always be true though. I'll always love Kate for bringing you into this world and allowing Dad and me to be your forever family."

"Me, too, Mommy."

"Lily, there's another thing I know right now: Kate has to leave. Her drug addiction changed her. It made her into a different person than the one I knew in college or the one who gave birth to you. It made her untrustworthy, selfish, and—like you said—mean. I can't let her stay here and hurt us anymore. Do you understand?"

She nodded.

"Okay, honey. I need to go downstairs and make sure Kate understands. Do you mind staying in your room until she leaves?"

A pause. "Should I say goodbye to her?"

"Do you want to?"

"No, but what if it's the last time I ever see her?"

Damn you, Kate! Lily should be pirouetting around the kitchen, showing off her new outfit and begging to put on lipstick. Seven-year-olds should be sheltered from scenes like this!

"If you want to see or talk to Aunt Kate sometime later, we'll make sure that happens," I said. "But for right now, if you don't want to say goodbye, that's the way it'll be. Okay?"

Another nod. This one more confident. "Thanks, Mom."

Kate was still in the kitchen, sitting at the counter with an unlit cigarette in her hand, a vacant look on her face.

"I mean it," I said. "You. Need. To. Go. If you choose not to pack your own belongings, I will. But you've got half an hour to get the hell out of my house."

"You can't be serious," she said, rifling through her back-pack. "I said I was sorry."

"I'm dead serious, and it's way too late for apologies. You come in my house, higher than a kite—"

"You don't know that."

"You put Lily in the worst possible position—hearing you berate me. Not to mention your profanities."

"Who are you to talk? You swear just like the rest of us." She fiddled with the matchbook that had been her apparent target in the backpack.

"I'm not gonna let you get me off on a tangent here. This isn't about whether or not I swear. It's about you disrespect-ing me and my home, and upsetting my child—and she is *my* child now—with conflict she's too young to be a part of."

She started to light the cigarette but stopped, perhaps deterred by my withering look.

"Where am I supposed to go?" she asked, biting her lip, every trace of a challenge gone from her voice.

"To quote Rhett Butler who, like me, figured out way too late when enough was enough: 'Frankly, my dear, I don't give a damn.'"

A look of fear flashed across her eyes. "But what about my bail conditions?" she asked.

"Did you worry about your bail conditions when you used cocaine this afternoon?"

She stared down at her lap and didn't reply.

"Let me guess," I said caustically, "You were called in to give a urine sample this morning and figured you were home free for a couple of days."

She didn't deny it, and her prolonged silence told me I'd hit the nail squarely on the head.

"It's too late today," I said, "but as soon as the court opens on the second of January, I'll be filing a motion to withdraw as your attorney."

She put down the cigarette and matches and looked up at me, her eyes brimming with tears. "Caroline, please! Please reconsider. I need you and don't know who else to turn to. I feel like I'm at risk for a serious relapse, and my world is crashing around me. That's why I was so hateful to you. I'm so, so sorry."

Her tears and plea touched me not at all. It was—finally—crystal clear: I needed out of this toxic relationship, a relationship that had long since ceased being a friendship.

"This isn't open for discussion," I said. "If you're afraid of *relapsing*—which, by the way, it seems to me you've already done—call Adam or Jake or your N.A. sponsor. I don't care who you call. That's not my problem either. Do you intend to pack or shall I?"

Without a word, she stood and trudged up the steps. I listened to be sure she went to the guest room rather than Lily's and collapsed onto a kitchen stool. A wave of relief flooded over me. *It feels so good not to care about her—and to tell her so!*

About ten minutes later, I heard Kate's duffle bags thumping to the floor upstairs, then the squeaky hinge on my daughter's door. As fast as an Olympic sprinter on steroids, I was up the steps.

I don't know what made me pause outside Lily's open door. The hand of God on my shoulder? Some telepathic message from my daughter saying, "Give me a minute, Mom?"

"...you know how Caroline overreacts, Lily," Kate was saying. "I'll leave for a while, she'll cool down, and everything will be back to normal."

Normal? I rounded the doorjamb but stopped in my tracks.

Lily's dark eyes—narrowly focused on Kate's—told me she needed to handle this herself. I backed away.

"Don't call her Caroline to me!" Lily yelled. "She's my *mom*, and she reacted just right. We don't want you here anymore. Get out of my room and get out of our house."

Kate stormed out of the room, grabbed her bags and headed for the stairs. "I hope you're happy," she said to me over her shoulder. "You've turned my daughter against me with your histrionics, and you'll regret it someday."

Lily and I stood at the head of the staircase until the kitchen door slammed behind Kate.

She was gone.

CHAPTER FORTY-TWO

—⚍—

Tuesday, January 1

David and Lily looked up from their pancake preparations as I wandered into the kitchen, still trying to clear my sleep-deprived eyes.

"Happy New Year, Mom," Lily said, apparently recovered from any ill effects of yesterday's emotional fireworks. "Do you want bacon or sausage? We can't decide."

I kissed her on the head and my husband on the cheek. "Just coffee for me, please."

"You'll be sorry when you see our feast," she said. "And Dad said we could eat in the family room so we can watch the Rose Ball Parade."

David laughed and looked at his daughter with unabashed adoration. "And since we can't make up our minds, we'll have both bacon and sausage. Then Mom'll really be sorry."

I sat at the counter, warming my hands on my coffee mug and watching the two people I loved most in the world puttering away contentedly.

"You were pretty restless last night," David said when Lily trotted off to the bathroom. "I was hoping you'd be relieved to be rid of Kate and would sleep like a baby."

"I am relieved she's gone," I said, twisting to stretch my stiff back. "But I kept asking myself if she had a right to be pissed. About the presentence report, I mean. Kate left her copy here on the counter. So I got up around two o'clock and read it—four times, actually."

"And?"

"And I need to do some legal research today to be sure."

He couldn't mask his disappointment. "You're not going to the office, are you?" he asked.

"No, I can do it on-line. And I promise not to obsess about it or let it wreck our day."

I sniffed at the air and forced a smile when Lily came back. "Is it too late to change my mind about breakfast?" I asked. "That bacon smells irresistible, and Chef David's pancakes look wonderful. Golden brown, just the way I like them."

"No, it's not too late," she said with a blink—she hadn't quite mastered winking. "But you have to do the dishes."

My dishwashing and cleanup chores accomplished, and with Lily and David scrunched together on the couch watching the parade, I sat at my desk in the corner of the family room and got down to what was no longer my business—Kate's defense.

The presentence report was beyond disastrous. When George Cooper and I had discussed the plea agreement, he'd given me his estimate of Kate's sentencing guidelines. I rummaged through a pile of papers and found my notes from that meeting. Cooper thought Kate's offense would be categorized at level fifteen: a base offense level of six; ten levels added for the undisputed monetary loss; two levels added because Kate's crime involved her abuse of a position of trust with the university; three levels subtracted because Kate accepted responsibility and pleaded guilty, saving the prosecutor the work and expense of trial.

I looked again at my copy of the sentencing chart. Since Kate's criminal history was relatively minor, Cooper thought her imprisonment guidelines would be twenty-one to twenty-seven months. Cooper agreed to recommend a "downward departure"—or that the judge sentence Kate three levels lower for her help in prosecuting Joe Ames and Thorpe Akani. That would make the range twelve to eighteen months, and we'd planned to argue for a year or less.

What we hadn't counted on was Helen Garrety's recommendation for two more two-level *increases*. I didn't agree that Kate's offense involved "sophisticated means," as Garrety believed it had. And I sure hadn't anticipated Kate would be tagged for being a manager or supervisor of Joe Ames and Barbara Hughes, Marty Braxton's mistress and sometime assistant. *Kate was only doing Ames' bidding, for God's sake. She didn't have anything to do with Barbara Hughes at all.* Although how I could prove that without implicating Marty Braxton was beyond me. The bottom line: Garrety believed Kate should serve between thirty-three and forty-one months in prison.

I was also struck by how badly Kate came off on a personal level in the presentence report and how lukewarm Helen Garrety was toward George Cooper's recommended downward departure.

After spending an hour studying case law on-line, I began formulating arguments to challenge Helen Garrety's recommendations. Then I caught myself. *What in hell are you doing, Caroline Spencer? This is no longer your concern.*

I typed a short motion, requesting to withdraw as Kate's defense attorney, and sent it electronically to the U.S. Clerk of Court. The motion would be filed when the courthouse opened for business in the morning, and someone else could handle Kate's sentencing hearing.

Good luck, whoever you are, I thought as I closed my laptop and went to join my family in front of the TV.

Wednesday, January 2

Just as I finished telling Rosalee about the blow-up with Kate, a deputy court clerk called me at my office.

"Judge Coburn wants to hold a hearing on your motion to withdraw as counsel," the clerk said. "Would ten o'clock tomorrow work for you?"

I looked down to see my hand shaking and wondered fleetingly if I was nervous or excited by the judge's quick response. "That's fine with me, but you'll have to contact Ms. Daniels. We're not in communication at this point."

"Oh, we will. I'll send you the notice as soon as it's firmed up."

Within minutes, I received an e-mail notifying me of the *ex parte* hearing scheduled in the case of United States of America versus Kathryn S. Daniels. *Ex parte*, meaning one-party, indicated George Cooper would not be present at the hearing, only Judge Coburn, Kate, and me.

Thursday, January 3

I dreaded seeing Kate in the courtroom and timed my entrance for the last possible moment. She sat alone at the defense table, a yellow legal pad and a pen in front of her. I hadn't noticed it in the previous days, but her shoulders appeared bony through the cream-colored cashmere sweater she wore, and her hair was once again lacking in luster. *Has she been using regularly?*

She turned to look up at me as I approached. "Hello, Caroline."

"Hello," I said, thumbing through the files in my briefcase and pulling out the ones I'd need.

While we stood as Judge Coburn took the bench, Kate slid her legal pad in front of me. I looked down and saw, scrawled across the bottom of the page, "You OWE me."

My breath caught in my throat. I felt my face flush and my knees buckle. Once seated, it was all I could do to croak, "Kathryn Daniels, in person, with attorney Caroline Spencer," when the clerk asked for our appearances.

The judge began the hearing without fanfare, clearly unaware of my distress.

He looked up from the paperwork on his desk. "Ms. Spencer," he said, "I'm never happy to see motions like this so late in the game. We've got sentencing scheduled in two weeks, the early date at your request, as I recall. There's no way substitute counsel could be up to speed by then. You've requested permission to withdraw as counsel because of 'an irreconcilable breakdown in the attorney client relationship,' preventing you from providing effective assistance of counsel. You're going to need to tell me more."

"Yes, Your Honor," I said. "Ms. Daniels and I became friends in college in 1989, and our friendship continued. I initially encouraged her to retain another attorney to represent her in this case so as not to jeopardize our friendship, but I nevertheless accepted the retainer. Shortly after Ms. Daniels pled guilty, she sold her home and came to stay with me and my family while awaiting sentencing."

I didn't want to go on with the story—it all sounded trite and childish. But I wanted even less to continue representing my former friend.

I took a deep breath and forged ahead. "Ms. Daniels became angry when the presentence writer recommended a longer sentence than she expected and was clearly dissatisfied with my work. I asked her to leave our home due to the adverse effect the conflict was having on my family. It's my opinion Ms. Daniels would be better represented by another attorney at this time."

"Are you in agreement with the facts Ms. Spencer has proffered, Ms. Daniels?" the judge asked.

"I'm in agreement with most of it," Kate said with an edge of petulance. "But I'm not dissatisfied with her work and don't believe I could be better represented by anyone else. And I certainly don't want to wait longer to be sentenced."

The judge leaned back in his chair, his hands crossed behind his head, and stared at the ceiling for what felt like an eternity. I kept my eyes straight ahead but could sense Kate fidgeting next to me in her chair.

Finally, he spoke. "Ms. Spencer, you were right to begin with: it would have been prudent for your friend to hire another lawyer. But she didn't, and you accepted the retainer, knowing full well it could strain your relationship. There's no conflict of interest here—just ill will. I trust that if I deny your motion to withdraw, you'll still give your client your best efforts?"

If he knew me and my competitive nature, he wouldn't have to ask. "Yes, Your Honor," I said. "But—"

"And Ms. Daniels, are you certain you want me to deny the motion?"

"Yes, very certain," Kate said.

"The motion is denied," Judge Coburn said without a trace of apology in his voice, which told me any further argument on my part would be futile. "Ms. Daniels, I expect you to cooperate fully with your attorney to keep this case on track. Ms. Spencer, I'll extend the deadline for submission of your objections to the presentence report by three days, but the sentencing hearing will remain as scheduled. Is there anything further?"

Bile rose in my throat, tasting of dashed hopes and resignation, and I struggled to speak. "No, Your Honor."

"Very well. We're adjourned." He rose and walked through the door behind the bench.

My albatross was back.

—ɯ—

The cold, steely look in Kate's eyes as we left the courtroom precisely reflected my feelings toward her. Her dilated pupils told me she was probably high, and I wondered what sort of scheme she'd come up with to beat the urine tests. The question fled as quickly as it had come, though, since I no longer cared.

"Sorry, Caroline," she said. "I had to do it."

It was a hollow apology, not worth the breath she'd expended to say it, and I knew it as well as I knew my own name.

I ushered her toward a bench outside the courtroom, tension tightening my neck muscles. At the same time, my course of action was suddenly clear.

"This is how it's going to be," I said, towering over her as she sat. "I don't want to see you until the sentencing hearing. We'll communicate by e-mail or through Rosalee. I take pride in my work, so I'll do my best to argue for the lowest sentence possible, but I'm doing it because it's my professional responsibility and for no other reason."

I walked toward the elevator.

"Caroline," she said, "don't you want to know where I'm living?"

"I'm not babysitting you for one more minute," I said looking back over my shoulder. "Call Rosalee and give her the address for our file."

—ɯ—

With focus unclouded by emotion, I finished my legal research and filed the written objections to Kate's presentence report a day before the deadline. My arguments were well crafted and supported by case law, if not slam-dunk strong. Rosalee sent a copy of my submission to Kate, who couldn't resist responding.

"Great job!" her e-mail to me read. "I knew my confidence in you wasn't misplaced. Thanks for all your work and your vigorous, professional defense of my position. And again, I'm very sorry for the hurt I've caused you. Give Lily a hug for me. –K."

Her shallow platitudes turned my stomach. *She wasn't saying "great job" when she stormed into my house a week or so ago.* I hit "delete."

—⚮—

"Looks like you finally got some good news," Rosalee said several days later as she brought in my mail and a fax from the probation office. "That Garrety woman agrees with your argument on one of the objections to her presentence report."

I scanned through the paperwork. "Hallelujah!" George Cooper and I had both objected to Helen Garrety's two-level increases for the "sophisticated means" and managerial role guidelines. Now Garrety had amended her calculations, agreeing with us that Kate should not be classified as a manager or supervisor of other participants in the crime. She persisted, though, in her assessment that the offense involved sophisticated means.

Buoyed by the small success, I had Rosalee e-mail a copy of the letter to Kate along with the message: "We've gotten the probation officer to lower the guideline range to twenty-seven to thirty-three months. The judge doesn't have to agree, but from what I hear, he usually sides with the probation office."

Kate must have been sitting at her computer. "Pardon me for not being elated," she replied within seconds, writing directly to me. "It still sounds like a shitload of time to me."

Bitterness and defensiveness rose in my throat. "As I've told you before," I typed furiously, "the guideline range is just the starting point for our downward departure argument. We're shooting for three levels lower than that. You should be thankful for any slack we can get."

I powered down my computer before she could respond, my hands shaking with adrenaline and frustration. *The ungrateful bitch!*

Chapter Forty-three

—m—

Friday, January 18

Kate, her parents, one brother, and her sister were waiting in the security line when David and I got to the courthouse for Kate's sentencing. Her parents and siblings, clearly unaware of the rift between Kate and me, greeted us with hugs and smiles. Once through security, they held the elevator, waiting for us to clear the metal detector. Despite their friendliness, it was an awkward ride to the second floor. Kate stared at the ceiling, while I looked down at my shoes, grateful David had persisted in his plan to come with me.

A motley crew of about twenty supporters, including Adam Larken, Kate's N.A. sponsor, and a few people I recognized from The Meadows, huddled nervously in small groups in the hallway outside Judge Coburn's courtroom. As Kate strode over to say hello, I struggled to suppress my negative thoughts. Some of Kate's friends were downright seedy looking. One young man, garbed in torn jeans and a faded t-shirt, personified my mind's-eye picture of a heroin addict, with pale, waxy skin like that of an embalmed body lying in state. Another, a middle aged man sporting a sparse but incredibly long beard, wore a black leather jacket, pants, and biker boots, and a bandana around his thinning hair. Still another, an overweight woman of indeterminate age with broken and yellowed teeth, stood at the edge of a cluster, fingering a cigarette—this in a pristine smoke-free building.

These were not the kind of folks I wanted the judge to associate with my client. I wracked my brain to think of a way to tactfully ask them to sit in the back of the courtroom, well separated from Kate, her family and university colleagues. A quick glance at her father showed me he shared my disdain, and I cringed to realize I was as concerned with appearances as Corbett Daniels.

Kate turned to me and seemed to read my mind. "These people," she hissed, barely audibly so Corbett, Margaret and I had to strain to hear, "have been true friends to me. Don't you dare pass judgment on them or even suggest they should not be here."

Before I could respond, George Cooper touched me on the elbow and pulled me aside.

"Oh, man," he said, "it's like a circus in here."

I nodded and followed him around the corner of the hallway.

"I'm afraid I've got some bad news," he said. "The sentencing hearing Judge Coburn started this morning is still going on, so we won't begin on time. He just took a ten-minute recess because the court reporter signaled she needed a break. I'm hoping they'll finish in under a half-hour so we can get going."

"I know how these things go, George," I said. "I assume we should be in the courtroom at one-thirty anyway, so we're all assembled when they call our case?"

"Right. But there are as many people inside as Kate has with her out here. And I'm warning you, it's an emotional hearing."

"Oh?"

"Yeah. A bunch of twenty-year-old gang-bangers 'befriended' two fourteen-year-old girls at a mall," he said, making air quotes with his fingers. "They slipped them some Roofies, and what the girls thought would be an afternoon of amusing, innocent flirtations ended up being a weeklong excursion through hell."

I felt an emptiness in the pit of my stomach and wanted nothing more than to extricate myself from this conversation. But George continued, "They took the girls to Minnesota, where they raped, sodomized, and beat them before they finally let 'em go. One of the thugs, Rickey Johnson, copped a plea and snitched on his three pals. The trial for those guys ended yesterday, and they were all convicted. Rickey is the one getting sentenced today, and even though he was one of the key witnesses at the trial, he's still despicable. We're gonna hear from one of the victims' fathers right after the recess. I doubt it'll be pretty."

"At least Kate should look good by comparison," I said weakly.

"Yeah. I hope it'll play in your favor," he said, distracted by another prosecutor who approached.

Why wouldn't it play in our favor? I thought, equally as distracted, as I walked back to rejoin Kate and gather the troops. I explained the delay and what Cooper had told me about the earlier sentencing to Kate and those around her.

"We all need to go in and be seated before the judge comes back on the bench," I said, though the last thing I wanted to do was sit in on such a sordid case. I'd had enough of those when I was a prosecutor. "He probably won't take a break between this sentencing and ours."

We took up the last three rows of the courtroom. I was begrudgingly impressed with the demeanor of Kate's less-than-impressive-looking friends. They were clearly awed by the imposing surroundings, stood promptly and respectfully when the judge appeared, and sat in rapt attention when the clerk called us all back to order. I'd imagined I would need to watch them as I watched Lily and her classmates on a field trip to the theater, ready to give my "evil eye" if anyone veered over decorum's centerline. Yet here, not one needed it. Like me, they were soon engrossed in the drama that unfolded before us. Kate and her situation were momentarily lost to us as we listened and watched the conclusion of Rickey Johnson's sentencing hearing.

"Ms. Sanchez," the judge said to the prosecutor, "you've advised me one of the victims' fathers would like to make a statement. He can do so from counsel table."

Victoria Sanchez stood and brushed her thick black hair behind her ear. "Thank you, Your Honor," she replied. "Bridgette Walton's father, Mr. Abraham Walton, has asked to be heard." She beckoned forward a man who had been seated behind her.

Abraham Walton was the blackest man I'd ever seen. His leathery face and hands were the color of wrought iron—or so they seemed against his crisply starched, stark white shirt. A wiry man, perhaps fifty-five years old, he moved as one twenty years his senior, hobbling to the seat next to the prosecutor. He placed his shaking hands flat against the tabletop and leaned toward the microphone, then paused as if to collect his thoughts. The courtroom waited in complete silence.

"Judge," Walton finally said, "my wife and I sat and watched the whole trial of Rickey Johnson's so-called friends. We wanted to see for ourselves that justice was being done to the hateful people who'd stolen our daughter. My wife was so happy Bridgette didn't have to come testify, and I thought she was right."

Walton's Adam's apple bobbed as he swallowed hard and cleared his throat. "But then Bridgette's friend Marie got on the stand," he said. "She was scared at first, but I watched her get stronger and stronger as the trial went on. It was like this sweet child got her power back by being able to testify against the gangsters who hurt her. I think my Bridgette would have too. I think she's strong enough to have handled it.

"So I really don't think the boy deserves any less time because he *spared* my child the pain of testifying. Especially not after inflicting a *week* of pain and terror on these girls. And as far as his voluntary confession, I say baloney. He knew DNA from his seed would be detected on the panties found in my daughter's closet. He testified to save his own skin, to get a break from this Court. He's nothing but a damned scoundrel and a rat. Ummh... I'm sorry for the language, Your Honor. That's all I've got to say."

"Thank you for your candor, Mr. Walton," Judge Coburn said. "Ms. Sanchez, do you wish to be heard?"

"Thank you, Your Honor. I have nothing further to add to my written sentencing memorandum and my motion for downward departure," the prosecutor said.

Judge Coburn looked over his glasses and honed in on Rickey Johnson. "This Court owes a debt of gratitude to Bridgette Walton's father," he said. "He saw the truth of this defendant and spoke it succinctly. Rickey Johnson deserves no further mercy from this Court. I've already granted him the three-level downward adjustment in the sentencing guidelines for his 'acceptance of responsibility.' And I use the term very loosely in this case. Rickey Johnson did what he had to do to get a shorter sentence: he pled guilty and admitted his criminal acts. But I don't for a minute believe he did so out of a sense of remorse. He didn't testify against his cohorts because it was the right thing to do. He did it in hopes of getting an even shorter sentence.

"I agree with Mr. Walton. Rickey Johnson didn't spare Mr. Walton's daughter by testifying. He kidnapped, assaulted, and raped her and her friend, and nothing he's said or done since has spared her. The motion for downward departure is denied."

In the back of the courtroom, my mind raced. *Will Judge Coburn's ire at Rickey Johnson extend to Kate? Should I ask for a continuance?*

Through my distraction, I managed to hear the judge sentence Rickey Johnson to the maximum term authorized by his sentencing guidelines, thirty years in prison without parole. *It's not enough.*

The judge looked up from the bench. "I see the parties in United States versus Daniels are present in the courtroom," he said. "I apologize for the delay. I'm going to ask your indulgence a bit longer. We'll take a fifteen minute recess."

CHAPTER FORTY-FOUR

George Cooper motioned for me to join him in the hall, and we moved out of earshot of the spectators. "I don't have a good feeling about this," he said. "Coburn's loaded for bear, and I don't think it bodes well for your client."

"I don't know. I was just thinking it would be easy to distinguish her from that scumbag of a defendant. But you know the judge far better than I. Can I ask for a continuance?"

"On what ground? It's not unusual for a proceeding to be delayed an hour or even more. You certainly can't tell the judge you're afraid he's lost his impartiality. Even if it's true."

My palms were sweaty. I wiped them on the skirt of what I'd always considered my lucky gray suit. *I should've ignored my superstitions and worn the red power suit.*

"Do you have any suggestions for me?" I asked Cooper.

"Not really. He likes it if we don't reiterate what we've already submitted to him in writing. So avoid long arguments if you can. You and I are in essential agreement on what should happen, but I can't give the judge the impression I've gone soft on crime, especially after what just happened in there."

"Do you think we still have a chance of getting our downward departure?"

"Sure. But we probably would've been better off to come back later for a reduction in the sentence, after Joe Ames and Thorpe Akani are convicted and sentenced. It's too late now, though. We've already filed our motion."

Cooper looked at his watch. "Look, I gotta hit the men's room before we go back in. Good luck."

"What's up?" Kate asked when I joined her outside the courtroom.

I marveled at how little she seemed to care that she and I were on the outs, demonstrating to me, once again, that our friendship had become toxic. "Cooper and I were just talking strategy," I said. "He thinks the Johnson sentencing may be a bad act for us to follow. I can't tell. We'll just have to hope Judge Coburn regained his composure—and his objectivity—during the recess."

"Que sera. I just want this over with," Kate said, striding back in to court. I also marveled at her composure.

As I walked back up the aisle of the formidable courtroom, my stomach churned, and I felt a wave of panic overcoming me. *No! This cannot happen now*. I plunged ahead through the swinging door of the bar and collapsed into the chair next to Kate's. At least it felt like I collapsed.

Okay, just go on—move through it. I pulled a legal pad out of my briefcase and went through the motions of studying my notes, frantically hoping I could calm myself before it was time to give my sentencing argument. As an ADA, I'd been able to question and cross-examine witnesses with no fear, but lengthier statements had sometimes been difficult—especially with too much downtime beforehand.

Just as more unsettling sensations began swelling within me, David tapped me on the shoulder. I spun around and saw he'd selected a seat in the left front row, just behind our table. He made direct eye contact, gave me a thumbs-up and sat down. God bless him—he'd sensed my panic and was there for me. It was enough to bring me out of myself and back into the courtroom. Maybe another time I'd be angry with myself for needing his rescue, but right then all I felt was gratitude.

Judge Coburn returned to the bench moments later, his face expressionless. My confidence returned as I began searching for clues as to his thoughts. I'd always considered myself a good reader of people. *I can make the most of this strained and strange situation. I can convince this man to be lenient toward my client.* With a strong, clear voice, I entered my appearance on behalf of Kathryn Daniels.

There would be no levity or informality during this hearing. Judge Coburn delved right in to Helen Garrety's presentence report and accepted her modified calculation of the sentencing guidelines. Kate was looking at twenty-seven to thirty-three months in prison when we moved on to the next phase, the argument for a sentence below the guideline range.

"Now I'll hear your arguments as to departure," Judge Coburn said. "Please begin, Mr. Cooper."

George Cooper rose, buttoning his suit coat. After the briefest glance at his notes, he began. He spoke in an informal yet eloquent manner, with nary an "um" or "ah."

"Your Honor, as I outlined in my motion for downward departure, Kathryn Daniels provided very valuable assistance to my office in two specific investigations. The first is the case captioned U.S. versus Joseph William Ames. Ames had been suspected of trafficking in substantial quantities of cocaine for several years, but he was well insulated from law enforcement. With information given by Ms. Daniels, and with her grand jury testimony, we were able to obtain a two-count indictment against Ames. As the Court is aware, one of the counts alleges Ames provided the cocaine that caused the death of twenty-three-year-old Yvonne Pritchard last fall. If necessary, Ms. Daniels will testify at his trial. However, we're already in plea negotiations with Ames' defense counsel, largely because of the solid case Ms. Daniels gave us."

Cooper took a sip of water. "The second case, which involved fraudulent documents, has not yet resulted in an indictment. Ms. Daniels gave a lengthy statement concerning one of the potential defendants, whom I can't name in open court for obvious reasons, but the investigation is ongoing. The FBI informs me the leads provided by Ms. Daniels are panning out, and we expect to indict at least three individuals as a result. These individuals would likely have gone undetected but for Kathryn Daniels' assistance.

"In summary, Your Honor, the government believes the defendant's assistance clearly warrants the three-level downward departure for which we've moved. Thank you."

Cooper unbuttoned his jacket and was halfway to his seat when Judge Coburn asked, "Would you care to comment, Mr. Cooper, on the probation officer's suggestion at paragraph seventy-one of the presentence report?"

Cooper resumed standing and shuffled through the papers on his table to find the report. "If I might have a moment, Your Honor?" Then, without glancing in the judge's direction, he studied the report as if there were no urgency to respond.

My thoughts reeled as I paged through the report to find the paragraph in question. Out of the corner of my eye, I saw Cooper leaning over the table and jotting a few words on his legal pad. *Don't piss off the judge*, I thought, while at the same time outlining an argument in my mind.

The lull couldn't have lasted more than a minute or two—and far too short a time for me to formulate a strong rebuttal—though it must've felt interminable for Kate and the spectators.

Judge Coburn interrupted the silence with derision. "For the benefit of those who have not studied the report, I'll quote paragraph seventy-one: 'According to Section 2B1.1, Note 18(A), in cases where the monetary loss determined under the guidelines "substantially understates the seriousness of the offense," an upward departure may be warranted. The National Institutes of Health lost more than the money the defendant embezzled. They bargained for solid research and got questionable data from an impaired person.'" He looked down at the prosecutor.

"Judge," George Cooper said with equanimity, "perhaps I should have been more clear in my letter to the Court dated January third. I'll read the pertinent paragraph: 'The government believes there are no appropriate grounds for upward departure.' I then went on to advise I would be filing a motion for downward departure. I thought it implicit in my comment that the probation officer's suggestion for upward departure was without merit. I can specifically tell you the National Institutes of Health found no fault with Dr. Daniels' research itself. In fact, the study is continuing under the leadership of her colleague, Dr. Braxton."

Without skipping a beat or tipping his hand, Judge Coburn turned to me. *I wish we were in front of Judge Judy—she always lets you know what she's thinking.*

"Ms. Spencer, your comments?"

"Your Honor, had I known Ms. Garrety's offhand suggestion would warrant this Court's serious consideration, I would certainly have included a detailed response within my objections to the presentence report. I agreed with Mr. Cooper that there was no merit to the suggestion."

Judge Coburn looked across the bench, avoiding eye contact with either Cooper or me, and spoke directly to the spectators. "Just because the prosecutor and the defense attorney agreed to buy a pig in a poke," he said, "doesn't mean I'm bound to buy into it too."

He glared at me. "Ms. Spencer, you were provided with adequate notice of the potential upward departure through the presentence report. However, if the parties wish a continuance, we can resume this hearing on March first. What's your preference?"

Shaking her head, Kate moved as if to stand in reply. While my hand shot over to still her movement, I faced the judge. "May I please have a moment to confer with my client?" I asked with all the courtesy I could muster.

Judge Coburn nodded, and I leaned my head toward Kate's, signaling her to whisper. "I do not want a continuance," she hissed, loudly enough for even the near deaf to hear.

"Hold it down, Kate," I said, flashing back to my days as an ADA when I'd have to calm the occasional hotheaded cop whose integrity was being questioned by a lying witness. "You've got to know this afternoon has turned into a nightmare. I think we'd be wise to take the continuance he's offered so we can regain some control of this situation."

Still shaking her head, although less perceptibly, Kate grinned. "I gots to know," she said.

"What?" I asked, more astonished by her expression than the question. *What was this mood swing all about?*

"You know. The line from 'Dirty Harry' when the bad guy just has to know if Clint Eastwood has another bullet in his gun."

"My God. Are you high?"

"No, but I might be two or three weeks from now."

"Kate, this is no time for foolishness. This is a bad situation."

"I know. Believe me, I know. But the suspense is killing me. And I just want to get it over with."

"But going ahead today may hurt your chances when you appeal the sentence," I said.

"I'm not going to appeal, Caroline. I'm guilty. I pled guilty, and I want to know now what my punishment is going to be."

"You're sure?"

"I'm sure."

I fleetingly thought of requesting a recess so I could have Kate put her choice in writing, but I was afraid of further irritating the judge.

After a quick silent cleansing breath, I rose. "Thank you for the time, Your Honor. My client wishes to proceed with sentencing today. For the record, and to preserve the issue for appeal," I said, as Kate kicked at me under the table, "I object to the proposed upward departure. Dr. Kathryn Daniels was a well-respected, conscientious scientist, and I submit her personal use of cocaine did not affect the quality of her research. As Mr. Cooper indicated, no one, including the NIH, has ever once questioned her results."

I flipped the page of my legal pad. "As Your Honor will recall from the employment section of the presentence report," I continued, "my client received an unprecedented early promotion to the position of associate professor based on her excellent evaluations and research skills. There is simply no evidence her research was flawed, and there is no valid ground for upward departure. That's all, Your Honor."

To my surprise and pleasure, he nodded. Maybe, just maybe, he'd accepted what I had said.

"Very well. If there are no other comments regarding departures?" Judge Coburn inclined his head, first toward me and then toward George Cooper. We shook our heads. "Then we'll move on. Ms. Daniels, do you wish to make a statement?"

Once again, I was caught off guard. I'd expected the judge to rule on whether he would depart upward or downward from the guideline range before proceeding to the final sentencing arguments. But no way was I going to question his protocol. I nodded to Kate, and we both stood.

"Thank you, Judge," she said in a clear voice. *If only she could sound halfway nervous*, I though with chagrin. But, like the Kate Daniels of old, she spoke with authority. "There's not much I can add to the written statement I've already submitted to you. However, I would like to say a few words publicly.

"When I graduated from medical school, I never could have imagined myself in the position in which I find myself today. I had a physician's knowledge of the pharmacology of drugs, but I had no clue what cocaine was doing to me on a personal level. Although I knew better, I became an addict, plain and simple."

Kate hung her head for an instant in what might have been contrition, then looked back up at the judge. "My long-term love affair with cocaine brought me here," she said. "I could have found a way to break from this despicable drug. But I didn't. Instead, I abandoned my principles and stole from the grant program. I abused the trust NIH placed in me. I brought shame upon the university that had so graciously hired me and promoted me. I caused my family and friends untold pain. For all of this I am profoundly sorry.

"I hope the sentence you impose, Your Honor, will allow me to return to the community as soon as possible so I can begin to make amends for my actions. Thank you."

What a tough act to follow, I thought, as the judge turned to me for my sentencing argument. I had urged Kate to prepare her allocution ahead of time and to let me read it. At first, she'd simply put me off, saying she hadn't gotten to it. But as the sentencing date approached, she flatly refused to discuss it. "I'm not an idiot," she had e-mailed me the last time I broached the subject. "I don't need you coaching me on how to be contrite."

Kate's short and forthright statement was just right. The judge regarded me with courtesy as I addressed him. He must have been moved by her words. And he must not have been put off by her confidence.

I lacked Kate's commanding oratorical style, and, in fact, stumbled over my first words. But my many years of courtroom experience took over, and I talked to the judge, hitting every point on my outline without missing a beat.

"Your Honor," I stated in closing, "Kathryn Daniels has seen the error of her ways. She sought treatment for the addiction that clouded her judgment and led her here, and she's made remarkable progress toward recovery. She's already paid dearly for her crimes with the loss of her livelihood and her stature within the academic and research communities. Dr. Daniels liquidated all her assets to make restitution, and I have with me a cashier's check for the full amount owed.

"Kathryn Daniels is a bright, resilient woman who has much to offer the community. Given the sentencing guidelines are advisory rather than mandatory, a term of probation is an option. I urge the Court to impose probation, and I do not believe a sentence of probation would depreciate the seriousness of her crime. However, if the Court elects to sentence her to a term of confinement, I would ask you to give her the opportunity to return to meaningful and productive work as soon as possible."

I glanced at my outline and saw with relief I'd reached the last item on my list. "Finally, if a term of imprisonment is imposed, we ask the Court to recommend Dr. Daniels be designated to serve her sentence at a facility in close proximity to her family in northern California. Thank you, Your Honor."

As I sat down, Kate smiled and dabbed a wadded tissue to the end of her nose. I snuck a peek up at Judge Coburn. *Is it a positive vibe I feel? I hope so.*

"Mr. Cooper. Your comments," he said.

Cooper stood. "For the reasons I've already set forth in writing and in court today, the government is recommending no upward departure but rather a three-level downward departure. I'd ask for a sentence somewhere within the resulting range of eighteen to twenty-four months' imprisonment, and the government has no objection to designating her to a prison in northern California. I'd also ask the Court to order restitution in the amount of $147,682, which Ms. Daniels and my office agree is owed, and Ms. Daniels is prepared to pay. Thank you."

The silence in the courtroom was as intense as the cacophony in my brain as Judge Coburn paused before pronouncing sentence.

He looked down at his desk, sorting through the many papers piled on it. The suspense was palpable. I'm sure I stopped breathing. I could see Kate's grip on the edge of the table tightening. After what felt like an eternity, Coburn found the single page he'd been searching for. When he began to read from it, my heart sank. I knew without question he would show no mercy toward my client. He'd listened to

Kate's plea and mine. But in the end he'd gone back to find the tough sentencing statement he'd prepared earlier.

"First, I'll address the prosecutor's motion for downward departure from the guideline range. I don't doubt the defendant's cooperation was very helpful. The United States Attorney's office provided me copies of her statements to authorities, and I have seen the indictment in the case of Joseph Ames. The sentencing guideline manual says I can't use the information she gave to determine her sentencing range. But I *can* use it to decide whether or to what extent I should depart downward to reward her cooperation."

The judge looked straight at Kate, his eyes icy. "This defendant was up to her eyeballs in criminal activity for a long time. Not only did she steal money from the university, she willingly consorted with drug dealers, con men and counterfeiters. She had in her possession a counterfeit passport while she was on bond in this case. And she didn't turn it in to the FBI until after she realized she might get a reduced sentence for it. This defendant was not, as she would have us believe, an upstanding citizen who engaged in a little aberrant behavior. She was a criminal, plain and simple. And I am denying the government's downward departure motion."

I felt devastated and betrayed. George Cooper had told me the judges, including Judge Coburn, rarely denied their cooperation motions. And now he'd done it twice in one afternoon. Worse yet, I knew I had virtually no chance of winning on appeal: A judge has almost unlimited discretion in deciding whether or not to grant a downward departure. I glanced over to the prosecution table, where George Cooper hung his head in dismay. He didn't meet my eye.

Behind us, Kate's mother struggled to contain her sobs. I could hear Corbett Daniels mumbling, "...son of a bitch... can't..."

Kate turned and glared him into silence.

"Next, the issue of upward departure," Judge Coburn said. "I intend to depart upward two levels because the defendant's conduct was more serious than the monetary loss reflects. I believe the probation officer—Ms. Garrety—correctly stated the facts: The National Institutes of Health lost more than money here. They gave the defendant a substantial grant, expecting valid, innovative research on a potential cure for cancer. I know there were no guarantees the research would be successful, but the defendant was obligated to give it her best shot, and she didn't.

"Mr. Cooper and Ms. Spencer told me there's no evidence the research was flawed, and I certainly can't go out and prove it was. But what the defendant herself told the probation officer is very revealing. I'm quoting from paragraph forty-six of the presentence report. 'Daniels admits she sometimes worked in the university research laboratory while under the influence of cocaine. She states in such cases, she double-checked the instrument readings and her data entries or had a laboratory assistant do so, just to make sure there were no mistakes.'"

Judge Coburn paused for effect, again speaking to the spectators. "What's to say the defendant's 'double-checking' or the 'double-checking' by a less trained laboratory assistant was sufficient to ensure accuracy? And even if it was, how do you account for the waste of time involved? This defendant squandered her God-given talent. She should have been using her skills and imagination for the benefit of the medical community. Instead she expended her time and energy obsessed with getting high."

At this, Corbett Daniels made a grand exit from the courtroom, with Margaret—sobbing uncontrollably—in tow.

"Shit," Kate said under her breath to me. "Why did he even come?"

But Judge Coburn was done with the caustic words. While he intoned the formal sentencing statement, I sat numbly, listening but not fully hearing the words. Somehow I managed to jot down the salient points: three years in prison, a ten thousand dollar fine, three years of supervision, and the agreed-upon restitution. Kate would have three weeks to "put her affairs in order" before turning herself in to serve the sentence. She had ten days in which to file her notice to appeal the sentence, and I was obligated to represent her until or unless relieved by the Court of Appeals.

And then it was over. Judge Coburn rose to leave the bench. Like robots, we stood too. Kate turned to me. "Don't worry, Caroline—you're done with me," she said. "I'm not going to appeal."

CHAPTER FORTY-FIVE

Friday, February 8

The morning Kate was scheduled to surrender to prison was a typical February morning in Wisconsin—frigid, with dingy piles of crusty snow everywhere you looked. Despite the parka I'd pulled on over my robe, the air bit me as I trudged to the driveway's end to retrieve my newspaper.

A front-page above-the-fold headline in the *State Journal* provided another jolt—"University Researcher Reports to Prison Today." The story, rehashing Kate's crime and punishment, described the conditions she'd find when she reported to the federal prison camp in Dublin, California, later in the afternoon. At least they'd printed a picture other than her horrific mug shot.

When I'd kicked Kate out and relinquished my role as her babysitter, Marty Braxton's wife Rita had jumped in with both feet.

I'd been surprised when Kate called Rosalee to report she was staying with the Braxtons—it took a lot of audacity to be a guest in the home of your former lover and his wife.

Rita, as I would come to learn, had experience dealing with two dysfunctional adult children of her own, and Kate's neediness didn't much faze her. After Kate's car lease expired, Rita ferried her to counseling sessions, N.A. meetings, and urine screening appointments. I seriously doubted Kate was remaining clean and sober, but at least she'd been able to avoid bail revocation.

The day we were notified where the Bureau of Prisons had assigned Kate to serve her sentence, Rita Braxton had called me with a complete travel itinerary. She would drive Kate to Chicago for a red-eye flight from O'Hare to San Francisco; Kate's sister, Elizabeth, would pick her up in San Francisco and drive her to Dublin, about forty minutes away. The schedule would easily allow Kate to report to the prison by two o'clock, as ordered by the court. I'd wanted to cut Rita off, but I had to admit her willingness to handle the details was a relief to me. Otherwise, as Kate's defense attorney of record, I might also have found myself assuming the role of travel agent.

Today's newspaper article triggered a few moments of angst, but I managed to push them aside. I sat at the kitchen counter with my second cup of coffee, engrossed in the cross-word puzzle, and startled when the phone rang.

"It's Rita," she said, "and I hope I didn't wake you. But I've been worried half to death and didn't know who else to call."

Shit! Can this ever really be over?

"You didn't wake me. What's wrong?" I asked, my back stiffening.

"After dinner last night, Kate said she wanted to go to one last N.A. meeting before she left, so I lent her my car. She was an hour late getting home—told me about an impromptu farewell party her sponsor had arranged—and I was frantic to get to Chicago on time."

My heart skipped a beat. "You made it, didn't you?" I asked before I could stop myself. *What do you care?*

"We made it on time," Rita said. "But Kate chattered incessantly the whole way down. And some of it didn't make much sense. Then she refused to let me park and go in with her—I mean, what was she going to do if her flight was cancelled due to weather or something? On the way home, all I could do was think of how bizarre she was acting and maybe she was back on cocaine. I did call and make sure the flight left, but there was no way to check to see if she actually got on. I tried to reach her sister Liz this morning, but only got her voice mail. And I don't have her cell phone number—stupid of me not to get it."

"Rita, please don't feel guilty about what you did or didn't do. This is Kate's responsibility, not yours."

"I should know that by now—I've been enabling my own kids for so long. And I guess I just fell into doing it with Kate, too. But she's such a nice person, and I feel sorry for the mess she's in."

I'm pretty sure you wouldn't feel that way if you knew about her and your husband!

"I'll call Dublin later this afternoon to make sure she got there," I said. "Don't give it another thought."

Before I had a chance to move, the phone rang again—this time Kate's N.A. sponsor, Luann.

"I didn't know if I should call, because it's violating a confidence," she said. "But I was expecting Kate at the meeting last night, and she called with a lame excuse. When I saw this morning's paper and realized she was supposed to go to prison today, I got really worried."

"She didn't go to the meeting?"

"No."

"You didn't have a farewell party for her?"

"Farewell party?" She sounded genuinely puzzled. "No. In fact, she told me she'd gotten a postponement from the judge and didn't have to go for three more weeks."

"Shit," I said, with a grimace. Kate was poisoning more decent folks—like Rita and Luann—and they didn't deserve it any more than I had.

"You don't think she'd run, do you?"

"I can't begin to guess anymore. Her friend Rita dropped her at the airport, but God knows if she actually got on the plane. From what Rita said about her behavior, I suspect she was stoned."

"I'm sorry. I should've seen it coming," Luann said.

Kate sure has a way of making other people feel sorry for her fuck-ups.

"I'll let you know if I hear anything," I said. "But this is her responsibility, not yours."

I hung up, found my cell phone and scrolled through it to find Liz's number. But the words I'd already spoken twice this morning echoed in my head. *It's Kate's responsibility, not yours.* With a sense of pride and relief, I switched the phone to silent, left it on the counter, and went back to my crossword puzzle.

Just as I filled in the last blank, I heard the insistent hum of the phone vibrating against granite. I reached for the phone. Liz. *Can't you all leave me in peace?*

But then I remembered what I'd heard recently on some talk show: Just because a phone rings doesn't mean you have to answer it. *How liberating! Why didn't I think of that?*

Wednesday, February 27

I sat at my desk, engrossed in highlighting a new Supreme Court case, and glanced up in irritation when the phone rang.

"Kate's sister Liz is on line one," Rosalee said through the intercom. "Can I put her through?"

At least six phony excuses flashed through my head, but I'd never had anything but respect for Liz. And I felt more than a little shame for ignoring her message three weeks ago. "Sure," I said.

"Hi, Caroline," she said. I could hear the nervousness in her voice.

"Before you go on," I said, "I need to apologize for not returning your last call. I'd just had it up to here with Kate and behaved childishly. I'm sorry."

"I think it's my sister who's behaved childishly. And I completely understand. Did you listen to my message?"

"Not until the next day," I said sheepishly. In her message, Liz had said that Kate hadn't voluntarily surrendered as scheduled to serve her sentence. She'd gotten on the flight from Chicago to San Francisco but had failed to meet Liz. At the time of the call, no one had known where Kate was.

George Cooper had subsequently called me to report the U.S. Marshals nabbed her two days later, after she'd tried to buy cocaine from an undercover cop. Her failure to appear had disqualified her from serving her sentence at the minimum-security camp, so Kate was sitting behind actual bars at Dublin's secure facility.

"Mom and I visited Kate yesterday," Liz said, "and there's something we thought you should know."

My stomach knotted, and I realized I was sitting on the edge of my chair. "What's that?"

"Let me start by saying our visit with her was hell. My mom held her tongue, but I was so angry about the whole voluntary surrender fiasco and all. I confronted Kate—told her she needed to grow up. I mean, I said it quietly because we were sitting in this depressing visiting room with other inmates and their families within earshot. But Kate lashed out at me. Who did I think I was telling her how to live her life? And on and on."

"Oh, man," I said absently. None of this was new or unexpected—I wanted Liz to get to the point.

"Then she started playing the blame game. 'If it weren't for our fucking father I wouldn't be in this mess.' Then Mom got defensive for Dad, and Kate laid into her for putting up with a 'pompous, selfish, womanizing bastard.'"

"I'm sorry. It sounds awful."

"Kate was so focused on her victimhood, it was like I didn't even know her. You were the next target for her blame. She said another inmate is helping her file an appeal because you were negligent in defense of her case. Or something along those lines."

My heart sank: I should've expected this but hadn't. I'd studied the U.S. Code section that allows prison inmates to challenge their sentences. I knew that alleging an attorney's substandard work was a common ground for appeal. "Ineffective assistance of counsel?" I asked Liz.

"Yeah. That's it. I don't know if she'll actually go through with it or not. But Mom and I thought I should at least call and warn you—and let you know she's being negative and hateful to everyone right now."

A finger painting of Lily's—prominently displayed on the side of my file cabinet—caught my eye. *Think of Lily— that's what's really important. Kate is not worth one ounce of angst.*

"Thanks for the heads-up, Liz. But it's your mom I feel badly for. She doesn't deserve this."

"No, she doesn't."

"What do you plan to do about Kate?" I asked.

"Nothing. She told us to get the hell out of the prison and out of her life. We decided to take her advice. You may want to do the same."

I didn't tell her I already had.

—⁘—

The Internet is an incredible yet awful invention. In the next few days, I checked on-line court records countless times to see if, in fact, Kate had filed her appeal motion. Finally, I found it. It still hurt to see the notation on the court docket sheet, showing she actually had. It pained me to see in black and white that Kate believed I had done an inadequate job in representing her.

I reviewed the court documents by computer. Kate claimed I hadn't given her an accurate estimate of the likely sentence when she decided to plead guilty, and I hadn't objected to the guideline calculations and the probation officer's suggestion for upward departure. She asked the court to overturn her sentence because of my negligence.

Although I knew intellectually that many of the "facts" Kate provided in her motion were outright lies, the overriding charge of negligence cut me to the quick. Try as I might, I was unable to refrain from questioning my work on the case. I told David as much when he came home that evening.

His vehemence surprised me. "You need to stop this second guessing," he said. "It's bad enough Kate filed the motion to begin with, but she's flat-out wrong to misrepresent what happened. And her whole 'poor me' thing is pissing me off!"

David was right. Kate had repeatedly ignored my advice. She was the one who'd insisted on going forward when we had the opportunity to ask for more time to present a stronger case. And she was the one with a prior arrest record, and the one who'd associated with all manner of criminals.

But I hadn't been vigilant enough to realize Kate's "cooperation" against Joe Ames and Thorpe Akani would be viewed so negatively by the judge. And I should never have let her tell the probation officer she'd worked in the lab under the influence of cocaine.

—w—

"I can't stop feeling guilty," I told Dr. Brownhill during one of our sessions.

"With all due respect, you *can* stop," she said, fingering the large silver bracelet she wore on one wrist. "But go ahead and tell me what you feel guilty about."

"My life goes on. Kate's is on hold, and will be for another couple years. Despite the hateful things she's done and said, I still wish I'd done a better job representing her. I was too quick to let her cooperate with the cops—maybe I still identified with them too much. If I hadn't, she might be out by now. Or at least at a halfway house."

"Who did the crime, Caroline?"

"Kate. But—"

"I'm sorry to interrupt you, but I need to make this point. The one who does the crime has to do the time, and that's not your fault. From what I read in the paper, she stole a lot of money and put it up her nose. And she didn't stay clean after she got caught. So unless you helped her steal the money or forced her to use cocaine, it's on her. I admit the criminal justice system isn't perfect. People don't always get the exact punishment they need or deserve, but who's to say this isn't what she deserves?"

"Do you think she deserved three years in prison?"

"As your psychotherapist, I shouldn't say. But do you want my opinion as a graduate of the university she embezzled from and as a former benefactor of federal grants?"

"Yes."

"Okay. I agreed with the judge. And I hate to see what you're allowing this to do to you. The motion Kate filed calling you ineffective was hitting below the belt. She knew your criminal law experience was on the prosecution end, and she still pressured you to take her case."

Dr. Brownhill took a sip from her mug of tea and looked at me. "Why don't you tell me the real reason you chose to represent her in the first place? You hedged when we talked about this before the sentencing."

I lowered my head and closed my eyes. "It's so hard!"

"I understand. But it's harder in the long run to keep secrets, and the toll it takes on one's psyche is immeasurable."

I nodded and told her what I remembered about that Friday in January 1991, shortly after I had begun taking Valium for anxiety. I had taken one pill to help me through a presentation in my afternoon Constitutional Law class. That evening, I skipped dinner and took another one to get ready for a top-drawer fraternity's party—I was going with a senior I'd been attracted to for a long time and was beyond nervous.

The party was disastrous from the beginning. Even through my Valium-induced haze, I could see my date had invited me only to get back at another girl. Embarrassed and self-conscious, I drank three cups of punch—made with grain alcohol—to ease my discomfiture. It wasn't long before I passed out.

I vaguely remembered being awakened and going upstairs with two guys, guys I considered friends, before I blacked out again. When Kate barged in, interrupting what would surely have turned into a brutal sexual assault, she found me naked. Both men had their pants down and were arguing over who would go first, at the same time shouting for others to come watch. In a rage, Kate wrapped me in a blanket and demanded her date take us to the nearest emergency room.

By this time, my loss of consciousness was of more concern to her than rape. Doctors pumped my stomach, detoxified my system, and hammered home how perilously close to death I'd been.

Mortified at having put myself in such a precarious situation by using alcohol on top of tranquilizers, I refused to snitch on the fraternity boys. Kate didn't push it either. Maybe she understood it would be a no-win situation, or maybe she identified with their pedigrees and prep school ways. I told myself that other than bruises and a bruised ego, I had come to no harm.

Kate had been uncomfortable with the profuse thanks I gave her for saving my life. "Don't mention it again," she had said. And I hadn't. To anyone.

I sat, spent, and wiped an errant tear from my chin.

Dr. Brownhill reached over and squeezed my hand, bringing me back to the present. "Oh, my dear," she said. "I'm so sorry for what you went through. And that you persisted in your silence for so long. It can't have been easy."

"I was usually able to block it out. I read some books about victims of sexual assault and attended a seminar or two—as an anonymous observer. Those things helped me get beyond my shame. But it all came back when Kate called in the favor. She took it for granted I'd repay her by representing her."

Dr. Brownhill nodded knowingly, but I sensed she wanted to move beyond discussing Kate. "Caroline, this was a major traumatic event in your life," she said, "and it had to have affected you in lots of areas. Tell me about your subsequent relationships with men."

"Oh, I didn't even date for about a year after the incident. But going home that summer really helped. I got to see two good men—my dad and my brother—up close. They're not glamorous guys, but they're reliable, constant and true. That's what I looked for in a partner. And—thank God—I found it in David."

"Speaking of David," Dr. Brownhill said, "I really think he needs to know."

"You're right," I said, raking my hair with my fingers and consciously formulating excuses to ignore her advice.

"Tonight," she said, looking straight through my defenses.

I didn't respond.

"It's important for your mental health," she said patiently. "Don't postpone it."

"Okay."

—ᴡᴡ—

The timing didn't seem right before or after dinner. And, in truth, I put off the conversation as long as I could. David was in bed reading when I went upstairs. I hurried to get ready for bed myself, intent on catching him before he dozed off, if only to fulfill my promise to Dr. Brownhill.

I climbed in beside him. "There's something I want to tell you about, if you're not too tired," I said.

He lowered his book to his chest and looked at me, then reached over and rubbed his thumb against my cheek. "Sure, but let's get this moisturizer goop off you first. It's distracting," he said with a grin.

"I should have told you years ago…"

I hadn't intended to alarm him, but clearly I had. The grin vanished, and he put the book on the nightstand. "What is it?"

For the second time that day, I recounted the humiliating experience I'd tried for years to forget. I thought the second telling might be even more embarrassing, but David listened intently, seemingly without judgment or pity. And, remarkably, the story didn't bring me to tears this time. David's tears did.

He engulfed me in his arms, his body heaving with sobs. "I'm sorry, honey," he said after a moment. "I want to kill those bastards—all three of them—for what they did to you."

Overwhelmed by his strength and goodness, I said a silent prayer of thanks. We held each other until the tears passed.

"I really wish Kate would've called the police," he finally said. "Like that girl's father said at the sentencing hearing—what was her name? Bridgette? You would've regained some strength by testifying against those assholes. And it wouldn't have haunted you all this time."

"Maybe you're right. But in grade school I learned it wasn't cool to 'tattle.' And even though this was more than a classroom misdeed, I still blamed myself for getting into the situation in the first place. I was mortified and ashamed."

He nodded.

"Any idea where those guys are now?" he asked, nonchalantly.

I pulled away and looked at him. "Don't even think of getting back at them."

"It's only in the movies that SEALS engage in vigilante justice," he said, smiling again. "Really. I'm just curious."

"I admit I've Googled them," I said. "The guy who was my ostensible date is the CEO of a company in San Jose, and I'm guessing he does okay. One of the would-be rapists died in a motorcycle accident about five years ago, and I'm not ashamed to say I was happy about it. I didn't find anything on the other guy, so I'm hoping he's a skid row bum. And, no, I'm not gonna tell you their names."

Later, holding hands under the covers, David turned to me again. "You know, I can see why you felt indebted to Kate—I sure do. But if she never mentioned saving your life again, why did you feel like she was using it to manipulate you into defending her?"

No sense holding it back. He already knows her true character.

I hadn't thought a lot about them since Kate went off to prison, but the seemingly innocuous incidents were permanently etched in my memory. I told David about Kate's "You'd do it for me" comment and the "You owe me" note.

He shook his head. "Can't anything about that woman be pure and simple?

CHAPTER FORTY-SIX

Monday, March 17

The adoption arrangements had proceeded as planned. Linda Wordsworth, our social worker, had finished and filed our new home study with the court. At our request, Julie Wutherspoon had arranged for another social worker to interview Miriam and Antonio at greater length, and we were waiting on the report. A private investigator David knew made discreet inquiries into the background of Miriam and Antonio's families, and—other than Miriam's father's bigotry—nothing remotely troubling turned up.

For fear it might scare her away and nix the deal, David had balked at my idea of asking for hair analysis to see if Miriam had used drugs during her pregnancy. But I'd had trouble letting it rest—I'd been so badly burned and deeply hurt by Kate's deception, and I'd come to doubt my own abilities to see and know the truth.

After sitting at my desk idly playing with paperclips and accomplishing nothing for almost an hour, I impulsively called Miriam and asked her to lunch. The minute the words left my mouth, I regretted it, with visions of an irate Julie Wutherspoon flashing through my mind.

"That would be great," Miriam said without hesitation. "But would you mind if we just went someplace like Perkins where I can get bland food? These kids have been giving me heartburn lately."

My breath caught in my throat as a wave of sadness hit me from behind. *I'll never know what that's like—carrying an unborn child who holds such incredible power.* I didn't reply.

"Can you still hear me?" Miriam asked.

"Sorry. You cut out on me there for a second. Perkins is fine. The one on the beltline?"

"Yes. That's great. Is twelve-thirty okay?"

Miriam was already seated at a table when I arrived ten minutes late. I began a profuse apology for mistiming the traffic, but she stood up, gave me a warm hug and brushed it off. "Not to worry. I'm free until two-thirty. It's great to see you."

This confident, radiant young woman—with clear skin and shiny hair—was the picture of physical and mental health. I felt like a fool for doubting her. And I was at a loss as to how to begin this conversation.

Miriam charged right ahead. "I'm really glad you called. Julie said we should let her and the social workers do the talking, but this adoption thing is a big deal, and I want to be sure about it. When I sign on the dotted line, it'll be too late. Can I ask you some more questions?"

"Sure. I'd like to ask you some too."

Our waitress was top-notch—she brought our order without chitchat or fuss, and left us alone to talk. Before I knew it, Miriam and I were baring our souls to one another. She told me about her adolescent struggles with bulimia and her ongoing conflicts with her demanding, perfectionistic father and her bitchy mother. I told her about my panic attacks, about defending Kate and the damage it had done to my confidence in judging people.

"I was going to ask you for a hair sample," I said, shaking my head.

Miriam burst out laughing. "Oh, my God!" she said. "I was going to ask you and David for them too. I kept telling Antonio I didn't want our kids ending up with closet addicts. He told me I was being paranoid."

We both agreed our fears were allayed and lab analysis of our hair was unnecessary.

"So other than having heartburn, how have you been feeling?" I asked when Miriam waddled back from her second trip to the restroom, her hands bracing her hips.

She looked down at what used to be her lap. "To be honest, I'm running out of gas. There's not much room for them to move around anymore, so the big kicks have pretty much stopped. But one or the other of them always seems to have the hiccups, and I've started having some of those Braxton Hicks contractions. It's kinda scary."

"Is your doctor concerned?" I asked, my heart in my throat. *Dear God, please let everything be okay—for Miriam's sake and ours.*

"She's concerned about my blood pressure. It was up when I was in for my last exam," she said, shifting in her seat. "Hey—do you want to come with me to my appointment this afternoon? Antonio couldn't get away today, so I was going to go by myself."

I set down my fork and napkin and looked at Miriam. Her eyes glistened, and I realized she was on the verge of tears, much as Lily would be if a shot awaited her at the doctor's office. Despite her maturity, Miriam was really a child having children—and without support from her own uptight mother.

My own sadness at never having experienced pregnancy dissolved, replaced by profound concern for this young woman. "I'd like that, Miriam," I said.

—⟨⟨⟨—

One glance at Miriam told me she'd also seen the alarm on the nursing assistant's face when she took her blood pressure. "Thanks for coming with me," she said in a small voice as we waited for the doctor.

"I'm glad to do it. They try to make these examination rooms bearable, what with the pastel walls and cheerful artwork. But you can't disguise the smell of alcohol and disinfectant, and there's no way to make a paper gown comfortable. It's like a recipe for claustrophobia."

She nodded. "You got that right."

If Dr. Winters was surprised at meeting the adoptive mother-to-be of Miriam's twins, she didn't show it. She said hello and shook my hand, then got right down to business.

"I'm going to check your blood pressure again myself," Dr. Winters said, wrapping the cuff around Miriam's arm. "Sometimes the nursing assistants don't read it correctly, and sometimes we get a more accurate reading after you've been seated for a while."

Dr. Winters was better at keeping a poker face, but she jotted a note in the file and immediately voiced her concern. "We need to get your BP down," she said. "And the protein level in your urine today is a bit high too. We'll do an ultrasound to see what these kiddos look like, and then we'll talk about where to go from here."

I watched in amazement as the doctor squeezed gel onto Miriam's huge belly and began the sonogram. She smiled and pointed to the images on the monitor, telling us the babies looked great. "You're at thirty-one weeks right now, and their weights look okay. But we need to keep 'em cooking for a while longer to get their lungs in a better position for delivery."

Miriam and I looked at each other in shock. We both knew twins often arrived early, but the average is thirty-six weeks. *No! This is more than a month too early.* I, for one, wasn't prepared.

—⚬—

"Thank heaven I went with her," I told David as we sat together on the couch that evening. "When the doc said Miriam had to be on bed rest for the remainder of her pregnancy, she fell apart. It was heartbreaking. She said she and her mother were fighting all the time, and there was no way she could be on bed rest in her parents' home. The doctor didn't want her driving, so I took her to Antonio's house. There's not much room there—his grandmother lives there too. I'm not sure what will happen."

"Don't even think it," he said.

"What?"

"I know you, Caroline. You're thinking the guest room is still available, and you're winding things down at work. You're thinking Ida could look in on Miriam if you weren't around."

He was right. "Why wouldn't it work?" I asked. "It would be to everyone's advantage if Miriam had a comfortable, quiet place to rest. There'd be a better chance she could maintain the pregnancy longer, and our kids would have better odds at survival."

"Think back to the last time we had someone living in our guest room. It turned into a nightmare, and we knew Kate a helluva lot better than we know Miriam. We've met her, what, two times?"

"She and I got to know one another pretty well over lunch and at the doctor's office today."

"Which probably wasn't the wisest idea either," he said. "When we first talked, Miriam and Antonio made it clear they don't want future involvement in the babies' lives—and we don't want that either. Which would be a lot harder if we became friends with them during the last month or so of this pregnancy. She's feeling vulnerable and would love to have a welcoming house to go to, and I'd like that for her too. But we need to look ahead toward our family's long-term wellbeing. And having her stay here would more than complicate things."

I didn't want to admit it, but he was right again.

Feeling a shiver run down my back, I pulled the afghan from the arm of the sofa and wrapped it around my shoulders. "David, what if the babies are born too early? Or if they're not healthy? I'm not sure I could deal with it."

CHAPTER FORTY-SEVEN

—w—

Wednesday, March 26

Judge Coburn's ruling on Kate's "ineffective assistance of counsel" motion came on the same day she arrived back in Madison. She didn't come of her own volition: She'd been transported, shackled and chained on the U.S. Marshal's bus, to testify at the trial of Joe Ames. George Cooper called me at my office to tell me.

"Hello, counselor," he said. "Just thought you might want to know your client got to the Dane County Jail this morning. Trial starts next week, and I'm going over to prep her tomorrow. Do you want to join me?"

"Uh, George... she filed a 2255 motion claiming I'm incompetent. I hardly think she'd have use for my services at this point."

"Standard jailhouse lawyer crap. You can't take it personally. Besides, Coburn's order came out today: he denied the motion."

Giddy with relief, I let my head fall back against my chair. "He did?"

"Yeah. It's on-line. Take a look. And call me if you want to sit in on the trial prep."

Judge Coburn's order was terse: He stated Kate had been advised before pleading guilty of all the possible penalties, and estimates of the sentencing guideline calculations were simply estimates, not guarantees. He cited the extensive research I had done to try to refute the application of the increased sentence for "sophisticated means." He noted I had prevailed in my "cogent" argument against the two-level increase for a managerial or supervisory role. He noted I had asked for time to confer with Kate before proceeding with sentencing after the issue of upward departure was raised—and correctly inferred Kate had insisted on proceeding.

The magnitude of the relief I felt amazed me: I hadn't realized how much I'd let her allegations get to me. I was off the hook, vindicated! Of course it meant Kate still had months to serve before being released, but I realized I truly didn't care. I was over the guilt.

Thursday, March 27

Cooper called again Thursday afternoon. "I need you to talk some sense into your client," he said without preface.

"I assume you mean Kate Daniels, and she's not my client. But you might as well tell me what's going on," I said, my curiosity getting the better of me.

"Carter Ellingson, Doug Connaboy, and I went to talk with her today. Seems she's had a major attack of amnesia.

Doesn't remember giving the statements implicating Ames. Says the transcript of her grand jury testimony is flat-out wrong. She's gone south on us."

"I'm really sorry to hear that. I haven't had any contact with her since she went to prison: no letters, no calls, no e-mails. So I have no clue what's going on. Any chance Ames has gotten to her? Is he at Dane County Jail too?"

"No," George said. "The marshals have him housed in one of the outlying county jails. We looked at the phone and visiting records for both of them—there's no indication of any direct or indirect contact."

"So what happens?"

"We bring her in to testify as scheduled. If she lies on the witness stand, which I expect she will, we'll introduce her grand jury testimony and try to convince the jury not to believe her now. And I'll prosecute her for perjury."

"You told her that, I assume."

"Oh, yeah. She didn't budge."

"It stinks, but I'm afraid there's nothing I can say or do to convince her."

He paused. "Could you appeal to her as the biological mother of your daughter?" he asked, almost in a whisper.

A sick feeling engulfed me, like a wave of noxious gas filling my airways. *He can't be asking this! Joe Ames is a jerk of the highest order, and I want nothing more than to see him rot in prison. But he is no threat to Lily.*

I couldn't withstand another personal entanglement with Kate Daniels: it just wasn't worth it. "No, George. I can't," I said and hung up the phone.

Friday, March 28

I was in my office again on Friday morning when Rosalee knocked. "George Cooper and another gentleman are here to see you. Can I show then in?"

Why can't he take no for an answer? I thought he was a reasonable guy. I almost snapped at Rosalee, then caught myself. *This isn't her fault.*

"Sure, Rosalee. I've got a minute."

But one glance at Cooper's face—drained of all color—and his downcast eyes, told me I'd been wrong about the reason for his visit. Rick Shelton, trailing behind him without a trace of his usual swagger, appeared stunned.

"She's dead, isn't she? Kate's dead," I heard myself say, as if disembodied.

Cooper nodded. "I'm sorry, Caroline. We wanted to tell you personally—before you heard it on the news."

I leaned back in my chair and squeezed my eyes shut, as if to shield myself from the news. "What happened?" I finally asked.

"Apparent overdose," Cooper said as he and Shelton sat down. "About six o'clock this morning, her cellmate started screaming, and staff found Kate dead on the floor. There was a rolled up piece of paper on the floor next to her—probably what she used to snort the drug. And there was a note."

"Suicide?" I asked, shaking my head. "That doesn't sound right."

Shelton opened the leather folder on his lap, took out a single sheet of paper, and gave it to me. I noticed his hands were shaking. "This is a copy."

Apparently written with a dull pencil on lined paper, about five by seven inches in size, the note read: "Tell Lily I'm sorry. No one likes a snitch. −K."

I closed my eyes again, this time to hold back the tears. Tears for my daughter, who would never have the chance to reconcile with, to ask questions of, or to know as an adult the woman who'd given birth to her. Once, after Kate went to prison, Lily and I had talked about our hopes for the future. We both hoped Kate would recover from her addiction and its self-centered focus. That she'd eventually return to find a place in our lives. And now, Lily would have to cope with the notion that Kate had intentionally taken her own life?

"I know this is difficult," Cooper said, "but please take a close look at the note and see if you think it was written by Kate or by someone else. Since it's printed, handwriting analysis isn't an option."

"You think someone else may have written the note? That this was murder?" I asked.

"We don't know," Shelton said. "But we have to cover all the bases. Joe Ames certainly had a motive, if not the means."

I wiped my eyes with the back of my hand, then studied the note. The printing was as sloppy as Kate's typical handwriting, though I'd never known her to print.

"It doesn't look like something she'd write," I said. "But shortly before her sentencing, she started signing her e-mails like that. You know, just a dash and a K. I just don't know."

"Did you show Kate a copy of the note Ames gave to Lily's friend that day last fall?" Cooper asked me.

I nodded. "Yes, I think so. But the printing on this note looks different—messier or something."

"It does look different," Shelton said, "but both notes mention Lily. And snitches."

CHAPTER FORTY-EIGHT

—w—

"Honey, your mom and I have some bad news to tell you," David said to Lily that evening, after she hung up her jacket and backpack.

"Bad news?" she asked, already in a panic. "It's not the babies, is it?"

"No. They're fine," I said. "Let's go in the other room. It's warmer in there."

David and I had a fire burning in the family room where we'd spent the last hour discussing how to break the news to Lily. Tell it to her straight, was what we'd decided, but we had no idea how she'd take it.

Lily sat next to me on the couch, leaning forward in anticipation, while David perched on the edge of the coffee table facing us and watching her closely. "Aunt Kate died sometime early this morning," he said.

As though someone pushed her "pause" button, Lily neither moved nor spoke—for seconds that felt like hours. *Dear*

God, she's not in catatonic shock, is she? That's only in the movies, isn't it?

Finally she blinked and shook her head. "What happened?" she asked.

I explained Kate had been brought to jail in Madison to testify in Mr. Ames' trial and sometime around six a.m. she'd been found dead in her cell. "The police are trying to find out exactly what happened," I said. "She may have taken or been given an overdose of drugs. Do you understand what that means?"

Lily nodded, her lips quivering. "You mean Aunt Kate might have killed herself or someone might have killed her?"

David put his hand on top of hers. "Yes, it looks like those are the two possibilities," he said.

"Do you think she's in heaven?"

"Oh, yes, honey. I do," I said, choking back tears as I hugged her. "And I know she's happier than she's been in a long, long time. But I'm sad you won't get a chance to know the nice, generous, funny person she was when I met her in college."

"We can always look at the photo album," she said with a sniffle. "Some adopted kids never even get to see what their real moms looked like. At least I got to know her a little."

Words caught in my throat, and all I could do was hold her.

—◊—

Hugh Coburn granted George Cooper's motion for a continuance in the trial of Joe Ames while investigators probed the suspicious death of the prosecution's star witness. I read with detachment the newspaper accounts: the autopsy revealed Kate died of cardiac arrest; there was no sign of physical trauma, suggesting she hadn't been forced to ingest drugs; toxicology tests were pending.

"Why don't I care?" I asked Dr. Brownhill during a session the week after Kate died.

"What do you think?" she asked.

"I think it's pretty frickin' frustrating that you answer my every question with a question," I snapped before I could think to censor my comments.

Her eyes twinkled. "Hurray, Caroline! It's always good to hear your honest feelings. But you know you're the one who needs to answer your own questions—I'm just here to make sure you ask them."

"So why do I care so little about how Kate died?" I asked aloud.

I tried to picture the scene: Kate on the cement floor of the cinderblock jail cell with its scarred beige walls. The Spartan furnishings—thin mattresses on steel benches covered with army blankets and worn sheets, a stainless steel toilet and washbasin. A hysterical cellmate, screaming for help. None of it moved me.

A moment later it hit me. "My friend Kate died for me months ago," I said. "That's why I'm not grieving now."

Dr. Brownhill inclined her head.

"And even Lily, the wonderful legacy she left us, understands Kate's chances for redemption in this lifetime were slim."

"Perhaps you're right. Keep in mind, though, our feelings aren't static. And don't be afraid of it if grief sneaks up on you or Lily in the weeks, or months, or even years to come."

The cell phone in my pocket vibrated. I jumped up in alarm and pulled it from my pocket. "Sorry," I said to her as I looked at the screen. "I need to read this text."

It was from Julie Wutherspoon. "Miriam's at St. Mary's. It might be time."

—⁓—

When David and I arrived at the hospital, Antonio stood outside the door to Miriam's room, his dark skin almost pale with worry. "The doctor's examining her," he said. "She was having pretty regular contractions, and the doctor said to bring her in."

With a feeling of utter helplessness, I patted his shoulder.

"It's really too soon, isn't it?" he asked me.

"A bit," I said. "A week or two more would be better for their lungs."

He sniffed and wiped the corner of his eye with his knuckle. "We've been following all the doctor's orders."

How will he possibly be able to give up these children?

The exam finished, Dr. Winters opened the door and invited us in. I was glad she was on duty: She was as calm and collected as Antonio was flustered.

"Miriam is dilated to about three centimeters, but labor isn't particularly strong yet," Dr. Winters said when we were seated on folding chairs around the bed. "We'd like to do amniocentesis to test the babies' lung development. If they're good to go, we'll let her deliver. Otherwise we'll administer a drug to stop the labor and hope she can carry the twins for at least a little while longer. Do any of you have any questions?"

We shook our heads.

"Antonio, why don't you stay? Miriam could use some moral support while we're doing the test. Mr. and Mrs. Spencer, there's a waiting area down the hall to the left."

David and I walked numbly to our appointed spot and sat together on a stiff, barely upholstered couch, miles away from one another. I had no words to explain the wildly mixed emotions I felt: sorrow—again—at my inability to bear children; a desire to comfort both Miriam and Antonio as they coped with this situation; fear they wouldn't relinquish the babies; fear the babies wouldn't survive, or would suffer birth defects; and excitement at the prospect of bringing home the babies, sooner than expected.

Then, as if he'd just realized I was present, David put his arm around me. "It'll be all right," he said.

We sat and waited for what seemed like forever, but was really only about an hour. "I feel like we don't belong here," I said to David. "Will they even bother to tell us what's going on?"

He put down the two-year-old copy of *Fish and Wildlife Magazine* he'd paged through at least four times. "I think they'll let us know. Julie had Miriam sign forms authorizing the doctors to communicate with us throughout the pregnancy and delivery."

"Yeah, but—"

"I'll go see if I can find out," he said.

But before he reached the doorway, Dr. Winters walked in and sat on the arm of a side chair. "The lung development's not quite where we'd like it to be," she said. "The babies are still thriving in utero, so we're going to give Miriam a medication to stop the labor and some steroids to help the lungs along."

"How long before it's safe for them to be delivered?" I asked.

"I'd like to see them get to thirty-six weeks, but we'll take what we can get."

"Is she going home to wait?"

"Oh, no. Not with her risk for preeclampsia. She'll be here until she delivers." She stood up to leave.

"Dr. Winters," I said, "this is a pretty awkward situation for us. Should we visit Miriam? Encourage her? We just don't know what to do."

"It's funny," she said with a kind smile, "Antonio just asked me if I thought he should come fill you in on the test results. I told him, no, that's my job. That's why the lawyers gave us consent to talk with you. And my answer to your question is also no. I think the kids need to be alone. The adoption agreement calls for you to be present when she delivers, and I noticed we have four or five numbers for you in the chart. We'll let you know when to be here, I promise."

We thanked her and left the hospital. Walking to the parking lot hand-in-hand, I marveled at the calm and strength radiating through my husband's skin. I felt anything but calm, and my legs threatened to give way.

It wasn't a panic attack per se. Instead of inducing anxiety, this downward spiral of catastrophic thoughts brought on a pervasive feeling of despondence. I couldn't stop focusing on the risks we faced: Miriam's dangerously high blood pressure, the babies' underdeveloped lungs, the possibility that Miriam and Antonio would change their minds.

"David, I have an awful feeling things are going to go wrong."

CHAPTER FORTY-NINE

—⚬—

Monday, April 7

I'd felt sorry for Miriam, being cooped up in a hospital for what might be days or weeks, without the benefit of family support. Antonio, while loving and devoted, had school and a job to contend with. And it was impossible for me to picture her high school friends visiting Miriam, confined to bed while she waited to deliver babies she wouldn't keep.

But I was less than pleased to learn, shortly after Miriam's labor was forestalled, that her parents were back in the picture.

Julie Wutherspoon knocked on my door one morning, clearly aggravated. "Got a minute?"

"Sure. C'mon in and sit down."

"Everything okay with Miriam?" I asked, but I already sensed this had nothing to do with the pregnancy itself.

"Long story short," she said, "Ted and Lucille Buffington, Miriam's parents, are threatening to bollix the deal. All of a sudden, they're at the hospital with candy and flowers, gushing about how they'll work it all out. Lucille's childless niece in Omaha got wind of the situation and put in a pitch for the kids, and now Lucille thinks 'it would be best for them to be raised by family.' Ted is behind it, too, because he'll do almost anything to keep his wife from bitching."

Paralyzed by the rush of blood to my head and the cacophony of my hateful thoughts, I could barely sputter. "We have a contract."

"A contract no judge in the world will enforce if Miriam doesn't agree to it after the birth. You know that."

I did know it, and it scared the bejesus out of me.

"And what's Miriam's take on it?" I asked, half-afraid to hear the answer.

"She's a good, honest kid who has strong feelings about who she wants to adopt her kids. If she'd wanted Cousin Betty, or whatever her name is, from Omaha to adopt them, she would've said so in the first place. My only concern is she's pretty vulnerable, and her folks may try to blackmail her for a college education."

"Is there anything we can do?" I asked, unable to mask my desperation.

"If you're praying people, I'd give that a shot. Otherwise, I guess we just wait. I'll keep you posted."

Too upset, even, for Rosalee's consolations, I grabbed my cell phone and headed out for a walk. The spring flowers outside the Capitol resembled a Monet painting through my tears. After three circuits around the square and fifty or so silent prayers, I was calm enough to sit and dial David's office.

As I waited on hold for him to finish another call, I thought of our guest room cum nursery. Maybe my Greek friend Karen was right about it being bad luck—or Karma, or whatever Greeks call it—to prepare the nursery until kids are born. Or, in this case, in our arms.

I wish we would've left those cribs unassembled in their Babies R Us boxes. It'd be some consolation, however small, to get our money back if this falls through.

"What's up?" David asked.

I told him.

"You know there are no guarantees in this life," he said. "It is what it is."

Quit talking in fucking clichés! I wanted to yell at him. But I couldn't argue with his underlying message. "No use crying over spilled milk," I said.

"Sarcasm's not your best attribute," he said, chuckling. "But if we don't laugh, we'll cry. And that won't help anything."

"I don't know about that," I said. "I just cried and walked and prayed my way around the square several times like a crazy lady, and I do feel better."

"Hey, whatever it takes. I love you and we'll get through this—however this turns out."

I sat a while longer after I hung up and finally gathered enough momentum to move. A fresh-squeezed lemonade from the Asian food cart would have been welcome, but I'd left my wallet in my office. *Just head back to the office*, I was telling myself, when Tom Robbins and Doug Connaboy walked up beside me.

"Hey, Sugar," said Tom, wrapping a hefty arm around my shoulder. "We were just talking about you. Got time for a word?"

I started to say no but realized the distraction was just what the doctor ordered. "If one of you'll front me the money to buy a lemonade, I'd be happy to chat."

The sunshine and positive regard from two old friends made the discussion bearable. Doug broke the news about the toxicology tests: Kate died from a heroin overdose. Analysis of the drug residue found in her cell revealed the drug was virtually pure.

Tom told me about the jail's in-house investigation: They'd reviewed the video from all of the security cameras and found no clues as to how Kate had gotten the drug. Although the jail deputies' union wouldn't allow across-the-board polygraphs, Tom had interviewed all of them and heard nary a rumor about staff involvement. The usual inmate snitches, who would roll over on their grandmothers if they could, knew nothing.

"Maybe she brought it in with her," Doug said, "although the marshals and the federal prison folks say it's unlikely. Carter Ellingson's had FBI agents interviewing staff and inmates alike in Dublin, California, and at every detention facility Kate was housed in along the way here. Nothing. Nada."

"What about Joe Ames?" I asked. "He's been the prime suspect in my mind, whether or not he ever dealt heroin before."

"He's been in lock-down at the Jefferson County Jail for weeks, and the only person he's been allowed to see or talk to is his lawyer. Benson's an asshole, but I don't think he'd stoop to this," Doug said.

"How about that Nigerian? Thorpe Akani. He had all sorts of tricks up his sleeve," I said, although I realized I might be grasping at straws.

"It's a remote possibility, since he's never been apprehended," Doug said. "But Ellingson got a fairly reliable tip that Akani was murdered in Nigeria a couple of months ago. He's still trying to confirm, but we're almost certain Akani couldn't have had anything to do with Kate's death."

"We'll never know?" I asked.

"Looks like it. Sometimes we'll get a confession or a useful tip months or years after the fact, but I wouldn't count on it in this case," Doug said.

"So it goes down as a suicide, and no one's responsible for giving Kate the drug."

"'Fraid so," Tom said, with another hug. "But if it's any consolation, Ames is going *down* in federal court."

"We'll see," I said, as I walked away. Nothing in this whole case had gone the way it was planned. I had little confidence things would change now.

CHAPTER FIFTY

—⟋⟍—

Wisconsin State Journal – Wednesday, April 16

MADISON – The trial of Joseph Ames will continue today in U.S. District Court. Ames is charged with providing the cocaine that caused the death of 23-year-old university research assistant Yvonne Pritchard last September. In January, Pritchard's mentor, Dr. Kathryn Daniels, received a three-year federal sentence following a guilty plea to a charge of grant fraud. At her plea hearing, Daniels told Judge Hugh Coburn she stole the grant monies to support her own cocaine habit.

Daniels testified before the Grand Jury last November and was expected to testify against Joseph Ames. She was transported from the federal prison camp in Dublin, California, to Wisconsin in March. However, just days before the trial was scheduled to commence, Daniels was found dead in her Dane County Jail cell. Judge Coburn granted the prosecutor's motion for a continuance in the trial while Daniels' death was investigated. The coroner has since ruled the death a probable suicide.

On Tuesday, prosecution witness Laquisha Abbott, who shared a Williamson Street apartment with Yvonne Pritchard, testified Pritchard said her source for cocaine was a "very attractive man" whom she had met through her university advisor. Abbott also testified that on the afternoon before her death, Pritchard complained about having run out of cocaine and told her she expected to get more that evening.

Assistant U.S. Attorney George Cooper introduced the transcript of Dr. Kathryn Daniels' grand jury testimony, during which she identified Joseph Ames as Yvonne Pritchard's supplier. According to the transcript, Daniels herself planned to meet Ames to purchase cocaine at Pritchard's apartment around 11:30 on the night of September 9. Daniels testified she was late, arriving during the early morning hours of September 10, only to find Pritchard dead.

Yesterday, Ames' defense counsel Edward Benson introduced stunning evidence of an alibi. On September 9, Joseph Ames' mother, Adelle Ames, underwent emergency surgery at St. Luke's Hospital in Milwaukee and remained in intensive care for two days. Testimony of family members and hospital staff, as well as ATM receipts and surveillance video, placed Joseph Ames at St. Luke's from approximately 9 a.m. on September 9 until 2 a.m. on September 10, when he was seen leaving the hospital.

As he left the courtroom, Cooper was asked to comment on the defendant's alibi but declined.

Closing arguments are scheduled to begin today.

I read the article while sitting in a waiting room at St. Mary's Hospital and handed the paper to David when I finished. We were both on edge: Miriam's parents hovered in the hallway, and we feared she would succumb to their emotional and financial pressuring.

The furrow in my husband's brow grew deeper as he read. "Just because Ames didn't personally deliver the coke doesn't mean he wasn't the supplier," I said while he refolded the newspaper. "That would be my argument if I were George Cooper."

"It's possible," he said, staring past my shoulder toward the TV.

He picked up the remote and raised the volume. A local news station was showing a clip of a news conference Ed Benson had staged outside the courthouse yesterday afternoon. Two trim, well-dressed women flanked Benson, both beaming at him. "...airtight alibi," Benson was concluding. "I have no doubt the jury will acquit my client of any involvement in the unfortunate death of Yvonne Pritchard."

The anchorwoman appeared on-screen. "That was Joseph Ames' defense attorney, accompanied by Ames' mother and wife, Adelle and Jolene Ames, who both testified on his be-half," she said.

David muted the commercial that followed and turned to me. "Do you think they conjured up the alibi?" he asked.

"Not from the way it sounds in the paper. Too much evi-dence coming from sources other than the family. But those women do look like they'd do anything for Ames..."

He raked a hand through his hair. "Did it ever occur to you Kate might have given Yvonne the coke that night?" he asked.

It hadn't occurred to me, and I found myself inexplicably defensive. *Am I feeling defensive for Kate? Or defensive of myself for never considering that angle?*

"How can you say that?" I asked, knowing full well my question was disingenuous. "She was a user, not a dealer."

"Stop and think about it," David said with equanimity. "Kate and Yvonne were friends, and friends have been known to share their stashes."

"Well..."

"It's the most logical explanation," he said, "assuming the roommate was telling the truth when she testified Yvonne complained about being out of coke earlier in the day. There's a record Yvonne called Kate at the lab that night, after she made three apparently unsuccessful calls to a throwaway cell phone—probably belonging to Ames. So Kate takes the sup-ply she has on hand over to Yvonne's, expecting she can go back and get more when Ames arrives later that night."

After believing Kate's version of the events for so long, David's hypothetical scenario didn't ring true. "Yvonne's call to Kate was sixteen minutes long and ended at nine forty-five. Kate was seen on video picking up Marty Braxton from the airport at ten-fifteen that night, and he confirms they went straight to the lab. She didn't have time to deliver coke to Yvonne."

"Sure she did," he said. "It's only half an hour from the university to the airport, and Yvonne's apartment wasn't that far out of the way. For all we know, Yvonne met her down on the street."

"I don't know. Maybe..."

Our speculation would have to wait, though, because a nurse summoned us to the delivery room. "We're thinking just a few more pushes and the first one should be here," she said.

The hair on the back of my neck rose as the Buffingtons followed the three of us down the hall. But at the doorway, the nurse turned to them. "I'm sorry," she said. "Miriam specifically asked that only Mr. and Mrs. Spencer be admitted."

Hallelujah! Maybe this will all work out after all.

Since Miriam carried twins who were still premature, she couldn't finish her labor in the more comfortable birthing suite. The stark lights highlighted how young and scared Miriam and Antonio appeared, and the solemn presence of surgical equipment in the delivery room frightened even me.

Her face contorted in pain, Miriam pushed in silence through a contraction. Antonio, holding tightly to her hand, looked at the floor, his eyes glistening with tears. Neither watched the birth of their first child. But—in total awe as we'd been when Lily was born—David and I did.

The first twin slid into Dr. Winters' waiting hands. "It's a boy," she said. "Would you like to hold him a moment, Miriam?"

"Yes, please," she whispered.

As the nurse gently placed the baby, still attached by his umbilical cord, on Miriam's chest, David sensed my apprehension and squeezed my hand. *I'm not gonna believe it till it happens. Please, please, Miriam—let us have your babies.*

Offering up a surgical scissors, Dr. Winters asked, "Have we decided who will cut the cord?"

Antonio stood speechless. Miriam, tears catching on her cheeks, responded in a surprisingly clear voice. "Mr. or Mrs. Spencer should do the honors. He's their son now."

"You're sure?" asked Antonio.

Miriam nodded.

Thank you!

But my elation lasted only seconds, interrupted by the insistent alarms on two medical monitors. The fetal monitor showed the second twin's heart rate faltering. Then we watched in horror as Miriam lost consciousness—her blood pressure having dropped to critical levels.

Dr. Winters made a quick assessment. "Ladies and gentlemen," she said with authority, "we need to deliver this child and save this mother. I'm sorry, but the non-medical folks will have to leave. Now."

While I wanted to go to the nursery and bond with our son, one look at Antonio said he couldn't be alone in the waiting room. And leaving him to deal with Miriam's parents would be an even crueler fate. Earning my love and respect for what had to be the millionth time, David put a fatherly arm around the young man's shoulder and led him from the delivery room to an out-of-the-way sitting area.

No small talk or discussion of criminal trials during this wait. We three sat in silence, Antonio between David and me on the couch, staring at a Spanish-speaking soap opera on the TV. Antonio, I realized, could understand the program, but I was sure he'd remember none of it later.

I also realized I was more dispassionate about the events that were transpiring than I ever would have imagined. The ups and downs of our years of infertility must've formed a callus on my psyche—protecting me from the hurt and disappointment of losing yet another opportunity for parenthood. Until I held the twins and knew them to be mine, I could invest only less-than-motherly emotions.

Even so, I was relieved to hear the nurses hadn't kept us posted on the touch-and-go nature of our daughter's birth. When we were escorted back into the delivery room, she'd already been resuscitated.

Antonio declined the nurse's offer to hold the child and rushed straight to Miriam's side.

"She's small—only three pounds, six ounces," the neonatologist told us while we stared in awe at the baby. "She'll need to be in an incubator for a while, but she was deprived of oxygen for only a very brief time, and she's looking great."

David had to support me while I cradled her, for my knees were weak. One look, one touch, and I was hooked for life. "Hello, precious Amy," I said.

As one nurse wheeled Miriam to a recovery area, another wheeled in a little bundle in a clear bassinette—the son we'd decided to name Luke.

David and I marveled at their tiny fingers, toes and ears. Perfect little miracles.

Monday, April 21

A tough cookie, our Amy's stay in the Neonatal Intensive Care Unit was blessedly easy—she required only Level II care and just needed to grow stronger. I overheard parents and staff discussing some very sick babies, saw anguished relatives struggling to be brave, and witnessed the grief when one baby died. And I thanked God that we didn't have to go through that pain.

Despite her relatively stable health, I couldn't bear to leave Amy alone in the hospital and spent most of my time there. David, who'd been a hands-on dad when Lily was born, stayed at home to mind Luke and Lily. With Ida McKinley's help, we kept our sanity.

Several days after the birth, while searching for my hairbrush, I came upon a newspaper I'd thrown into my tote bag to read when I found the time. As Amy slept soundly, I sat on the couch in her room and opened the paper.

JURY RETURNS VERDICT

Wisconsin State Journal – Saturday, April 19

MADISON - On Friday, after seven hours of deliberation, the jury returned a verdict in the federal case against Joseph Ames. Ames was acquitted on the charge that he provided the cocaine that caused the death of 23-year-old Yvonne Pritchard last September. He was found guilty of a less serious charge, distribution of cocaine. Evidence at trial reflected that over a three-year period of time he provided cocaine to the late university researcher, Dr. Kathryn Daniels, and he also introduced small quantities of cocaine into the Dane County Jail.

Although Daniels had been expected to testify against Ames, she was found dead in her jail cell in March of this year, as a result of a heroin overdose. The death was ruled a suicide. Investigators were unable to learn how she obtained the drug.

U.S. District Judge Hugh Coburn scheduled Ames' sentencing for July 16.

It hardly seemed possible that only seven and a half months had passed since Kate had awakened me with the phone call about Yvonne's death. I'd felt a lifetime's worth of emotions in that brief span of time. I'd learned more about addiction than I'd ever wanted to know—and still couldn't explain it. I'd been horrified at Kate's criminal behavior, proud when she walked down the road to recovery and redemption, and devastated when she veered off-track again. I mourned for our friendship, shattered by lies and anger. I mourned for Lily, who would never know the smart, caring, fun-loving woman who had been my friend.

But an almost inaudible baby gurgle was all it took to bring me back to the present. I stood quietly beside Amy's incubator, stroking her butter-soft cheek and marveling at this wonderful new life. I looked up to see David, carrying Luke in an infant seat, and Lily, carrying a bouquet of yellow roses. Their luminous smiles made everything right.

ACKNOWLEDGMENTS

Heartfelt thanks: To my parents, Margy and the late Fred Amthor, who instilled in me a love of the written word. To my children, Carlos and Lauren, who have enriched my life immeasurably. To many friends who encouraged me—oh, so long ago—to write: Virginia Chiles, Ann Bloor, Catherine Spinelli, and Janine Frank. To Kathy Groft Steffen for her enthusiastic instruction and Rachel Berens-VanHeest for her insightful editing. To Mike Bell for the title. To Claire Ogunsola for her beautiful cover photography and design. To my faithful reader-friends, Jane Erickson and Corinne Hollar, for plodding through every draft with patience, kindness, and attention. And, to my loving husband, Nick, for his steadfast support and good humor.

About The Author

Leslyn Amthor Spinelli lives with her husband near Madison, Wisconsin, and enjoys winters in San Diego, California. *Taken for Granted* is her debut novel.